C000091198

THE LAST KING OF ROME

LUCIUS TARQUINIUS SUPERBUS

LAURA DOWERS

BLUE LAUREL PRESS

ISBN: 978-1-912968-00-8

DRAMATIS PERSONAE

THE TARQUINS

    LUCOMO — FIFTH KING OF ROME

    TANAQUIL — WIFE TO LUCOMO

    SERVIUS TULLIUS — SIXTH KING OF ROME

    TARQUINIA — DAUGHTER OF TANAQUIL

    LUCIUS TARQUINIUS — SEVENTH KING OF ROME

    ARRUNS TARQUINIUS — BROTHER TO LUCIUS

    LUCILLA — SISTER TO LUCIUS

    TULLIA — DAUGHTER OF SERVIUS TULLIUS

    LOLLY — DAUGHTER OF SERVIUS TULLIUS

    TITUS — SON OF LUCIUS AND LOLLY

    ARRUNS — SON OF LUCIUS AND LOLLY

    SEXTUS — SON OF LUCIUS AND LOLLY

    CASSIA — DAUGHTER OF LUCIUS AND LOLLY

    TITUS BRUTUS — SON OF LUCILLA

    IUNIUS BRUTUS — SON OF LUCILLA

ROMANS

    ACACIUS ARCO — SENATOR

AETIUS — A SHEPHERD

AULUS FLAVONIUS — SENATOR

AXIA QUINTILLA — NOBLEWOMAN

BRUSCIUS — ASTROLOGER

CAMILIA SEGESTES — NOBLEWOMAN

CNAEUS SUDENNUS — FRIEND TO SERVIUS TULLIUS

COLLATINUS — PATRICIAN

COSSUS — FRIEND TO LUCIUS

CUTU TAPHO — SERVANT

DANAOS — DOCTOR

ELERIUS — FRIEND TO SEXTUS

GALLIO BURRUS — SENATOR

HOSTUS VENTURIUS — PATRICIAN

ISSA — MAID TO TANAQUIL

LUCRETIA — WIFE TO COLLATINUS

LUSIA — INFORMANT TO TANAQUIL

MACARIUS — A SHEPHERD

MANIUS — FRIEND TO LUCIUS

MATIA — FRIEND TO LOLLY

METELLA — A BROTHEL-KEEPER

NARCISSA — WIFE TO QUINTUS SANCTUS

NIPIA — SLAVE

NONUS LUCCEIUS — PATRICIAN

PLACUS — TUTOR

QUINTUS SANCTUS — SENATOR

RESTITA — FRIEND TO TARQUINIA

SILO — SLAVE

SISENNA VICTOR — MERCHANT

UTICA — CLEANING WOMAN

OTHER CHARACTERS

BELLUS — A LATIN

Rufus — Gabii leader

Turnus Herdonius — Latin leader

Venza Cae Rusina — Veientes merchant

Vulso — a Gabii

The inevitable course of fate overwhelms the wisest of human intentions. The jealousy that Servius had aroused by ascending the throne pervaded his household, and hatred and disloyalty were rife even among his own family.

— LIVY, HISTORY OF ROME 1.42

He [Tarquin] always kept himself protected by armed men, for he had taken the throne by force — neither people nor senate had consented to his usurpation. He accepted that there was no hope of his being accepted into the hearts of his subjects, so he ruled by fear.

— LIVY, HISTORY OF ROME 1.49

PART I

579 BC–574 BC

1

The shepherds did not like the city.

As far as Aetius and Macarius were concerned, Rome was an alien world they would venture into only to sell their wool, and then only as far as the forum. Rome was too noisy, too smelly, too dirty, too busy for their liking. They preferred their hilltop huts where the wind rustled through the thatched roofs and the bleatings of their sheep could be heard just outside the mud walls.

And yet the city, with all its busyness, its bright colours and noisy citizens, held a strange fascination for them. Sometimes, when the day's work was done, Aetius and Macarius would sit on the grass, a plump wineskin between them, look down on the metropolis and muse on how the rich folk spent their days.

They grew to wondering this more and more often, until rich folk became their usual topic of conversation. What would they do, they asked one another with playful smiles on their lips, if they had bronze, even gold, to spend? Then they would throw their heads back, fix their eyes on a distant point in the wide sky and say they would buy pewter plates and silks, and laugh at their foolish dreams. They were foolish, they knew, to imagine having any wealth at all. To be a shepherd was to be poor. To be a shepherd meant having to work from dawn to dusk and bartering every item they and their families needed to survive. There was no room in their lives for beautiful but useless things.

And then the sickness came, a sickness that killed off most of their flock and made their lives so much harder than they already were. The sheep were diseased so they couldn't eat their meat nor could they sell the carcasses on. Aetius and Macarius had to listen to their children crying and begging for food and watch as their wives went hungry so the little ones wouldn't starve. The two shepherds would escape to their lookout point and with no wine to sweeten their mood would look down on the rich folk in the city and declare the unfairness of their lot.

It was at such a time that salvation came to them in the guise of two strangers. Word had spread, the strangers said, of the shepherds' misfortune. What would they do, the strangers asked, to drag themselves out of the mire? Clutching at fortune, Aetius said he and Macarius would do anything.

'Anything?' the strangers queried.

'Anything,' Aetius assured them.

'Well then,' the strangers gestured at the grass, 'let us talk.'

The strangers understood what would motivate the shepherds most and so began with how much they would pay. Aetius and Macarius listened eagerly to what would be required, and with only the slightest hesitation, agreed. Their wives, when they told them later, said they were mad. But then they looked at the gold ingots the strangers had given their husbands and their scolding words died in their throats.

When the chosen day came, Aetius and Macarius left

what little remained of their flocks in the care of their wives, who sniffed back their tears and held them tight as they said their goodbyes, and made their way to the city.

They hoped to pass unnoticed. Their short woollen tunics were not so very different from those the plebeians wore, but Aetius and Macarius knew their leather cloaks set them apart, not least because they stank so of sheep. They knew too that their straw hats were out of place in the city, but they wore them to hide their faces and they kept their heads down, looking up only to check the painted shop signs that told them which streets they walked along. They were heading for the Capitoline Hill, but it was a place they had never been, and after turning into streets that seemed to head straight for it, would find these often doglegged to the right or left and lead them further away. With each blunder, their uneasiness grew, and in desperation, asked the way of a passing citizen. He directed them with a dirty, crooked finger to the domus of the King.

There were armed guards stationed either side of the open double doors. The guard on the left demanded to see the shepherds' petition before he would allow them to enter. Aetius delved into his leather satchel and extracted the papyrus the strangers had given him. He held it, hand shaking, beneath the guard's nose. Aetius, having no learning, had not been able to read what was written there, but the strangers assured him it would guarantee entry to the King's domus, entry and an audience. As he held the papyrus up for the guard to inspect, Aetius realised he was hoping a flaw would be discovered, some error that would see he and Macarius turned away, their mission over before it had begun. But the guard nodded his approval and waved them through.

The vestibulum of the domus was crowded and noses wrinkled in distaste at the pungent odours coming from the two shepherds. Here, packed in like the shepherds' sheep when they were waiting to be shorn, were the Romans who had some complaint to make, some dispute they needed settling, or some respect to pay to the King for a favour previously bestowed. And just beyond here, the King would come, sit in his stately chair, listen to each person's petition and deliver a judgement. No one was turned away for being too low born or unimportant. Aetius and Macarius would be seen and heard by the King and their opportunity would come. But when? The 'when' was starting to bother Aetius.

Macarius put his mouth to Aetius's ear. 'Are we sure about this?'

Aetius glared at him. 'We agreed. We took the gold.'

'But the doors are guarded and we won't get past all these people. I didn't know it would be like this.'

Aetius's jaw clenched at Macarius's stupidity. What had he expected if not this? An empty domus, perhaps, and no guards at all? That they would just walk away?

'It will be all right,' he said, but he was worried all the same. His mind had been so occupied with the deed itself that Aetius hadn't considered the possibility that they would have to wait to see the King. How long would it be? An hour? Longer? The longer he and Macarius waited, the greater the likelihood of their turning tail and scurrying back to the safety of their huts. The deed undone, they would have to return the gold. Their wives would cry, their children starve. No, that couldn't happen. They had to see the King before their courage deserted them.

'We must make the King come here and see us now,' Aetius whispered to Macarius.

'How?'

Aetius pulled hard on his beard, the sharp pinprick pain

helping him to think. 'We'll make a scene,' he decided, 'make a lot of noise.'

Macarius shook his head. 'We'll just get thrown out.'

'Not if we demand to see the King. We've got a dispute, haven't we?' Aetius held up the petition. 'Our story is that I've stolen some of your sheep and you want the King to make me pay you for them.'

'You think he'll come?' Macarius asked doubtfully.

'He's there somewhere,' Aetius gestured beyond the vestibulum to the rooms stretching out before them. 'He'll be curious about the noise. I would be, wouldn't you?' Macarius didn't look convinced. 'It's the best we can do. Now, do it.'

Macarius made a space between himself and Aetius and took a deep breath. 'Do I have to wait all day to get justice from the King?' he said loudly.

'You don't deserve justice,' Aetius returned on cue. 'All I did was take back what was mine.'

'You stole my sheep.'

'So you say. I say they were mine. I'll let the King decide who's in the right.'

They carried on like this for a few minutes, their voices growing louder, their arm-waving wilder, until a lictor, a member of the King's personal bodyguard, appeared.

As guards went, the lictor wasn't particularly intimidating. 'You two, you must be quiet,' he insisted, hitching the fasces further up his shoulder, 'or I will have you removed.'

'Don't you tell me what to do,' Aetius yelled into the lictor's face. 'I've a right to be heard. You get the King to hear me. Go on, you get him.'

The lictor looked Aetius up and down and sneered. 'The King doesn't come at the command of peasants.'

'Who you calling a peasant?' Macarius pitched in, genuinely outraged.

'I'm a Roman citizen,' Aetius said, pushing Macarius back, 'and I demand to see my king.'

The lictor shook his head in scorn and waved over two guards who were peering around the doorway of the tablinum. The guards sauntered over, enjoying the unaccustomed drama, and took hold of Aetius and Macarius. Aetius felt himself being pulled towards the doors and began to struggle ferociously, determined not to be thrown out before they'd done what they'd come for. Macarius did the same, clutching at the other people waiting in the vestibulum who tried to slap away his hands.

'What is all this noise?'

Aetius and Macarius froze, the guards too. The lictor spun around.

An old man was standing in the tablinum. He wore his white curly hair long in the fashion of his Etruscan ancestors and he had on the finest toga Aetius had ever seen, saffron-dyed linen decorated with elaborate embroidery. His kid leather shoes were long and pointed, extending far beyond where his toes would have ended, and the tips curled up, making them wholly impractical footwear for any kind of physical labour. *So, this is how a king dresses*, Aetius thought.

'Now look what you've done,' the lictor hissed at Aetius and gave him a vicious kick in the shin. 'I am sorry, my lord,' he said to the King. 'I shall have these troublemakers thrown out at once.'

King Lucius Tarquinius, known to his family as Lucomo, stepped towards the shepherds. 'From what I heard, you are demanding justice?' he said to Aetius and gestured to the guards to release their prisoners. 'I'm not accustomed to having justice demanded of me in so rude a fashion.' He took in their appearance and concluded, 'You are shepherds, yes?'

'Yes, my lord king,' Aetius said, feeling for the knife he kept in his belt, checking his struggle with the guard hadn't dislodged it.

'You people must learn your country manners have no place here,' Lucomo said with a shake of his finger and he began to turn away.

Their opportunity was fading. 'You must hear me,' Aetius cried desperately.

The lictor shushed him but Lucomo halted. 'Must I?' he said, raising a bushy white eyebrow.

'I beg you.' Aetius dropped to one knee and curled his fingers around the knife's handle. He flicked a glance at Macarius.

No one else was watching Macarius. No one noticed him moving behind the lictor and then behind Lucomo. No one noticed him, in fact, until he pulled out the axe he'd hidden beneath his cloak and brought it down upon Lucomo's head. There was a dull crack and blood spurted. The onlookers gasped. A woman screamed. Aetius rammed his knife into Lucomo's stomach and a crimson stain blossomed over the expensive toga. His legs buckled, pitching him forward. Aetius scrambled to get out of the way as Lucomo smacked into the tiled floor. The axe handle juddered, the blade embedded deep in the old man's skull.

The guards' sense of duty returned and they once again took hold of Aetius and Macarius, bundling them to the floor and pressing their knees into their backs so they couldn't move. Aetius met Macarius's eyes in grim understanding and they both ceased their struggles.

There was no point. They were dead men.

———

The screams brought Queen Tanaquil running.

She had tutted when Lucomo rose from his desk, curious to discover the cause of the shouts coming from below. 'Ignore it,' she admonished testily. 'Finish your papers. Whatever it is, the guards will take care of it.'

But Lucomo was in one of his stubborn moods and had waved her away, flinging open his office door and shuffling out, for the pointy toe slippers had a habit of slipping off. Putting her own papers aside, Tanaquil followed after him, stopping at the top of the stairs to watch as he crossed the courtyard, losing sight of him as he entered the tablinum. She banged the balustrade lightly with her clenched fist. Why couldn't Lucomo leave well enough alone? Why must he always interfere? She leant over the balustrade, straining her ears, but heard only murmurings.

Tanaquil straightened, thinking she might as well return to her work. She turned back to the office door. A shudder suddenly went through her body and it fixed her to the spot. It made her reach out a trembling hand to find something solid to steady herself. Her heart began to hammer and she had a sudden presentiment. Something was wrong. Something was terribly wrong. Lucomo!

She spun around and stared down into the tablinum, to the spot where she had last had sight of her husband. She could hear voices, perhaps every other word that was said, but she could see nothing. But something was wrong, she could feel it, sense it. Out of the corner of her eye, she saw a guard shift at his station. She opened her mouth to call out, to get his attention, but her throat was tight, she couldn't utter a sound.

She was too late. She heard the screaming and Tanaquil ran, her sandals slapping on the stones. From the courtyard, she could see through into the atrium. The lictor and guards were bending over something on the floor. Her step faltered as she feared what the something was. *No, no, oh please, Jupiter, no.* She rushed towards the men and pushed them out of the way. A cry escaped her throat. It was Lucomo. He was lying face down on the stones, his blood spreading around him and an axe sticking out of his head.

Tanaquil fell to her knees beside her husband. She wanted to touch him but she didn't know where to lay her hands. Part of her wanted to tug the axe out of Lucomo's head but the sight revolted her and she couldn't bring herself to put her fingers to the bloody instrument. Hot tears were running down her cheeks. And then hands were tugging at her, gripping her beneath her armpits and pulling her backwards onto her feet.

'Help him,' she screeched to the lictor who held her.

She heard the lictor give orders. 'Take the King to his cubiculum. And fetch the doctor.'

Tanaquil saw one of the guards reach out to the axe handle. 'No, don't touch it,' she cried with sudden lucidity. The blood would flow more freely, she realised. Thanks be to Jupiter she hadn't touched the axe.

She watched as the guards lifted Lucomo, his body sagging between them. Blood dripped in heavy globules as they carried Lucomo through the domus and up the stairs to his cubiculum. Her eyes followed the trail of blood, and while her mind was telling her Lucomo couldn't survive losing so much, her heart was praying to Asclepius to save him.

In his cubiculum, the guards laid Lucomo on his bed, stepping back and staring down at the man they called king. As she joined them, she realised they didn't know what to do now they had got Lucomo here. That was understandable. She didn't know what to do either.

But someone had to take charge.

'Who did this?' she asked. Her voice sounded strange to her.

'It was two shepherds,' the lictor answered. He turned to her and his face was ashen. 'The guards have them. They started an argument, deliberately, I think, to get the King to come down. They attacked him — it happened so fast.'

'Secure them in the domus and keep the petitioners in the vestibulum. I don't want this incident to be spoken of until we know how serious the King's injury is.'

The lictor stared at her. 'The King is dead, lady.'

She returned his stare unflinchingly. 'We don't know that yet. My husband may survive this attack. The doctor will tell me. Lictor, the people must not think the King is dead.'

'Yes, of course,' the lictor nodded. 'I will have the domus doors locked.' He took a last look at Lucomo, then hurried out.

As he left, another man entered. His olive complexion showed his stubble clearly and a white band surmounted his short black hair. 'I didn't believe it when they told me,' he breathed, his eyes on Lucomo.

'Don't just stand there, Danaos,' Tanaquil said to the doctor, 'help my husband.'

Danaos moved to the bedside. He put his fingers to the axe blade where the metal met the bone. He prodded gently and Lucomo twitched.

Tanaquil grabbed at his arm. 'He's alive?'

Danaos clicked his tongue against his teeth. 'The blade has gone in deep, lady. It's cleft the skull.'

'But he moved, he moved.'

Danaos studied the axe handle, then extended a finger and pushed the wood. Lucomo twitched again. 'It's the axe. A semblance of life, nothing more.'

Tanaquil's hands rose to her mouth to stifle her cry. For

the briefest of moments, she thought Asclepius had answered her prayer and Lucomo was still alive, that he would live. But Danaos had crushed that hope as quickly as it had come.

'Take that thing out,' she ordered, flicking her fingers at the axe.

Danaos gripped the handle with both hands and tugged the blade free. It made an obscene sucking sound and Tanaquil felt vomit rising in her throat. She swallowed it back down, watching as more blood poured from the wound, and now she could see spongy grey matter beneath the red and she knew it to be Lucomo's brain.

'Turn the King over,' Tanaquil ordered the guards.

Tanaquil hadn't seen Lucomo's face since he left her. Now, as the guards wrestled the lifeless body onto its back, Tanaquil found she didn't recognise the man on the bed. This was not Lucomo, this thing with bulging eyes and slack mouth.

Danaos bent over Lucomo and put his ear to the King's lips. After a long moment of listening, he straightened and looked at Tanaquil. 'There is no breath, lady. The King is dead.'

Tanaquil gestured for Danaos to step aside. She moved to the bed and sat on its edge, not caring if the blood on the sheets stained her dress. She closed her eyes and pressed her lips against the side of his mouth, wincing at the cooling skin. Placing her palm over Lucomo's staring eyes, she slid the delicate skin over the orbs to close them.

———

Tanaquil closed her eyes. She wouldn't cry, not in front of Danaos and the guards. And besides, there wasn't time for grief, not yet. The King was dead. Rome had no ruler. When it became known, there would be change, and the manner of Lucomo's death might mean there would be chaos. She couldn't let that happen to Rome, not after all she and Lucomo had achieved together.

'You will stay here,' she said to Danaos, rising from the bed.

'There is nothing I can do,' Danaos said, perplexed by her command. 'The King is dead.'

'I'm not a fool, you Greek, I know he's dead. You will stay here.'

'Lady, I don't understand.'

'The King is not dead,' Tanaquil told him, irritated she had to explain to him as she had had to explain to the lictor. 'He is injured and you are tending to him.'

Understanding crossed Danaos's face. 'Oh yes, I see.'

'You stay here too,' she told the guards as she left the room, closing the door behind her. She needed to be alone for a while. She went to her own cubiculum next door to Lucomo's and collapsed onto her bed. Burying her face in the pillow so as not to be heard, she allowed herself to weep.

But she was too old to have too many tears in her. Soon, her throat was sore and her head was throbbing, but her eyes were dry. Moving to the bowl of water kept on a stand in the corner of the room, she dampened a linen cloth and pressed it to her eyes to soothe them. She knew she didn't have long, that she would have to present herself to the people and pretend she wasn't grieving, that her husband was still alive. She took a few deep breaths and exited, making her way to Lucomo's office.

The office was just as they had left it, the papers messy on the desk, Lucomo's cup of honey water half drunk. He would never finish it now, she reflected. She tidied up a little, setting the papers in a pile and gulping down the honey water, almost believing she could taste Lucomo on the cup's rim.

The lictor appeared in the doorway. 'Your instructions have been followed, lady,' he said, and she could tell he was examining her face, no doubt trying to determine her state of mind.

'I'm ready to see the men who attacked the King. Have them brought here.'

The lictor hurried away. When he returned, ushering the guards in with their captives, Tanaquil was perfectly composed.

The shepherds were terrified, Tanaquil could see that clearly, the younger man especially. Mucus, mixed with blood, slid from his nose to soil his lips and chin, and she could smell the acrid odour of urine. The other, the elder, was watching her, his eyes wary.

'What are your names?' she asked him and was proud her voice sounded strong.

'My name is Aetius. He is Macarius.'

'Roman names. Why did you try to kill your King?'

Aetius started. 'He's... he's not dead?'

'No, not dead. You wounded him, nothing more.'

'But the axe—'

She cut him off. 'Why did you try to kill your King?'

'We were paid to.'

'Who paid you?'

Aetius shook his head. 'I can't tell you.'

'You will tell me.'

'I cannot. We made an oath we wouldn't tell.'

'You made an oath to traitors?'

'Please, lady,' spittle dripped from Aetius's mouth, 'we're just shepherds. We don't know their names.'

'You don't know who you were working for? I think that

unlikely.' Tanaquil nodded to the guard who held Macarius. The guard punched him in the stomach and Macarius doubled over, spluttering.

'I ask you again,' she said, fixing her eyes on Aetius. 'Who hired you?'

Aetius shook his head.

She nodded again and this time the guard kicked Macarius in the ribs.

'Tell them, Aetius,' Macarius begged when he could catch his breath again.

'Shut up,' Aetius spat.

'So, Aetius,' Tanaquil said, 'for the last time. Who sent you to kill the King?'

Aetius looked at Macarius cowering beside him. 'The sons of Ancus Marcius.'

Tanaquil's breath caught in her throat. Of course, it was obvious now the name had been spoken. Ancus Marcius had been king before Lucomo. Lucomo had served Ancus well and Ancus had favoured him highly. When Ancus died, the senate, knowing Lucomo to be an honourable and capable man, had elected him to be king. But Ancus's sons had objected, claiming their right superseded that of Lucomo's, that one of them should be king. But the senate paid them no attention and Ancus's sons had slunk out of Rome, protesting against the people's lack of respect for their nobility. Secure on the throne, Lucomo and she had grown complacent over the years, not considering the Marcius family to be a threat. Now, she knew how reckless they had been to think so.

'They paid you to kill the King?'

Aetius nodded. 'They gave us gold.'

'And where are they now?'

'We don't know,' Aetius said. 'The rest of the gold was to be sent on to us when…'

'When you had butchered my husband,' Tanaquil finished.

Macarius was mumbling he was sorry. Tanaquil ignored him. To Aetius, she said, 'Did you really expect to survive this?'

Aetius shook his head.

'And so the gold was to go to your families. I suppose you have families?'

'Yes,' Aetius said and began to sob.

'And you would be heartbroken to have anything happen to your families?'

'Please, lady,' Macarius said, pawing at the hem of her dress, 'they have nothing to do with this. It was us. Aetius, tell her it was just us.'

'We beg you, lady,' Aetius said, 'have mercy.'

'Mercy?' she said, bending down to him so their faces were only inches apart. 'Mercy from the woman whose husband you have attacked?'

'We didn't want to do it,' he cried.

'But you did it all the same.' Tanaquil drew back her arm and struck him across the face, feeling the sting in her palm. She enjoyed the pain, it gave her strength. 'Take them away and lock them up,' she said to the guards. 'Then discover their families and have them taken up as well.'

'No,' Aetius cried. 'Please, I beg you, my Queen. They are innocent of this.'

'No one is ever innocent,' she said as the guards dragged Aetius and Macarius away. To the lictor who remained by her side, Tanaquil said, 'Find Servius Tullius.'

2

The lictor had anticipated Tanaquil's command and despatched a messenger to fetch the King's son-in-law as soon as he had secured the domus. The lictor had instructed the messenger to speak to no one but Servius Tullius. Servius had been in the forum on business when the messenger found him, telling him as quietly as he could that the King had been attacked. The news had stunned Servius. He didn't stop to question the messenger but hurried home.

Servius ran up to the domus, kicking up dust into the faces of the guards. Breathlessly, he yelled at them to unlock the doors. They hurried to obey and had barely opened the heavy wooden doors before Servius burst in, pushing his way through the petitioners who had been detained on Tanaquil's order. Spotting an opportunity to escape, they all tried to exit at once, but the guards forced them back and re-locked the doors.

The lictor was waiting at the top of the stairs. He stepped forward to meet Servius.

'Is it true?' Servius asked. 'Has the King been attacked?'

'Sir,' the lictor said, keeping his voice low, 'the King is dead.'

Servius stared at him. 'Dead?'

The lictor nodded.

'And what of the Queen?' Servius asked. 'Was she hurt? Where is she?'

'In there.' The lictor pointed to Lucomo's office. 'She wasn't there when it happened. She came down once it was… when it was over.'

'Thanks be to Jupiter,' Servius breathed. 'How is she?'

'I don't know, sir. She's wept, I could tell by her eyes, but she did it in private. I knew she'd want to see you, so I sent the messenger to find you.'

'Thank you for that.' Servius patted the lictor's arm, a gesture of familiarity he was not apt to bestow nor one the lictor would normally have welcomed. But this was no ordinary day and the lictor appreciated the gratitude. He stepped to one side, allowing Servius to pass.

Servius knocked on the office door. The voice he knew so well called, 'Come in.'

Tanaquil was sitting at Lucomo's desk. She looked worn, tired. Her grey wiry hair, normally kept so tidy in a bun at the nape of her neck, had come loose and thin strands hung around her jaw. The counterfeit blush, carefully applied that morning, stood stark against her pale cheeks. The lictor was right, Servius thought, she had been crying; her eyes were red and bloodshot. Tanaquil gasped his name and held out her arms.

Servius rushed to her and she cradled herself against him. He stroked her hair, feeling awkward. He'd never done this before, never comforted Tanaquil, it had always been the other way around. 'I can't believe it,' he said softly. 'Lucomo dead.'

'The axe broke his head open,' Tanaquil said, pulling away and dabbing at her eyes.

'And those who did it?'

'Under guard. I've given orders for their families to be captured too.'

'Why did they do it?' he asked, pulling up a stool. He took her hands, drew them onto his lap and rubbed them gently.

Tanaquil licked her cracked lips. 'They were hired by the sons of Ancus Marcius.'

Servius cursed under his breath. 'But it's been almost forty years. To act after all this time.'

'Yes, we thought we were safe.'

'But then, Tanaquil, they'll be coming to Rome to take the throne. We must—'

'They won't come. They won't come because they won't know Lucomo is dead. Not yet. We won't announce his death until we are ready.'

'But the senators and the patricians—'

'Servius, listen to me,' Tanaquil grasped his hands and held them to her breast. 'If we tell the world the King is dead, there will be war. I am too old to fight a war, my boy. But we have you.'

Servius jerked his hands away. 'Me?'

'Yes, you.'

'But I'm— I'm nothing, Tanaquil.'

Tanaquil pushed away the short dark hair sticking to his forehead. 'You are far from nothing, Servius. You are a gift from the gods. Oh, don't look at me like that, it's true. Lucomo and I never told you the story of what happened when you were young, did we? I shall tell you now. You were asleep, just a boy of about eight, and as you slept, your head became a ball of fire. People thought your head was aflame and the slaves rushed to bring a bucket of water to throw over you, but I had been called to see you for myself and I told them to stand back. I saw you were in no danger. You slept peacefully. I stayed and watched the flames lick your pillow, yet the linen did not burn, and you did not cry out. Eventually, you awoke and the flames flickered out, and there you were, staring at me, wondering why I was staring at you.'

'I don't remember any of this,' Servius said, dumbfounded.

'It was a sign you were to be a beacon in our household,' Tanaquil said. 'Lucomo and I decided to raise you as if you were our own son because we knew Rome would have need of you one day.'

'Need of me? What do you mean?'

'You will serve as regent until we announce Lucomo's death. There will be no outcry or unrest. Rome will be safe.'

'And when Rome knows Lucomo is dead? We can't keep his death a secret forever, Tanaquil. When it's known, the senate will want an election.'

'There will be no need for an election, my boy. You will do well as regent and it will be the easiest thing in the world for you to take over as king.'

'You want to make me king?' Servius gasped. 'But what of Lucius and Arruns? They're your grandsons, Tanaquil. Surely, one of them should succeed if there is to be no election?'

Tanaquil sighed impatiently. 'Lucius is not yet two years' old, Servius, Arruns is only six months. Even if one of them were elected to be king, a regent would still be needed until they were old enough. Do you not see that you are the obvious, the best, the only choice? Rome needs you, Servius.'

Servius ran his hands through his hair. He felt them shaking. 'Is that why you adopted me? You meant for me to succeed Lucomo? Have you been planning this all these years and never once thought of telling me?'

Tanaquil gave him a hard stare. 'What good would it have done to tell you?'

Servius looked away. 'And all this time I thought you loved me, not that you were grooming me to be Lucomo's successor.'

'Oh, Servius, don't be foolish, of course we loved you. You were as a son to us. We trusted you, we gave you our daughter in marriage. Do not doubt us. Do not doubt *me*. Not today.'

'And if I don't want to be king?'

Tanaquil drew herself up and gave him a withering stare. 'And why would you not want to be king, Servius?'

'Why not? Tanaquil, how can you ask that? I saw how kingship burdened Lucomo, don't forget. And besides, what if the people decide they don't want me as king?'

'They *will* want you, Servius, we shall see to it.'

Servius stood up and began to pace the room. 'I don't know, I just don't know.'

'The throne is yours, Servius, if you are man enough to take it,' Tanaquil said coldly. 'Don't let those cowards who ordered this attack benefit from your lack of confidence. Because that is all it is. You will obey the will of the gods who gave me a sign of your destiny.'

'I can't think… I can't think what I should do.'

Tanaquil beckoned him to her. Servius, feeling like the child he had been when first taken into the Tarquin household, knelt and laid his head in her lap.

'If you cannot put your mind to this, my boy,' Tanaquil said, her fingers playing with his hair, 'then you must let me do your thinking for you.'

'I'll do whatever you say, Tanaquil,' Servius said, letting his eyes close.

———

The sky was turning dark when Servius left Tanaquil and made his way across the domus to his private apartments. His mind was reeling, his body a strange mixture of energy and exhaustion. The death of his father-in-law somehow didn't seem real, so suddenly had Lucomo been taken. And yet, here was his adoptive mother asserting that he, Servius Tullius, was to be the next King of Rome.

His eyes were on the flagstones as he walked along the corridors, not noticing the servants who backed into corners and stood ramrod straight against the walls as he passed. He reached the door of his cubiculum without knowing how he got there. He lifted the latch and almost hit his head as it failed to open.

'Who is it?' a trembling female voice called out.

'Tarquinia?' he called angrily, 'why is the door locked?'

'Servius, is that you?'

'Of course it's me. Open the door.'

He heard the bolt being drawn back; a moment later, the door was flung open. His wife, Tarquinia, stood before him, her face red and swollen and a terrified look in her light brown eyes.

'Oh, Servius,' she hurled herself at him, her fingers clawing at his shoulders, and pulled him into the room. 'Where have you been? I've been here all alone.'

He hadn't given Tarquinia a thought, he realised guiltily, not once since he heard the terrible news. He put his arms around her waist and drew her to him.

'I've been with your mother. I was in the city when it happened.'

'I was at Fulvia's house,' she said, gulping dry sobs. 'We were going shopping and then Nipia came running in and told me Father had been attacked. I wasn't sure what to do, whether to stay at Fulvia's or come home. I didn't know if you were coming to get me...'

Servius felt another stab of guilt. Why hadn't he considered Tarquinia's safety? For all he had known, there could have been more assassins. The plan might have been to remove the entire Tarquin family. Ye gods, what a fool he was. What else hadn't he considered?

'You did the right thing,' he assured her. 'But you haven't seen your mother yet?'

'I came straight here and locked the door,' Tarquinia said. 'I was frightened, Servius.'

'Yes, of course you were. But you should see your mother. She's very upset.'

'*I'm* very upset.'

'I know, but I think it would be good for both of you to be together. And she may want to talk to you about... about other things.'

Tarquinia wiped her eyes and sniffed. 'What other things?'

Servius didn't want to tell her what he and Tanaquil had talked about. It seemed wrong somehow to talk of becoming king so soon after Lucomo's death, especially with Tarquinia so touchy.

'Go to her now,' he said instead, pushing her towards the door. He didn't just want Tarquinia to be with her mother for their sakes; he wanted to be alone for a while, get his brain in some sort of order.

But Tarquinia hesitated. 'Is Father... does he look awful?'

The way she spoke made Servius wonder for a moment whether she knew Lucomo was dead. He quickly thought back over her words. She knew there had been an attack, but she hadn't said she knew Lucomo had been killed.

'Tarquinia,' he began kindly, 'Lucomo didn't survive the attack.'

'I know,' she said as if he was being stupid. 'I'm not a child, Servius. I know Father's dead. But I don't want to see him if he looks horrible. I don't think I could bear it.'

Relieved, he said, 'Wait until tomorrow to see him. He'll have been looked after properly by then.'

She nodded and stepped out into the corridor, but once more paused and looked back. 'Are you all right, Servius? I know how you loved him.'

He smiled at her, absurdly grateful someone had thought to ask him how he felt. 'I will be. I just need a bit of time.'

'I know. It won't be easy for you.'

'What won't be easy for me?'

'Being king.'

He stared at her in astonishment. 'How do you know about that? Tanaquil's only just told me.'

'I've known for years you would become king when Father died,' Tarquinia shrugged. 'It's why we married.'

'You knew then?'

'Mother told me the night before our wedding. I'd asked her why I had to marry you — oh, don't look at me like that, it was only a question and I was a little in love with Publius at the time — and she said you would be king after Father and that my marriage to you would help with that.'

'You never told me,' he said accusingly.

'I didn't think to tell you,' she protested. 'And I never imagined it would be because of something like this, or that it would happen so soon. I thought Father had years left.'

She began to cry again and took a step back into the room, wanting Servius to comfort her. But Servius was furious. It seemed all the Tarquins had been in on this plan for him to become king from the very beginning, and yet no one had bothered to ask him whether he wanted a part in it or whether he thought it was right for him to be king at all. Was his opinion of so little value?

'If this hadn't happened now,' he said, trying to control his temper, 'if your father had lived for another ten or twenty years, Lucius and Arruns would be old enough for the throne and one of them would succeed. Not me.'

'Oh, Servius,' Tarquinia sighed, 'you're not going to be difficult, are you?'

'Difficult!' he roared, unable to hold his anger back any longer.

'Yes, difficult,' Tarquinia shouted back through her tears. 'This *has* happened now. Father's gone. Lucius and Arruns are babies. The senate won't elect one of them king. So, who else is there?'

'Someone of high birth.'

Tarquinia's mouth opened, closed, opened again and then puckered. Servius knew why she was struggling to respond; she hated to hear him speak of his origins. He wasn't sure whether he believed the rumour that he was the son of a slave, or the son of a whore, depending on who was telling the story. He didn't want to believe it and yet it was always there, in the back of his mind, tormenting him. Tarquinia refused to countenance the possibility that she had been married off to anyone other than a nobleman. The idea cheapened her in her eyes, he knew and understood. It was of small consequence that she loved him as he knew she did. Love wasn't enough in the Tarquin family.

'I won't listen to you talk like this, Servius,' she declared at last. 'I'm going to Mother. Will you be here when I return?'

He told her he would.

'I won't be long,' she promised and left, closing the door quietly behind her.

Servius peeled off his toga, leaving just his tunic. Leaning over the bed, he punched the middle of the pillow to create a hollow for his head. With a sigh, he lay down, closing his eyes as he sunk into the pillow. He was going to be king, at least, he was if Tanaquil had her way, and why wouldn't she? Tanaquil always got what she wanted. But this! What Tanaquil wanted was against Roman law. And yet, he also knew she was right. Lucomo had brought stability to Rome. Change didn't always disrupt; sometimes, change was necessary and good, but it could also be terrible. And now he thought about it, who better than himself to take over the reins of office? He had, after all, observed monarchical rule from the inside, he knew how it worked and what it could do. And there was Tarquinia. She thought it only right and natural that he should take over from Lucomo, it wasn't just a desire on her part to be called queen. Maybe everyone else would think it right and natural, too.

Servius wanted to believe that but the rumour of his birth had haunted him since he was old enough to understand the gossip. He played over and over in his mind what Tanaquil had told him of the vision she had witnessed when he was young. He supposed there was some truth in the fact that he had risen in the world, whatever his origins. He had married the King of Rome's daughter, and he knew he was not a stupid man; he had brains and he knew how to use them. He didn't doubt he could do all that was required of a king, but did he have the right to sit on the throne? Would he not feel an impostor, a fraud?

He turned over onto his side, staring at the wall. In the end, it wouldn't matter what he thought or what he wanted. Tanaquil was determined he would become king and Tanaquil would let nothing stand in her way.

————

Lucomo had been wrapped in his shroud and his body removed from the cubiculum to lie in an empty room. The bed she had shared with Lucomo had been stripped of its soiled linen and the mattress thrown out, so all that remained was the wooden frame and the crisscrossing rope supports. A new mattress was laid on the ropes and the servants set about making the bed with fresh linen.

That night, when her mind was so tired she could think no more, Tanaquil retired to the cubiculum and bent her body into the bed that felt so cold without Lucomo in it. He would never be with her again, not in this life, at least. She was alone at last, now the servants and her daughter had left her, and she suddenly understood what she had lost.

She and Lucomo had been married for many years and it had been a happy marriage. And yet, she had not wanted to marry Lucomo. She had shouted at her parents that no matter what they did, no matter what they threatened, she would not stand before the priest and utter the words that would bind her to him. She had not objected to Lucomo's looks nor his manner; he had been quite handsome back then and very courteous. She objected to him because he was unworthy of her, she being of a rank above him. But he had been rich, oh yes, he had had plenty of money, and that, so her parents told her, made all the difference.

So, she had married Lucomo and those early years had not been easy for her. Her friends sniped constantly about her husband of low birth, how she had demeaned herself by marrying someone so inferior, and she had pretended she didn't care. And in a way, she hadn't, for she had come to realise her friends could say what they liked but it was she who wore expensive silks imported from Phoenicia and she who had gold chains to hang around her neck while they wore cheap jewellery, had to mend what good clothes they had and make a dozen other petty economies.

But in those moments when Tanaquil had been alone, her friends' words would play on her mind, and then they had had the power to sting her pride. So, one night, when she and Lucomo lay in bed, she had twined her fingers in his chest hair and suggested they leave Tarquinii and move to Rome. In Rome, she told him, they would have a chance to make something of themselves. In Rome, money mattered, and well, they had plenty of that. In Rome, nobility could be purchased and public office attained.

And that was what she wanted, for her husband to be somebody important. She allowed herself a small smile at the memory. Lucomo had certainly not disappointed her and she had loved him for it. Yes, she had fallen in love with her husband. What a joke!

His rise to power had been heralded by a portent, too, she remembered. When she and Lucomo had trundled into the city sitting atop a wagon packed with their belongings, an eagle had dropped out of the sky and plucked the cap from off Lucomo's head. He had yelped in alarm as the shadow of the big bird fell across them and ducked his head as the clawed feet scraped through his long black hair.

But Tanaquil had kept her eyes on the eagle, watched it soar and circle the wagon three times as though reluctant to leave. It had flapped its wide wings and hovered above them for a thrilling few seconds before dipping and dropping the cap back onto Lucomo's head.

As the eagle flew away, Tanaquil had kissed her astonished husband and said it was a sign from Jupiter that Lucomo was destined for greatness. And so, once they had found themselves somewhere to live in Rome, Tanaquil told Lucomo that henceforth he was to be Lucomo no longer but Lucius Tarquinius, a true Roman, although Tanaquil found it impossible to address him as anything other than Lucomo in private and so, to her, Lucomo he remained. And as any true Roman, he began to make valuable friends and acquired a reputation that brought him to the attention of King Ancus and a position in the royal household. This memory made Tanaquil cry out into the darkness. King Ancus, who had so loved Lucomo that he had consulted him on all matters of politics and made him tutor to his sons, those very sons who had conspired to murder him.

Lucomo was dead! Those three words seemed impossible. He was dead and she was still alive. Tanaquil had always thought she would die first. The possibility of her dying young had been great, as it was for any woman who bred; indeed, with her first son, she had laboured so long and so greatly, the midwives thought her poor exhausted body would give out. But she had lived and Lucomo had given thanks to both Jupiter and Juno for her deliverance with the sacrifice of a kid. And when her childbearing days were over, she had thought she could look forward to a few more years working alongside her husband before leaving him to carry on as king alone.

And now, all that was over. Lucomo had left *her* and what was she to do now? She was too old to enjoy power for its own sake. And her pride, so important to her in her youth, had all but gone, for only the young cared what other people thought. *What is there left to me?* she asked the empty room.

The answer came immediately. Vengeance! She would see those murderers die and revel in their deaths and Lucomo would be avenged. And those setters-on of his murder, the sons of Ancus Marcius, would never become kings of Rome. She had Servius Tullius, no son of her body but of her moulding, and in the end, perhaps that was better.

Servius had disappointed her a little, it was true. She had expected his eyes to shine with excitement at the thought of becoming king but his eyes had had fear in them. Perhaps she had been too precipitate in telling him of her plans so soon after the attack. She should have told him tomorrow when the horror would, Jupiter willing, have receded and he understood what needed to be done.

Worn out with grief, Tanaquil slept soundly that night. She rose early, calling for her maid to dress her hair and pick out her most expensive dress. When dressed, she sat down at her dressing table and held up the bronze mirror to watch her warped reflection as the maid applied her makeup. Tanaquil instructed her to cover up the dark patches beneath her eyes and to flesh out the hollows of her cheeks with the powder of crushed rose petals.

When she could find no fault with her appearance, Tanaquil called for the lictor to accompany her to the balcony at the front of the domus. The lictor seemed determined to let her know how sorry he was for her and she wished he wouldn't. To stop his chatter, she asked what the news abroad was and the lictor reported the attack was known all over the city and that there was a crowd waiting in the street to hear the latest.

'I know,' Tanaquil said, 'I can hear them.'

'We could post a proclamation on the front doors,' the lictor suggested.

'No, I will talk to them.'

'Are you sure that's wise, lady?'

'Yes, I am sure. Is Servius Tullius ready?'

'I'm here, Tanaquil,' Servius called, hurrying along the corridor. He was wearing Lucomo's royal robes as Tanaquil had instructed before they parted the previous evening. 'How are you? Did you get any sleep?'

'I did,' she said, a little ashamed of just how well she had slept.

They reached the balcony. She and Servius lingered in the shadows, Tanaquil's eyes raking over the crowd gathered below. 'Do you think they are here because they want to find out how badly hurt the King is or to hear the grisly details of the attack?'

'Both, I expect,' Servius said. He turned to the lictor. 'Word hasn't got out, has it, that the King was killed?'

The lictor assured him it had not.

'That's something, at least,' Servius said, examining Tanaquil's face. 'Are you up to this?'

'When I say, you come out,' she said. She moved into the sunlight, blinking away the black spots that appeared before her eyes. The crowd quietened when they saw her.

'Go—,' she began, and the sound was too feeble, it would not carry. She cleared her throat and began again. 'Good people of Rome. You will have heard the King was attacked yesterday. This attack was completely unprovoked and the assailants apprehended before they could escape. The King was wounded but is now resting. Until he is once again able to stand before you, I ask that you obey his appointed regent, and beloved son, Servius Tullius. He will dispense justice and take upon himself all other duties until the King is well once more.'

Tanaquil knew he would be nervous; she fancied she could almost hear his heart thumping as Servius joined her at the balcony. She clutched at his hand in the folds of his clothing and gave it a quick squeeze.

'People of Rome.' His voice came out strong and she breathed a silent sigh of relief. 'My heart is heavy at this attack on my beloved father and filled with hate for those who dared to hurt him. But they will not succeed in bringing this state to ruin. Rome is too strong to be blown down by such a feeble wind. The King will recover to stand before us once again. Until that time, I am proud to serve you in his place as regent and I promise you all that I will give my last breath for Rome.'

The people cheered, and she saw a blush flood Servius's neck and cheeks. *This is going to work*, she thought, *I was right*. Servius raised his right hand in salute to the people below and then stepped away from the balcony, back into the shadows.

Tanaquil followed, lifted her thin arms and placed her hands on his shoulders. 'You did that well, Servius. Now, come.' She led him down the stairs to the atrium. The servants had cleaned as best they could, but Tanaquil saw some of the stones were tinged with red. *Lucomo's blood will never be wiped away completely*, she thought, *and perhaps that is as it should be*.

She had not told Servius she would call the senators to the domus, so she wasn't surprised that he hesitated when he saw them waiting. She put her hand to the small of his back, a gentle reminder if he needed it that there was no turning back. A large, carved wooden chair, the one Lucomo had always used when hearing petitioners, stood empty and the senators were giving it a wide berth. There was no mistaking the reverence they had for the inanimate assemblage of wood.

Servius turned a horrified face to Tanaquil. 'I can't,' he whispered.

'Do you think I have the time or patience for your qualms, Servius?' Tanaquil hissed. 'You've said the words. It's time to take your place.'

'As regent,' he protested.

Tanaquil looked hard into his eyes. 'You are king now, Servius. Sit.'

Servius held her gaze for a long moment, then stepped up to the chair.

———

Servius didn't look up as the door to the office opened.

His mind was on his papers, and there were many of them. He had helped Lucomo with the work of being a king, it was true, but he had had no real idea of just how much there was to do. The attack had made no difference to the people; they carried on the same as normal. Every day there had been petitioners in the domus, asking him to intercede in a dispute or pass judgement on a matter, whether that matter was a disagreement over shop boundaries or a legal case to be heard in the courts. And those were only the domestic matters. As soon as news spread beyond Rome that Lucomo had been attacked, emissaries had been arriving from the other Latin states, ostensibly to pledge their support but really to find out how matters stood in Rome. Servius now understood why Tanaquil had wanted to preserve the illusion of Lucomo still being alive and he thanked the gods he had listened to her. Had Lucomo's death been announced, Rome would now be under siege by every foreign potentate who thought his country had a chance to move in and take it over.

Tanaquil closed the door behind her and took a seat by the desk. 'You've worked hard this last week.'

Servius crossed out a line of text. 'That pleases you?'

'It pleases me greatly,' she said. 'I like to see things are carrying on. And you like the work?'

'It has novelty,' Servius shrugged nonchalantly. Tanaquil may have been right, but the little boy in him wasn't willing to admit it. Truth was he felt a little ashamed of how he had behaved. What other man, when offered the throne, would have quailed and protested he was unfit?

Tanaquil nodded and he could tell from the look in her eyes she understood him better than he liked. He returned his gaze to the paper before him, a proposal from the senate. She asked him about it and he grew animated as he told her what the senators were suggesting and what he was willing to cede. By the time he finished, there was the slightest smile rounding out her cheeks. He reddened.

'You're enjoying it,' she said, giving his hand a playful slap, 'admit it.'

'Oh, very well,' he said, throwing up his hands in surrender, 'I am. So far.'

'Get used to it, it's going to get a lot busier.' She took a deep breath, her shoulders rising and falling. 'I'm going to announce Lucomo's death.'

'It has been eight days,' Servius agreed after a moment. 'We can't go on saying there's no change in his condition. We're prepared, aren't we?'

'I think so,' Tanaquil said thoughtfully. 'You will address the senate. You will tell them Lucomo never regained consciousness and that he slipped away in his sleep. His end was peaceful.'

Tanaquil's face hardened and Servius knew she was fighting against the memory that Lucomo's death had been anything but peaceful.

'Do you think there will be opposition to me becoming king?' Servius asked.

'Some, perhaps, but from what I've heard, the senate is as eager for a quick accession as we are. They know you, Servius, they trust you. Any other candidate would be a risk. There will be a vote and the majority will agree that an election is not necessary. You will be made king. Don't worry.'

Was it really going to be this easy? That he could step into Lucomo's shoes and everyone would thank him for it? Servius glanced at Tanaquil and saw no doubt in her eyes. He had known her for so long now that he trusted her implicitly. If Tanaquil said there would be no opposition, there would be no opposition. It *was* that simple.

'And once that's done, we'll need to arrange Lucomo's funeral,' he said carefully, studying her face for any sign he had said the words that would wound her.

But he needn't have worried. Tanaquil's expression didn't change. 'My dear boy,' she said with a rueful smile, 'I've already begun.'

———

Lucomo's body had been washed and anointed, a wax mould taken of his face and a gold piece for Charon placed in his mouth to pay for the ferry that would take him across the River Styx to the Underworld. He would soon be welcomed into Elysium, Tanaquil thought, as she watched the bier carriers lift him onto their shoulders and carry him out of the domus, as befitted such a favourite of the gods.

Too many days had now passed for Tanaquil to cry afresh;

her crying was done. As they had agreed, Servius told the senate of Lucomo's passing and a proclamation was nailed to the senate doors to inform the people. Now, his shrouded body was ready for burial and the streets of Rome were already lined with citizens who wanted to see the late King embark on his final journey.

Tanaquil joined Servius, Tarquinia and her grandchildren — Lucius, Lucilla and Arruns — and together they led the procession from the domus, the loud music played by the hired musicians walking behind them making it impossible to think of anything beyond putting one foot in front of the other.

The bier was set down in the forum so everyone could see it. She watched as the people clustered around the body while the funeral lament was sung, some reaching out their hands to touch it. The professional mourners began their wailing and tearing of their hair, letting the dead know a great man was about to join them. When all the crowd had seen the body, the procession set off again. They had a slow walk to the cemetery, for though it was less than a mile distant from the walls of the city, the sheer volume of people and the stately pace of the bearers meant it took almost an hour to reach the funeral pyre.

The time for sacrifice had come. A man unlatched the door of a small wooden cart and released a pig, pushing it out of its wooden cage and towards a stake hammered into the ground. Putting a rope around its neck, he tied the other end to the stake.

Servius moved towards the animal, a knife ready in his hand. The pig must have sensed its death was near for it began to squeal and try to escape its leash. The man held the squirming animal tight, hooking his arm around its middle and squeezing it against his side. Servius waited while the man put his hand beneath the pig's chin and pulled its head back, exposing its neck. *Do it now*, Tanaquil urged, and it seemed as if Servius read her mind, for he stepped forward and quickly, cleanly, cut the pig's throat, its blood spraying the bottom of his toga.

The pig died quickly, its legs twitching as its blood pumped into the earth. When it had stopped moving, Servius took a heavy cleaver and cut off its head, splitting this in two a moment later. He gave one half to the man, who put it on the funeral pyre alongside the body. Servius carried the other half to the altar that stood to one side, the bloody flesh and bone an offering to the goddess Ceres. The pig's blood was sticky on Servius's hands and Tanaquil knew he would be wishing he could clean them, but he had to endure the gory mess until the end. Someone put a flaming torch into his hand and he held it to the kindling at the base of the pyre. It took only moments for the logs to catch.

Tanaquil and the others moved out of the wind's direction as the fire started to smoke, but still their eyes smarted. Four-year-old Lucilla was being very good, standing still and quiet by Tanaquil, but Lucius, only two years old, grew restless and tugged at Tarquinia's hand, demanding to be taken home, while Arruns, a babe in arms, started to bawl, not liking the roar of the fire nor the smell of the roasting flesh. Tarquinia appealed to her mother and Tanaquil agreed she could take the children back to the domus.

Many of those who had followed the funeral procession from the city stayed for an hour or so, just long enough to honour the dead king, but mindful of the business that awaited them in their shops. The patricians and senators remained, having no shops to open and acutely conscious of what was expected of them.

It was night by the time the pyre had been reduced to ash

and the bones of Lucomo found among the debris and placed in an urn. The house servants had journeyed from the domus with carts laden with food for the funeral feast, and in the light of charcoal braziers, began to lay out bread, cheese, eggs and honey and pour out cups of wine. A bowl of water was presented to Servius so he could, at last, wash the pig's blood from his hands. Tanaquil accepted bread and honey and a cup of wine and watched as the urn containing Lucomo's ashes was buried. Servius put his hand on her back and asked how she was feeling.

'A little numb,' she said, 'but pleased for Lucomo. He can rest now.'

'And when he's in Elysium,' Servius said, squeezing her shoulder, 'he'll be welcomed with wine and song.'

'That will not be until he is avenged, Servius,' Tanaquil said, pouring her wine over the fresh mound of earth that showed where the urn was buried. 'Not until the blood of those who killed him waters the dirt.'

———

They returned to the domus when the night had become black, their way through the narrow streets lit by torchbearers. The front doors had been shut upon the most curious and persistent, feeling that after a long day of public show, the Tarquins could at last allow themselves some privacy.

Servius yawned as he entered the triclinium. As soon as they returned to the domus, he had gone to his office, conscious he had urgent papers to read. He had meant to work for only a little while, but he had been at his desk for over an hour.

He saw Tanaquil sitting alone. 'Are you all right?'

She forced a smile onto her face and patted his hand. 'I'm

fine, my boy, thank you. Come and sit by me.' She patted the seat cushion beside her.

'Where's Tarquinia?' he asked as he sat.

'She's gone to bed with a headache. Lucius was very naughty after they left.'

'Oh, that makes a change.'

They both laughed and fell into a companionable silence. Servius broke it. 'I miss Lucomo. I only realised today how much.'

'Well, you've been busy. You've hardly had time to think.'

'So have you and you've had more to cope with. Managing the servants, making sure all the little jobs are done, seeing to the children, arranging the funeral. You've done all of that as well as helping me. You're magnificent, you know. I couldn't have borne all this without you.'

'Of course you could,' Tanaquil said, smiling with pleasure despite herself. 'But I'm glad I've been able to help you.'

'Help me? You've done everything. You've told the secretaries and lictors and guards what to do, shown me how to act and talk to the senators—'

'Enough, Servius. Lucomo and I had to learn all this too. We didn't just know how to rule a nation straightaway, you silly boy. There's no shame in allowing an old woman to help.'

Servius nodded. 'You've been the best of mothers, Tanaquil. I don't know how to thank you.'

'There's no need. If I've been a good mother to you, then you've been more than I could have hoped for in a son. But you will have to be strong now, Servius,' she said, her expression hardening.

'What do I have to do?'

'Have you forgotten about the shepherds?'

Understanding spread across Servius's face. He had indeed forgotten about Aetius and Macarius. 'I have to execute them.'

'Yes, you do,' she nodded. 'Tell me how.'

She was testing him, Servius knew. He thought for a moment. 'With swords on the Field of Mars,' he decided. 'We will show the sons of Ancus Marcius we are strong.'

'Good. And what of the shepherds' families?'

Servius frowned. 'They played no part in the murder.'

'Did they not?' Tanaquil's thin eyebrows rose. 'Do you imagine those men did not discuss their plan with their wives? Did their wives not wonder where the gold came from?'

'They're women, Tanaquil.'

'They are traitors, Servius.'

'Very well,' he sighed. 'The children, too?'

Tanaquil nodded. 'I want no one left alive who will have reason to hate you, my boy.'

3

A proclamation had been made in the forum that the late King's assassins were to be executed.

It was all anyone talked about in the city. Men wondered how the executions would be carried out; women speculated as to whether the wives and children would be killed along with the men. Few, if any, expressed sympathy. The way the people of Rome saw it, the men and their families had acted treacherously and now had to pay the price.

The executions were to take place in the morning. As the appointed hour drew near, men shut up their shops, letting down the awnings and fixing them in place with wooden bars, while women set aside their spinning and their cleaning, and taking their children by the hand, made their way to the Field of Mars.

The royal guards had made a square in the centre of the field and here waited Aetius and Macarius, their wives and their children. All were bound with ropes and the men's faces were bruised dark purples and reds, their lips split, and blood matted their hair. The women and the children had not been touched. Their faces bore nothing but fear.

People found spaces for themselves, elbowing their closest neighbours aside to ensure they got a good view. They laughed and joked, not considering nor caring their good humour might heighten the prisoners' fear.

Trumpets sounded to announce the arrival of the royal family. There was more shoving as a passage was made through the crowd, the royal guards forcing onlookers back to allow Servius and the women through. People murmured to one another as they looked on Servius. He looked grim, they commented, and poor Tanaquil there, losing her husband in such a way. But that was the way of the world, they shrugged, they lived in violent times. And there was Tarquinia, the women looking her up and down, their eyes devouring her silk dress and gold necklace and bracelets, working out how much they cost and how long it would take for them to save up to be able to afford such trinkets, knowing they never would.

Servius, Tanaquil and Tarquinia took the seats that had been set out for them. The crowd stopped their talking and waited.

Servius gestured for the lictor to pronounce the prisoners' crime and the judgement passed upon them. The shepherds' wives began to cry, and one rushed towards Servius, begging him to spare her and her son. A guard took hold of her, dragging her back to the others and cuffing her around the mouth to keep her quiet. She fell to her knees, blood dripping from her lips.

The women and children were to die first, Tanaquil had insisted. The shepherds were to feel the most exquisite agony and see what their murderous actions had wrought. At a nod from Servius, two guards took hold of the women and the children, the other four guards pulled Aetius and Macarius aside.

The children were crying now, not knowing what was happening, only aware their mothers were frightened. They sobbed as they watched the guards approach and tried to back into their mothers even as the guards drove their swords into their stomachs. The women clutched at their dying children, holding their hands over the wounds as if they could stop the blood pouring out of their offspring.

One of the women realised there was nothing she could do to stop her children from dying. Her hands, slick with their blood, ceased their attempts to close up the rips in their abdomens. She let their bodies tumble from her lap to lie face down in the dirt. Pushing herself up onto her feet, the woman faced Tanaquil and Servius. There was a frightening intent in her movement and the guards held back, wary.

The woman opened her mouth wide, tilted her face to the sky and screamed. It was a terrible sound, high, keening, more animal than human. She raised her hands to her face, dragging them across her cheeks. When she pulled them away, her cheeks were streaked with the blood of her children. She opened her eyes and they stood out white against the red. She fixed them on Servius.

'I curse you,' she screamed into the sudden silence of the crowd. 'King Servius Tullius, I curse you. May your reign be marred by discord at your hearth. May your loins bring forth monsters who will cause you pain and strife. May your end be full of blood and pain and come at the hands of your children. And may you suffer eternal torment in the Underworld. I call on Poena to avenge this murder of my innocent children. Poena, hear me.'

The woman raised her arms to the sky. The clouds above her head swelled and turned dark. The Field of Mars became shrouded in grey. The goddess of punishment had heard her servant.

Servius clutched the pommels of his chair. His wide-open eyes stared at the woman, then at the louring clouds. His breath started to come fast, his heart pounded in its cage. A dark shape was forming in the grey clouds, a strange, human-like form with wings. It hovered in the sky until the edges became solid. Then, a piercing scream rent the air and it folded its wings back to dive straight at Servius.

It was coming nearer and nearer, its scream louder and louder. Servius couldn't breathe, he couldn't move. The shade struck, bursting into him, through him. For a horrible, shocking moment, he felt as if his body had exploded into a million pieces and then become whole again.

Servius could breathe again, he could move. He jerked around, looking for the shade. He couldn't see it. Where was it? He peered up into the grey sky and saw something dark, distant. It was going away from him, towards the city.

'Servius,' Tanaquil cried and touched his hand.

Servius wrenched his eyes to her. She looked as scared as he felt. Beside her, Tarquinia was crying, burying her face in her hands. 'Did you see it?' he cried.

Tanaquil nodded, her lips pressed so tightly together they were no more than a thin line.

'What does it mean?'

'I don't know.' She shuddered, and the movement brought some sense back to her. She looked at the crowd. They had seen it too and there was shouting and screaming and crying. 'Servius, we must—,' she swallowed a few times, 'we must calm the crowd.'

Servius took five deep breaths, feeling light-headed. *Pull yourself together*, he told himself, *act like a king*. His legs feeling as if they would collapse under him, Servius manoeuvred himself to a standing position. Trembling, he held out his arms and shouted for silence. The crowd obeyed. *What do I say?* he wondered, and looked to Tanaquil for help.

'Order the guards to kill the others,' she said.

Servius called out to the guards. 'Continue.'

He saw the guards hesitate a moment, but then they obeyed. One of the guards stabbed the woman in her heart and she crumpled to the ground; the other woman died as swiftly. The guards were keen to make quick work of Aetius and Macarius too. Swords were thrust into their bellies and driven home. Both men fell to their knees as their guts pushed out. The guards raised their swords above their heads, bringing them down upon the exposed necks and severing their spines. The shepherds' bodies slumped to the ground.

No one cheered. No one clapped. Servius couldn't bear it any longer. He stumbled down the two steps from his chair and held out his hand to Tanaquil. He felt her fingers clasp him, felt them trembling. He heard Tanaquil call to Tarquinia and heard the rustle of her silk dress as she too got to her feet. Servius was glad when the guards lined up around them, cutting them off from view.

'Move on,' he told the guards.

———

There were those in Rome who hadn't left the city to watch the executions, those who were perhaps too squeamish or simply uninterested. But some of those people looked up at the sky when it turned dark and wondered at the small black shape that appeared and flew over their heads. Wondering what the thing was, they watched as it headed towards the Capitoline Hill and there lost sight of it.

They could not have known but the shade found the Tarquin domus and passed through its walls. The domus was empty save for a few domestics working in the kitchen and the children in the nursery who had been deemed too young to attend the executions.

The shade sought out the nursery. The nurse left tending the three children was struck immobile by its presence in the small room. Rooted to the spot, she stared wide-eyed and open-mouthed as the shade settled first on Arruns in the cot, making him wail, then Lucilla on the bed playing with a doll. It made her fling herself face down on the mattress and cry into the blankets. And then it found Lucius, sitting on the floor playing with a set of wooden animals, carved for him by one of the servants. It folded around the small boy like a cloak and Lucius screamed. Then the shade peeled away from him and disappeared through the ceiling.

The noise from the children was overwhelming and it startled the nurse into movement. She went first to little Arruns, picking him up and cradling him to her chest. She moved to Lucilla, pressing her hand against the little girl's back, begging her to stop crying. The little girl cried all the louder and kicked her legs. The nurse then bent to Lucius, pressing Arruns tighter to her to stop him falling. She begged Lucius to stop screaming, but his eyes were screwed tight and he just kept on. She couldn't bear it any longer and slapped him hard. Lucius stopped screaming and stared at her, his little body racked by deep gulping breaths.

Terrified, the nurse bundled Lucius to her and called Lucilla over. Feeling alone on her bed, Lucilla obeyed, and the nurse pulled the little girl into the tight circle. That was how Tarquinia found her and the children when she, Tanaquil and Servius arrived home.

'What does it mean?' Servius demanded, wrenching off his toga and throwing it on the floor. 'Tanaquil, what?'

Tanaquil raised the cup of wine to her lips, having to use both hands to keep it steady, and drank, holding the cup out for the servant to refill it. She drank the second cup down. 'The shepherd's wife cursed us,' she said only when she felt the wine warming her blood.

'I know. But you saw, you saw that thing, everyone saw it. It entered me. I felt it go into me and then—,' Servius tried to describe how it had felt when the shade had invaded his body. Tanaquil stared at him as he talked. 'And then it came here. It touched the children. Ye gods, Tanaquil, are we doomed?'

'We shall counter the curse,' she said. 'We must go to the temple and make a sacrifice. There is an ox, I've seen it, a large one. We must sacrifice it to Jupiter and have the priests counter the curse.'

'Will it work?' Servius asked.

'How do I know?' Tanaquil snapped. 'Poena heard that woman, so we must appease her too. The priests will know what to do. Send to them, tell them we will come when it is dark.'

'Let's go now,' Servius pleaded.

'No,' she said. 'We've exposed our fears enough for one day, don't you think?'

'You want to cover this up?' he said, laughing hollowly.

She closed her eyes against his sarcasm. 'Send to the priests,' she repeated. 'The counter-curse will work.'

'And we will be safe?'

'We will be safe.'

'You can promise that?'

She opened her eyes and stared at him. 'I promise, my boy. Nothing will happen. The children will not know of this, they will not remember. The people will not talk of it, we will see to that, and it will be forgotten. Just a story, nothing more. Now, go to your wife and put her to bed. She will stay up all night with the children if you let her and that is not good for them. But send to the priests first.'

She watched Servius as he went to his office, calling for his secretary. It was a terrible thing that had happened, but she meant what she had said to Servius. Nothing would hurt her family.

Nothing.

4

Nonus Lucceius was feeling restless. He had been laid up in bed for the best part of a week with a stomach complaint, the result of a badly cooked dinner at his wife's brother's house, and his rectum felt raw from all the visits made to the latrine.

His stomach and bowels had settled over the past two days and he felt in need of company and a little exercise. Nonus bathed and shaved, treating himself to a dab of rose water upon his temples and wrists, and felt ready to brave the streets of Rome. He made his way to the forum, stopping at some of the shops on the way to gaze longingly at the bowls of fresh figs and olives on offer, only to have the burning between his buttocks remind him he should abstain from food not provided by his own kitchen for a while. He walked past the House of the Vestals and headed for the Janus shrine. As he hoped, he found his friend Hostus Venturius sitting at a table in the shade of the Curia drinking a cup of wine.

'Salve, Hostus.'

Hostus looked up. 'Salve, Nonus. How's your belly?'

'Better,' Nonus said, pulling a stool over to the table. 'If my wife's brother ever asks you to dine with him, refuse.'

Hostus laughed and ran a linen cloth over his bald head to wipe away the sweat. 'You missed all the excitement.'

'The executions? I know. Couldn't be helped.'

'I was right at the front. Saw everything. You should have seen the faces of Servius and the women. I thought the Lady Tarquinia was going to faint. And Servius.' Hostus made a face. 'I don't envy him one little bit. That woman's curse was terrible.'

'I heard the shade entered him. Is it true?'

Hostus nodded. 'Saw it with my own eyes. It went straight through him. I don't think he could move.' He shuddered. 'I don't want to imagine what it felt like.'

'I expect they made a sacrifice to counter it?'

'Probably, but curses like that can't be undone easily. It was powerful to manifest the way it did. Serves them right.'

'You don't wish the assassins had succeeded, do you?'

'Why not? It's about time we had a new king.'

'We've got a new one,' Nonus laughed. 'So, you should be happy, yes?'

'Happy! That we've had the son of a slave foisted upon us as king?'

'Oh, come on, you don't believe that rumour, do you?'

Hostus grunted. 'And Servius has just taken the throne. What about an election, eh? When are we going to have an election to see who should be king?'

'I don't see the problem,' Nonus said. 'Elected or hereditary, it's all the same to me.'

'Then you're a fool. All right then,' Hostus said, wagging his finger, 'you don't mind a hereditary monarchy. But how can a monarchy become hereditary when the Queen can't give her husband any children? How long has Servius Tullius been married to Tarquinia? Years now and still no sign of a babe. She's probably barren, so that's your hereditary monarchy gone straight out of the window.'

Nonus waved his hand dismissively at Hostus. 'Tarquinia was very young when they married. Some women take time to bear fruit.'

'Well, I'd have got rid of a bitch if she hadn't whelped by now. Here, have some of this bread.' Hostus tore off a piece of the bread he had bought and passed it to Nonus.

Nonus's stomach had begun to grumble, and deciding he couldn't go far wrong with bread, put a small piece in his mouth. 'He could divorce Tarquinia and marry again. He's got the throne now, so being married to a Tarquin is no longer necessary. He could have any woman and she could give him an heir.'

Hostus shot his friend a disgusted look. 'Roman kings shouldn't have heirs.'

Nonus shrugged and cast his gaze out over the forum, his eyes attracted by a fight between two dogs being encouraged to bite each other by a gang of young boys. 'It begs the question, though, doesn't it, that if not Servius Tullius, then who?'

'What are you talking about?'

'You name me another man who is fit to be king.'

Hostus opened his mouth to reply, then shut it again. He stared fiercely at his friend.

'Exactly,' Nonus grinned. 'The grandsons of old Tarquin are too young, mere babies.'

'There you go, talking about heirs again. A king doesn't have to come from the Tarquin family. We could choose any of the patricians to sit on the throne.'

'You, for instance?'

'Or you,' Hostus countered irritably.

Nonus shook his head. 'I wouldn't want the throne if it

was offered to me. And it wouldn't be. My family's not old enough.'

'Mine is,' Hostus muttered, not daring to say it too loudly. 'And I'm not alone, Nonus. There are others who don't like having this king thrust upon us.'

'If our only objections are his breeding—,' Nonus began.

'What is he going to do?' Hostus cut in, 'that's what we want to know. Who's he going to be for? The patricians or the plebeians?'

'You make it sound like he has to choose between the two. Why can't King Servius simply be for the good of all Rome and leave it at that?'

'I never took you for a naive man, Nonus. Foolish, yes, but not naive.'

Nonus bridled. 'I didn't come here to be insulted, Hostus.' He made to get up.

'Oh, don't be so precious, you sound like your wife,' Hostus chided and waved Nonus to stay where he was.

Nonus's mouth pursed but he kept his seat. 'I suppose you've heard something that prompts such a question?'

'I've heard King Servius isn't interested in protecting the rights of the patricians, that he was always telling the late King he should tax us more and that we should be made to give up land and hand it over to the poor. I mean, I ask you, what kind of ideas are they?'

'Perhaps we patricians have too much?' Nonus suggested.

Hostus looked at Nonus as if he had just said something shocking. 'You can't mean that?'

'No, no,' Nonus said, holding up his hands, 'I'm merely putting the other side of the argument. Debate. Is that not what we Romans do best, after all?'

'And that's another thing,' Hostus carried on. 'Can Servius Tullius even be called Roman?'

'The late King was not Roman,' Nonus pointed out. 'He was an Etruscan, he came from Tarquinii, both he and the Lady Tanaquil.'

Again, Hostus's mouth opened only to shut again. He found comfort in another piece of bread. 'Well,' he said, olive oil running down his chin, 'don't say you haven't been warned when all of Rome starts to fall about your ears, my friend.'

———

Tanaquil lifted the latch of the kitchen door and stepped inside. All chatter ceased. The head servant put down his knife and hurried over to Tanaquil, bowing his head, ready for her instructions.

'Where is she?' Tanaquil asked, feeling sweat prickle on her skin from the heat coming off the kitchen fire.

'In the storeroom, domina,' the man replied, gesturing towards a door at the back of the kitchen.

'Show me,' Tanaquil said.

She followed him around the large wooden table which still bore the uneaten remains of their dinner and which would serve to fill the bellies of the kitchen staff. The man opened the storeroom door, the uneven wooden bottom scraping against the stone floor. The room was dark for there was no window in the small space.

'Fetch a light,' Tanaquil ordered and he hurried away, returning promptly with a lamp, its flame flickering wildly. He handed the lamp to Tanaquil.

Tanaquil stepped inside and signalled he was to close the door. Holding the lamp at shoulder height, she asked, 'Is it you?'

'Yes, my lady. It's Lusia.' A willowy woman with long

black hair stepped away from the wall and into the faint yellow glow. 'Please allow me to say how sorry I am for your loss.'

Tanaquil wasn't interested in Lusia's words of consolation. 'What have you to tell me?' she snapped.

Lusia swallowed nervously. 'I was in the forum earlier today, my lady, by the Janus shrine, trying to buy some—'

'I don't want to hear about your shopping trip, Lusia.'

'No, my lady,' Lusia stared down at her feet, took a deep breath and began again. 'While I was there, I overheard two men talking about King Servius and their words were not kindly.'

'What did they say?'

'You will forgive me for repeating their words, my lady?'

'Yes, yes,' Tanaquil said, waving the lamp in her irritation. The flame dwindled and bloomed, and a few drops of oil spattered onto her thumb. She winced as they burned her skin. 'Speak.'

Tanaquil listened as Lusia recounted the meeting between the two men. When Lusia came to what they had said about Servius, she felt the muscles in her neck tighten.

'You know the names of these men?'

'I heard only their first names, my lady. They called each other Nonus and Hostus.'

Tanaquil's eyes narrowed. 'One was bald, the other had white hair?'

'Yes, my lady. You know them?'

Tanaquil ignored her impertinent question. 'You've done well,' she said, and turning quickly, opened the door. 'Pay her,' Tanaquil told the man who had been waiting just outside for her to emerge. Thrusting the lamp into his hand, Tanaquil strode out of the kitchen.

'What was all that about?' Tarquinia asked, popping a grape into her mouth as her mother returned to the dining room.

Tanaquil didn't answer. Instead, she moved past her daughter and peered at Servius lying full-length on the couch beside her. 'Is he asleep?'

'Yes,' Tarquinia sighed, looking down at her husband. 'He'll probably start snoring soon.'

'I need him awake. Shake him.'

Wondering what had so agitated her mother, Tarquinia leant forward and shook Servius's shoulder. Servius grunted, mumbled to his wife to leave him alone and pushed his face back into the cushioned seat. Tanaquil gestured for Tarquinia to shake him again, resuming her seat on the couch opposite.

Tarquinia's second shove was more forceful than the first. Servius hitched himself onto his elbows. Opening his eyes with difficulty, he peered at Tarquinia. 'What?'

Tarquinia pointed to Tanaquil.

'I need your brain working, Servius,' Tanaquil told him as he turned his head towards her. 'Sit up and attend to me.'

Servius pulled his legs around to hang over the couch and faced Tanaquil. He felt dizzy and a little nauseous; he had eaten and drunk far too much at dinner.

'You should water his wine,' he heard Tanaquil say, 'if it makes him this stupid.'

'He doesn't always drink so much, Mother,' Tarquinia retorted and he made the weakest of smiles in her direction for her loyalty. 'It's been a very unpleasant few days.'

'For us all, daughter, but you and I don't drink ourselves witless.'

'I'm not witless,' Servius protested, wondering what he had done to deserve Tanaquil's displeasure.

'I'm pleased to hear it,' Tanaquil said, folding her hands over her stomach and waiting for him to look at her. 'Well, are you ready to listen?'

Servius belched and nodded.

'You need not stay to hear this, Tarquinia,' Tanaquil said. 'You can go to bed.'

'I won't be sent off to bed,' Tarquinia whined. 'I'm not a child.'

Tanaquil's eyes closed briefly in irritation. 'Very well, stay and listen, if you prefer. Servius, there is talk in the city, some murmurings among minor patricians complaining there wasn't an election.'

'I knew it,' Servius declared. 'I said there would be oppo… oppo—'

'Opposition,' Tanaquil finished for him, unwilling to wait. 'And yes, you said it. At present, it seems to be nothing but talk between two old men who have nothing better to do, but we must stop it before it spreads.'

'Who do they want as king?' Tarquinia demanded indignantly. 'Who is there better than Servius? The old fools.'

'Yes, daughter, I know.'

'But how do we stop them?' Servius slurred. 'We can't stop people from talking. And besides, maybe they are right. There should be an election. I could stand down—'

'NO,' mother and daughter shouted in unison.

'You will not do that,' Tanaquil said quietly, stroking her throat, a little embarrassed by her outburst. 'There is no need. If there was an election, you would be elected anyway, I know it. Why waste money buying votes?'

'Would they have to be bought?' Servius asked sourly.

'It's how these things are done,' Tanaquil said, 'you know that, Servius. Don't make difficulties. As if I don't have enough to do.'

Servius muttered an apology. 'Then how do we stop the talk?'

'All it will take is the personal touch, my boy. Let the people of Rome see you and you will win them over. Listen to them when they talk to you. Be gracious.' Tanaquil glanced at her daughter, considering. 'Take Tarquinia with you. Let them see the daughter of a king on the arm of a king.'

'That's all I have to do?' Servius asked doubtfully.

Tanaquil smiled. 'You'll be surprised what personality can do, Servius. Mind you, you'll have to try. None of your brooding, you hear me. Look up, smile, greet people warmly.'

'I can do that,' Servius assured her, a little annoyed by her criticism.

'Then do it,' Tanaquil said. 'Tomorrow. You will go into the city. A small, spontaneous procession. The King showing himself to his people.'

'Tomorrow!' Tarquinia scrambled up from the couch. 'But what shall I wear? I shall have to look the part, won't I? I must go and see what I have.' She hurried from the room.

'At least your wife is pleased,' Tanaquil smiled mockingly. 'Tarquinia does so like to show off.'

'And why shouldn't she?' Servius said quietly. 'She has little else to occupy her.'

Tanaquil knew what he meant and recalled what Lusia had reported the two men had said about Tarquinia's lack of children. The lack of children between Servius and Tarquinia was a worry to her too. She knew Tarquinia bled regularly and was seemingly healthy in every other respect. Tanaquil had often wondered if the trouble lay with Servius for she had never heard of him siring a child on any woman.

'You should go to bed, Servius. I don't want you leaving

it too late tomorrow. You want as many people to see you as possible and give them time to talk.'

'Very well. Will you come with us?'

Tanaquil shook her head. 'You want to show them you are the future. I will just remind them of the past.'

Servius climbed clumsily off the couch, wobbling a little as he straightened. 'Thank you, Tanaquil.'

'Don't be silly, my boy. Get to bed.'

Tanaquil watched Servius as he left the room. He was still so unsure of himself and yet, he was ambitious, she knew. She had seen it as he grew up, always wanting to be involved, always asking Lucomo why he pursued such-and-such treaty, why he attacked who he did. Servius had far more knowledge of kingship than he realised. All he needed was approval from the people. Well, tomorrow would see to that. Let the patricians try to overrule the plebs and just see what they would risk.

She yawned, realising how tired she was. She rose from the couch and made her way to her cubiculum.

———

Tarquinia woke him with a poke to his ribs and an abrupt, uncompromising, 'Servius, you have to get up now.'

Servius did not need telling twice. He climbed out of bed, called his servant to wash and shave him and put on his finest toga. Tarquinia looked him up and down from her seat at the dressing table as her hairdresser poked and prodded her curls into place, then ordered him to hold out his hands like a child to be inspected. She tutted and scolded him for getting his hands so inky and ordered fresh soap and water to be brought up from the kitchen, along with a small brush so they could be scrubbed clean.

Tarquinia looked beautiful, he thought, as she watched the scrubbing take place. The dress she wore was not a new one — there had been no time to buy a new one — but the way her hairdresser had styled her hair with braids and tortoise-shell combs was new and it suited her well. There was an amber necklace he hadn't seen before around her neck as well as a gold bracelet on her wrist, his present to her on her last birthday. The jewellery made her look older as well as more beautiful. She had been so young when they married, only a girl of fourteen, and he, a moody, old-before-his-time man of twenty-five. She had not wanted to marry him — there was a lad, Publius, she was keen on — but Lucomo and Tanaquil were not to be dissuaded from their plan of bringing Servius into the family and Publius's family had been told to keep their son away from Tarquinia. Once married, Tarquinia had done her best to forget Publius and be a good wife. Servius couldn't remember if he had ever told her he loved her.

'You look magnificent,' he said.

Tarquinia's face broke into a wide, toothy smile. She leant forward and kissed his cheek. 'I do, don't I?' she said, picking up her hand mirror, holding it at every angle to get a complete picture of her appearance.

He gestured at his toga. 'Will I disgrace you?' he asked, only half-joking.

She set the mirror down and turned to him, her expression reproachful. 'Don't begin like that, my dear. You are the King and you must act like it. Show any sign of weakness and the patricians will be on you like dogs.'

Servius laughed. 'How like your mother you sound.'

'Oh, do I?' she asked unhappily.

The lictor entered the room carrying a crimson cushion with a gold band upon it. Tarquinia took the band and placed it upon Servius's head.

'There,' she said, standing back to examine him. 'Now you really are a king.'

He smiled and took her hand. 'Ready?'

———

They decided to walk through the city. A litter had been suggested for Tarquinia, but she had refused, saying she intended to walk by her husband's side. And so, the procession began, Servius and Tarquinia at the head, their bodyguards immediately behind.

At first, the people had stared. There had been no announcement of the procession and they had been going about their daily business when the entourage first entered their streets. They had been too startled to even bow their heads as their king and queen passed.

But word quickly got around. The further into the city Servius and Tarquinia went the more packed the streets became. The bodyguards had to divide in two, some going ahead to force the people back, the remainder staying behind. And then the cheers began, and women called out to Tarquinia, cooing over how beautiful she looked and praising her dress. Tarquinia was so very pleased and she gave them her most gracious smiles.

Servius was pleased, for himself as well as her; the people, it seemed, were for him as Tanaquil said they would be. But these, he noticed, were the plebeians, the labourers and the shopkeepers, the butchers and the bakers. Would the patricians come out of their houses to see him and Tarquinia? Would they bow their heads before him?

Their little procession was heading for the forum, and as they emerged from the claustrophobic street into the openness of the square, Servius began to recognise a few patrician faces. Here they were, then, no doubt having come out of the senate to see what all the fuss was about. There was Ursus Gratidia and Libanius Manilius. Were their heads bowed? It was difficult to tell. He thought Baro Pomponia and Pertacus Ammianius were bowing, but Flavius Alectus and Pinarius Longus seemed to be standing as tall as they could.

Here, the press of bodies was so great that even the body-guards were having trouble holding the people back. They began to shout and shove, causing those on the end of their shoves to protest loudly and fiercely. Servius and Tarquinia could do nothing but stand still. The air seemed to be standing still too. Servius could hardly breathe and the smell of so many unwashed bodies was forcing its way into his nostrils. He saw Tarquinia raise her hand to cover her nose and shook his head almost imperceptibly at what would doubtless be perceived as an insult. She let her hand drop to her side. *Smile and wave*, he reminded himself, *we must smile and wave.*

A young boy suddenly broke free of the crowd and pushed his way under elbows to hold up a small posy to Tarquinia. She bent down to take the posy — the flowers were dry and wilted — and thanked the boy. As she did so, a cry, louder and harsher than all the others, shouted, 'Son of a whore,' and something dark came flying through the air. It struck Servius in the face and dripped into his mouth. He could taste and smell what it was: shit.

And then there were screams and shouts and pushing and pulling. Tarquinia was tugging at his arm and he looked into her blotchy face and saw that she too had been hit with the ordure. Lumps were clinging to her hair and there was a brown smear across her cheek.

They had to get out of there. Where on earth were the bodyguards? He scanned the crowd. The guards ahead seemed to be trying to find whoever had thrown the shit but there wasn't time for that. Servius grabbed Tarquinia's arm and pulled her back the way they had come, shouting to the bodyguards behind to clear the way.

Servius had no notion of how he and Tarquinia reached the domus. He just kept a tight hold of her and run as fast as they could, heedless of their dignity. The guards on the front doors started towards them as they approached and Servius shouted at them to keep away anyone who ventured too close. He pushed Tarquinia inside the domus and followed, watching as the doors closed.

———

Tarquinia was sobbing.

She had fallen to her knees and was holding her head. Her hair had fallen out of its pins, the tortoiseshell combs lost, and her dress was ripped and torn.

From her room, Tanaquil heard her daughter's crying and came running down the stairs, holding up her dress so her feet wouldn't get caught in its folds. She hurried to Tarquinia. 'What happened?'

'We were assaulted in the forum,' Servius snarled. 'Someone threw shit at us.'

'Who?'

'I don't know, I didn't see.'

'Animals,' Tanaquil spat. Her hands explored her daughter's body, feeling for injuries. Finding none, she grabbed Tarquinia's head and made her daughter look at her. 'You're not hurt, Tarquinia, so stop crying.' She got to her feet, wincing as her knee bones cracked. Servius looked so angry. His clothes were dirty and dishevelled and the excrement was flaking from his jaw. 'Are you hurt?' she asked him.

He shook his head.

'Are you sure? Let me see.' She stepped towards him and lifted her hands to his face.

He swatted them away. 'Stop fussing. See to your daughter. She's the one who needs you.'

He was furious with her. He thought this was all her fault. 'I know you're angry,' she began cautiously.

'Angry?' He glowered at her. 'Oh, Tanaquil, I'm beyond angry. *You* told me to go, *you* told me I would be received well.'

'Servius—'

'Is this what you wanted? Me to look a bloody fool? Because that's what you've made of me. The people of Rome didn't see a king and queen today. They saw two cowards running away.'

'That's not true,' she said, her eyes filling with tears. 'Servius, where are you going?'

Servius was heading up the stairs and didn't answer her. He had turned away from her, blamed her for this mess. Hatred welled up in her. She had had to endure the horrific attack on Lucomo and now her children had been publicly abused. Servius and Tarquinia hadn't deserved this insult. S*he* hadn't deserved this.

Watching her daughter as she clambered to her feet with the aid of a servant and followed haltingly up the stairs after her husband, Tanaquil resolved that Servius would see she was not to blame. She would find whoever had thrown the filth and make them pay. She would put this right and Servius would know he could trust her. Servius would love and need her again.

5

Tanaquil had grown unaccustomed to giving dinners. She had given plenty in the early years of Lucomo's reign, when it had been crucial to cultivate friends and craft alliances with those who would be useful to them. Back then, the dinners had been created to impress. She and Lucomo had still to shake off their origins and their dinners had been more Etruscan than Roman in style, reflected in both the food on offer and the way it was served. The Romans had been impressed by their Etruscan opulence back then, but as time passed, Tanaquil thought it politic for them to become more Roman in every aspect of their lives. Once alliances had been forged and friendships made, and once Lucomo was secure on the throne, she had not found it necessary to entertain nearly quite so much or to bestow her favours so extravagantly upon those lower down the social scale.

But today, she had a good reason for giving a dinner. She needed information.

Camilia Segestes was a woman close to her own age although, Tanaquil thought with some satisfaction, Camilia had not aged so well as she. Camilia's hair had turned white in her late thirties and eleven pregnancies had left her body bloated and shapeless. A healthy, some might say greedy, appetite had had its effect too, so that her eyes had sunken into her puffy cheeks to become mere black pebbles in a sandy complexion, and three chins bobbed upon her collar bone.

Axia Quintilla was quite different. She was younger than Tanaquil and Camilia, having only just celebrated her forty-sixth birthday, and had been less fecund than Camilia, providing her husband with a mere four children in all the years of their marriage. Her body had escaped the ravages of pregnancy and Tanaquil had to admit she kept herself well, not skinny but not plump either, and she still managed to turn the heads of her husband's friends, or so Tanaquil had heard.

But it was not for their personal appearances nor their maternal achievements that Tanaquil had invited them to dine. If there was one trait both women shared it was their willingness to talk, especially about the affairs of other people.

And Tanaquil wanted them to talk. The fracas in the forum had unsettled her greatly. She could not erase from her mind the fury Servius had felt towards her, nor could she shake off the belief that the sorry episode had been her fault. Guilt lay heavy upon her.

'Do try the sea urchins, Camilia, they're delicious,' Tanaquil said, pointing to the dish before them on the table.

Camilia dipped her pudgy finger into the sauce and stuck it in her mouth, her eyes closing at the taste. 'Oh, they are good,' she said. 'We never have them at home.'

'We have them often,' Tanaquil said. 'Sea urchins are a favourite of my daughter.'

As Tanaquil hoped, the comment provoked a new line of conversation.

'Oh yes, how is Tarquinia?' Axia asked earnestly. 'Has she recovered from her horrible ordeal? I heard there was almost a riot.'

'She was very shaken. I doubt she will ever get over it entirely.'

'It was disgraceful,' Camilia said. 'I wasn't there — I don't like to go out at that time of day, the streets are so hot and you simply can't avoid the people — but I heard about it. To throw excrement! I mean, one just isn't safe in Rome these days.'

'And the King? How is he?' Axia asked, irritated by Camilia's interruption.

Tanaquil paused to give the impression she was seriously considering her answer. 'Servius was saddened by the incident more than anything,' she said eventually. 'He thought he had the love of the people. It was quite a blow to discover there are some who hate him.'

'*Do* people hate him?' Camilia asked.

'Well, someone must,' Tanaquil said, 'to say and do what they did. I would just like to know who it was so I could talk with them, ask them why they dislike Servius so. I know Servius would like to know so he could do something about it.'

Tanaquil saw the look that passed between Camilia and Axia. Would they need more prompting or would they speak now?

'I expect he doesn't dislike the King,' Camilia simpered. 'Not really. It was just one of those things. He lost his temper, that's all. It was the heat probably. It can make one feel so irritable, don't you find?' She dipped her finger in the sea urchin sauce again.

'Who lost his temper?' Tanaquil asked quietly.

Camilia froze. 'I.. I..,' she stammered, her face turning

pale, 'that is, I don't know. Whoever it was. I don't know.' She looked away, nervous under Tanaquil's penetrating gaze.

'Oh, I suspect you do know who it was, my dear,' Tanaquil said silkily, forestalling any idea Camilia might have of leaving by gesturing for the servant to refill her cup. 'You must tell me.'

Camilia gave a tight shake of her head.

'I insist,' Tanaquil said in a tone that would have been charming in another situation. 'You will have me guessing all night else. If you won't tell me what you know, Camilia dear, it will make me wonder whether you played some part in the attack and... well, let me just say I would be very unhappy to believe that.'

'No, you mustn't think.... my dear Tanaquil, please don't think I had anything to do with it.'

'But you know who did?'

'My husband told me,' Camilia said with a little strangled laugh, 'that is, he thinks he knows who was behind it, but of course, that is only a guess on his part.'

'Of course, just a guess as you say, but tell me anyway. Who?'

Camilia licked her lips, then cast a quick glance at Axia, who gave the smallest of nods for her to continue. 'Hostus Venturius. We had him round to dinner recently and he said the most dreadful things about Servius, I mean the King. We thought perhaps he had had a little too much wine and thought no more of it, but now my husband thinks maybe Hostus meant what he said.'

Hostus Venturius again, Tanaquil thought. 'And what did Hostus say exactly?'

'He said the King's mother had been a slave in the kitchens and that the late King...,' Camilia trailed off, unwilling to continue.

'Sired a bastard on her and that Servius is in fact the illegitimate son of my husband?' Tanaquil finished for her equably.

Camilia nodded, her bottom lip curling into her mouth.

'Let me tell you, my dear,' Tanaquil's voice was deceptively charming, 'that rumour is completely unfounded. My husband never forgot himself in that way. He was entirely faithful to me.'

Tanaquil was lying. Lucomo had not been faithful to her, nor had she ever expected him to be. She knew every woman Lucomo had slept with since their marriage; she had even chosen a few of them for him, mostly when she was recovering from childbirth and she really could not face having him inside her. He had been grateful to her for her solicitousness, and when she asked if Servius was his natural son after she had witnessed the flaming portent, he had not hesitated and promised her he was not. She had trusted him and believed him, and indeed, she had never seen any resemblance in Servius to Lucomo.

'Oh no, of course not, I've never believed it for a moment,' Camilia blustered. 'I'm merely repeating what I've heard others say.'

'Of course you are,' Tanaquil said. 'But this Hostus is spreading this malicious rumour, from what you say.'

'I've heard him say it with my own ears,' Axia confirmed, eager to prove herself a friend, 'and he said it to my husband too.'

'So, it was this Hostus who attacked my son-in-law and daughter the other day?' Tanaquil asked, selecting an olive from the dish before her and popping it into her mouth.

'I don't know whether he actually did it himself,' Axia said, 'or whether he got one of his men to do it. I do know it was him who shouted out the King was the son of a whore.'

'Indeed? Well, my dears, I must thank you for sharing this information with me. It is a relief to know most of the people do love the King, and that you do too.'

'Oh, we do,' both women agreed vehemently.

Tanaquil smiled at them both and bade them try another dish.

———

Hostus was feeling good.

He had just completed the purchase of a plot of land in the east of the city and was planning to build an insulae that would bring in a lot of money in a year or so. He had got the land at a good price, too. All he had to do was clear it of rubbish and the foundations could be dug.

Hostus was heading for his favourite brothel. He'd received a message from his friend Aulus Quintilla at breakfast that morning that if he was free around noon, Aulus would be pleased to meet him at the brothel, enjoy a girl or two, and then while away the afternoon playing dice. Hostus should really have been going over his estate accounts but it was too good an invitation to turn down. He had a fancy for a Cretan woman today and knew the brothel had at least three to choose from. *Or I can have all three*, he laughed to himself, *if I can manage it*.

He arrived at the brothel door, drawing the ragged curtain aside to enter. The brothel-keeper, an old fat woman who looked like she'd been dipped in grease, was sitting at a small table, counting the bronze ingots earned so far that day.

'Good day, sir,' she greeted Hostus with a gummy smile. 'What can we do for you today?'

'A Cretan, Metella,' he said. 'Any available?'

'I've got one just finishing. She'll clean herself up and I'll send her in to you. Number three's empty.' She gestured towards the corridor to her right where small cubicles were curtained off and from where grunts came in rhythmic intervals.

'Is Aulus Quintilla here yet? I'm supposed to be meeting him.'

'Not seen him yet, sir,' Metella said.

Hostus dipped his hand into his purse, withdrew a bronze ingot and threw it on the table before Metella. She added it to her pile and Hostus went along the corridor to the third cubicle. The stone bed was covered with a straw mattress which he noted ruefully had taken some pounding. He squeezed it and considered for a moment whether it would do. His knees were bony and he knew he would feel the hard stone through the straw if he went on top. He decided he would stand and penetrate the whore from behind to save his knees. He didn't want to waste energy complaining to Metella about the bedding.

He undressed and lay down on the mattress, eyes closed, hand idly caressing his cock. A few minutes later, the curtain was drawn back and the girl he ordered came into the cubicle. He sat up and looked her up and down. She was wearing a thin, threadbare dress that fell to the middle of her thighs and which emphasised the almost skeletal nature of her body. Metella didn't feed her girls well, Hostus knew. *This girl's too thin*, he thought, *it'll be like humping a bag of bones*. But he had already undressed and didn't feel like going back out to Metella and demanding a fatter bitch.

'Come on, then,' he said testily, 'get that off.'

The girl understood his gesture rather than his speech, for she had not learnt the Roman tongue. There was no point; what men wanted from her could be expressed in a universal language. She pulled the dress over her head and started towards the bed.

Hostus pushed her in front of him and applied pressure to her back to make her bend over. She did so readily and made no noise when he pushed into her. *At least she's tight*, he thought, and he grabbed her hips and pulled her back roughly with every thrust. By the gods, it felt good to fuck like this. His wife made such a fuss if he used her in this way. She would keep whimpering all the time he was in her and then sulk afterwards for hours, so that to enjoy her from behind for a quarter of an hour was hardly worth the trouble. No, he decided, a man needed a whore to hump like this.

Hostus closed his eyes and tilted his head back as his pleasure grew. He was close to climaxing when a cloth was clamped over his mouth. He tried to move, to look around at what was happening to him, but an arm, strong and unyielding, enclosed his chest and tugged. The girl gave the smallest of screams as the assailant dragged Hostus, his cock rapidly shrinking, from the cubicle. She curled into the corner of the bed and watched as her client disappeared from sight.

———

Tarquinia bent her head and kissed the small, furrowed forehead. The soft mouth pursed and relaxed, pursed and relaxed, then the pink, fluffy head fell to the side. Arruns was asleep and Tarquinia knew she had to hand him back to the nurse who was waiting to lay him in his cot. But he felt so wonderful in her arms, she wanted to keep hold of him, to feel his warmth and warm him with her own body. She would have liked to press his little mouth to her nipple and have him suck but her breasts were not filled with milk, nor had they ever been. She smiled wanly at the nurse, who was old enough not to find babies enchanting any longer, and handed the little body over to her more experienced hands.

What was wrong with her? Tarquinia wondered. Why had she not conceived a child? Other women she knew, her friends, even servants, found themselves pregnant all the time, often when they had no wish to be so. Yet she, who wanted a child so badly, bled unfailingly every month. She wanted to blame it on the curse the shepherd's wife made, for she remembered that unhappy woman had cursed Servius's loins, but her mind knew this could not be the only reason. She had not once been pregnant. She had never conceived, let alone miscarried or given birth to a dead child. Her womb had never been seeded. She had to admit to herself there was something wrong with her.

And Servius was so good. He never complained of having a barren wife, never upbraided her for not being able to conceive. He just said it would happen one day when the gods wanted to bless them. Until that happy day, Tarquinia would have to content herself with visiting the children of her dead brother.

Her eldest brother, Lucius, had been killed in an attack Rome carried out on Rutuli, his battered body brought back to Rome for burial. His wife, though she had not known it, had been pregnant with little Arruns, and the news of her husband's death sent her into a despair. She put on little weight and took no care of herself, so that when Arruns was born, two months early, she had not the energy to recover and her life simply drained away. Arruns was left to the care of a woman who had lost her baby only a week before and whose milk had not yet dried up. The three children, Lucilla, Lucius and Arruns were left motherless and fatherless. It wasn't fair.

Tarquinia left the nursery. She always felt depressed after visiting and cursed that she had put herself through it again.

She sighed. She knew she should be looking over the house-hold stores, making sure the servants weren't eating more than they were allowed or selling on the food, but she didn't want to go into the kitchen and have to be that woman. She wanted Servius. She wanted to find him and nestle against his chest, feel his arms around her and have him tell her every-thing was fine.

She asked one of the lictors where her husband was and he told her the King had gone down to the cellar with Tanaquil. Perplexed as to what Servius and her mother were doing down there, Tarquinia made her way to the cellar stairs. It was a dark, narrow space and she went carefully. As she descended the stairs, she heard a strange noise coming from behind the door. Reaching for the latch, she opened it as quietly as she could.

Her eyes had to adjust to the gloom for only a single lamp burned in that dark space. She made out the figure of a man, naked, his wrists and ankles tied with ropes to hang between two wooden poles. His back was a mess of ragged flesh and blood and the yellow lamplight illuminated slivers of white that Tarquinia realised was the man's exposed ribs and backbone.

What in Jupiter's name was happening? She dragged her eyes away from the bloody, slumping figure to the man before him who held a whip in his right hand. Tarquinia thought she recognised him as one of her mother's litter bear-ers. He paused only long enough to allow the tortured man to recover a little before making the whip scorch across his back once again. She had to turn away. A voice called out, 'Again,' and Tarquinia recognised it as her mother's. She looked up and saw Tanaquil sitting on a stool, her face impassive as she watched the whip fly. And alongside her, leaning against the wall with his arms folded over his chest, was Servius, his forehead corrugated as he concentrated on the scene before him.

The whip struck again and sliced a strip of flesh from the man's back; it peeled away to hang along the crack of his backside. The cry that came from the man had been terrible and Tarquinia couldn't bear to watch any longer. Vomit rising in her throat, she pulled the door shut as quietly as she had opened it and hurried back up the stairs.

Back in the cellar, Hostus Venturius slumped between the two wooden poles. The last strike of the whip had robbed him of his life and paid him back in full.

6

Sisenna Victor tugged the leather tarpaulin over his wagon and tied it securely to the wooden frame.

He'd had a very successful trip. He'd sold all his timber, not at quite the price he had hoped but not far beneath it, and he'd loaded his wagon with cloth he already had a buyer for back in Rome. But perhaps even better than his successful trading was the information he had learnt.

Sisenna climbed up onto the wagon and flicked the leather reins against his ox's flanks, the cart jerking forward uncomfortably as the animal moved off. As he trundled out of Veii, he played the scene over in his mind. His buyer, Venza Cae Rusina, was a talker and as he examined the timber in Sisenna's cart, he'd asked for the latest news from Rome. Sisenna told him about the executions of the shepherds and their families and Venza asked if it was true they'd been paid by the sons of Ancus Marcius to kill the King. Sisenna confirmed it was and then Venza had asked Sisenna if he'd heard about the assembly meeting.

'What assembly meeting?'

'The one all the rich folk called yesterday,' Venza said,

counting out bronze ingots. 'The one where they agreed the treaty we have with Rome is as dead as your king. You didn't know? Caused a right to-do, it did. Two of the younger men, Vilia and Mute, said that with the King dead, the treaty he made all those years ago should be torn up. They said you Romans have been taking advantage of us for years.' He grinned, showing the gaps in his teeth. 'Well, I know that's true, don't I?'

Sisenna rolled his eyes and waved him to continue.

'Well, the old men in the assembly didn't want to hear talk like that, said they were too old to go to war again and walked out. But that didn't stop the others. They all voted with Mute and Vilia. So this, my friend, may be the last bit of business we have for a while.'

'Veii voted to go to war with Rome?' Sisenna asked, wanting to be sure he had heard correctly.

'So we're told. Men are already being called up. And a friend of mine, Marmarce, he's a blacksmith. He's been instructed that the only work he's to do from now on is the mending and making of weapons. So, that seems to settle it, don't you think?'

Sisenna said it certainly did and expressed his sorrow that business was going to be next to impossible with Venza, for a while at least, and that he hoped things would settle down soon.

'If only the rich folks didn't want to get richer,' Venza said, 'then you and I could do business the same as always. I hate rich folk. They always claim to be doing the best for us poor folk, but really they're only doing the best for themselves.'

Sisenna stored Venza's information away in his mind. The news had unsettled him. If Veii was about to declare war on Rome, was he even safe at this moment? It was just as well, he thought, his business was done and he could be on his way. He bid Venza a hasty farewell.

When he arrived back in Rome, he put his ox and cart away, made sure his goods were stored correctly and washed himself, knowing he couldn't appear at the royal domus with the dust of the road on his clothing and the smell of ox shit following him around.

———

Servius was dreaming.

He was standing in a river. It looked like the Tiber but he wasn't sure. He was naked and the water lapped and rippled around his thighs and caressed his genitals. The water should have been cold yet he did not feel so. He looked down. Tendrils of red in the water were tickling his skin. He raised his hands to his head and ran them through his hair. He held them, palms up, before his face and they were wet, not with river water, but with blood.

His heart began to beat faster, harder. His hands went again to his head, feeling in vain for a wound that would explain the blood. He looked around for help. There were people on the riverbank but he couldn't make out their faces. It wasn't that he couldn't see them — it was that they had no faces. But somehow, he felt they were watching him, even without eyes. He tried to move, but the water seemed to be holding him fast. He pushed but it would not give and, over-balancing, he fell beneath the water. It rushed over his head and into his mouth. He couldn't breathe. He tried to push up, to break the surface of the water, to get free of it, to get to the air.

And then something had grabbed him and it was pulling him, up and up and...

'My lord!'

His eyelids broke apart; sleep crusted his eyelashes. He heard breathing in the darkness.

'It's Issa,' a voice said. 'My mistress wants you.'

Tanaquil! 'Is she ill?'

'No, my lord. But she wants you to come at once.'

Before Servius could question her further, he heard Issa's footsteps walking away. He swung his legs to the floor and felt Tarquinia stir behind him.

'Where are you going?' she asked, her voice thick with sleep.

'Your mother wants me,' Servius said, wondering what Tanaquil could want at this time of night.

———

Servius found Tanaquil sitting on a chair in his office with a thick woollen blanket around her shoulders. A man stood before her.

'Tanaquil?' Servius jerked his head at the stranger.

'You need to hear this, Servius,' Tanaquil said. 'Sit down.'

Servius did as he was told. 'Who are you?' he asked the man.

'This is Sisenna Victor,' Tanaquil answered for him. 'He has a timber business that takes him to Veii, amongst other places. He keeps me informed.'

Another of my mother-in-law's spies, Servius thought with amusement. *Just how many does she have?*

'Sisenna, tell the King what you told me,' Tanaquil ordered.

Sisenna looked at Servius and cleared his throat. 'I have just come from Veii, my lord. While I was there, a meeting of the Veientes nobles was held at which the death of the King was discussed, as well as your accession.'

'Well, it is news, I suppose, even in Veii,' Servius said, wondering why he was being bothered with this.

'Just listen,' Tanaquil said. She nodded to Sisenna to continue.

'They agreed your unelected accession provided them with an opportunity,' he said. 'They declared the treaty they had with Rome over and that they are under no obligation to continue peaceful relations with us.'

Servius looked at Tanaquil. 'Which means...'

'Which means they are planning to attack Rome,' Tanaquil nodded.

'They were already making preparations when I left,' Sisenna said. 'Men were being called to serve in the army and the blacksmiths were working through the night.'

'Making weapons,' Servius said ruefully. His dream returned to him. Had it been a portent? He covered in blood while faceless entities looked on?

'You may go, Sisenna,' Tanaquil said, gesturing to Issa to show him out. Sisenna bowed to both Tanaquil and Servius, knowing he would receive his payment from Issa as she showed him out the back door.

'We can trust his information?' Servius asked when they were alone.

'Certainly we can trust it.'

'Then I'll address the senate first thing in the morning.'

'And say what?'

'That we must be prepared to fight.'

'You will not try diplomacy with the Veientes?'

'Diplomacy?'

'Why not?' Tanaquil asked. 'Make another treaty. It worked before.'

But Servius was not thinking of diplomacy. He was all for talking with Rome's neighbours — treaties were usually so much less costly than battles — but if his unelected accession made the Veientes think they had been presented with an opportunity, then why should he not think the same? Here was an opportunity to show Rome, to show those damned patricians, he was fit to be their king. And nothing would prove that better than a show of force, a victory against a common enemy.

'We should fight,' he said, 'and not wait for them to reach the walls of Rome. We go out and we meet them on the battlefield.'

Tanaquil smiled. It was good to hear a man talk so fiercely; it had been a long while since anyone she knew had done so. Lucomo had brought so much stability to Rome, it had become as if there was nothing left to fight for.

'Well, do you agree?' Servius prompted.

'You want to show what you can do?'

He laughed at himself. 'Ye gods, am I so obvious?'

'Only to me,' she said, reaching out and stroking his cheek. 'And I think you're right. We could try diplomacy and I suppose it may work for a while. But it would be good to show how strong we are by teaching Veii a lesson.'

'Will the senate agree, do you think?'

'Oh, yes, you won't have any trouble getting them to commit to a war. They'll be eager to provide men and money.'

'An army with me as leader?'

'There is no other choice, my boy. As king, it is your duty to lead.'

'And to win?'

'If you can. But of that, Servius, I have no doubt.'

———

It had been a cold autumn, not the best time of year in which to battle, but Servius had had little choice. The Veientes, confident their stores of food and drink would be enough to see them through the coming lean months of winter, had made their declaration of war against Rome as expected. The declaration had come hard on the heels of Sisenna's information. Rome had not had the luxury of making similar provisions and needed a swift victory if the army was not to starve.

The day had begun overcast and by mid-morning rain was falling steadily. It had turned the field of the Romans' camp to mud and the soldiers were struggling to lift their booted feet out of the sucking ground. Servius's commander and friend, Cnaeus Sudennus, had decided he would not wait for the Veientes to show their shields on their horizon and had organised the men into lines. This had kept them occupied for a while, but now they had been standing still for over an hour and the sound of creaking wet leather filled the air as bodies twisted to relieve aching muscles.

Cnaeus walked up to Servius, who was standing in front of the lines, scanning the far side of the field where the Veientes would appear. He studied Servius's profile and noted the grim determination set there. Servius had never been martial-minded, though he had had experience of battle during the late King's reign, but it seemed to Cnaeus that when Servius addressed the senate and told them of the danger that was coming to Rome, he had been relishing the idea of dirtying his sword with Veientes blood.

Despite his dislike for public speaking, Cnaeus thought Servius had spoken well. He had mounted the dais and addressed the senators in a firm, clear voice. The senators listened and muttered amongst themselves when they heard what Veii was planning. And when they heard Servius tell them he intended to lead the army into battle, they had cheered, Cnaeus as loudly as any of them. The senate had not dallied either, acting swiftly to gather an army. To Cnaeus, it felt almost as if Rome had been waiting for someone to fight and by early autumn, Servius was ready to march out of Rome at the head of a thousand men, and with Cnaeus by his side.

Rome had so far fought two battles with the Veientes. The first had been no more than a skirmish; the Romans had unexpectedly encountered a cohort of Veientes and had had no choice but to fight. The fighting had been fierce and many men had been lost in that first encounter without a decisive victory on either side. But it had been a valuable learning experience for the Roman commanders who, like Servius and all patricians, had been trained in arms as soon as they had been old enough to hold a wooden sword. For the youngest men, all their training had been nothing but theory, for Rome had enjoyed peace for so long. They soon discovered that sword practice was nothing compared to facing an enemy intent on splitting open stomachs and watching guts spill out. It took that first skirmish to make those youngsters realise just what being at war truly meant.

Now, they could call themselves true soldiers, Cnaeus reflected, as the rain continued to fall. He hadn't had a wash for three days, not a proper one, and the smell of his own sweat offended him. His face, like Servius's, like all the other Roman soldiers, was grimed with dirt. The dirt mixed with the crusted blood of minor cuts and mingled with a large purple bruise that spread over his cheekbone and blackened his left eye. He ached all over. He was starting to regret his eagerness to join the army. Just how many more battles must they fight, he wondered, before this war would be over?

Servius suddenly noticed Cnaeus and nodded towards the opposite side of the field. 'They will come soon. I can hear them.'

'Can you?' Cnaeus strained his ears but all he could hear was the noises the men behind him were making.

'They're there,' Servius said, almost to himself. 'Are the men ready?'

'They're ready.'

'How many do we have?'

'Eleven hundred, not counting the wounded.'

'And our scouts estimate the Veientes have less than eight hundred men, yes?'

'Yes. Should be easy.'

'Don't get complacent, Cnaeus,' Servius snapped. Then his face softened and he turned towards his friend. 'Just in case Bellona deserts us, eh?'

'The goddess is on our side, Servius, I know it,' Cnaeus said. 'And when we win this battle, we'll sacrifice ten doves to thank her for her goodness to us. Wait, look there.'

Servius turned to where Cnaeus was pointing. On the crest of the hill, the Veientes were moving into position. He nodded. 'Prepare the men.'

————

Servius felt Cnaeus move away and, a moment later, heard him giving orders to the men to make ready. The clatter from the ranks was almost deafening after the quiet of waiting. His fingers tightened around his sword's hilt and he felt all his energy flow into it. Drawing his sword, he pointed its wet silver tip towards the Veientes ranks. He pulled his right foot from the mud and began the steady march towards them, knowing his army was no more than a few feet behind him.

When the two armies were less than fifty feet apart, Servius yelled his war cry and charged. His ears filled with noise, his sword met flesh. Bodies closed around him as he pressed deeper and deeper into the Veientes ranks. He lost all sense of awareness, all sense of time passing. His sword stabbed, withdrew, stabbed again, until he could hardly move for Veientes dead.

'Servius!' Cnaeus cried, his face and breast covered in blood. 'They're retreating.'

Servius looked to the far side of the field and made a quick count. Perhaps two hundred Veientes were running away, fleeing into the trees for cover. Many never made the wood, hacked down before they got there by Roman soldiers reluctant to see their enemy escape.

'Sound the trumpet,' Servius croaked, his throat cracked and dry. 'Assemble the men. Count our numbers.'

'We haven't lost many men, Servius. But look how many we've killed.' Cnaeus gestured with his bloody sword at the bodies littering the ground. 'And most of them down to you, I'd say.'

'Don't be foolish,' Servius chided, a sheepish smile creeping onto his lips. 'Is it over, do you think?'

'Ye gods, it must be, mustn't it? If that's all the men they have, there can't be anyone left for us to fight.'

Servius arched his back, groaning as his spine cracked. 'I'll send a messenger to the Veientes camp with the terms we'll accept of their surrender.'

'And send word to Rome while you're about it,' Cnaeus said, bending to wipe his sword on a dead man's tunic. 'Tell them of your victory.'

'*Our* victory, my friend. And let's get the surrender in writing first.'

'Ever the cautious one,' Cnaeus said laughed. 'Allow

yourself to enjoy your victory, just a little, won't you? You are king, after all. And I'll tell you something, Servius, this has proved it. If anyone doubted you were fit to be king before, those doubts have been quashed here and now.'

Servius gave him a sideways glance. 'I have been one of those doubters, Cnaeus.'

'I know,' Cnaeus said, 'that's why I'm telling you this. You're my friend and my king and I'm very proud of both. No more doubts, Servius. You are the King of Rome.'

'I know it, now.'

'Good. And now, I'm going to count our numbers as you ordered, my King.'

'And find ten doves,' Servius shouted after him.

'What's that?' Cnaeus frowned.

Servius grinned. 'Bellona will be expecting a sacrifice, won't she?'

7

Tarquinia checked the calendar, counting off the days, counting twice, just to be sure. She clapped her hands to her mouth, hardly daring to believe. By her reckoning, she was thirteen days past the time when she should have expected to bleed. She shut her eyes tight.

'I beg you, Juno,' she whispered, 'please let me be pregnant. And please let this baby live.'

But she couldn't rely on prayers alone. She would have to make a sacrifice. A goat, yes, a goat would be best. Juno would be pleased with a goat.

Tarquinia smoothed her hands over her flat belly. Inside there, she felt sure, new life was growing. She wanted to tell someone, have someone share in her happiness, but who? Servius was not at home; he had been invited to dine with Cnaeus Sudennus at his house and would no doubt come home late, having spent the afternoon recounting their battles and adventures. Tanaquil was out for the afternoon, some meeting with the Vestal Virgins.

The door opened and her maid entered carrying clean bed linen.

'Nipia,' Tarquinia addressed her, feeling a little foolish, 'I have news.'

'Yes, domina.' Nipia stopped what she was doing and stood ready to attend to her mistress's words.

'My blood hasn't come,' Tarquinia said. 'I think I'm pregnant.'

'May Juno bless you, domina,' Nipia said politely and bowed her head. She returned to her work, taking off the soiled bed sheets and replacing them with the clean ones.

What did you expect? Tarquinia thought, chiding herself for feeling disappointed at Nipia's conventional response. *She's only your maid. What a silly goose she must think you.*

The afternoon was an agony of restless waiting and almost too-much-to-bear joy. When Servius came home later that day, reeling a little and with wine sour on his breath, Tarquinia rushed to him and squeezed him tight. He laughed and asked her what she was about to accost him so. With flushed cheeks and bright eyes, she told him her news.

Servius sobered instantly. He embraced his wife and buried his face against her neck, wetting it with his tears. He was going to be a father at last.

————

Tanaquil studied the wax death masks of her family on display in the atrium. The masks had been created in the first hour after death, before time had slackened the skin or decay set in, and were perfect facial representations of the people they had once been.

On the top shelf were her mother and father, both long dead and buried in Tarquinii. Beneath them were three masks, the first two being of her sons, Arruns and Lucius. Arruns had died of a fever in his fourteenth year; Lucius had been killed in battle. Next to their likenesses was Lucomo, dear Lucomo, the man whom she had thought not good enough to marry. Her death mask would sit alongside Lucomo's one day, staring soullessly at anyone who passed through the atrium.

But not too soon, she told herself sternly. She still had work to do. Servius still needed her, although she thought sadly, not as much as he had at first. His victory over Veii had not only secured his kingship in the eyes of the patricians; it had proved to Servius himself that he *was* the King of Rome, not an imposter merely acting the part.

After the Veientes had been defeated, Servius returned to Rome to celebrate a triumph. He had ridden into Rome, his crown upon his head and followed by carts laden with spoils and captives to the adulation of all Rome. No one dared whisper behind their hands about Servius any longer.

And Servius had come home not only with treasure but with ideas. When he had told her of them, Tanaquil realised how lazy Lucomo had been. Yes, her husband had worked hard to make treaties and forge alliances, but once achieved, he had considered his duty done. From that point on, Lucomo had concerned himself only with domestic affairs, acquiring clients, listening to petitioners and filling his money chests. Servius wanted to do things, make changes, make Rome better, make it the envy of all the Latin tribes. Enraptured, Tanaquil had listened to Servius's ideas and wanted to be a part of them.

Tanaquil knew the changes Servius wanted to make would benefit Rome, it was true, but in her mind, there was a better reason for pursuing them. If Servius succeeded, he would be not only popular but powerful, and he could change forever the way Rome thought about kings. Roman kingship could become truly hereditary.

Tanaquil had never believed in the concept of an elected

monarchy. To her, such an arrangement was messy and unnecessary. Under the present system, a man could become king simply because he had proved himself a good soldier, not because he had any brains in his head. Such a man knew how to hold a sword but could not be relied up to know how to rule a kingdom. But a man who had been brought up in the royal household, a man who had been trained from the earliest age to rule! Such a man was fit to be a king.

And that was why Rome needed to change. Rome needed a royal dynasty.

Tanaquil's eyes returned to the death masks of her two sons. Her sons were gone, but now Tarquinia was at last pregnant and in her belly might be a great Roman, an admirable successor to Servius. And if not, if the child were lost or if it were only a girl, then there were still Tarquins who could succeed Servius, her grandsons, Lucius and Arruns. They were fit and well, and though young, they seemed intelligent enough.

Of course, there was no guarantee the boys would stay fit and well. Children died, even adults died, well before their time, she reminded herself, looking at her sons' masks. And the Tarquins were burdened now with misfortune, all because of that wretched woman's curse. Tanaquil closed her eyes at the memory. She and Servius had sacrificed the ox that very night after the executions, and the priests had assured them that Jupiter would be pleased and Poena appeased, but Tanaquil couldn't be sure.

Nothing was certain. The only thing Tanaquil knew for sure was that the future of the Tarquins as Rome's royal family could be secured, or destroyed, by the children.

———

Her labour had begun in the late morning.

Tarquinia had been spinning wool in the garden, enjoying the cool breeze of the spring day, when a pain wrenched through her body. She had cried out, clutching her swollen belly and Nipia had hurried to her mistress, putting her arm around her waist and helping her to her room.

They had only gone a few feet when Tarquinia's waters broke. The sudden gush of fluid down her legs had made her cry, not just because of the pain but from embarrassment. She hadn't wanted to make such a mess. She felt suddenly, horribly undignified.

Nipia had managed to get Tarquinia to her bed before scurrying off to send for the midwife and fetch the birthing chair. Tarquinia had been left on her own, struggling to find a position, sitting or standing, that would ease the pain. She hadn't expected her labour to come on so suddenly, nor to intensify so quickly. She had thought she would feel mild twinges and spasms for a few hours before her pains truly began. In that way, she would be able to prepare herself for the birth. She would have time to talk to the midwife and remind her of her duty. She would have time to make sure her room had everything she could want: food and drink to see her through the labour, clean clothes to keep a respectable appearance. And then the baby would come and she would be in bed with the child in her arms and looking beautiful when Servius walked in.

Tarquinia hadn't imagined this, this pain and mess and fear she felt. Her mother had told her the pain would be great but she had not, could not, have imagined it would be so very cruel.

Nipia came back with clean linen towels over her arms. She laid them on a table and told Tarquinia the midwife had been summoned.

'I want my mother,' Tarquinia panted.

Tanaquil had been sent for and now sat on a stool, silently praying to Juno and watching as her daughter clutched the arms of the birthing chair and screwed up her face in pain.

———

Servius was at the senate house.

When he had left Tarquinia that morning, there had been no sign her labour would begin that day, and as the matters to be discussed mounted up, his mind was too occupied to spare even the smallest thought for his wife. Servius returned home only when night was coming on, his way lit by torchbearers and his person protected by bodyguards.

As he passed through the atrium, he heard a low-throated scream that turned into a shuddering moan. His mind weary from the day's work, Servius's first thought was that some animal had been set loose in the house, but then he remembered Tarquinia and realisation coursed through him. He rushed through the house to their cubiculum, his momentum so fast he almost ran into the closed door. With his hands on the door frame, he pressed his ear to the wood, his heart pounding. He heard murmurings and the padding of feet. And then a cry, the unmistakable protest of a baby.

It took him a minute to collect himself. When his breath had returned to normal, Servius opened the door with a trembling hand. The birthing chair stood in the middle of the room. There were bloodied towels in a heap beneath it. He looked away and to the bed. Tarquinia was climbing gingerly into it, wincing as she settled. Nipia fussed around her, trying to make her more comfortable. Tarquinia leant into the pillows and closed her eyes, excessively weary. She had not even noticed Servius. Neither had Tanaquil, who was on the other side of the bed. She put a leather cord around her daughter's neck and Servius saw a small figure of Juno bob against Tarquinia's swollen breasts. Protection for the mother, he thought grimly, all too aware that Tarquinia, having survived the birth, was not out of danger yet. Many women died in the days after childbirth from fever.

Tanaquil straightened and turned. She saw Servius and gave him a rueful smile.

'Tarquinia's asleep already. Come and greet your daughter.'

Servius's mind registered Tanaquil's last word and he felt the smallest sinking feeling of dismay. A daughter, not a son. After all this time, after all the believing Tarquinia barren and then the joy of her pregnancy, to not have a son to carry on his line was like he had been punched in the stomach. He felt winded.

Tanaquil waved him over to the woven willow basket behind him where a small body squirmed. Servius looked down into the basket and rested his gaze on his new daughter. Any disappointment he had felt disappeared on the instant. This little creature was his, made from him, a part of him. The pink face was all screwed up and wrinkly, but it was the most beautiful thing he had ever seen. It didn't matter that she was a girl. She was whole, she was healthy, and she was his.

———

Tarquinia had the house all to herself and was glad of it. Servius was in the city on business and Tanaquil had declared she really couldn't stand another sultry Roman summer and had travelled to the coast with a friend to spend a month or two by the sea. For once, Tarquinia could be alone with her daughter, her Tullia. She loved her mother dearly, but she would interfere, telling her how the baby should be held, when she should be washed, how she should be fed... On and on went the list of things that, according to her mother, she was doing wrong. And yet, the baby thrived.

Tarquinia gazed down at the child in her arms, at the little mouth puckered around her nipple. How she loved this small bundle of flesh, more than she loved anything, even Servius. What a pity this little thing would grow up. If only her daughter could stay this small and needy.

Her pleasant solitude was not to last. Tarquinia had moved from the garden to the atrium, it being the coolest place in the house. She had not been there long when the front doors opened and her young nephews entered with their nurse.

'Why are you sitting here, Aunt?' Lucius asked, coming up to Tarquinia.

'It's too hot anywhere else,' Tarquinia said, drawing a fold of her dress over Tullia's head and covering her breast. She knew Lucius was only a boy, but she didn't want him to see her naked breast.

Arruns moved to stand beside his brother. 'Can I see?' he asked.

'Later,' Tarquinia assured him. Had he been on his own, she would have shown Arruns the baby, but not with Lucius looking on. 'She's feeding at the moment and then she will need to sleep. You can see her when she wakes up.'

'She can play with us then,' Arruns said.

'She's too young for that,' Tarquinia laughed. 'When she's older, you will play together.'

'We don't want a girl playing with us,' Lucius said to his brother.

'Why not?'

'She'll spoil everything. Girls always do.'

'If you say so,' Arruns said glumly.

'Well,' Tarquinia took hold of Arruns's hand and drew him towards her, angry at the way Lucius always forced his opinions on his brother, 'if Lucius doesn't want to play with Tullia when she's older, then you can play with her all by yourself, Arruns.'

'I'll only play with her if Lucius will,' Arruns said, pulling his hand away.

Tarquinia met Lucius's eyes and saw smug satisfaction in them. 'You should go to your lessons,' she said, wanting Lucius gone, and gestured to the nurse to take the boys away.

''bye Tullia,' Arruns waved as he was led away. Lucius gave the bulge beneath her dress a contemptuous look before following.

If only Lucius could be sent away, Tarquinia thought as she watched the boys go, *then I could be truly happy*.

———

Cutu Taphu handed Lucius the wooden sword and told the boy to stand ready, pointing a warning finger at him not to start until Cutu said so. Lucius was always so eager to fight.

Cutu took a few steps back to make room for the boys and then called, 'Begin.' Lucius charged at Arruns, who held his sword awkwardly with both hands, pointing it feebly at his brother who swiped it aside easily. Cutu shook his bald head, disgusted by Arruns's ineptitude with the sword. That boy would never make a decent soldier, no matter how much training Cutu gave him.

'Lift your head up,' he bellowed at Arruns who was trying to make himself small before Lucius's onslaught.

Arruns obeyed and promptly received a blow from Lucius's sword to his mouth that ripped open the delicate skin of his lip. Arruns backed away, his sword arm at his side while his other hand tentatively pressed two fingers to his bleeding lip and inspected the evidence of the damage.

'Come on,' Lucius demanded, his brother's blood fuelling his desire to inflict another such blow.

But Arruns's face was screwing up and turning red. Lucius straightened and let out a puff of air. 'He's blubbing again, Cutu. Tell him to stop.'

'Boy,' Cutu said, 'stop that and be ready.'

But Arruns wasn't listening. He dropped his sword on the ground where it puffed up dust and buried his face in his hands, his sobs getting louder and longer. Lucius appealed to Cutu again, but Cutu had no patience left. He walked off to sit in the shade of an awning at the back of the domus.

'You've ruined everything,' Lucius screamed at Arruns, who raised his blotchy and crumpled face to his brother, still crying. Lucius strode towards him and began slapping Arruns's sweaty head. Arruns brought his arms up over his head and curled himself up in a ball, lying on his side where Lucius started to kick him.

Cutu watched the two boys in amusement. That Lucius, he was a one all right, had a right temper on him. Arruns was a cry-baby, always had been. A slave girl, a spoil of the war with Veii, offered Cutu a cup of water and he took it without a word, gulping it down. She stood by him, watching Lucius hitting Arruns, and he saw how much it upset her. *Women*, he thought, *they always wanted to mother something*.

'He'll be fine,' he said to her, gesturing at Arruns. 'He needs to learn to stop whimpering every time he gets hurt.'

The girl wasn't convinced. 'He is only a boy,' she said, wincing when Arruns let out a high-pitched scream as Lucius's foot made contact with his groin.

'He'll be a man soon enough,' Cutu shrugged. 'Crying won't do him any good then.'

The girl cast one more look at the boys, then returned to her work. Cutu shifted his backside on the bench and leant his head against the wall, watching the boys through half-open eyes. A minute later, at the periphery of his vision, he saw a dart of red emerge from the doorway and knew what it meant. Tarquinia had heard the fight.

'Stop that,' Tarquinia screamed, flapping her arms as she ran towards the two boys. 'Stop it. Get away from him. Leave him alone.'

Lucius didn't stop. Tarquinia grabbed Lucius by his arms and pulled him backwards. He fell against her legs, almost knocking her off balance. Arruns was still curled up, having resolved to accept the blows rather than try to escape them. Furious at being prevented from hurting his brother, Lucius turned on Tarquinia, kicking at her, but she held his wrists above his head at arm's length and his little legs couldn't reach her. He tried instead to pull out of her grip.

'Let go of me,' he said, tugging with all his strength.

'You stop this,' Tarquinia insisted. 'Stop it now.'

Lucius stopped and let his arms go limp. He looked up at her, his face full of hate.

She studied the small, oval face, so like his father's had been at his age, she remembered. Lucius was so like his father, petulant, spoilt, quick to temper. 'You little monster,' she hissed.

Lucius spat and Tarquinia blinked in surprise as she felt the gobbet of spittle slither down the side of her nose. Shocked and disgusted, she slapped him hard across the face.

'TARQUINIA!'

Tanaquil was striding towards them. Lucius held a hand to his flaming cheek and stared at his grandmother.

'Did you see what he did?' Tarquinia screeched at her mother.

Tanaquil took a cloth tucked into the neck of her dress and handed it to her daughter. 'Wipe your face.'

Tarquinia snatched the cloth and scrubbed her nose and cheek. 'He's a little shit.'

'I'll deal with this, Tarquinia. Why don't you go inside and lie down?'

'You are going to punish him, aren't you, Mother?' Tarquinia demanded.

'I'll deal with him,' Tanaquil said, putting a hand on her daughter's shoulder and gently pushing her towards the doorway. Tarquinia shot Lucius one last dark look then disappeared into the domus.

Tanaquil looked down at her grandson. 'Why do you do it, Lucius?'

'She hurt me,' Lucius said, thrusting out his arms to show where Tarquinia had grabbed him. Tanaquil glanced down at his wrists. The skin was red, not bruised.

'She is your aunt, Lucius,' Tanaquil reminded him. 'She can do as she likes with you.'

'No, she can't, I won't let her.'

Arruns, sensing it was safe to move, unfurled himself and clambered to his feet. He looked reproachfully at his brother. 'You didn't have to do that,' he sniffed, rubbing himself to ease the pain. He had to rub himself all over, for Lucius had spared no part of him.

'Lucius, apologise to your brother,' Tanaquil said.

'Won't,' Lucius pouted.

'You will.'

'I won't.'

'It doesn't matter, Grandmother,' Arruns said.

'It does matter, and Lucius will say he's sorry,' Tanaquil

said, her hands on her hips. She grabbed Lucius's shoulder and pulled him around so he was standing in front of Arruns. 'Apologise.' She saw the full red lips pucker and knew he was thinking whether it would be easier to get it over with or continue to stand firm. In the end, the increasing pressure of her fingers digging into his flesh convinced him.

'Sorry,' he mumbled, staring down at his feet.

'It's all right,' Arruns said, and Tanaquil wished he wouldn't forgive so readily. And it was most certainly not all right. Even now, she could see where the red marks on Arruns's face and arms would soon turn into bruises, and there were many of them. Lucius was a little brute and no mistake.

'Arruns,' she said, 'go inside and clean yourself up. Have Nipia see to your cuts. I will come and see you later.'

Arruns nodded and, limping slightly, went into the domus. Lucius was about to follow when Tanaquil said, 'Not just yet, Lucius. You need to explain yourself.'

'What?'

'Why did you attack your brother like that?'

'He wouldn't fight me.'

'So you hit him?'

Lucius shrugged. 'Why not?'

'Why would you want to hit him?'

'He ruined it all. I was winning.'

'Your arms training is not a competition,' she said. 'You do it to learn how to fight, not so you can beat your brother.'

'There's no point to it if we don't try to win,' he said, and Tanaquil felt she could not argue with such logic.

'I won't have you treating your aunt in that way either,' she said. 'Spitting at her, indeed. Why do you imagine we will tolerate such behaviour from you?'

'Because one day I'm going to be a king and then you'll all have to do what I say.'

Tanaquil was taken aback. She stared down at her grandson, astonished at his words. 'You'll be a king, will you?'

'Yes,' he said defiantly.

'You may and you may not,' she said. 'And besides, even if you were to become king, that is a long way off. You will be much older than you are now.'

'So what? I will be king and then you won't be able to order me about.'

'Lucius, I won't be here.'

Lucius frowned. 'What do you mean?'

'I will be dead.'

The frown remained on Lucius's face as he studied hers. 'How old are you now, Grandmother?' he asked.

'That is none of your business.'

'I suppose you will be dead by the time I'm old,' he said matter-of-factly. 'But Arruns won't, nor will Aunt Tarquinia. She'll just be old like you are now.'

'But Aunt Tarquinia may have a son,' Tanaquil said, 'who may become king before you. Have you thought of that, Lucius?'

It was obvious he hadn't. His face clouded. 'But I was here first.'

'It doesn't work that way,' she said, pleased to have thrown his composure off a little. 'In Rome, kings are elected. They don't inherit.'

'Uncle Servius became king,' Lucius said, thinking hard. 'And I've heard him say he wasn't elected.'

'The circumstances were very different when he became king. Exceptional. They won't occur again.' That awful time when she had lost Lucomo felt so long ago. Had it really only been five years? 'And now, enough of this. Go indoors and have a wash, then get to your lessons. You will have no food for the rest of the day.'

Lucius stamped his foot and it amused her to see his childish impotence. He was still a child, she reminded herself, despite his ambition. She watched him go, then looked around the stable yard and settled her gaze on Cutu. She ambled over to the awning.

Cutu saw her coming and got to his feet. 'My lady.'

'Why did you let my grandson behave like that, Cutu?'

'He was just doing what boys do, my lady,' Cutu shrugged. 'There's no real harm done.'

'He could have seriously injured his brother.'

'A few kicks and punches, my lady, that was all.'

'I am not so concerned about the fighting but what lies behind it, Cutu,' Tanaquil said, holding out her hand for a cup of water. It really was so very hot, even in the shade, and she began to wish she hadn't returned home just yet but stayed at the seaside with her friend. The slave girl gave her a cup and she took a few delicate sips. 'My grandson Lucius has a very strong temper when he doesn't get his own way. It is not good for him to be indulged in it. It's not good for anyone else, either,' she added grimly.

'He'll make a good soldier,' Cutu said defensively.

'But an undisciplined one,' Tanaquil pointed out. 'I won't have it. If he begins to act like that again during your training, I expect you to check him. Do I make myself clear, Cutu?'

Cutu bit back the response he wanted to make, that no amount of telling off would ever make Lucius a kind and obedient child, and nodded. 'Yes, my lady.'

Tarquinia was pacing the room when Tanaquil entered. 'What punishment did you give him?' she demanded.

'He's to have no food for the rest of the day,' Tanaquil said, taking a seat on a couch.

'No food! Is that all? For what he did, he should be whipped.'

'He's just a boy, Tarquinia,' Tanaquil said, smoothing her dress over her knees. 'He'll learn to control his temper. I've instructed Cutu but disciplining the children is really your job.'

'Mine?' Tarquinia was indignant.

'Yes, yours. You run the household. Seeing to the children is part of that role.'

'I try to discipline Lucius—'

'By calling him names?' Tanaquil raised a sceptical eyebrow.

'He is a little monster.'

'Well, what if he is? Do you think insulting him will have any effect? He needs careful handling.'

'I'll get Servius to handle him. I'll get him to handle him by having him thrown in the Tiber,' Tarquinia said sulkily.

'Oh, really, Tarquinia.'

'You make it sound like it's all my fault he's a little monster. It isn't. And I love Arruns and Lucilla.'

'They are all are your brother's children. Cannot you love Lucius too?'

Tarquinia fiddled with her belt. 'I've tried, Mother, really, I have, but I can't. He hates me.'

'I'm sure he doesn't. He just doesn't like to be thwarted—'

'And he takes it out on me.'

'You must make him love you. Handle him better.'

'Is it not his place to do as he's told?' Tarquinia stared at her mother defiantly. 'I am the adult, he the child. There should be no need for me to handle him.'

Tanaquil sighed. Her daughter was right, of course, but Tanaquil just wanted life to be quiet. She didn't want to have the domus resound with the noise of a child's tantrum or her daughter's shrill shouts and cries.

'Maybe we can all try a little harder to get along,' she suggested. *After all,* she thought, smiling to herself, *Lucius may be king one day.*

PART II

574 BC–539 BC

8

Servius put his hands on his hips and surveyed the scene before him. At last, his plan to build Rome a new temple had been realised. The foundations had been dug and the first stones were being laid as he watched. He couldn't help feeling just a little bit proud.

'It will be magnificent, Servius,' Tanaquil called from the litter, holding back the embroidered curtain to look out.

He turned to her, grinning. 'It will, won't it?'

'Worthy of the goddess. Diana will be pleased, my boy.'

Tarquinia, sitting opposite her mother in the litter, swatted irritably at a fly buzzing around her head. 'We've seen enough, haven't we? Can't we go now?'

'Must you be so impatient, daughter?' Tanaquil snapped.

'I'm not impatient, I'm uncomfortable,' Tarquinia retorted, smoothing her hand over her stomach.

She was pregnant again and she wasn't enjoying her condition at all. Her morning sickness had been acute, so much so she actually lost weight during the first two months. Her skin had lost all its colour and she felt tired all the time. The sickness passed eventually and Tarquinia began to gain weight. But the fatigue didn't leave her, not until Tanaquil overruled the doctor who wanted to give her evil-tasting potions and told Tarquinia she was to eat more red meat and, once a week, the testicles of a goat. Desperate to feel better, Tarquinia had not protested, even though she gagged at the testicles. Her mother had been right; she soon began to feel better.

But that wasn't the end of her suffering. During her sixth month of pregnancy, Tarquinia's hair started to fall out. At first, it had been just a few strands caught in the comb, but then her hair started coming out in clumps. Wigs had to be purchased to hide her bald spots and this distressed her greatly, worried Servius would begin to find her unattractive. The thought terrified her. She found comfort in food and her weight ballooned alarmingly. Tanaquil had joked her daughter was twice the woman she had been. Tarquinia hadn't found her words funny.

Servius rested his arm on the litter's canopy and ducked his head in. 'What do you think of it, my love?'

'Yes, very nice, Servius,' Tarquinia smiled as best she could. 'Now, please. You said we would move into the new domus today.'

'And we are, I just wanted to show you the temple,' Servius said, disappointed at Tarquinia's lack of interest. 'I'll just have a word with the foreman and then we'll be on our way.'

'Really, daughter,' Tanaquil scolded when he had gone, 'cannot you show just a little enthusiasm? For your husband's sake?'

Tarquinia glared at her mother. 'It's a temple, Mother. I've seen temples before.'

'That may be so, but this one has only been built because of your husband's hard work and perseverance. Because of your husband, the people of Rome have a place to worship Diana.'

'And I'm sure the goddess is very grateful,' Tarquinia said, swatting at the fly again. 'Ye gods, let us please get to our new house before nightfall.'

Tanaquil saw it was useless to persevere. She drew the curtain of the litter to shield herself from the sun and from the stares of the passers-by.

Servius finished his conversation with the foreman and came back to the litter. He told the bearers to take up the litter and he walked alongside as they made their way to the Esquiline Hill.

Servius had been building there, too. He had decided that, grand though the domus on the Capitoline was, it had never been intended for a large family and had become too small. It was showing its age, too. Lucomo and Tanaquil had taken up residence there back when Ancus Marcius died, and it seemed that barely a month could go by without roof tiles needing to be replaced, flagstones relaid or plaster crumbling from the walls. Servius had decided it was time for Rome's king to have a home that reflected his status.

Work on the new domus had begun almost a year earlier and had raised a few sceptical eyebrows among the patricians. The Esquiline Hill was not where Rome's rich had ever thought of living before, but Servius wanted to change that. Rome was growing every year; more people were coming to live and work there and the city was in danger of becoming overcrowded. New parts of it had to be made fit to live in and he, Servius, would lead the way.

Tarquinia complained during the entire journey to the Esquiline Hill. Even for the strongest bearers, carrying a fully occupied litter across uneven streets and up and down hills was hard work, and the men shuffled and stumbled their way along. Tanaquil, although aware her daughter's pregnancy made the journey very uncomfortable, found her complaining extremely wearing and was glad when they arrived. She had so little patience these days and there was only so much of her daughter's complaining she could take.

The bearers set the litter down outside the front doors of the new domus and Tarquinia cried, 'Thank the gods for that. Help me out, Servius, I need to pee.'

Servius took Tarquinia's hand and helped her down from the litter. She waddled through the front doors, ignoring the people who had gathered to see the King and Queen arrive. 'So much for making a dignified entrance,' Servius murmured to Tanaquil as she joined him on the front steps.

'That's my daughter for you,' she said. 'Now, let us see this new home of yours, shall we?'

They entered the new domus hand in hand. Tanaquil's eyes quickly noted the familiar furniture, brought on carts from the old domus over the last few days.

'That's in the wrong place,' she said, pointing to a small round table that had come from the old tabiculum. 'Are the frescoes finished?'

'Yes, all done,' Servius said, and as they walked through, Tanaquil saw that the walls were indeed decorated to her specification. The decorators must have only just finished because the smell of the paint still lingered.

'The floors need sweeping,' she said, noticing the stones were covered with plaster dust.

'Do you want to give the servants their orders or leave it to Tarquinia?' Servius asked with a hint of amusement at her scrutiny.

'It's your house, not mine.'

'It's *our* house, Tanaquil. And besides, the mood Tarquinia's in, I doubt if she'll want to do anything. She'll probably come out of the latrine and go straight to the cubiculum and sleep.'

'Very well, if you want me to, I'll see to the servants. Tell me, when are the children arriving?'

'I told Nipia to bring them over when their lessons are done. They haven't seen the domus yet. Do you think they'll like it?'

'Oh, I should think so. There's more room here for them to make a nuisance of themselves.'

'Being nuisances is what boys do. And you can't accuse Lucilla or my little Tullia of ever being naughty.'

Tanaquil smiled and shook her head. She knew Servius could never bear to hear criticism of his darling daughter. 'I know, I know. I'm old, my boy, that's all. I long for a quiet life.'

'You weren't destined for a quiet life,' Servius said. 'And what's all this talk of being old? You're not old.'

'Don't be ridiculous, Servius, I am seventy-two,' Tanaquil said, settling into a chair. 'I can't pretend I'm a young woman anymore and nor should you.'

'Well, I don't care how old you are.' He pulled over a footstool, lifted her legs and put her feet up on it carefully. 'Don't think of retiring any time soon. I'm going to need you.'

'Why?' she asked, peering at him. 'What are you planning now?'

'Wait and see,' Servius said, grinning mischievously.

———

'Well, what do you think?'

Tanaquil's breath caught in her throat. For an instant, looking up at her from behind his desk, she suddenly saw

Servius as a boy, eight or nine years old, eyes wide and
bright, eager for her approval. She shook her head; the
memory threatened to bring tears and Servius wouldn't
understand why. She found herself remembering such things
more often of late and she knew she was becoming the very
thing she had so often despised, a sentimental old woman.

'Go through it again,' she said, covering up her weakness
by searching for a chair. 'You talked so fast before, I couldn't
take it all in.'

'Sorry, I'll go slower this time.' Servius took a deep
breath and began again. 'The current legislative system is
blatantly unfair and favours only the highest level of our
society.'

'The patricians. Of which class, need I remind you, you
and I are a member.'

'Yes, yes,' Servius held out a hand to stop her, 'but it
isn't fair.'

'I hope you have a better reason than that, my dear,'
Tanaquil said, raising a thin eyebrow. 'Fairness doesn't
interest the patricians a great deal.'

'Agreed, but that's no reason not to try and change them.
Listen, this is how the current system works. The *comitia
curiata* advises the King and they always advise me on
matters close to their own hearts and their own money
chests.'

'You can't blame them for that, Servius. We all look after
our own interests.'

'I don't blame them and I'm not asking them to forsake
what's good for them. But is it not my duty as king to
consider all members of our society, Tanaquil, not just those
who have been favoured by Fortuna?' Tanaquil looked away
quickly, but not quickly enough. Servius had read her thought

in her expression. He slumped in his chair. 'I know what you're thinking,' he sighed.

'Do you?' Tanaquil asked warily.

'You're thinking this idea of mine, fairness for all, is because I'm not a patrician, not really, just the son of a slave.'

'May the gods have pity on me,' Tanaquil moaned, rubbing her forehead. 'Servius, when will you ever forget–'

'My lowly birth?'

'The gossip about you?'

Servius picked up his stylus and twiddled it between his fingers, not looking at her. 'I've tried. I can't forget it.'

Tanaquil wished she could reassure him, once and for all. She wished she could lie to him, tell him she had known his parents, that they had been of her class. But she didn't know the truth about his origins and she could not deceive him. For all her pride, this man before her, a man of indeterminate and suspect parentage, with whom she shared no bloodline, was as a son to her. Even before she had witnessed the portent marking him out for a special destiny, she had been drawn to the boy. She had liked his face with its big brown eyes and wide mouth, and she had liked *him*. It had been as simple as that. Tanaquil wondered how long Servius had been thinking about this… what else could it be called but reform? It wouldn't be easy. This wasn't the same as building a new temple or domus; it wasn't even the same as extending the property rights of the plebs or keeping the corn merchants in line. What Servius was proposing was changing the very fabric of Roman society.

She tapped the papers on his desk. 'Carry on.'

Encouraged, Servius stopped sulking and sat up. 'We get rid of the *comitia curiata*. We replace it with another assembly made up of plebeians. We call that assembly the *comitia centuriata*.'

'What of the senate?'

'The senate stays as it is.'

'I see,' Tanaquil nodded her approval. 'And how do we decide who makes up this assembly of plebeians?'

Servius's grin widened. 'We carry out a census. Every citizen of Rome has to register his details. They have to tell us their rank, who lives in their house, what property they own and how much money they earn.'

'And from this we establish what?'

'How much tax each man should be paying, if he has workers that can be used in the army when the need arises. And then, we put each man in a specific group that sets out his voting rights. You see what this will mean, Tanaquil? Every man in Rome will have a say in how Rome is run. Every man, regardless of his background, will have a voice.'

Tanaquil stayed silent, considering his words. 'It sounds complicated,' she said after a moment.

Servius held his hands out. 'It's complex, not complicated,' he assured her.

'It's ambitious. There will be a great deal of opposition.'

'Yes, from the patricians, I know.'

'They'll fight you hard on it.'

Servius gave a nonchalant shrug. 'Let them. I'm the King of Rome.'

Tanaquil threw back her head and laughed. Reaching across the desk, she grasped his hand. 'Yes, you are, my boy.'

9

Placus kicked a stool over to the wall beneath the awning and sat down with a loud harrumph.

The boys had been a pain in the backside all day. Lucius simply refused to attend to his lessons, and his refusal had encouraged Arruns to behave just as badly, so that in the end, Placus had slammed the boys' wax tablets shut, snatched the styli out of their hands and told them to get out of his schoolroom. He knew that that was what Lucius had wanted all along and he had to restrain himself from slapping Lucius's self-satisfied face when he'd grinned up at him in triumph and rose from his stool slowly, as if he had all the time and the right in the world to abandon Placus. Arruns had, at least, looked shamefaced as he slunk out after his brother.

Should he tell Tanaquil or Tarquinia about this incident? Placus wondered. Would it make any difference? He knew Tarquinia hated to be drawn into anything that involved Lucius and she would just tell him to inform her mother. Tanaquil would only give him an earful for not exerting a more controlling influence over his pupils. Placus knew he wouldn't win whatever he did, so he decided to take the opportunity to rest his bones in the sunny yard and drink a jug or two of wine.

Settled under the striped awning, Placus watched through half-closed lids as Lucius and Arruns each collected a wooden sword from the chest kept in the yard for arms training and began to play. It would end in tears, Placus knew, it always did. Lucius would forget he was supposed to be playing with Arruns and instead try to beat the shit out of him. But the sound of wood on wood was strangely pleasing to the ears and soon, Placus's eyes closed. He dozed, his head resting against the stone wall. He was roused by the sound of crying.

Lucius was in the middle of the yard, swinging his wooden sword around him. Arruns was a few feet away, his back to his brother, holding his hand up to his mouth and whimpering. Placus sighed and rose from the stool, pulling his tunic away from the back of his thighs where sweat had made it stick. He ambled over to the boys.

'What's the matter, Arruns?'

'It's nothing, Placus, ignore him,' Lucius said.

'You hit my finger,' Arruns yelled.

'Show me,' Placus said.

Arruns held out his hand, curling three fingers to leave his index straight. There was a small red mark on the skin.

'It's not cut,' Placus said in a tone meant to be soothing but which came out bored.

'It really hurt,' Arruns insisted.

'You're going to get hurt playing with swords. That's what happens.'

'You're such a baby,' Lucius said and thrust his sword at Arruns's belly.

Arruns tried to swat it away but he was too slow and the point poked deep into his skin. It was too much for the boy after the assault on his finger. He started crying again and Lucius shouted at him, calling his brother all the bad names he could think of.

Placus had had enough. He barked at Lucius to stop, shaking the boy's shoulder vigorously to show he meant what he said. Lucius stopped, though not before poking his tongue out at Arruns. Lucius sloped off in disgust and put his sword back in the chest, slamming the lid down and slumping onto it with his arms crossed. Arruns went off into a corner and crouched on the ground, resting his head on his arms.

Satisfied the altercation seemed to be over, Placus returned to his stool, reminding himself not to doze off again but to keep an eye on the boys while they were out here in the yard. He believed Arruns would soon run out of tears and then would simply take himself out of Lucius's company, probably going off to find his Aunt Tarquinia, who would give him a cuddle and agree what a nasty boy Lucius was.

Two little girls emerged into the sunlight. Tullia Prima, the eldest, was holding her sister's hand and led her over to where Arruns was sitting. Tullia Secunda, who was known to everyone as Lolly, a nickname coined by her sister who had been unwilling to share her name when the new baby came along, wanted to go to Lucius and her body angled in his direction. Tullia spoke to Arruns who stood up and showed her his injured finger. Placus had no doubt Arruns was exaggerating how painful the blow had been. Tullia let go of Lolly's hand, placed her arms around Arruns's waist and laid her head against his shoulder in sympathy at his ordeal. Placus smiled to himself. That Tullia, she was such a compassionate little thing, always ready to provide comfort to anyone who asked for it, whether they deserved it or not. Placus glanced at Lolly, who was not paying any attention to her sister and cousin. Her eyes were fixed on Lucius, still sitting sulkily on the chest and pretending not to notice the girls. Now that one, Lolly, she was trouble, in Placus's opinion. A right little madam, even at only five years old. Lucius must have grown jealous of the attention Arruns was getting from Tullia, for he got up from the chest and strode over to the three children.

'He's a cry-baby,' he told Tullia.

'You hurt him,' she said reproachfully. 'You're mean.'

'I hardly touched him. I didn't cry when he hit me. Look.' And he showed Tullia his left shin where a large black bruise was already emerging.

Lolly bent and kissed the bruise. 'All better,' she said to Lucius, who curled up his mouth in distaste and gave her a shove.

'Are you going to play anymore?' Tullia asked.

'Only if he stops crying,' Lucius said.

'I'm not crying,' Arruns retorted. 'And I don't want to play with you.'

'I'll play with you,' Lolly said, slipping her hand into Lucius's. She didn't let go, not even when Lucius tried to prise her fingers away.

'Girls can't play with swords,' he said.

'We can play something else,' Arruns sniffed, his tears drying.

'Chase?' Tullia suggested.

'It's too hot now,' Arruns shook his head.

'Kings and Queens?' Lolly piped up.

Placus saw both Arruns and Tullia open their mouths to say no, but Lucius snatched at the idea.

'Yes, we'll play Kings and Queens. I'll be the King—'

'And I'll be the Queen,' Lolly said quickly, jumping up and down.

'You can't,' Lucius said, 'you're too young.'

'I want to be the Queen,' Lolly stamped her foot.

'Tullia has to be the Queen,' Lucius said, ignoring her, and he set about arranging things.

He ordered a servant to drag over two sacks of grain to the centre of the yard. Set side by side and with a wooden board placed across them, Lucius declared this his throne. A large upturned jug served as Tullia's seat placed alongside. Lolly hopped over to the rear wall, and sitting cross-legged on the ground, began picking wildflowers to fashion into two crowns. She skipped back to Lucius and told him to bend down, placing the chain over his curls. Tullia ran over to her sister and bent her knees to bring herself down to Lolly's height. Lolly put her floral crown on her sister's head. With great dignity, Lucius processed to his throne. He ordered Tullia to take her seat on the upturned jug.

'You two are our subjects,' he told Arruns and Lolly.

Lolly threw herself on the ground, her arms stretched out on either side in abject obeisance to her lord. Arruns looked at her and it was obvious by his expression he was trying to decide whether or not to play along. He glanced at Lucius, who was scowling at him, then dropped to his knees. Placus was pleased Arruns had at least some sense of pride that prevented him from prostrating himself before his brother.

Placus closed his eyes once more, at ease now and feeling free to doze. There would be no more tantrums between the brothers today so long as Lucius could be the mighty king and the others played their parts as his devoted subjects.

———

Tanaquil had observed the children from an upstairs window. She had watched as Lucius arranged everything to his liking and seen the way Lolly had been quick and eager to indulge him. The display irked her. It wasn't good for Lucius to have everything his own way.

Watching Lucius and the way he treated those about him reminded Tanaquil of his father, her son. He too had been wilful and full of his own importance. Many times had she and Lucomo punished him with a rod to his back for some misdemeanour. The beatings had never seemed to do much good. It was only as he grew older that her son's truculence had diminished, around the time he had been sent to fight the Veientes. She had welcomed the battles he would face. War, she knew, made men out of boys.

The game she had witnessed set Tanaquil to thinking. 'We need to talk about the childrens' marriages,' she declared at dinner that night.

Servius looked at her over the rim of his cup. He glanced at Tarquinia, whose eyes were fixed hard on her mother.

'There's no need to look at me like that,' Tanaquil told her daughter. 'It has to be discussed.'

'The girls aren't old enough to make any decisions about who they should marry,' Tarquinia protested.

Tanaquil glanced at Servius, who lowered his eyes. Tanaquil knew then he had not discussed the matter with Tarquinia, despite Tanaquil telling him months before that he must. It was up to her then. 'There's no question of *who* the girls should marry,' she said. 'The girls will marry Lucius and Arruns.'

'Oh no, they won't,' Tarquinia said, setting her cup down so violently the wine slopped over her hand. She hastily wiped it away with her napkin. 'I'm not having my girls married off to them.'

'Why not?' Tanaquil asked.

'Why not? Because… because…' Tarquinia spluttered then turned to Servius. '*You* tell her why not.'

Tanaquil looked at Servius as if innocently awaiting his explanation. He did his best to avoid her gaze.

'It does make sense, Tarquinia,' he said apologetically.

Tarquinia's eyes widened. 'You've discussed this,' she said, her eyes moving from Servius to Tanaquil. 'Haven't you? Without me.'

'We've talked about it, yes,' Servius admitted. 'Just talking, my dear.'

'We did rather more than that, Servius,' Tanaquil said, too impatient to play along with his pacification attempts. 'Let's not pussyfoot about. Tarquinia, we want one of the boys to succeed Servius to the throne when he dies. That will be made much easier if a daughter of King Servius Tullius is their wife. People like continuity and they like bloodlines.'

'I don't—,' Tarquinia began, unable to find the words to express her horror at what was being proposed. 'Why are we talking about Servius dying? And since when is it a given the monarchy will become hereditary?'

'It's been done once,' Tanaquil said, picking apart a boiled egg and squeezing the hard yellow yoke onto her plate, 'it can be done again.'

'You can't know that.'

'No, Tarquinia, I can't and I also won't be here to see one of the boys become king after Servius, but what we decide now will make such an outcome likely.'

'Oh, so, now you're a prophet,' Tarquinia tried to laugh but couldn't manage it.

'Don't use that tone with me,' Tanaquil glared at her. 'I made your husband king, I can make one of your daughters queen.'

'And which one gets given to Lucius? Which of my daughters are you going to sacrifice to that monster?'

'He's not a monster, my love,' Servius said, reaching out to pat her arm.

Tarquinia slapped his hand away. 'He is a monster,' she spat.

'He's a handful at the moment,' Servius conceded, 'but I'm sure he'll grow out of it.'

'He's got bad blood,' Tarquinia said.

'Lucius has your blood, daughter,' Tanaquil said coolly, 'or have you forgotten?'

Realising her arguments were falling on deaf ears, Tarquinia threw her napkin onto her plate and climbed off the couch. 'It seems you two have my daughters' futures all planned out, so you don't need me.' She flounced out of the room, banging the dining-room door after her.

'I told you to talk to her about this,' Tanaquil scolded.

'I was going to,' Servius insisted, 'but there never seemed a good moment to broach the subject.'

'Did you think it was just going to go away?'

'I didn't think anything, Tanaquil. I do have plenty of other matters to occupy me, you know.' He poured himself another cup of wine, feeling he needed it.

'Tarquinia doesn't like Lucius,' Tanaquil said.

'Well, that's not news. She's never liked him. She is fond of Arruns, though. She won't object to him marrying one of the girls. And don't be too hard on Tarquinia, Tanaquil. She just wants the girls to be treated well by their husbands.'

'All mothers would like that,' Tanaquil snapped, 'but there's no way of knowing how their daughters will be treated by their husbands. A woman is either fortunate in her husband or she isn't. She doesn't find out until after the wedding.'

'You have to admit, though, Lucius's character doesn't bode well for a happy marriage. I tell you, I'm not too happy myself about giving one of my girls to him.'

'I've told you, he'll grow out of it,' Tanaquil said. 'His father was just the same at his age.'

'If you think it's for the best, Tanaquil.' Servius knew it didn't matter what he or Tarquinia thought or wanted. When the time came, their daughters *would* marry their cousins.

10

Lucius had waited for a night when the moon was covered by cloud. He had told his grandmother he was going out, ignoring her protests that her old friend Abito was coming to dinner and she wanted all her family present. He wasn't a child anymore. He was eighteen and he didn't have to do what Tanaquil said. Lucius found Arruns and told him that if he wanted to have some fun, he should go with him. Arruns, who knew of his grandmother's wish, hesitated, but a hard punch on the shoulder from his brother persuaded him to agree.

Lucius has taken him to his friend's domus on the Sacra Via. Cossus had been a friend of Lucius's from the age of twelve when Tanaquil had thought it time to extend the boys' circle of acquaintances. The sons of her friends and important patricians were invited to take lessons with Lucius and Arruns and so the next generation of Rome's leading citizens became allied. Tanaquil had hoped these new friends would have a positive effect on Lucius, showing him just how privileged his position as prince was and how he should learn to respect other people's opinions and failings.

If that had been her aim, then Cossus had been a poor choice on Tanaquil's part. He brought out and encouraged Lucius's worst character traits. Cossus would treat his parents with scorn, even contempt, call them old fools or worse, and go out of his way to act in a manner he knew would displease them. He would join with Lucius to torment slaves and throw rubbish at people in the streets, for no better reason than they were bored. And perhaps most unfortunately, he shared Lucius's opinion of Arruns, always careful because Arruns was a prince after all, to follow Lucius's lead in insulting and mocking his brother but disparaging him roundly, none-theless. Poor Arruns! He put up with it all and still Lucius was his idol.

When they arrived at his house, Cossus greeted Lucius with a hearty embrace and Arruns with a bored nod. There, they had waited, drinking several cups of wine, while Cossus sent out his slave to fetch his other friends. One by one, they arrived.

When night came down, they donned dark cloaks and made their way out of Rome through the Quirinal gate. Their journey only took about half an hour and they squatted behind a dense row of hedges that bordered the village they had chosen for their fun. There was no movement in the village save for the livestock that snuffled and squeaked in their pens. Fine wisps of smoke seeped through the thatches of the huts but no light showed beneath doorways or through cracks in the mud walls.

Lucius's blood had quickened. This was better than having to endure a boring dinner with people he didn't know or care a fig about. He was ready, he was eager. What would be more enjoyable, he wondered, to go in quietly or shouting? To take the peasants unawares or to scare the shit out of them with their noise?

'What do you think?' Lucius asked Cossus.

Cossus grinned. 'It's more fun to go in shouting but it alerts them, gives them a chance to fight back. This is a new tunic. I don't want blood on it. Leastways, not mine.'

'Silently, then. We'll enjoy the look of surprise on their faces.'

'Lucius,' Arruns squatted down beside them, leaves and twigs cracking beneath his feet, 'I don't think this is a good idea.'

Lucius and Cossus both laughed. 'Go home, brother,' Lucius said, 'if you've not got the stomach for this. I won't have you showing me up by pissing yourself.'

'I won't,' Arruns declared indignantly, 'I'm not leaving.'

Cossus grunted. 'Then get ready.'

There were seven of them in all, seven young men eager to cause trouble and shed blood. They checked their weapons, spat on their hands, prayed to Mars and ran silently toward the village.

Lucius ran past the nearest dwellings, heading for the largest hut in the middle. He kicked the wooden door and it flew open, banging against the wall behind. The inhabitants, woken by the sudden noise, jumped from their straw beds on the floor, crying in alarm. A man reached to the wall for a heavy stick, but before he could grab it, Lucius stabbed him with his sword. A woman cowering in the corner began screaming as her husband fell to the ground. Lucius quickly sized her up. Past forty, scrawny and plain. Not worth his effort. He put his sword in her throat to stop her screaming.

He wiped his sword on the woman's clothing and looked around the hut. By the gods, did people really live like this? There was nothing but a few rags, some wooden utensils and a dried-up loaf to be seen in the dim light afforded by the embers of a dying fire. Nothing worth taking for his own.

Lucius used his sword to swipe bowls and cups from a shelf; they crashed and smashed pleasingly on the floor. He was about to leave when he heard the smallest of noises, like the catching of a breath. He turned back.

Against the rear of the hut was what appeared to be a pile of blankets covered by a wolf's pelt. Lucius was by the mound in one stride. He pulled the pelt away and a cry came from beneath the blankets. Lucius grabbed a handful of the fabric. Something firm was beneath the coarse wool and he closed his hand around it and pulled. An arm emerged, then the blanket fell away to reveal a young girl's face.

Lucius laughed. There was something worth taking after all. He threw his sword on the floor and used both hands to drag the girl out from her hiding place. She tried to pull away, but she was young and small and no match for Lucius. She pleaded with him to spare her, her eyes flicking between him and the sword that had killed her parents.

Lucius struck her across the face. She fell back, blood streaming from her nose to soak her thin tunic. Hurting and senseless, she was easier to handle. He tore her tunic, exposing her small, pointed breasts that had only just budded. She was very young, no more than thirteen, he guessed. He spread her legs and shuffled up between them. She moaned as she started to come round and he felt the excitement course through him. It would be more fun if she knew what was happening to her.

He pushed into her. She screamed, her hands scratching and clawing at his chest. He was too excited to last long and he quickly spilled into her, his spittle dribbling onto her face as he grunted out his pleasure.

Lucius left the hut. He'd decided not to kill the girl, his small act of mercy. As he emerged into the cool night air, he swelled with triumph at the sound of screams that punctuated the quiet. Was Arruns the cause of some of those screams, he wondered? *He had better be*, he thought, and set off to find his brother, wanting to make sure he hadn't lost his nerve and run out on him. He'd searched two huts before he found Arruns.

'How many have you got?' Lucius asked, spying bodies on the floor of the hut.

'Only those two there,' Arruns replied.

'Women?'

Arruns shook his head.

'Never mind,' Lucius said, and taking hold of his brother's arm, led him back to the hut he had wrecked.

The girl had curled herself up into a foetal position and was crying into the blankets she had once more tried to cover herself with. Her whole body shook as Lucius and Arruns entered, her eyes opening wide in renewed terror.

'You can have this one,' Lucius said, then as Arruns hesitated, 'go on.'

Arruns went to the girl, who was trying to move as far she could away from him, but there was nowhere to go. Arruns pulled on her legs, laying her flat on her back once again. There was no fight left in the girl. She lay acquiescent beneath Arruns, her immature body jolting with every thrust.

In less than an hour, the small village had been ransacked, the men killed or wounded, the women raped. One or two of the group helped themselves to an animal, and they started the journey back to Rome, the squeals of the pigs and bleats of the goats joining in with their shouts and whoops celebrating a successful night hunting.

'How many more?' Servius asked his secretary, gesturing at the people in the vestibulum waiting to see him.

The secretary checked his wax tablet. 'Six you should see, my lord, the rest you can dismiss if you want.'

Servius sighed. He had a duty, he knew, to the people, but such a lot of this was a waste of time; so much of what came out of these petitions was just complaining. But occasionally there was a valid case, some matter he could put right with a nod of his head or a flick of his hand, and those were the ones he enjoyed, the cases he could be justifiably proud of.

'I'll see all of them,' he said, 'just see if you can hurry things along.'

The secretary nodded, wondering how he was expected to make the audiences go faster when Servius would insist on asking so many questions. Just then, there was a commotion at the far end of the hall, raised voices, the sound of a scuffle and Servius instructed the secretary to find out what was happening. The secretary folded shut his wooden wax tablet and went off to investigate. He came hurrying back a few minutes later, a look of alarm on his face.

'It's a man and a girl from a village on the banks of the Tiber a few miles north of here,' he reported. 'He says they were attacked last night.'

'Another raid?' Servius threw down his pen in annoyance. 'I thought we were clamping down on those. But why have they come here? They should appeal to the senate for help.'

The secretary stepped closer, his mouth close to Servius's ear. 'The man claims to have recognised one of the raiders. He says it was Prince Lucius, my lord.'

Servius stared at the secretary. 'Prince Lucius raided this man's village?'

'So the man claims.' The secretary made to go, paused, then turned back to Servius. 'Shall I dismiss the petitioners?'

'Why?' Servius asked sharply.

'If the man's claims are true, we don't want them hearing it, do we? It'll be all over the city before nightfall.'

Servius's jaw tightened. 'If the man's claims are true, then it should be made known. Word always get out and then I should be accused of covering up for my wife's nephew. You leave those people where they are. Bring the man and the girl before me.'

The secretary returned to the vestibulum and Servius heard his murmurs. Servius knew the secretary thought he was wrong to keep the people there, he had seen it in his face. Tanaquil would think him wrong too. But Tanaquil, thankfully, wasn't here and he would have the truth. *Damn Lucius*, he thought, *he knows how hard I'm working to stop these unprovoked attacks on our neighbours.* Servius would fight for Rome when he had to, but raids! Raids were senseless. They achieved nothing save to rouse up the peasantry and cause problems for the senate.

The secretary returned, shepherding the man and girl forward until they stood before Servius. They were a sorry sight. The man was about twenty-five. His ragged dark hair was matted with blood, his mouth and cheek were swollen and bruised and there was a dark red stain on his clothing above his hip. The girl's nose was swollen and cut, both eyes were blackened and the clothing she wore was far too big for her, obviously not her own. No one who looked upon the pair could doubt they had been attacked.

Servius addressed them. 'I am sorry for your trouble. My secretary tells me your village was attacked last night.'

'Yes, my lord king,' the man said thickly, his tongue as swollen as his lips. 'Our homes were entered and ransacked, our men attacked and our women raped. Some of our live-stock was taken too.'

'There were killings?"

The man nodded. 'Most of the men in my village were killed. I would be dead too but for the sword missing its mark.' He pointed to the red stain on his tunic. 'A neighbour of mine was bashed about the head and hasn't woken up yet. All the other men are dead, some of the women too. The bastards killed them when they'd had their pleasure.'

Servius winced. 'And this girl?'

'Raped twice, my lord. She's only twelve years old. She was a virgin until Prince Lucius found her. Now, no other man will have her for a wife, despoiled as she is.'

'You accuse Prince Lucius of raping her?'

'He took her first. I saw him go into her family's hut. Then I was stabbed and fell down. I couldn't move, else I would have gone to her. But I heard her screaming, begging with him not to touch her. I saw him leave, then come back later with another man. They both went into the hut and Prince Lucius watched while the other raped her.'

The girl had started to weep as her companion recounted her ordeal. The man put his arm around her shoulder and she flinched at his touch.

'You accuse the Prince, yet how can you be sure it was him?' Servius asked, hoping the man was wrong. 'By my remembrance, the night was dark, there was no moon to see by.'

'Our roofs were set alight. Straw burns fast. There was plenty of light to see by and I saw Prince Lucius as clear as I see you now. I've seen him before. I've come to Rome many times. I know it was him.'

Servius spoke to the secretary. 'Bring Prince Lucius here.'

———

The banging on his door woke Lucius. He blinked open his eyes, feeling the crust on his lids crack and break apart. Sunlight came thinly through the narrow window, enough to hurt his eyes. He shut them again.

He and his friends had returned to Rome and made straight for a tavern, the wriggling animals they had stolen lost on the way. They had caroused for hours, until they had started vomiting over the floor and the tavern keeper told them to leave, a big stick in one hand and three of his biggest men behind him.

Cossus had wanted to make a fight of it, but the others had had enough for one night. They pulled and pushed Cossus out into the street, the tavern keeper shouting and slamming the door behind them. They had sung each of the company to his own home, until only Lucius and Arruns remained, entering the domus through the back yard.

Arruns had pulled his brother into a drunken embrace and kissed him sloppily on both cheeks and then they parted, each to their own cubiculum. Undressing would have taken too much effort and so Lucius had not even tried. He collapsed onto his bed still wearing his tunic, all stained and smoky from the night's adventures. And this was how the secretary found him.

'Prince Lucius.' The secretary shook Lucius's shoulder without ceremony. He didn't like Lucius. He had seen him grow up and witnessed too many of his tantrums to have any reverence for his person.

'Go 'way,' Lucius mumbled, trying to shrug him off.

'The King demands your attendance at once.'

'The King can go fuck himself.'

The secretary grabbed a handful of tunic and tugged, making Lucius slide half off the bed. 'He wants to see you *now*.'

Lucius grunted and pushed himself up. With a great effort, he swung his legs to the floor. 'All right,' he snarled at the secretary. 'I'll be along as soon as I've bathed.'

'There's no time for that. You must come at once.'

Half asleep and barely able to keep his eyes open, Lucius followed the secretary along the corridor to the tablinum. 'What's this about?' he asked.

'You'll find out,' the secretary said peremptorily.

'Just tell me, you dog.'

The secretary didn't answer and Lucius was forced to cease his questioning. Every step jarred his brain and he cursed Servius for making him get out of bed. *I'll piss in his wine later,* he thought.

They reached the tablinum. 'Yes, Uncle?' Lucius sighed.

He glanced towards the vestibulum, hearing the murmur of voices. Oh, by Jupiter's great cock, there were plebs there. He looked down at his tunic. It was a mess, stained with blood and beer, and by the smell of it, vomit. He was in a disgusting state and yet here he was, on display to these peasants. If he could, he would have their eyes burned out for seeing him like this.

Servius looked him up and down and Lucius saw his top lip curling in distaste. 'Where were you last night?'

Lucius blinked at him. 'Wh— where was I?' He laughed. 'Oh, please tell me this isn't because I wasn't at dinner.'

'No, it's not because you weren't at dinner,' Servius roared, rising and banging his fists on his desk and sending his stool crashing to the floor. The noise hushed the onlookers and knocked the fug out of Lucius's brain. 'It's because of them,' and he thrust out his arm and pointed behind Lucius.

Lucius glanced over his shoulder. There were two people in the room he hadn't noticed before, a man and a girl. The girl was hiding behind the man but she was peering out around his elbow, her frightened eyes on Lucius. Lucius wondered why she looked familiar.

'Well,' he said, turning back to Servius, 'who are they?'

'Their village was attacked last night,' Servius said. 'This man claims you were among the attackers. Is it true?'

Lucius licked his lips. Why was Servius doing this to him, humiliating him in front of all these people? He thought quickly. He could deny it, say he'd been with Cossus in one of the city's brothels and get a girl to confirm it if he had to.

But why should I? Lucius straightened and raised his chin. 'Yes, it's true.'

Servius closed his eyes and took a long, hard breath. 'Why?' he growled.

Lucius shrugged. 'Because I could. Because I wanted to.'

The man behind him bellowed in rage. 'You killed our men and raped our women because you felt like it?' He lunged at Lucius. Servius's guards reacted quickly and pinioned him to the ground. He thrashed and spat curses at them.

'Stop,' Servius said, 'leave him alone. Let him up.' The guards released him and the man clambered to his feet. Fresh blood was leaking through his tunic for his struggle had reopened his wound. 'You, control yourself,' Servius ordered him sternly. 'Now, you will both go with this man.' He pointed to one of the lictors who hovered in the doorway. 'He will take you to the kitchens and you will be fed. Send for the doctor too,' he added to the secretary, who clicked his fingers at his junior and gave the instruction. 'You will be looked after and you will be safe. We'll talk later.'

The lictor led the man and girl away and Servius told the secretary to remove the people from the vestibulum. The rest of his interview with Lucius would be private now he had acknowledged his guilt.

'What is the matter with you?' Servius asked as soon as the heavy double doors had closed. 'What is it that goes through your head?'

'I don't know why you're making such a fuss,' Lucius said, rolling his eyes. 'We—'

'Who?' Servius snatched at the word. 'Who was with you?'

'A few of my friends. And Arruns.'

'Arruns?' Servius's mouth fell open. 'Your brother was with you?'

Lucius's mouth curved upwards in an unpleasant smile. 'Don't look so surprised, Uncle. He isn't the good little boy you think he is, you know.'

'Arruns took part in the killing?'

'He took part in all of it.'

Servius ordered the secretary to fetch Arruns. 'Whose idea was it?' he asked Lucius. 'Yours, I warrant.'

'What if it was?'

'Ye gods, do you know what you've done?'

'Yes, I had some fun.'

'You've endangered everything I've been working towards, that's what you've done. How can we be at peace with our neighbours if we carry out such senseless attacks?'

'Peace is for women,' Lucius sneered, 'and for slaves.' The look Lucius gave Servius was full of meaning and loathing.

'I know what you think of me, Lucius,' Servius said, breaking the stare. 'You think I have no right to be king. Well, maybe you're right. You certainly wouldn't be the only one to think so. But I am king and I won't have you ruining everything I'm trying to do for Rome.'

'It was one raid,' Lucius said. 'One. We should raid when the fancy takes us. Why not? It's good for us. It's what

Romans should do. In my grandfather's time, there were always raids and he never complained. Raids keep us ready for battle. Not that with all your talk of peace we'll ever get the chance to go to war now. You'd rather let the Latins raid us and do nothing.'

'I have never shied away from war when it's been necessary, Lucius. If the Latins were to—'

'Oh, don't give me that. If you had your way, you would have us all spinning wool with our women.'

Servius laughed hollowly. 'You see, that's the difference between us, Lucius. I am ready to fight when there's no other option. You'd rather fight than have peace. And that, let me tell you, is why you're not fit to be a king. You understand nothing about ruling, Lucius, nothing. You don't grow prosperous through battle. You grow prosperous through trade, and in order to trade, you need to be on good relations with your neighbours.'

'It was one little village—'

'Those people live by the Tiber. They are Romans. Those men you killed and the women you violated were your own people, Lucius. And yes, it was one little village last night, but then you get a taste for it and then you raid another, and another, and suddenly, we have everyone against us and we have nothing but war.'

Servius broke off as the secretary returned shepherding a sheepish-looking Arruns before him. Arruns tried not to look at his brother.

'Arruns, come here,' Servius pointed to a spot beside Lucius. 'Lucius tells me you were with him last night.'

'Yes, Uncle,' Arruns said, hanging his head.

'You killed and raped?'

'I did, Uncle.'

'I——,' Servius broke off and smacked the table. 'I don't understand. You, of all people, Arruns.'

He looked to Arruns for a response but Arruns said nothing.

'I know young men like to fight,' Servius continued, his voice adopting a pacific tone. 'I was young once. And I know there are times when we need to fight to preserve what's ours. But when we attack our own people in senseless raids, we're damaging Rome. We hurt ourselves and we hurt the monarchy of which you,' and he jabbed a finger at Lucius, 'are so proud to be a part. What do you imagine the people of Rome will think when news of what you did last night spreads?'

'Well, you've seen to it that it will spread, haven't you?' Lucius sneered. 'You could have said nothing but you made sure you humiliated me in public. I'm going to be the gossip of every tavern and brothel in Rome.'

'And you deserve to be. The people must know that they can trust their king, that they can trust *me*. They must know that anyone who transgresses the law will be exposed and punished, regardless of their family name.'

'We are not family,' Lucius said.

'We *are* family,' Servius insisted, 'whether you like it or not, Lucius. You may not have my blood, but you may have my throne one day. You'll be happy to be known as my heir, won't you? Well, you carry on like this and you won't be. You won't be elected king because the senate won't trust you.'

'Maybe I won't need to be elected,' Lucius muttered.

'You will need the senate's approval, Lucius, don't think you won't. And you won't have your grandmother by your side to help you as I did. Think on that.'

Servius saw his remark had hit home. Lucius's face fell.

'It won't happen again,' Arruns promised, looking from Lucius to Servius.

'You can promise me that, Arruns?' Servius asked.

'Yes, I can and I do,' Arruns said vehemently.

Servius looked to Lucius. 'And what about you?'

Lucius pouted, refusing to make his uncle any kind of promise.

'Both of you will pay restitution to the man and the girl,' Servius said. 'My secretary will work out a suitable amount for her violation and for the damage caused to the village. You will also make a sacrifice to Jupiter and to Pax to atone for your misdeeds.' He sighed. 'Even so, all the gold in Rome will not undo the damage you have done this night. Mark me, I will not tolerate any further raids. I promise you, Lucius, Arruns, you do this kind of thing again and I will have you both banished, never to return to Rome again.'

———

Tanaquil rubbed her fingers against her temples and pressed hard. She'd had a sharp pain behind her eyes for almost three days now and she fancifully thought that maybe she could force the pain away with her fingers. It didn't work, just as none of the potions prescribed by her doctor had done the slightest bit of good. She knew the only way the headache would go, or even just recede a little, would be through rest. All she wanted to do at this moment was lie down on her bed and sleep the pain away. But she couldn't. Now, she had to deal with this.

'Men will do this sort of thing, Servius,' she said, trying to keep the tiredness out of her voice.

'You're condoning the rape and murder of innocent Romans?' Servius said incredulously.

'Of course not,' she said. 'But Lucius was right. Lucomo authorised raids on our enemies, and those he didn't authorise… well, he turned a blind eye to. You went on a few raids yourself, if you remember.'

Servius held up his hands in an acknowledgement but his face told her he wasn't going to be placated by the reminder. 'It was a different time, Tanaquil.'

Tanaquil knew he was right. When she and Lucomo had arrived in Rome, it had been a vicious place, entirely in tune with Tarquinii and Veii and Volsci and all the other tribes who believed in fighting one another constantly. In her opinion, Rome was still vicious at heart, but over the years, it had at least acquired the appearance of a civilised society. 'I think it is time,' she said.

'Time for what?'

'Time for the boys to be married.'

'Oh no,' Servius said, shaking his head vehemently, 'not after this. I'm not having my daughters married to men like them.'

'What man isn't like them?' Tanaquil asked. 'Don't tell me you never ravished a woman on one of your raids.'

'It's what you do,' he said after a moment's hesitation, his tone regretful. 'You kill the men and rape the women. By Jupiter, most of the slaves in Rome were captured during raids.'

'Quite. They're nothing, they're nobodies. Those people the boys killed and raped don't matter, Servius. They're peasants.'

'But my daughters…'

Tanaquil rose, walked around the table and put a hand on Servius's shoulder. 'The children have grown up together. Lucius and Arruns will treat the girls well.'

'When Tarquinia hears of what Lucius and Arruns have done, she won't agree to the marriages.'

'Then we won't tell her.'

'You want us to deceive her?'

'If it's best for the family, yes.'

'But she'll hear about the raid from her friends when she gets back from her holiday,' Servius said. 'You know what they're like. They love nothing better than to gossip.'

'If she hears of it, she hears of it,' Tanaquil shrugged. 'It won't matter. She may rail against us and shout and cry but in the end, Tarquinia always does as she's told. And I promise, things will be better when they're married.'

Servius turned his face to hers. 'You really believe that?' he asked hopefully.

Tanaquil bent and planted a kiss on his forehead. 'You've always trusted me, my boy. Trust me in this.'

———

Tanaquil didn't bother to knock. She opened the door and found Lucius standing naked in the middle of his bedroom while a girl washed him down, dipping a cloth into a bowl of warm water on the floor. The water was grey with tinges of red.

Lucius looked around at his grandmother and Tanaquil could see the indecision in his face as to whether he should protest at her entrance. In the end, he said nothing. She walked over to the bed and sat down, pleased Lucius didn't try to cover his nudity as she suspected Arruns would have done. It seemed nothing could embarrass Lucius.

'Have you come to tell me off too, Grandmother?' he said.

'Don't take that tone with me, Lucius,' Tanaquil retorted. 'You know you're in the wrong.'

'I'm not,' Lucius said. 'Everyone raids.'

'Not these days. And I'm not here to chastise you. Servius has already done that. I'm here to ask you to behave in future, Lucius. No, you listen to me. I chose Servius to be king when your grandfather was murdered. *I* chose *him* because I knew he was the best man to rule Rome. And I've never regretted my choice, not once. He was a good king from the very beginning and he is doing his best to be a great one. And you are not helping.'

'What have I done?' Lucius was pouting just as he had when a boy and he'd been denied something he wanted.

'You are not a child, Lucius, stop acting like one. I want you to be someone Servius can rely on, not his enemy.'

Lucius, saying nothing, turned away from her as the girl worked her way around his body. Just as she knew he wasn't one to be easily embarrassed, Tanaquil knew he also didn't respond well to being told what to do.

'Well, Lucius?' she prompted, wanting an answer. 'Can you do that for me?'

His back was to her now as she waited. She could have asked again but she held back. She was in control here and she wanted him to acknowledge it.

'Yes, Grandmother,' he said at last.

'Good,' she said, rising from the bed and heading for the door. With her hand on the latch, she turned back to Lucius. 'And you and your brother are invited to supper with me tonight. It will be just us three to chat about how things will be from now on. And unlike last night, Lucius, you will be there.'

———

Tarquinia returned from her holiday in the country with a slightly sunburnt face and a declaration she was glad to be home. Servius embraced and kissed her and ordered wine and dates to be brought while he took off her sandals and rubbed her feet as she reclined on one of the triclinium's couches.

He listened with strained attentiveness as she recounted the details of her stay: how tall the sons of her friend had grown, how the estate was managing following the blight that had affected the barley crop and how uncomfortable her bed had been. She prattled on and Servius let her, wanting to put off the announcement that the girls were to be married next month for as long as he could.

But he knew he couldn't put it off indefinitely, and after she had eaten her fill, he broached the subject. Tarquinia stared at him while he talked, not interrupting once. The silence that followed struck him as ominous. Where was the shouting? Where were the tears?

'So soon?' she said at last.

'Well, not that soon really,' he said. 'They are all old enough.'

Tarquinia shrugged. 'As you and Mother decide,' she said and saying she was tired, left the room to retire.

When Servius went to bed, earlier than normal as a courtesy to Tarquinia, he expected her to treat him coldly, but he was surprised. She greeted him civilly, if not exactly lovingly, and made room for him in the bed.

'Where will they live?' she asked as he pulled the bedclothes up to his chin.

'Your mother thinks they should live with us here in the domus.'

Tarquinia grunted. 'We will be able to keep an eye on them, at least.'

'Yes, I suppose we will. You're agreeable, then?'

'No, of course I'm not agreeable,' she snapped, 'but I know I won't be listened to, not if Mother has anything to do with it.'

'Tarquinia!'

'And I will not pretend to the girls that I am happy about it, so don't ask me to.'

'Very well, my love,' Servius said, aware her response was the best he could hope for.

————

Servius fixed a smile on his face as his daughters entered. As always, his heart swelled to see them. These girls of his had taken their time to enter his life and he treasured every moment he spent in their company.

Tullia, so like her mother in looks and temperament, docile and amenable, conformable to the wishes of others, was a girl to be cosseted and protected. Lolly was different. She had a character all of her own. Not everyone approved of her determination to have her own way all the time, Tarquinia for one, but it was a delight to him to see his little madam stamp her foot and give her orders, the tender rosebud mouth pouting. Tarquinia wondered where Lolly got her character from but Servius knew she'd inherited it from both her grandparents. From Lucomo she had inherited her sense of entitlement and pride, from Tanaquil her single-mindedness and brains. What, he sometimes wondered, did either of his girls get from him?

'Get on with it, Servius,' Tarquinia said sharply. 'Girls, attend to your father.'

Both girls were standing before him expectantly. His smile held in place, he began, 'Your mother and I—'

'Your father and your grandmother,' Tarquinia corrected.

'We've decided,' Servius said with only the slightest flicker of his eyelids betraying his annoyance, 'it is time you were both married.'

Tullia blushed. Lolly's eyes widened in interest.

'Who are we to marry, Father?' Lolly asked.

'Lucius and Arruns,' he said.

'And which am I to have?'

'You, Lolly, will marry—'

'Lucius?'

He shook his head. 'Arruns, as the younger.'

'No,' she cried. 'Why? I don't see that age matters at all.'

'Lolly,' Servius said sternly, 'you will do as you are told and you will marry who I say you will marry.'

Lolly opened her mouth to retort, but her father's expression seemed to change her mind.

'So, I am to be given to Lucius?' Tullia asked quietly.

'You are, my dear,' Servius nodded.

'And may Vesta protect you,' Tarquinia murmured from her corner.

Tullia turned to her. 'Why, Mother?'

Tarquinia folded her arms and glanced at Servius before answering. 'Because, my poor Tullia, in marrying Lucius, you're going to need all the good fortune you can get.'

———

'What do you think Mother meant by that, Lolly?' Tullia asked as the girls returned to the garden where they had been spinning their daily quota of wool.

Lolly picked up a cushion from a stone bench and began hitting the slave who stood by the nearest column. 'Why — do — you — get — to — marry — Lucius?' she demanded, each word a hit for the slave whose only defence was to turn his head away.

'Oh, Lolly, don't do that,' Tullia said, snatching the cushion out of her sister's hand. 'You'll burst the stitching.'

'I don't give a fig about the stitching,' Lolly spat, pushing the slave away. She flung herself down on the bench.

Tullia sat primly on the very end of the bench, smoothing the cushion on her lap. 'I wish you were to marry Lucius, Lolly. I'd much rather marry Arruns.'

'By the gods, why? Why would you want to marry *him*?'

'He's kind.'

'He's boring.'

'He's not,' Tullia said shyly. 'He's really not.'

'Ugh, next you'll be telling me how lucky I am.'

Tullia bit her lip. She did think Lolly was lucky and she really did wish she could marry Arruns. Lucius frightened her a little. She couldn't deny he was the more handsome of the two brothers, but that only made her feel more inappropriate for him. She wasn't pretty, she felt sure, although it was difficult to tell exactly what she looked like, for her bronze mirror provided a warped reflection only. But no one ever said she was pretty, not like they did to Lolly. And her mother's words were still in her head. She knew her mother didn't like Lucius. Tullia didn't know what exactly her mother had against him, but she trusted her and if she didn't approve of the marriages… but then, her father thought the marriages a good idea, and she trusted him too. It was rather confusing.

'Father didn't say when.'

'Mmmm?' Tullia murmured, bringing her mind back to her sister.

'I said Father didn't say when we will marry,' Lolly repeated.

'I expect it will be soon.'

'I wonder if I have time to get Father to change his mind and let me marry Lucius?' Lolly mused, twirling a loose strand of hair around her finger.

'You heard what he said,' Tullia reminded her.

'Oh, I'm sure I can get around him. Men are stupid like that.'

Tullia winced to hear her sister speak so of their father. Their father wasn't stupid, and Lolly shouldn't speak of getting around him as if he were a man with no backbone, as if he were weak. He wasn't weak, he was kind and loving, and he deserved to be treated better than the way Lolly treated him.

Lolly put her feet on the cushion on Tullia's lap, banging the stuffing down to get comfortable. Tullia glanced at her sister, lying on the stone bench with her eyes closed, no doubt scheming how to get their father to change his mind about her future husband. Ashamed of herself, Tullia couldn't help hoping, just a little, that Lolly would succeed.

———

Servius picked a grape from the bowl on the table and popped it into his mouth. 'Lolly wants to marry Lucius.'

'There's a surprise,' Tanaquil murmured, easing off her sandal and reaching down to massage her little toe. The leather of her sandal had been rubbing her corn all day and the toe was swollen and red.

'I wonder... should we say yes?'

Tanaquil groaned. 'Must you always give in to that daughter of yours?'

'It's not giving in,' Servius protested, sitting down beside her and gently lifting her foot onto his lap. He began to rub the offending foot, his hands passing over the cracked, hard skin and thickened yellow toenails. 'It may make more sense. I've often thought Lucius and Lolly were better suited. Tarquinia thinks so too, although she'd rather not have the marriages at all.'

'I'm not discussing Tarquinia's opinions again,' Tanaquil said flatly. 'And I have my reasons for choosing which of them will marry one another.'

'The eldest together, the youngest together. Was that not the reason?'

Tanaquil tutted. 'Do you really think it's that simple? What does age matter? They're all young enough for that not to be a consideration.'

'What are your reasons then?'

Tanaquil pushed his hands away. 'Tarquinia is not entirely wrong about Lucius. He is—'

'A monster?' Servius suggested with a laugh, thinking of Tarquinia's favourite word for her eldest nephew.

'Headstrong,' Tanaquil said. 'He has a high opinion of himself, he thinks he's better than everyone else. Well, in that, I cannot say he is entirely wrong.'

'You like Lucius, don't you?'

'I do.' She smiled ruefully. 'Oh, I know he's had his moments—'

'That's putting it mildly.'

'But he reminds me of his father in so many ways and though he was a handful, he was also...' she searched for the right word, 'impressive. I like a doer, Servius, you know that. That's why I loved you. Arruns is a pleasant young man, but he's easily led. You've seen for yourself how he does whatever Lucius tells him to do. The raid on the village proved that. Do you imagine Arruns would have gone raping and killing if Lucius hadn't put him up to it? Arruns would make a poor king. The senate would walk all over him, perhaps even get rid of him. But Lucius, ah, now there's a man they'd have to watch out for.'

'I'm not dead yet, Tanaquil,' Servius reminded her.

'You're not a god, Servius, you're not immortal. We have to think of the future.'

'If I'm not immortal, then you're nearer to the grave than I am, Tanaquil. You won't be here to see Lucius become king, so why does it matter to you?'

'Of course it matters to me,' she said sharply. 'It matters what we leave behind us, else why do we bother to have children, why do we bother to build, to educate ourselves? And you're wrong. I will know of what comes after me. I'll see all that happens here when I'm in Elysium.'

'But you won't be able to change anything,' Servius pointed out. 'If you don't like what you see, for example.'

'You don't know that,' she said, her lips twitching in amusement. 'I've had dreams where my father and mother have come to me and told me what to do when I've been unsure. And I've woken up and done what they told me and I have changed things. The dead can speak to the living. And what we do today will lead the way for tomorrow and all the tomorrows ahead of us. Do you understand?'

Servius nodded.

'My reason for wanting Tullia to marry Lucius is that she will be good for him. Her good nature will temper his bad one. She'll teach him to think before acting. She'll change him, you'll see, that's what women do for their husbands. Can you imagine if Lolly was allowed to marry Lucius? Ye gods, what a mess we shall all be in then. That little madam will bring out the very worst in him.'

'Lolly's not that bad,' Servius protested.

'She's your daughter, of course you think that. But I see her with an old woman's eyes, my boy, and let me tell you, your eldest daughter got all the good Tarquin blood and your youngest all the bad. Arruns will be good for Lolly as Tullia will be good for Lucius. Have I ever put you wrong before?'

'No, Tanaquil, you haven't.'

'No, well, let that be enough for you.' She put her feet back in his lap. 'And rub my feet again. I'll tell you when you can stop.'

11

The rich glow of the sun cast its colour over the fields of barley and embraced the forms of the men and women tending the crop. The estate was thriving. The crop was doing well, thanks to the good weather of the past few months, and most of the livestock had bred successfully, so much so that their enclosures were full of squealing from the young as they played with their siblings, while their mothers grunted in contentment as greedy mouths sucked on their teats.

Lucius squinted against the sun. 'It almost makes me wish I was a farmer.'

'Course it does,' Manius said sardonically. 'You'd give up Rome to live in the country and worry about the price of grain and how many pigs have been born, not forgetting to sacrifice all the time to Ceres to pray it doesn't rain too much or too little.'

'You do it.'

'Yes, but I'm me,' Manius prodded his chest with a dirty finger. 'I'm not the nephew of a king.'

'Much good it's done me,' Lucius muttered, throwing away the stem of barley he'd been fiddling with.

Manius studied his friend for a long moment. 'What's the matter?'

'Nothing.'

'Something's wrong. You're, I don't know… subdued. And you show up here without telling me you're coming. Not that you're not welcome, of course, but you usually let me know.'

Manius waited. He'd known Lucius too long to believe that there wasn't a good reason for his friend's visit. Like Cossus, Manius had been one of those boys invited to take lessons with Lucius and Arruns. Unlike Cossus, Manius was the kind of friend Tanaquil had hoped Lucius would make. Manius was clever and interested in his lessons, but he also enjoyed the physical exercises that were a part of all Roman boys' daily curriculum. He and Lucius would have wrestling matches and fight fair — sometimes he would win, sometimes Lucius — and he would always make a show of including Arruns in their games. He had felt sorry for Arruns, suffering under his brother's bullying, and knowing he had influence with Lucius, had led him to not be so hard on Arruns, at least not when he was around. He couldn't stop Lucius's bullying entirely, he knew, especially when Cossus was with them, and he did his best to distance himself from Lucius's other best friend. Manius understood perfectly the relationship he had with Lucius; he was the friend Lucius turned to when he wanted to talk. Cossus was the friend Lucius turned to when he was feeling frustrated and needed to break free of his bonds. So, Manius knew it would only take a little prodding for Lucius to tell what was troubling him.

'I had to get away from Rome,' Lucius blurted out just when Manius thought he would have to probe some more. 'The constant disapproval was getting on my nerves.'

'Disapproval from who?'

'From Servius,' Lucius snarled, 'who else? Ever since those peasants came to Rome to complain about the raid, he's done nothing but watch me to make sure I don't misbehave again.'

Manius knew about the raid. Accounts of Lucius's public dressing-down by Servius had quickly spread around Rome and friends had written to Manius to let him know this latest gossip. Manius had written to Lucius to find out the truth and had not been surprised to learn Cossus had been party to the raid. He had written that Lucius had been in the wrong but softened his admonition with the offer of a stay at his country farm. Lucius had not replied nor taken him up on his offer at the time, and Manius thought the affair must not have been as bad as reported.

'I thought Servius would have forgotten about that by now,' he said.

'Don't you believe it,' Lucius laughed bitterly. 'Of course, he doesn't come out and say anything, not with Aunt Tarquinia there, but he's always ready to remind me how much I disappoint him.'

'He must be the same with Arruns.'

'Oh, no, not Arruns. *He's* a good little boy. It doesn't matter that Arruns was with us that night and did everything we did. Arruns said he was sorry, so all is forgiven and forgotten as far as Servius is concerned.'

Manius could hear that Lucius was working himself up into one of his tempers and he wasn't in the mood to deal with one of those. 'Well, you're out of Rome now,' he said placatingly. 'You can forget about him.'

'I wish I could. But you know what he's doing back in Rome? Arranging our marriages to his daughters.'

'You and Arruns? That's good, though, isn't it? Wedding the King's daughters. You couldn't make a better marriage.'

Lucius made a face at Manius and didn't answer.

'Which one are you getting?' Manius asked.

'Tullia.'

'Tullia, eh? Well, she's all right. You won't have any trouble with her.' He laughed. 'It must have put Lolly's nose out of joint, though.'

'Why would it upset Lolly?'

'You're not serious?' Manius frowned. 'You've always been Lolly's favourite.'

'Have I?'

'Oh, don't pretend you haven't noticed. You could have had Lolly any time you wanted. All you would have to do is snap your fingers and she would lie naked on your bed with her legs spread for you. But you're getting Tullia instead. Never mind.'

'Lolly's a pain,' Lucius said. 'Tullia's easy.'

'So, what are you complaining about exactly?'

Lucius shot a sharp look at Manius. 'All right, I don't mind marrying Tullia. I've got to marry someone and it's best that it's her if I'm to be king. I just can't stand being told by Servius that I've got to.'

'And the gods know you hate to be told what to do.'

'Doesn't everyone?' Lucius snapped.

'Lucius, these things are always arranged. My parents decided who I would marry. I didn't argue with them. I was grateful.'

'You're telling me I should be grateful to Servius?' Lucius asked incredulously. 'Never.'

Manius held up his hands in a gesture of defeat. 'Will I be invited?'

'I doubt it. Why? Do you want to be?'

Manius shrugged. 'Any excuse to go to Rome.'

'And while you would be visiting every brothel in the city, I'd be ploughing my new wife.'

'What I'd give to have a life like yours.'

'What's so wonderful about my life, Manius?'

'You really want to know?' Manius said, suddenly angry. He splayed his left hand and with his right, began counting off the fingers. 'You're the grandson of one king, the nephew by marriage of another. You're being lined up to be the next king through a highly advantageous marriage. Top that off with your nobility and your wealth, all of which you've got without having to lift a finger to get them. Now, stop your whining, will you?'

'That's what you think, is it? That because I've got gold and people to do what I want, I should be content?'

'Yes, actually, I do.'

Lucius hurled his cup to the ground. It shattered into pieces, drops of wine sprinkling the flagstones. 'Then you really have no idea.'

———

Lolly knew about curses. She had listened, rapt, when her grandmother had spoken, just once, of the curse the Tarquins suffered under. The story fascinated her, how the woman had called on the goddess Poena to hear her words and how the goddess had responded. She remembered how Tanaquil had trembled as she spoke of the shade that had appeared, how it had entered her father and found the Tarquin children. She had never known her grandmother to be frightened of anything, but Lolly had seen how even mention of Poena's dark agent had made Tanaquil draw her shawl tighter around her shoulders and pray at the household shrine for their gods to protect them. That was power, Lolly thought, to call on a god and have your greatest desire granted. She wanted to have power like that. After all, she had none as the daughter of Servius Tullius and she would have even less, if she wasn't careful, as the wife of Arruns.

She knew what she had to do.

Lolly opened the small chest she kept hidden under her bed, moving aside the dried flower crown she had put on Lucius's head all those years ago and the lock of his hair she had picked up off the floor after it had been cut, and took out a small rectangular piece of hammered-thin lead. She unclasped the brooch that pinned the shoulder of her dress together, the fabric falling down to expose her left breast, the nipple hardening quickly in the cold stone room. She angled the sharp pin and began etching the words of the curse she had devised to the goddess Discordia into the lead, speaking them softly as she wrote.

'May Tullia Prima, first daughter of Servius Tullius, never find pleasure in the marital bed. May her womb dry up and shrivel. May her body bleed in vain. May her husband be disgusted by her person. May his phallus shrink and never seed her womb. May Tullia Prima never conceive a child of Lucius Tarquinius. Goddess, hear me.'

She kissed the tablet then stabbed the pin into her breast. The wound produced a single drop of blood. She rubbed her finger over it, spreading it over her white skin and pressing out more. Her finger wet and red, she pressed it to the lead tablet, smearing the red liquid over and into the words. Then she folded the long edge of the lead over and over until it became a thin tube and this she stuck into a crack in her wall.

There, it was done. Tullia was cursed and her marriage would be barren. Lolly licked her finger, tasting the metal tang of her own blood. If anyone was going to have a child by Lucius, it would be her. On that, Lolly was determined.

———

The domus had been decorated with flowers and herbs. Archways were decked with green leaves and blossom picked that morning from the garden, and incense was burning in each room, the cloying smell wafting throughout the domus as the guests entered.

Lucius, sitting on a stool in the corridor of the garden, watched as they came into the courtyard and mingled amongst themselves. They were all dressed in their best clothes, the products, no doubt, of recent trips to the forum to visit silk merchants' shops, and many of the women, and some of the men too, wore elaborate, expensive gold and silver necklaces and bracelets. All were smiling and laughing. *As if there's anything to smile and laugh about*, Lucius thought, *being married off to the King's daughters as if me and my brother are a pair of prize bulls Servius wants to put out to stud.*

Lucius had woken that morning hoping the marriages would not go ahead. But Servius had returned to the domus after a visit to the temple where he had sacrificed a sheep to ensure it was a propitious day for his daughters to be married. With a smile, he assured both Lucius and Arruns that the priest had declared the dead animal's entrails to be good and the marriages would go ahead. Arruns had told Servius he was very glad; Lucius had said he would go and get ready.

And now, there was Servius, striding into the courtyard with his arms wide, greeting everyone with a smile. Tanaquil and Tarquinia followed. Tarquinia seemed determined to show them all up by overdressing, Lucius thought sourly. She wore a wig she had bought specially and it was ridiculous, bright orange and studded with hairpins and combs. Her dress was a vulgar choice too, dark purple embroidered all over with intricate gold thread that clashed with her wig and a crimson shawl edged with an Etruscan pattern. No doubt she thought it looked queenly.

Lucius heard Servius mention his name and to pre-empt a summons rose from his stool. He wasn't about to be whistled for like the family dog. Moving to the small crowd gathered around Servius, he fixed a smile on his face and accepted as gracefully as he felt able the ebullient congratulations. Tarquinia asked him where Arruns was, breaking off as his brother came down the stairs two steps at a time, a heavy fold of his toga falling off his shoulder, and apologising for his lateness. Tarquinia fussed over him, putting the cloth right and smoothing his hair.

A collective aahh went up as Tullia and Lolly entered the courtyard. They were in their wedding clothes; immaculate white dresses that hadn't yet been washed to grey and flame-coloured veils covering their faces. Through her veil, Lucius saw Tullia give him a shy smile. He didn't return it.

Servius clapped his hands and ushered the guests through to the atrium. Lucius lingered in the courtyard, knowing it would take a few minutes for the guests to find their seats and for the priest to get into position. Arruns, who had started after Servius, halted and turned back.

'You could at least smile, Lucius,' he admonished.

'What, and be a grinning fool like you?'

Lucius registered the hurt look on Arruns's face and felt a little ashamed. He hadn't meant to mock his brother so, not really. He just wished Arruns wasn't so ready to please Servius all the time. It always seemed to him that when it came down to it, Arruns always sided with Servius, leaving Lucius to stand alone.

'Forgive me, brother,' he said, putting his hand on Arruns's arm. 'I'm in a foul mood. Ignore me.'

'But why? You should be happy.'

Lucius wished he could explain why he felt the way he did but he didn't really understand it himself. He seemed to feel angry all the time without it being directed at anyone or anything in particular and even he was growing tired of it. 'Arruns, do you ever think of the family curse?' he asked.

Arruns paled. 'No, I don't and you shouldn't either. It was so long ago.'

'But I feel it. I feel it on me, in me.' He gave an involuntary shudder.

'You're imagining it,' Arruns said, but his tone was unconvincing. 'Nothing awful has befallen us, has it? We are all well and today is a happy day, Lucius, the start of a new tomorrow. Please, think no more of it. For me?'

Lucius forced a smile and nodded. 'Very well, just for you, brother, I will try to enjoy the day.'

Footsteps sounded on the flagstones. 'Come on, you two,' Servius waved them towards the atrium impatiently, 'we're all waiting.'

With one last glance at one another, Lucius and Arruns made their way to their brides.

He had tried, he really had, but Lucius had not been able to remain sanguine. He had put on a good show throughout the ceremony, even returning Tullia's smiles, but he had had to pretend to be happy for too long and his patience had grown thin. By the time the wedding feast was coming to an end, Lucius hated everyone and everything there.

The wine had flowed freely and many of the guests had forgotten their sense of decorum and were truly enjoying themselves. The atrium long since abandoned, the wedding party had spilled throughout the domus and into the garden. Some male guests had brought dice and played drinking games while their wives discussed the furnishings and the dresses their fellow female guests were wearing.

Lucius gulped down his wine. He held out his cup for it to refilled and watched as Tullia timidly did the same. He looked at her as the wine was poured. Tullia's cheeks and nose were bright red, her neck and chest a scarlet blotch. Her pupils were dilated and her eyelids struggled to stay open. Lucius knew she wasn't used to drinking so much wine and he wondered how she would behave when really intoxicated. Would she be one of those women who lost her inhibitions or one of those who simply fell asleep? He was a little surprised she had indulged at all. *Perhaps she's scared*, he thought with relish. His eyes moved downward over the scarlet flesh to the high mounds of her breasts. They were firm beneath the dress. He would enjoy them later. As a wife, Tullia would do, he supposed.

Someone started to clap and the guests quietened. Men held their dice in their hands or left them lying on the table and women ceased their chatter. Servius was on his feet and smiling stupidly at the company, like his daughter, having partaken rather too freely of the expensive, full-bodied wine.

'I thank you all for your blessings on this day and for sharing this important event with us.' He looked down at Tarquinia seated beside him and held out his hand. She slipped hers into it. 'It has been truly wonderful. But now it is time for my sons, for so they truly are, to take their wives to their beds.'

There was cheering and clapping and some hearty, dirty laughter that filled Lucius with loathing. Servius gestured for Lucius and Tullia, Arruns and Lolly to rise from their couches. Arruns was the first to obey. He clambered off the couch and held out his hand to Lolly. Tullia looked at Lucius as if waiting for him to move before she would. Lucius took his time, finishing his cup of wine before dabbing his mouth with a napkin. Then, and only then, did he rise. Tullia hurried to do the same.

The guests followed them to their bedrooms. They arrived at Arruns's bedroom first and Lucius had to witness his brother taking Lolly unsteadily in his arms and carrying her over the threshold of his bedroom door. As the bedroom door closed, the guests all cheered.

Then they moved along the corridor, turned the corner and the party arrived at Lucius's cubiculum. Her cheeks dimpling, Tullia put her arms lightly around Lucius's neck and almost jumped into his arms. He had to react quickly to avoid dropping her.

'Am I too heavy?' she whispered in his ear.

He shook his head, and paying no further attention to the shouts of 'Good luck' and 'Enjoy yourself, lad', carried his wife over the threshold.

Lucius dropped Tullia onto her feet as soon as the door was closed.

'I'm glad that's over,' Tullia said, laughing nervously and straightening her clothes. 'I know it's part of the ceremony but I was dreading it.'

She was looking at him, her eyes wide, seeking some kind of affirmation. By Jupiter, she was so damned needy.

He quickly untied her knotted belt and threw it on a stool. 'Get undressed,' he said, gesturing at the rest of her clothes.

Tullia took a quick look at the bed against the wall. Her chin wobbled, her face crumpled, and she began to cry.

'Why are you crying?' he asked harshly. Tullia sniffed and he could see she was trying to stop her tears. Her chest shuddered and her throat tightened, but she didn't answer him. 'Just get undressed, will you?'

Tullia turned her head to the side and hooked her fingers under the shoulders of her dress. The soft fabric slid off her body, pooling at her feet. She paused for a long moment, seemingly undecided what to do next. She was undressed but not yet naked. She glanced up at him. Lucius met her eye and gestured she was to continue. His heart was beating fast, thrilled to be seeing the girl he had known all his life doing his bidding and exposing her soft pink flesh to his unrelenting gaze. Tullia unwrapped the linen from around her breasts and dropped it on the floor. Her nipples stood up prominently. He watched as she hooked her fingers into the fabric of her subligaculum and dragged it down over her slim hips and thighs, letting it fall to her feet. Now, she was naked and trying feebly to cover the dark triangle of curly hair between her legs with one hand while the other crossed her breasts.

Lucius enjoyed her embarrassment. He kept her standing there while he undressed, she turning her head away. He climbed onto the bed and propped himself up on his elbow, his long legs stretched out. Still, she kept her eyes on the floor.

'Tullia,' he said, a wicked smile on his lips, knowing she would have to look at him. Her eyes widened as she saw him in all his nakedness, his cock already beginning to swell in anticipation. 'Come here.'

She hesitated for a moment but then obeyed. Without him

needing to tell her, she lay down beside him, her arms by her sides, her eyes staring at the ceiling. He looked down along the length of her body. He moved his hand to her stomach, laying it flat, and felt the heat of her skin seep into his own. He moved gently, massaging the muscles he could feel tensing, creating wider circles each time until his fingers brushed over her hip bones and gripped, digging into the flesh. Intent on what his hand was doing to her, he was surprised when Tullia's hand caressed his cheek.

'I'm so happy if I please you, Lucius. Father told me I would. I'm so happy to know he was right.'

Servius again telling him what he would like! Lucius slapped her hand away. She gave a cry of shock and tears threatened to fall again. *I'll give you something to cry about*, he thought, angling his body over her and pushing her legs apart with his knee. His fingers explored her roughly and she twisted beneath him as he tried to get his index finger into her. He pressed himself against her, his penis prodding her folds. Using his hand to guide himself to her centre, he pushed into her but only just the tip. He saw her lips curl into her mouth at the slight penetration, gave her the smallest of moments to stop moving against the strangeness of the sensation, and then thrust hard. She cried out, loud and sharp in the otherwise silent room and he felt her hymen break and heat and wetness engulf him. She was crying freely and loudly now as he moved in and out of her. He was not gentle. When he had finished a few minutes later, he collapsed on the bed beside her, panting. Her sobs had turned to whimpers and the noise annoyed him.

'Shut up,' he said, saying it again when his words seemed to have no effect. He turned his back to her, slammed his head against the pillow and fell asleep to the sound of his new wife's crying.

12

Tarquinia had never imagined there were so many people in Rome. The Field of Mars was big, the largest open space inside Rome, and yet it was filled almost to bursting. The only uncrowded space was where she stood, a few metres from the altar. By her side stood Tanaquil, who had been strangely quiet all morning, in fact, for several days now. Tarquinia looked at her mother from beneath lowered lids, blinking because the smoke from the brazier fires was making them smart. She thought Tanaquil looked a little pale and tired.

'Are you all right, Mother?' Tarquinia asked.

'Of course I am,' Tanaquil answered quickly. 'Why do you ask?'

'You've been very quiet these last few days.'

Tanaquil shook her head. 'I've been thinking, that's all. It's a great thing Servius has done, daughter. I almost believed he wouldn't manage it but look.' She gestured at the crowd.

'He's very proud,' Tarquinia said, remembering the previous night when Servius had made love to her with an energy she had not experienced before. She knew his excitement about today had been its cause.

Servius had worked so hard and so long for this day. This reform had meant sleepless nights, oil lamps burning long into the night as he and his secretaries scribbled down their ideas and turned them into something the senate would approve. And all that work culminated in this magnificent ceremony which would change Rome forever: the inauguration of the census.

And yet, despite her pride in her husband, despite this moment of history Servius was creating, Tarquinia just wanted to go home. She had awoken that morning to a dull pain in her left temple. She had suffered with terrible headaches ever since her first pregnancy but they had worsened over the past few years. Where once she had suffered maybe one or two migraines a year, now she would suffer four or five. And the symptoms were more painful too. Often, it felt like her brain was swelling and pressing against the inside of her skull. At other times, she would have to lie down on her bed, blocking out the sunlight coming through the narrow window because any kind of light hurt her eyes. Nothing could chase away the pain entirely but Nipia made a soothing lavender balm that she would massage into Tarquinia's temples and which at least gave her a little ease. Her family had little sympathy for her headaches. She didn't think they even believed her when she said her head was killing her. They merely thought she was looking for sympathy and attention. Neither Tanaquil nor Servius would think well of her if she were to say she had a headache and wanted to go home.

She wouldn't do that to Servius, anyway. If she left now, before the ceremony was barely underway, it would look bad for him. When could she decently leave? she wondered.

There was the offering to Mars, that would take at least half an hour, followed by the sacrifice of the ewe. Oh, how she wished she could go before that, she was feeling sick already. It would be almost two hours, she decided, two hours before she could leave and go home. Her head would really be killing her by then. She closed her eyes, willing the dull ache away but knowing it was useless.

Arruns came up to her. 'You're looking a bit peaky, Aunt, are you feeling all right?'

'Just one of my headaches coming on,' she said as a wave of dizziness hit her.

'Oh,' he nodded knowingly and was about to turn away when Tarquinia stumbled against him.

'Lucius,' he called, 'bring a stool here, quick.'

Tarquinia closed her eyes, nausea rising. Arruns steadied her and then gently pushed her down onto the stool Lucius had deposited by her.

'What's the matter with her?' she heard Lucius ask Arruns.

'I just felt a little dizzy, that's all,' she said, keeping her eyes closed. 'I'll be all right in a minute.'

'It's probably the smell,' Lucius said, wrinkling his nose. 'All these plebs in one place. It's enough to make anyone vomit.'

'Lucius,' Arruns laughed uneasily, 'don't.'

'Don't what? I had no idea there were so many plebs in Rome, did you?'

'Well, we'll find out just how many there are,' Arruns said. 'That's what the census is for.'

'I know what the census is for, Arruns,' Lucius said, clicking his fingers at his slave to put another stool by Tarquinia. He sat down and yawned. 'Such a stupid thing to do.'

Tarquinia opened her eyes slowly, fighting the impulse to close them again. 'Stupid? This is your uncle's greatest achievement.'

'It's his greatest mistake. Oh, come on, Aunt, you're a Tarquin. You can't think this is a good idea.'

'Yes, Lucius, I do.'

He stared at her in surprise. 'Really?' he said, his tone implying she was more stupid than he thought.

The pain behind her eyes ratcheted up a notch. 'And what exactly do you have against the census?'

'He's giving power away, Aunt,' Lucius said, shaking his head in bewilderment. 'He's giving it to the plebs for no good reason.'

'He wants to be fair to them.'

'Did they ask him to do it? Did they threaten him? No, so, why do it? I'll tell you why—.' He broke off as if deciding saying more was a bad idea.

'Why, Lucius?' Tarquinia prompted, suspecting she already knew the answer.

He looked at her and she could see cruelty in his expression. 'Because he's one of them, isn't he?'

'One of them?' Tarquinia repeated.

'Lucius,' Arruns warned.

'Aunt,' Lucius laughed, 'we've all heard the rumours about Uncle Servius.'

Tarquinia wanted to hit him, wanted to smack that smug smile from his handsome face, but she didn't have the strength. 'I'm going to tell your grandmother what you said,' she said, her lips pursing. 'I'm going to let her deal with you.'

'I'm not five years old any more, Aunt,' Lucius said, unperturbed by her threat. 'You can't take a rod to me. And anyway, Grandmother agrees with me. She thinks the census and reform are mistakes. She just doesn't want to upset Uncle Servius by telling him so.'

'That's not true,' Tarquinia whipped her head around, searching for Tanaquil. Her mother was standing next to Servius, watching the procession of men as they queued at the tables to register their names with the scribes. Tanaquil's face was unreadable. *Could Lucius be right*, Tarquinia wondered, *that Mother doesn't approve of this*? The possibility troubled her. Servius relied on Tanaquil's approval. She knew he thought Tanaquil wholeheartedly supported his reforms but Tarquinia was suddenly unsure. She had never heard her mother talk about improving the lot of the common people, had never heard her say the old system needed changing. Tarquinia doubted her father would ever had thought of doing what Servius had brought about. Lucomo had believed there was a proper order to the world with the plebs at the bottom and him sitting at the top. Her father would, Tarquinia knew, have told Servius he was being a fool, just as Lucius was saying now.

'You know it's true,' Lucius drew her attention back to him. 'You just don't want to admit it.'

'Do you enjoy putting me and your uncle down, Lucius?' she sighed.

Lucius's mouth curled into a smile that turned his handsome face cruel. 'Just speaking the truth, Aunt. That's what you taught me to do.'

Tarquinia couldn't take any more. She rose. 'I was never able to teach you anything, Lucius. You're bad. You were born bad and nothing anyone will ever do will change that.' She walked over to Servius, slipped her hand into his and kissed his cheek.

'What was that for?' he asked in surprise.

'Because you deserve it, for this.' She gestured at the

crowd. 'And because I love you. You're a good man, Servius, and I'm proud of you.'

Let Lucius and Tanaquil think what they wanted, she decided, as Servius squeezed her hand. *They can think Servius is a fool for doing this for the people. I know my husband is the king Rome needs.*

———

Tarquinia had been right to worry about her. Tanaquil hadn't felt well for a long while and the last few weeks had been bad. She knew death was only a breath or two away.

She was glad; she really didn't feel like going on any longer. Her body had been failing for years and her mind, she knew, had not been as sharp as it once was. Dimwitted was no way for her to be and she didn't want to be talked about as an object of pity: 'Poor Tanaquil, her mind is going, you know.' She refused to let the doctor treat her, wouldn't let him force ill-tasting potions down her throat or rub foul-smelling ointments on her chest. She didn't want to be made better for a few days only to weaken again. She wanted to die.

But not just yet. Not until she had talked to Lucius.

Tarquinia was by her bedside. She had heard her crying and felt her daughter's hand in hers. She forced her eyes open. Tarquinia was leaning over her, her eyes puffy and the tip of her nose bright red.

'I must talk with Lucius,' Tanaquil said.

A frown creased Tarquinia's forehead. 'Why Lucius?' she asked.

'Please,' Tanaquil sighed, not having the energy to explain and pleased that Tarquinia obeyed without further query.

When Tarquinia returned, Lucius a few steps behind her,

Tanaquil said she wanted to talk with Lucius alone and Tarquinia left them, casting a resentful look at her nephew. Tanaquil gestured with a crabbed finger that Lucius was to sit, following him with her eyes as he took the stool Tarquinia had occupied. *He looks so like his father*, she thought. Lucius was so handsome and yet there was that hint of cruelty in the full-lipped mouth and the eyes that tried to avoid making contact. Even now, Lucius was looking everywhere but at her.

'Lucius,' she said, 'I'll be dead soon and I need to talk to you before I go.'

She paused, partly to catch her breath but also to give him an opportunity to speak, a small part of her hoping he would be kind to her, take her hand, say he would miss her. But he didn't and she chided herself for her hopes. Lucius was not kind, never had been. It was ridiculous to hope for kindness from him now.

'I know you want to be king. And I want you to be king, but I fear it, too.'

'Why do you fear it?' Lucius demanded angrily.

'You know there is a curse upon our family.'

Lucius made a gesture of disgust. 'You've countered that curse. It has no power over me.'

'The gods have power over you, Lucius. Poena has been placated all these years, but she may not always be so kind. Never believe the gods will always love you, Lucius. They are fickle.'

'So, I will continue the sacrifices to Poena, Grandmother.'

'There is more. Something I haven't told you. I consulted an astrologer. I asked him to cast your horoscope.' She had to stop talking. Her chest was hurting.

'What did he predict?' Lucius asked urgently, shaking her arm. 'Grandmother, what did he predict for me?'

He was merciless, she remembered, and would carry on shaking her until she answered. She fought the pain in her chest. 'The astrologer predicted you would be king but that your reign would begin in blood and end in despair.'

'What?' Lucius spat. 'End in despair?'

'Don't let it come true, Lucius, please.'

He shook his head. 'But if it's been foretold—'

'Change the prophecy.' She clutched his wrist and dug her fingers into his skin. 'Change it.'

'How?'

'Your nature will decide your fate. You must fight it, Lucius.'

'I can't help how I'm made, Grandmother.'

'You must try. If your reign is to begin in blood, then I fear it will be Servius's blood. And if Servius were to know what the astrologer predicted, he may act against you to prevent it. I will not have this family turn against itself. You must cease to be his enemy. Only then will you change the prophecy.'

Her crabbed claw released him, her energy spent. Her eyes closed. She heard Lucius scrape back the stool and leave the room. She thought she heard Tarquinia speaking to her, but the voice was distant and growing fainter. The room was growing darker too.

It was time to die. Lucomo was waiting for her.

———

Lucius had arrived at Cossus's house cursing the lack of privacy at the domus that necessitated his journey. There were too many people coming and going at the moment, all eager to pay their respects and commiserate with the family over Tanaquil's death.

The domus felt strange without Tanaquil. He had always been in awe of his grandmother; without her, he felt free. He had always done what he wanted, he knew, but his pleasure had been spoilt knowing he would have to answer to her afterwards. Now, there was no one to answer to, no one to reprimand him or express disappointment, no one whose person he respected as he had respected her.

Lucius had told no one of what Tanaquil had said to him in their private interview before she died. He had gone through all Tanaquil's papers while the rest of the family were in bed, trying to find the horoscope she had spoken of, wanting to see the truth of her words for himself. But he had been disappointed. He found no horoscope in her chests.

Lucius needed to know his fate and so had entrusted Cossus with finding an astrologer to cast his horoscope. Cossus hadn't asked any questions and done as Lucius asked. Now, the horoscope was ready and the astrologer waiting to deliver it in person at Cossus's house.

'Has he told you what he found?' Lucius asked Cossus the moment he crossed the threshold.

'No,' Cossus said, 'and I haven't asked. He's in the tablinum.' He led Lucius through the house to the study. 'There.'

He gestured at a middle-aged man sitting on one of the stools. He was plainly nervous, his right leg jiggling up and down. He started up at their approach.

'Leave us,' Lucius said curtly to Cossus.

'Now, wait just a minute,' Cossus began, angry at Lucius's tone. 'This is my house—'

'Cossus,' Lucius snarled, shooting his friend an uncompromising glare.

'All right,' Cossus said and left Lucius alone with the astrologer, deliberately not closing the door.

Lucius closed it. 'Your name?'

'Bruscius, Prince Lucius,' the astrologer said and bowed.

'You have my horoscope?'

'Here in my bag.' Bruscius rooted in his satchel for the parchment.

'I trust you have told no one you have cast my horoscope?' Lucius said, moving to the table as Bruscius unrolled the parchment upon it.

'No one, Prince Lucius, I assure you. All my clients enjoy complete confidentiality.'

Satisfied, Lucius stared down at the paper. It was a mass of symbols and images, only a few of which he recognised. 'Tell me what you learnt,' he ordered.

Bruscius began pointing to the illustrations, explaining each one in turn and how they related to one another. Lucius didn't want a lesson in horoscopes. He grew impatient and snapped, 'Yes, yes, forget all that. Just tell me. Will I be king?'

'Oh yes, my prince, yes,' Bruscius assured him, pointing to a symbol that meant nothing to Lucius.

'When?'

Bruscius licked his lips. 'It is difficult to say. It could be a few years or it could be ten or more.'

'As long as that?' Lucius said, disheartened.

'Possibly,' Bruscius shrugged.

'And how? How do I become king? Does Servius die or does he abdicate?'

'This is your horoscope, my prince, not the King's. I cannot say,' Bruscius said uneasily, knowing he was risking Lucius's displeasure.

Lucius kicked the leg of the table, knocking over a pile of papers. 'Is there blood? Does my reign begin in blood?'

'Yes, yes,' Bruscius said, pleased he could confirm something.

'Whose blood?'

'Not yours, my prince,' he said. 'Perhaps a battle, perhaps you defeat your enemy. And yours is a long reign, a good reign. All your subjects will love you.'

'You can see that?'

'Oh yes, yes, here.' Bruscius pointed to another inscrutable section of the parchment.

'How does my reign end?'

Bruscius made a show of studying the horoscope but it couldn't help him. That part of Lucius's future was indistinct, unclear to him. He did what he always did when asked a question by the client he didn't know the answer to: he made it up.

'You die in your bed, Prince Lucius,' Bruscius murmured.

Lucius stared at the horoscope. After a long moment, he said, 'Very well. Roll it up.'

Bruscius did so and passed the parchment to Lucius. He timidly held out his other hand, palm upwards. Lucius fished into the leather pouch on his belt and took out a small bronze ingot, pushing it into Bruscius's hand.

'Remember,' he said, 'no one is to know of this.'

'No one will know,' Bruscius assured him.

Lucius turned on his heel and opened the door. Cossus was waiting just outside and Lucius had said goodbye before Cossus could even speak.

Cossus watched his friend leave, then turned to Bruscius. 'Well?'

'The prince was pleased, sir,' Bruscius said.

'Told him what he wanted to hear, did you?' Cossus grinned.

'I told him the truth as I divined it,' Bruscius protested.

'What did you tell him?' Cossus asked.

Bruscius swallowed. 'The Prince swore me to secrecy, sir.'

'Did he?' Cossus said, stepping into the room. 'Well, you really shouldn't tell me, then.' His hand came up and grabbed Bruscius by the throat. He squeezed hard. 'But you're going to.'

Bruscius made a squawking noise. 'Sir, please.'

'I'll rip your throat out if you don't tell me,' Cossus promised calmly. 'Is he going to be king?'

Bruscius nodded as well as he could.

'When?'

'I couldn't tell.' Cossus's grip tightened, making Bruscius's eyes bulge. 'It's true. The horoscope didn't tell me that. I told the Prince it could be five, ten years.'

'Ten years?' Cossus said disgustedly and let Bruscius go. 'By the gods, I've got to wait that long?'

'It could be earlier,' Bruscius said, rubbing his throat gingerly.

Cossus spat on the floor. 'All right, stop your snivelling. Go on, get out. And keep your mouth shut.'

Bruscius picked up his satchel and scurried out. Cossus and Lucius didn't have to worry about his discretion. Bruscius wouldn't breathe a word.

13

'Are you really going to eat all of that?' Lolly raised her eyebrow at the plate of pastries Matia was picking from. 'You shouldn't, you know. You'll get even fatter.'

Matia froze in mid-reach, her eyes wide at the insult. She dropped the bun back onto the plate, seeing Lolly's lips purse in wry amusement, and her chest began to heave with resentment. She had a good mind to get up and leave but she knew she would need an excuse. One didn't just walk out on the daughter of the King of Rome.

'Husbands are so mindful about our bodies,' Lolly said, helping herself to a cake smothered in honey. 'And they are so hypocritical. It doesn't matter how fat they get but we must not.'

'Your husband isn't fat,' Matia said, glad to be able to contradict Lolly. 'He has a fine figure.'

'You think so?' Lolly asked in surprise. 'Arruns is getting a big belly. It's not noticeable beneath his toga, of course, but when he's undressed...' She blew out her cheeks and spread her arms wide to show Matia the enormity of her husband's stomach.

Matia took a sip of her wine, determined not to be drawn on Arruns's alleged obesity. She liked Arruns, he was always extremely courteous to her, and thought it mean of Lolly to disparage him in this way. But that was Lolly, she reflected, a mean bitch. Why did she put herself through this time and time again? It was always the same. Matia would come away from a meeting with Lolly determined not to have supper or see an entertainment with her again and yet, when the next invitation came, Matia always dashed off a reply that said she would be delighted to attend. She was a fool, that was the only explanation.

'His brother keeps himself so much better,' Lolly was saying. 'But then Lucius has always been very fit.'

It hadn't taken Lolly long to get onto her favourite subject, Matia thought. For as long as she could remember, Lolly would do her best to turn any conversation onto Lucius. Matia knew exactly what Lolly would say now. It was always the same: how handsome Lucius was, how clever, how good a husband to her sister, and wasn't Tullia lucky. Matia turned her mind towards concocting some believable excuse so she could leave. Could she say she didn't feel well? No, Lolly would only say it was because she had eaten too much. She had a prior engagement she had forgotten until now? Again, no. Lolly would only say she was more important than anyone else and Matia should let them down rather than her. Oh, what was Lolly saying now?

'And it makes a difference, doesn't it,' Lolly held out her cup for it to be refilled, 'if a man is fit and not carrying any extra weight?'

'A difference to what?' Matia asked, realising Lolly had deviated from her usual topic.

'To their potency,' Lolly said.

'Potency?'

'Well, of course, you goose. If your husband is fat, it means he sweats and grunts on top of you like a pig. I told Arruns he could stop all that. I told him, if you want to get fat and make that much noise and stink, you can do it away from my face.'

Matia sat up. 'So Arruns...,' she jerked her head to suggest what she couldn't bring herself to say out loud.

'Has to penetrate me from behind,' Lolly nodded. 'I find that far more agreeable.'

'You don't find it... uncomfortable?' Matia wanted to say undignified or bestial but knew Lolly would think she was hopelessly provincial.

Lolly shook her head. 'Arruns is so small, I barely notice when he enters me.'

'Really?'

'Oh yes. With some men, a small penis doesn't matter, they know how to use it, but Arruns...' Lolly didn't bother to finish the sentence.

'My dear Lolly, I would never have guessed,' Matia said, glad she had come now to hear this. 'I mean, he's really quite broad in the chest.'

'You can't go by that,' Lolly dismissed. 'Some men are pigeon-chested yet have the most enormous phallus.'

'Lolly, how would you know such a thing?'

Lolly burst out laughing. 'Oh my, what must you think of me, Matia? I must sound quite the whore. My dear, no, believe me, I'm not trying any man I fancy. But I make sure our slaves are healthy; I see them naked to make sure they're not diseased or malformed and I have seen the most unpromising upper-body specimens who are quite extraordinary below.'

I bet you have tried your slaves, Matia thought. Poor Arruns, to have such a wife as Lolly.

'Do you know, Matia,' Lolly was still talking, 'I almost envy my sister. Lucius is, so she says, not lacking in that area. But, of course, Tullia is such a quiet little thing, quite the mouse. She doesn't know how fortunate she is to have a husband with such a large phallus.'

'Tullia has told you how big Lucius is?'

'Of course, we're sisters. We share all our little secrets.'

'It's a pity that's all you can share. Wouldn't it be more fun to share husbands?' Matia giggled.

'Yes,' Lolly murmured, her eyes gazing off into the distance, 'wouldn't it?'

———

There was a banging coming from the other corridor. Tullia threw down her wax tablet on which she had been writing a letter and went to investigate.

The door to Lolly's old cubiculum was open and the banging was coming from inside. Tullia put her head around the door frame. Utica, one of the women who came in daily to clean, was sweeping cobwebs from the ceiling and the sound Tullia had heard was the knocking of the broom against the walls. The bed had been pulled into the middle of the room and a bowl of steaming hot water was beside it, ready to clean the wooden frame.

'Why are you cleaning in here?' Tullia asked.

'Been told to, lady,' Utica said, taking the opportunity to rest her arms for a moment. 'Going to be occupied again.'

'By whom?'

Utica opened her mouth to answer but closed it at the sound of footsteps.

Lolly entered. 'Why have you stopped? Oh Tullia, you're here. You, get on with your work.'

Utica resumed her cleaning, making a face. Lolly brushed past Tullia. She put a hand on the bed frame and wiggled it, checking its sturdiness.

'Who is this being got ready for, Lolly?' Tullia asked.

'For me, of course.'

'For you?'

'Yes, me, you little goose,' Lolly said, watching Utica critically. 'I simply can't stand sleeping next to Arruns any longer. I don't get a wink of sleep with his snoring all night.'

'You're having separate rooms? But doesn't Arruns mind?'

'He doesn't know yet. He'll find out tonight.'

'Oh, Lolly, you should have asked him first. He may not allow you to come back here.'

'Allow me?' Lolly's eyes blazed. 'I don't have to ask his permission.'

'He's your husband, sister.'

'And I never wanted him,' Lolly snapped. She shoved the bed frame aside. 'Don't stand there saying foolish things, Tullia.'

'They're not foolish,' Tullia protested. 'Arruns will be upset.'

'Oh yes, and we can't upset Arruns, can we?'

'But how... how...' Tullia blushed, her eyes darting towards Utica, who was pretending not to be listening.

'Oh, spit it out,' Lolly sighed.

'Babies, Lolly,' Tullia whispered. 'How will you become pregnant if you sleep apart?'

'Oh, I'll let him have me now and then.'

'It will serve you right if Arruns—,' Tullia broke off.

'If Arruns what?' Lolly raised her eyebrows at her sister.

'If he takes another woman to his bed,' Tullia said defiantly.

Lolly laughed. 'He's welcome to, if he thinks he can manage it. Just as long as it isn't you, sister dear. I won't have you in his bed.'

'Lolly!'

'Oh, don't pretend you haven't thought about it. Why, how you blush, Tullia.'

Even Utica was laughing at her now. 'I don't know how you can say such things, Lolly, I really don't,' Tullia said, her cheeks burning. 'I would never betray Lucius.'

'Would you not? Not even for Arruns?'

'Never. I am a good wife.'

'And I'm a bored one,' Lolly said flatly. 'Don't lecture me, Tullia. You're no good at it.'

She wouldn't stay to be laughed at. Tullia hurried back to her own room. She picked up her wax tablet and tried to resume her letter. But Lolly's words kept coming back to her. Lolly was mean to say what she did but she was right. Tullia did think of Arruns in that way and she knew it was wrong. What a bad woman she must be!

———

Arruns watched Cossus throw his arm around the whore's shoulder and stumble out of the back door with her. At last, Arruns could talk to his brother without Cossus listening in and laughing at him. Lucius wouldn't laugh, at least Arruns didn't think so, but if he did, Arruns could take it from him. Lucius would know what to do. Lucius would help him.

'Lolly's moved back into her old room,' Arruns said.

Lucius belched. 'Why?'

'She says I snore too much, that she can't get any sleep.'

'Sounds about right.'

Arruns leant closer. 'I'm not happy about her leaving me. Do you think I should forbid it? Tell her to move back?'

'Why are you asking me? She's your wife.'

'What would you do?'

'I'd tell her to get her arse back in my bed where it belongs,' Lucius said, brushing crumbs from his toga. 'Actually, I think it's a good idea. Maybe I'll tell Tullia to go back to her old room.'

'You wouldn't do that.'

'I would if I wanted. I'd have the bed to myself and I could do as I please. I could have that pretty little slave, the one with the red hair. You can have her now Lolly's gone. You should think yourself lucky, brother.'

'Lolly's my wife, she should be by my side.'

'Then tell her that's what you want,' Lucius said, bored with the conversation. 'But it's Lolly, remember. She only does what she wants to do.'

'Or does what you want,' Arruns muttered. 'Hey, that's an idea. You could tell her to move back.'

'Don't involve me,' Lucius said, waving his hands.

'But she'll listen to you, I know she will. Oh, please, Lucius.'

Lucius leant back in his chair and sighed. It pleased him to have his brother beg him, and to know that Lolly listened to him. He wondered if it was true. 'Yes, all right,' he said, thinking it was one way to find out. 'Anything to shut you up.'

———

Lucius found Lolly in the garden. She was lying on cushions thrown on the ground, arms over her head and legs splayed, only the folds of her dress covering her modesty.

Lolly angled her head back at his approach, smiling upside down at him. 'Hello.'

'Hello. You look very relaxed down there.'

'I am. Isn't it lovely to be able to lie here and do nothing?'

'Shouldn't you be spinning something?'

'Oh, don't be a bore, Lucius,' Lolly said, twirling a strand of hair around her fingers.

'Is that what Arruns is?' Lucius asked, settling down beside her on the cushions. 'Is that why you've started sleeping apart?'

'Oh, let me guess,' she said, 'he's sent you here to ask me to move back. Typical. He's so spineless, he won't ask me himself.'

'He thought I could persuade you.'

'To move back into his bed? Is that what you want for me?'

'I'm here for my brother,' he said, flustered a little by her manner.

'How strange you must find that. I've never known you to help him before.'

'What's your answer?' he said, pulling a fold of her dress down to cover her calf.

She sat up and rested her chin on his shoulder. 'My answer, Lucius, is no.'

Lucius felt her breath on his cheek, the point of her chin digging into his flesh. 'Then I'll tell him,' he said, moving slightly so his shoulder slipped from beneath her chin.

'Is that all?' Lolly said, sounding disappointed. 'You didn't try very hard. I don't think you want me to share my husband's bed.'

'I don't care what you do,' Lucius said, looking away from her.

'If he was any kind of man, he'd make me move back,' Lolly sighed. 'You wouldn't let Tullia move out of your bed, would you?'

'No, I wouldn't.'

'Unless that was what you wanted,' she purred. 'So you were free to take your pleasures where and when you wanted.'

'And if my pleasure lies with my wife?' he said, eyeing her sideways.

She laughed, a soft silky laugh that quickened his heart. She rubbed her leg against his. 'Then, Lucius, you're not the man I took you to be.'

14

Lolly pulled the hood of her cloak over her head and stepped out the back door of the domus. It felt strange, and a little exciting, to go into the city in disguise. She had borrowed her maid's dress, leaving off her jewellery and cosmetics and tying her hair back with a leather thong, so that anyone glancing at her would not have seen the daughter of the King but only a pretty young woman. The impression she was nothing special would be reinforced by her being alone, for Lolly would never normally leave the domus without a guard or a slave to accompany her. Rome, even in the daytime, could be dangerous.

Lolly knew where the shop she sought was though she had never been there before. She hurried along, hood up, head down, watching her feet as they moved swiftly over the ground, ignoring the grit and dirt that clung to her toes and crept inside to torment the soles of her feet.

As she drew nearer to her destination, she realised she was entering an area of Rome she had never visited before and curiosity as to the kind of plebs who inhabited it made Lolly lift her head a little and study her companions on the streets. They looked the same as those on any other street and she chided herself. What had she expected? Hunchbacks and crones? She examined the sides of the buildings, looking for the sign of a horse. A few more steps and she found it, carved into the stone beside a striped brown and blue awning.

The front of the shop had tables spilling onto the street and these held an assortment of herbs and spices in woven baskets and small wooden bowls. A man was standing behind the table, eyeing her with curiosity. What she was after would not be on display, Lolly knew, but shame held her back from asking the man for the item she sought. She hesitated, peering into the dimness of the shop's interior.

'You want my wife?' the man asked.

Gratefully, Lolly nodded, and the man called into the shop. A female voice shouted, 'Coming,' and a moment later, a fat woman emerged from the doorway. Her husband pointed at Lolly.

'What you after, love?' the woman asked. 'Come on, speak up. You're blocking the way.'

'I want… something special,' Lolly said.

The woman's eyes narrowed. 'You'd best come in,' she said and beckoned Lolly inward, past the table with its baskets and into the shop, where she had to duck her head to avoid hitting the bags and herbs hanging from the ceiling. 'Now, what can I get you?'

'A love philtre,' Lolly whispered, holding her hood so it covered half her face.

The woman smiled, revealing the gaps in her teeth. 'There's no need to look so scared, my sweet. I get lots of women coming to me for such things.'

She moved to a wooden crate at the back of the shop covered by a rough woollen blanket. Pulling the blanket back, she reached inside, pulling out a small glass bottle. 'Here you go.'

'Will it work?' Lolly asked, taking the bottle and inspecting it, watching as the liquid inside ebbed and flowed as she tipped it first one way, then the other.

'If you do it right. You have to put it in his drink or food every day and say prayers to Venus. You do that, my sweet, and the man you want will be yours, body and soul.'

'I'll take it.' Lolly tucked the bottle into the purse tied to her belt. The woman named her price and Lolly paid it without hesitation. No price was too high for something that promised so much.

———

He had drunk too much, Lucius decided, and groaned. Why did he always do this? It wasn't that he minded the hangover the next morning all that much; he minded the way he invariably made a fool of himself. Sometimes, he would remember the things he'd said or done and cringe in embarrassment. At other times, he wouldn't remember a thing and this was worse, for then his friends would say he did this or said that and he would never know if they were speaking the truth or lying.

Lucius mumbled he needed to piss and left the table, pulling his arm out of Tullia's hand as she tried to help him up. He didn't want her help, didn't want anyone's help. He stumbled out of the room. They were probably talking about him, Servius and Tarquinia, all of them, now he was gone. Tarquinia would be telling Tullia she shouldn't allow him to drink so much, as if Tullia could stop him doing what he wanted. If Tullia started moaning at him when they went to bed, he'd bloody well give her something to moan about.

Lucius steadied himself against the wall. *I mustn't fall down,* he told himself. He didn't think he'd be able to get up again if he did. He flinched as something touched his shoulder.

'No need to jump so,' a silkily soft voice said. 'It's only me.'

'Tullia?'

Hands crept around his ribs and splayed across his chest, squeezing gently.

'I was just thinking of you,' he said, his eyes closing.

'Nice thoughts?'

'No. Don't nag me. I'm only a little bit drunk.'

'You're slurring your words.'

'I am?'

'Stop talking.' Her hands moved down and spread over his hips, teased the top of his thighs and moved to his groin.

'This isn't like you,' Lucius said, wondering what had got into his wife.

'You like it, don't you?' her voice purred as her hands delved beneath his tunic, giggling as her fingers closed around him. 'Oh yes, you like it.'

Lucius moved his feet, wanting to stand up straight, but he fell sideways and slammed against the wall. He grabbed at the hands holding him and pulled her against him.

'You're not—,' he said, peering into the face now inches from his.

'I'm Tullia,' Lolly said, using her real name.

'Not...,' he searched for the right words, 'my Tullia.'

'I could be, if you wanted.' He felt the heat of her body as she pressed herself against him. 'Do you want?' Her hands began to massage their way up his thighs. It felt so good and Lucius heard himself moaning as his neck arched, pushing himself against her. *Touch me again*, he mentally begged. But then her nails painfully raked his skin.

He shoved her away. 'What you doing?'

'Showing you what you're missing, Lucius.'

'I'm not a fool.' He heard his own voice, loud in the corridor. She put her fingers to his lips and he swatted them aside. 'Go away. Leave me alone.'

Lolly smiled and stepped away from him. 'One day soon, Lucius, you'll ask me to stay.'

He closed his eyes, listening to her retreating footsteps, and slid down the wall, his legs unable to sustain him any longer. Tullia found him there fifteen minutes later, his chin upon his chest and snoring, and ordered the guards to carry him to their bed.

———

Lucius looked over to where Lolly was standing at the opposite side of the temple.

She was pretending not to notice him, he knew. Maybe she thought he didn't remember what had passed between them the previous night, but he did. Well, most of it, not the ending. He remembered being annoyed with her but he wasn't sure what about. He'd found thin red scratches on his thighs that morning and it tormented him that he couldn't remember how they had got there. What had Lolly done to him? More to the point, why had she done it?

She must have felt his gaze upon her because Lolly suddenly turned her head towards him and met his eye. There was determination in her expression, and something more, something almost victorious.

Lucius dragged his eyes away. He had to put the previous night out of his mind. It was nothing, Lolly's idea of a joke, probably. And if it wasn't a joke... well, that was something he didn't want to get caught up in.

Yes, Lolly was pretty, he thought now he bothered to look at her properly, and she was a damn sight more intelligent than her sister, but that didn't mean he wanted to bed her. There were other women he could have affairs with if he wanted, easy affairs, no complications. Lolly was too close to home for comfort. Going to bed with her would cause him no end of problems. No, he would forget their little encounter and stop thinking of Lolly naked in his bed.

He *would* stop thinking of her.

———

Lucilla had invited the whole family to dinner. Servius and Tarquinia declined, Servius claiming he was too busy and Tarquinia that she wasn't well enough, so it was only the younger generation who followed the torchbearers to Lucilla's house on the Capitoline Hill.

Lucilla welcomed them to her home and playfully accused her brothers of not visiting her often enough. Arruns agreed, apologised and promised he and Lolly would make more of an effort in the future. Tullia immediately asked to see Lucilla's children, Titus and Iunius, and headed off to the nursery. Lucilla asked Lolly if she wanted to see them too but Lolly shook her head, curling her hands around Arruns's arm as if she couldn't bear to be parted from him.

Lolly could put on a good show when she wanted to, Lucius thought as Lucilla led them through to the dining room. He had heard her shouting at Arruns not an hour earlier, complaining she would have to wear a dress to Lucilla's she had worn a hundred times before and which was little better than rags because he was too mean to buy her a new one.

Lucius stole a look at Lolly as she walked in front of him. He had seen the dress often, it was true, but he thought it suited her very well. The rich red showed off her white complexion and thick dark hair. The dress Tullia was wearing was a new one, Lucius reflected, and it had been a waste of his money, for she didn't look nearly as attractive as Lolly. Maybe he should choose Tullia's clothes for her in future, stop her wearing those dowdy browns and yellows. If Lolly were given the allowance Tullia had, she would choose grandly, Lucius felt sure. Lolly wouldn't show him up.

There I go again, he upbraided himself, *thinking about Lolly*. Ever since she had touched him in the darkness of the domus, she had been on his mind. Whenever he thought about her hand on his cock, he touched himself, imagining her sinking to her knees and taking him in her mouth.

No! He thrust the thought away angrily. *I won't have a woman clouding my mind in this way.*

———

Lucius was thinking about her again, Lolly could tell. The way he stared at her and tried not to, the way he tried to avoid talking to her. Oh yes, he was thinking about her all right.

Lolly put her fingers to her breast, feeling for the phial she had slipped into her cleavage as she dressed. She had warmed Lucius up with her approach in the domus. Now, she would make sure of him and put the love philtre in his drink. She couldn't wait any longer.

Lucilla offered them wine and was about to signal to a servant to pour when Lolly begged to be allowed to do it. Surprised at her sister-in-law's request, not least because it seemed so out of character, Lucilla agreed with a shrug and gestured Lucius and Arruns to the couches. Tullia returned to the dining room as they made themselves comfortable and declared Lucilla had the most delightful children.

Lolly moved to the table where the wine jug and cups stood. With her back to the company, she took out the phial and poured a small amount of the liquid into one of the cups, making a mental note of its decoration, a group of dancing girls, before filling the others. She raised Lucius's cup to her nose and sniffed. There wasn't any telltale smell, she noted with relief. Under her breath so as not to be heard, she began her prayer.

'Most bountiful goddess! Oh, Venus, Queen of love! Deliver to my arms he who has fired my soul and let him find pleasure in my body and love in my heart. Let him leave me satisfied but yet still desiring, sated but unfulfilled, so he returns to my arms and to my bed. Oh, most blessed goddess! Grant me this and I will make offerings to you of rose, myrtle and wine. In most earnest and true thanks for your bounty. Oh, goddess, hear me.'

She turned to the couches and handed out the cups, saving Lucius until last. He took his cup without a word of thanks, keeping his eyes from her. But she remained standing by him and he looked up, frowning. She glanced at the cup then back at him. Perplexed, he raised the cup to his lips and took a mouthful of the wine.

Lolly watched him swallow, yearning to kiss his throat. He'd done it. Lucius had drunk the love philtre. She took her placed beside Arruns. Ignoring his curious stare, she gulped down her wine, almost choking as it burned her throat.

———

Lolly had found it difficult to remain attentive throughout the dinner. She had heard the chatter going on around her, the inanities that Arruns uttered, the pathetic replies Tullia made and the gossip that Lucilla spouted. She only had eyes and ears for Lucius.

Lucius said little and only picked at the food that lay before him, even the dish of oysters Lucilla had ordered specially, knowing how Lucius liked them. He seemed preoccupied and Lolly worried she'd made him feel ill.

She found the evening interminable and was actually grateful to Tullia when she began to yawn, covering her mouth daintily with her hand and pretending she wasn't tired. Lolly nudged Arruns in the ribs and gestured she wanted to leave. Arruns made their thanks to Lucilla and apologised for not staying longer. The party broke up, Lucilla insisting they meet again soon.

Arruns and Tullia chatted all the way back to the domus, he holding Tullia's arm so she wouldn't stumble along the uneven narrow streets, telling the torchbearers not to walk too fast nor move too far ahead and leave them in darkness. Lucius held out his arm to Lolly, and she curved her fingers around his wrist, feeling his pulse throb into her body.

They spoke not a word on the journey home. Lolly wished Lucius would say something to her, anything, but he kept his eyes looking straight ahead and she didn't dare speak to him. Back in the domus, the four bid each other good night and parted, Tullia and Lucius to their bedroom, Arruns and Lolly to their separate rooms.

Lolly closed her door and leant her head against the wood. Her head ached so, all that worrying about Lucius and whether the philtre would work. She was a fool. Had she really expected Lucius to fall in love with her after a mouthful of wine? And what if he had? She shuddered to imagine Lucius falling to his knees, declaring he loved her in front of the others. What a fool he would have looked. He would never have forgiven her.

She kicked off her sandals and slipped her dress off her shoulders. Stepping out of her underwear, she lay naked on the bed. The chill air of the small stone room cooled her skin quickly and eased her aching head. It wasn't long before she fell asleep.

————

Lolly awoke with a start. A noise had broken into her unconscious, a sound she recognised as the opening and closing of the door, then the sliding of a bolt home. Someone was in her room. She opened her mouth to scream as a figure loomed over the bed but a smell, familiar and welcome, wafted over her, oil and sandalwood, and she realised who it was.

'What have you done to me?' Lucius growled. 'Why can't I stop thinking about you?'

Lolly, her body trembling, sat up and felt for him in the darkness. Her fingers found his chest and she smoothed her hand over his skin. He was breathing hard, his chest rising and falling beneath her hand. 'Do you want me?' she whispered.

In answer, he grabbed her hand and she felt his lips upon the inside of her wrist. She curled her fingers around the back of his neck and pulled him down onto her.

————

'You're a disgrace to the name of woman.'

The voice floated over Tullia's head and she jerked

around to see who had spoken. 'Oh, it's you,' she said with relief.

Arruns grinned. 'Look at you, just sitting there, not doing anything. Shouldn't you be hard at work spinning or ordering the servants about?' He sat down beside her.

'I suppose I should,' she said solemnly, her gaze on the garden before her.

Surprised by her tone, he said, 'I was only joking, Tullia.'

She gave him a thin smile, laying her hand briefly on his. 'I know. Don't mind me.'

A moment passed before he spoke again. 'What's the matter?'

Tullia squeezed her eyes together and bit her lip.

'It's Lucius, isn't it?' Arruns prompted.

She nodded. 'I think I must have done something to upset him, but I don't know what.'

'No,' Arruns shook his head and waved his hand decisively, 'I can't believe you could do anything wrong. Not you.'

'Then why is he being so cruel to me?' she burst out imploringly. 'Ever since that dinner at Lucilla's I only have to open my mouth and he's snapping at me to hold my tongue. If I touch him, he shakes me off. What have I done, Arruns? Has he said anything to you?'

'Tullia, you know Lucius doesn't confide in me.'

'If only he told me what I'd done wrong, I'd mend it. I've tried to apologise but that seems to annoy him even more.'

'Maybe you should just stay out of his way.'

'What kind of wife would I be then?'

'But if he doesn't want you—,' Arruns began but broke off as Tullia burst into tears. 'Oh, Tullia, I didn't mean—'

No, he hadn't meant to say his brother didn't want her for he knew how hurtful such a remark was. Arruns understood how Tullia felt. How often had Lucius grown bored with him and told him to bugger off, never caring how much his words wounded? Maybe he had deserved to be shoved aside — he could be a nuisance, he knew — but not Tullia, never Tullia. She didn't deserve that. She deserved to be loved and looked after.

Feeling awkward, Arruns put his arm around Tullia's shoulder, half expecting her to pull away. But she didn't. She curled into him and pressed her face to his chest. He felt the hot moistness of her tears through his tunic and laid his cheek against the top of her head. He found it strangely pleasant to hold her.

'If it makes you feel any better,' he said, 'Lolly's been off with me too. But I suppose that's nothing new.'

'Poor you,' Tullia said, sniffing and lifting her head. 'You're such a good man, you don't deserve it.'

'Oh, I'm used to it. I stay out of her way so I don't annoy her too much.'

'Poor you,' Tullia said again and smiled weakly.

'Well, I mustn't complain. I've got you to talk to.'

'And I've got you.'

'Makes it better, doesn't it?' Arruns asked hopefully.

Tullia nodded. 'Much. I don't know what I'd do if I didn't have you, Arruns.'

Arruns, embarrassed, smiled and squeezed her shoulder. Tullia put her head on him once again and they stayed that way for a long while.

————

Arruns wandered through the domus, his mind on his troubled marriage. He was not happy, Lolly not happy, but what could be done about it? He thought perhaps having a child would bring them together, but with Lolly in a separate room and doing her wifely duty only rarely, there seemed little chance of that. What was to be done, then? Separation? Servius would never agree to a divorce, and even if he did, what then? Could he and Lolly continue to live in the domus as brother and sister or would he have to leave and find a home of his own? If he moved out, he wouldn't see Lucius all that often, or Tullia.

Tullia! How it would hurt not to see her every day. They had become so close since that talk in the garden, it was hard and unpleasant to imagine not being near her. He would rise in the morning looking forward to seeing her and they would sit together and chat, about everything and nothing, it didn't seem to matter. With Tullia, he had found it possible to laugh and relax, something he never did with Lolly.

He wandered into the garden and sat down on one of the benches. Looking up, he saw Tullia at the far end. She was moving along the paths, bending down every now and then to smell a flower or rub the leaves of a herb between her fingers, bringing them to her nose, breathing in their scent. Every movement of her body was gentle and graceful. How different to her sister.

Tullia turned the corner of the path and gave a little cry of alarm. 'Oh, Arruns, you made me jump. What are you doing there?'

'Nothing. Just sitting.'

'Were you watching me?'

Arruns nodded. Tullia looked to the ground and he saw her cheeks redden. 'You're very pretty.'

'Oh, I'm not. Lolly's the pretty one, everyone says so.'

'I don't say so.'

'Well, that's because you're kind.'

'And is Lucius kinder to you these days?'

'No,' she said, keeping her eyes down, 'but I've learnt to accept it.'

'You shouldn't have to do that,' Arruns said angrily. By the gods, did Lucius not know what a treasure he had in Tullia?

'I do it, Arruns, it saves me pain. You mustn't worry about me.'

'Do you love him?'

Tullia looked at him. 'He's my husband.'

'That's not an answer.'

Tullia bit her lip. 'No, I don't.'

'Lolly doesn't love me. Do you think it's because we don't have children? Women like to have children, don't they?'

'*I'd* like to have them,' Tullia said.

Arruns heard the sadness in her voice. 'You will.'

She shook her head. 'No, I won't. Lucius doesn't touch me anymore. He even said I should go back to my old bedroom like Lolly has. So, how am I supposed to get pregnant?'

Arruns sighed. 'I'm sure he would miss you if you did leave him. Lucius probably just has something on his mind. He'll be attentive to you again and you'll have a baby.'

'I do hope so,' she said. 'My greatest desire is to be a mother.'

'Lolly has never said that or anything like it,' Arruns said glumly. 'But I feel sure she would love our children if we had any. Should I sacrifice to Lucina? Do you think that would help?'

Tullia hesitated, then took his hands in hers. 'I don't think Lolly would want you to do that. I'm sorry, Arruns, but she doesn't want your children, she told me so.'

Arruns stared at her. 'No, she wouldn't say that.'

'I'm not lying to you. Lolly doesn't want to get pregnant by you. She takes steps to prevent it. Why do you think she moved out of your bed? And when you do sleep together, she uses a sponge and vinegar, you know, inside herself, to stop your seed. I know too that she sends her maid to buy potions from a woman with a spice and herb shop near the Temple of Vesta. I've never been there myself, but Lolly says her potions can prevent a woman from conceiving or even make a man impotent.'

'But I'm not impotent,' he protested.

'I never said you were.'

'We made love all the time before she moved out of our room.'

'Then she should have been pregnant by now, shouldn't she?' Tullia snapped, instantly regretting her harshness as Arruns's indignant expression changed to one of hurt.

'Does she hate me so much?' he asked quietly.

'It's Lolly,' Tullia shrugged. 'It's how she is.'

'I've never heard you speak about her like this before. You sound as if you don't like your sister.'

'I don't like her,' Tullia said before she could stop herself. 'In case you haven't noticed, Arruns, Lolly's not a very nice person.'

He laughed and leant in closer. 'Shall I tell you a secret? I don't like my brother very much.'

'But you adore Lucius!'

'Oh, I love him, but I don't always like him.'

'What a pair we are,' Tullia mused. 'You know, Lolly once said we should have each other's husbands. I thought she was being silly, but maybe it would have been better for all of us.'

'What? If you and I had married?'

They stared at one another for a long moment until Tullia

blushed and looked away. Thunder rumbled across the sky. 'We should go in,' she said quietly.

They walked into the house, their hands brushing against each other, neither pulling away. They exchanged no words, didn't say where they were going, but somehow they seemed to agree they were going to Arruns's bedroom. They reached the door and halted outside.

'When is Lucius back?' Arruns asked, slipping his hand into hers.

'Not till late.'

'So...'

She looked up at him. 'Should we? I don't know.'

'Only if you want.'

'You will be kind, won't you, Arruns?'

'I'm not my brother, Tullia. If you had been my wife, I would have loved you.'

Tullia smiled shyly, then squeezed his hand and drew Arruns into his bedroom.

15

Tarquinia rose and rubbed some feeling back into the flattened and reddened skin of her knees. She hoped the goddess
Vesta would answer her prayers for she didn't know if she
could bear the discord within her family much longer.

Despite all Tanaquil's planning and Servius's assurances
that the marriages would work, the children had arranged
matters to their own satisfaction. Tarquinia had heard the
gossip of the household servants and seen with her own eyes
how her daughters had slipped into the beds of the other's
husband. She had been shocked by Tullia; Tarquinia had not
thought her eldest daughter capable of such deceit. But she
didn't blame her. She knew Tullia was miserable with Lucius.
What woman wouldn't be?

Well, Lolly, apparently, although that was no surprise to
her. Hadn't she told her mother and Servius so before the
girls were married? It had been over a week since she had
been sure her daughters were cuckolding their husbands, a
week of torment over whether to tell Servius or not. He
would be so upset, so disappointed. If she did tell him,
Tarquinia feared he would make a public display of the girls

as he had with Lucius after that damned raid. She didn't want her daughters, however disgracefully they were acting, exposed to such gossip and become the talk of the taverns. She could confront them but she doubted her daughters would listen to her. Lolly certainly wouldn't and Tarquinia would die before she appealed to Lucius to stop seeing Lolly and return to Tullia.

Was this part of the curse? Tarquinia wondered. The wretched woman had wanted the Tarquins to experience discord and strife, and nothing was more destabilising to family unity than having the younger generation sleeping with each other's spouses.

Tarquinia came to a decision. If the affairs hadn't ended by the start of the new month, she would tell Servius and let him deal with them.

———

Lolly pushed herself up onto her elbow and laid her hand on Lucius's chest. He murmured an appreciation of her touch and gave a hard squeeze to her fleshy hip.

'Lucius, I've been thinking.'

Lucius opened one eye. 'Don't,' he said and shut it again.

'No, listen,' she insisted, prodding him.

Lucius wiped his hand over his face, licked his lips and finally opened his eyes. 'What?'

'Do you love Tullia?'

'No.'

'Do you love me?'

'Yes.'

'And you would prefer to have me all to yourself, yes?'

'Where is this going, Lolly?'

Lolly began plucking at the blonde hairs framing his

navel. 'I just think it would be better for us both if Tullia was out of the way.'

'I can't divorce your sister,' he said, closing his eyes again. 'Servius wouldn't allow it.'

'I'm not talking about a divorce.'

'Then what are you talking about?' he asked impatiently.

Lolly paused before answering. 'What if Tullia were to die?'

'Die?'

'Oh, don't be obtuse, my love,' Lolly said, 'you know very well what I mean.'

'You want me to kill Tullia?'

'Why not?'

Lucius withdrew his arm from around her waist and sat up, drawing up his knees to rest his elbows. 'Are you serious?'

'Perfectly.'

'But what good would come of it? It's not as if I could marry you.'

'You could… if Arruns was also dead.'

Lucius's eyes widened. 'Kill my brother?'

'How is that any worse than killing your wife, my love?'

Lucius stared at her for a long moment, then scrambled over her to get off the bed. He began to pace the room. Lolly watched him, for once not noticing his physique or the lithe way he moved, both of which normally aroused longing in her. She concentrated on his face, trying to read what was going on behind his eyes.

'No,' he said at last, 'he's my brother, I can't. You will not talk of such things.'

'But—,' Lolly began.

He rushed at her and grabbed her shoulders. 'No,' he said

through gritted teeth. He shoved her away and snatched up his clothes from the floor.

'Lucius, don't go,' Lolly called after him as he headed for the door.

He cast a contemptuous look back at her, then pulled the bolt to the side and strode out.

'Oh, that went well,' Lolly murmured and massaged her shoulders, noting the red marks that would turn into bruises by the next day. Although a little disappointed, she had expected Lucius to react the way he had. For all his bluster and swagger, for all his talk, she knew Lucius's heart was not made of stone as hers was. His heart was penetrable. Lucius felt little love for others, it was true, but she knew from seeing him with Arruns that he suffered guilt. A worthless emotion, Lolly felt; it served no useful purpose and made one weak.

No matter, she would work on him. Only a feeble-minded woman took a man's first no for a final answer. The direct approach had failed. Well then, she would try the indirect way. Whisper in his ear when they were in bed about how badly her sister treated him, how Tullia never cared about what he wanted or tried her best to please him. She would move on to how badly Arruns treated her. Perhaps when the bruises appeared, she would show him those and say Arruns had made them.

She would find some way of convincing Lucius that Arruns and Tullia should die.

———

'You've been avoiding me,' Lolly said, pressing her hip against Lucius's arm as he sat at his study desk.

'I'm busy,' he said, refusing to look up.

'Stop being busy,' she said, lifting his arm aside and sliding into his lap.

'By Dis, Lolly,' he hissed, 'someone will see.'

'I don't care if they do,' she said, nuzzling his ear. 'I've missed you, my love. Tell me, are you angry with me?'

'Go away.'

She bit his neck. 'Are you?'

'No.'

'Then why have you not come to my bed?'

'I… I thought you were bleeding.'

'Liar. You *are* angry with me.'

'Can you blame me after what you said?'

'Yes,' she said sharply, causing him to at last look at her. 'I blame you for being a sentimental fool. If only you knew.'

'If only I knew what?'

'No, I shan't tell you,' she said, turning her head away. 'You'll stay angry with me.'

'I will if you don't tell me,' he warned, and clamping his hand around her jaw, turned her face towards him.

'I'll show you,' she said and rose from his lap. She held out her hand. 'Come on.'

With Lucius's hand in hers, Lolly led him out of the study and to the garden, along the stony path that led to the enclosed arbour. Putting her finger to her lips so he would be quiet, she pointed and whispered, 'Look.'

She knew what he would see as Lucius peered carefully around the hedge because she had made sure they were there: Arruns and Tullia sitting together on the stone bench. Standing on tiptoe, she peeped over his shoulder. Arruns and Tullia were talking in low voices and she saw Lucius half-turn towards her, no doubt to ask what was so wrong about them talking when Arruns pressed his lips to Tullia's neck in a very unbrotherly kiss. She felt Lucius stiffen as Tullia angled her body towards him and kissed Arruns fully and deeply on the mouth.

Lolly tugged Lucius's hand. He turned to her and she saw the fury in his face. Worried he would attack Arruns and spoil her plan, she pulled Lucius away from the arbour and hurried him back to the study.

'You see?' she said, pushing him down into the chair. 'They are deceiving both of us.'

'The bitch,' Lucius hissed. 'How dare she?'

'How dare Arruns?' Lolly countered. 'Does he not think of me, how hurt I must be that he is betraying me with my own sister? And you. I know a man may take his pleasure where he will, but could he not have found a woman other than his own brother's wife?' Once again, she slid onto his lap and this time, he didn't complain. 'You're angry,' she said, putting a hand on his chest. 'How your heart beats.' He stared at her, his breath coming hard and fast. 'Take your anger out on me.'

Lifting her dress to her hips, she straddled him and slipped her hands beneath his tunic, stroking him until he became hard. He didn't remind her of where they were, didn't say they should retire to their room. Lucius didn't say a word as she sank onto him and began to move.

———

Lucius's head was between her breasts, his breath blowing hot on her skin. They had moved from the study to Lolly's bedroom, and as Lolly told him he could, Lucius had been rough with her, holding her down on the bed and thrusting into her hard. She had bit her lip, determined not to cry out, revelling in the pain, relishing his anger. He had worn himself out and now she felt she had him just where she wanted him.

She played with his hair, curling strands around her fingers, while her other hand stroked the damp skin between his shoulder blades.

'That's nice,' he murmured and kissed the jutting bone of her breastbone.

'I do love you, you know, Lucius.'

'I know.'

'And you know I only want what's best for you?'

'I know.'

'That's why I showed you how they were deceiving us.'

He lifted his head and rested his chin on her. 'What does she see in him?'

'What does he see in her?' Lolly countered. Although she was not hurt by Arruns's infidelity, she did feel a little insulted by his choice of lover. That he could be aroused by such a mouse as Tullia!

'I should have confronted them,' Lucius said, rolling over onto his back.

Lolly, able to breathe easily again, turned onto her side to face him. 'What would you have done?'

'I'd have shown her,' he growled.

'Shown her what, my love?' When he didn't answer, she said, 'Would you have hit her?'

'I'd have smashed my fist into her face.'

'Just the once?'

'No, again and again until her face was nothing but blood.'

'Her face would mend in time. And then another man would take her fancy and she'd be at it again.'

'Then I'd hit her again. Or I'd keep her locked up.'

'My father wouldn't let you, you know that, my love. And what about your brother? He is not innocent in this, you know.'

'I'll pay Arruns back, don't you worry.'

'How? Hit *his* face until it's nothing but blood?'

Lucius fell silent and Lolly knew her moment had come.

'And there would be talk in the city. It would get around that your own brother had made you a cuckold. I know you, Lucius, I know you couldn't bear that, to be gossiped about and laughed at. And I couldn't bear it for you.'

She watched Lucius as he stared at the ceiling, knowing he was thinking how he could pay Tullia and Arruns back for their treachery.

'How can we do it?' he said coldly.

Lolly's heart began to beat faster. 'Poison,' she said, trying to keep the excitement from her voice. 'It's quiet and simple.'

'Poison is a coward's weapon. I should fight Arruns.'

'My love, if you fight your brother, people will want to know why. And besides, *you* don't have to do anything. You can leave it all to me.'

'Tullia, too?'

'Tullia, too.'

He nodded, satisfied. She put her fingers to his eyes and she felt his lids flicker. 'Rest,' she purred and kissed him lightly on the mouth. He needed little persuading.

Lolly smiled down at him as he slept. How fortunate it had been to learn that Arruns was sleeping with Tullia. It had made her task of convincing Lucius that their siblings should die so much easier.

16

Lolly donned her heavy woollen cloak, pulled up the hood to cover her head and so concealed, returned to the shop by the Temple of Vesta. The woman who had served her the love philtre raised an eyebrow when Lolly said she wanted poison.

'What you looking to kill?' she asked.

'Vermin,' Lolly answered. 'Rats.'

'Rats?' the woman said. 'Why don't you just get a cat?'

'I don't like cats,' Lolly replied, thinking quickly. 'They make me sneeze.'

'I've heard they can do that,' the woman nodded. 'Very well.' She went to the back of the shop again, this time to a different chest. The lid creaked as she opened it. 'This'll do the trick,' she said, holding up a large brown bottle. 'Put a spoonful on the food you put down and those little bastards will soon be dead.'

Lolly took the bottle. 'It will be quick, then?'

'Oh, it'll be quick,' the woman promised.

'Will it hurt?'

'What does that matter? They're only rats. You want them dead, don't you?'

'Yes, I… how does it kill them?'

'Look, love,' the woman said impatiently, 'I can't tell you what it does to the little bastards on the inside. All I can tell you is it kills them.'

'Can you tell that they've been poisoned?' Lolly pressed.

The woman put her hands on her hips. 'All right, my sweet, you tell me, and you tell me true. Is it really rats you want this poison for?'

Lolly swallowed and raised her chin defiantly. 'Not rats, no.'

The woman nodded, unruffled, not shocked. 'Well, if you don't want to leave a mark on the body, then that one won't do you any good.' She went back to the chest and rummaged through it. Lolly heard the clink of glass. 'This is what you want. It's a lot more expensive than the other.'

'That doesn't matter,' Lolly said, taking the bottle and handing the other back. 'How much?'

The woman told her. 'That's just for the bottle. My silence will cost you more, my sweet.'

Lolly's skin turned cold. 'How much more?'

'Quite a bit more, but not so much you can't afford it. Not a lady like you.'

Lolly told her to name her price. When she did, Lolly felt like laughing out loud. The sum named may have been a great deal to the woman, but it was nothing to Lolly. She had plenty in her purse, enough to cover the cost of the poison and the woman's discretion.

'How do I do it?' she asked, delving into the leather pouch and handing over the bronze ingots.

'Just put a spoonful in a bowl of strong-tasting soup or sauce, or into a cup of wine. Add some honey to the wine and the drinker will never notice the taste. They'll start to feel ill in a few hours.'

'How soon will they die?'

'There's no saying,' the woman shrugged. 'Some it takes after a few hours, others linger on for days. But they all die in the end.'

'And the deaths will look natural?'

The woman smiled. 'People die all the time, my honey. Who's to say what takes them off?'

Lolly tucked the bottle into her pouch, satisfied. She nodded at the woman and left the shop, taking care to adjust her hood.

———

Tullia accepted the plate her sister offered her with a smile.

Why was Lolly being so nice to her? It wasn't usual. Tullia's mind turned to the night she had just spent with Arruns and sweat pricked out on her top lip. Maybe she should end the affair. No, not maybe, she knew she should end it. How could she live with herself knowing how cruel she was being to her sister who had no idea of her treachery?

It wasn't fair to Lucius either. It wasn't his fault he didn't love her. She was his wife and she had a duty to be faithful to him. But oh, Arruns… their time together meant so much to her. Not once since their marriage had she ever felt Lucius cared anything for her while she wholeheartedly believed Arruns when he said he loved her. For so long she had thought herself unlovable, that there was something wrong with her and that was why Lucius had no time for her. Arruns made her feel worthy, wanted, desirable even. Could she give him up just like that?

Tullia forced herself to listen to what her sister was saying.

'You really are looking very pale, Tullia,' Lolly said. 'Are you eating properly?'

Tullia felt like saying Lolly sounded exactly like their mother, but she knew that would annoy her sister. Instead, she said, 'Yes, Lolly, I am. I feel fine. There's nothing wrong with me.'

'Well, I don't think you look well. It's not morning sickness, is it? You're not pregnant, are you?'

Tullia flushed. A few months earlier she would have shook off the suggestion, knowing it was impossible, for Lucius hadn't touched her for so long. But Arruns had. He'd been inside her so many times, had so many opportunities to seed her womb. And she hadn't cared that she might become pregnant by him. For him, she was willing to risk the dishonour and the shame.

'I… I don't think so, no,' she said in a voice barely above a whisper.

'Lucius does his duty, doesn't he?' Lolly asked.

Tullia steeled herself to deliver a rebuke. 'That's really none of your business, Lolly.'

'Oh, come, Tullia, we're sisters. We can tell each other anything. I would tell you about Arruns if you asked.'

'But I wouldn't ask,' Tullia snapped.

'All right, there's no need to bite my head off,' Lolly said, punching her cushion.

Tullia groaned inwardly. 'I'm sorry, Lolly. Maybe I am a bit under the weather and it's making me irritable.'

Lolly smiled graciously. 'You must let me give you something to make you feel better. It's something I take myself now and then.'

Tullia watched with reluctant interest as Lolly took out a small bottle from her purse. 'What is it?'

'Just a tonic.'

'I'd rather not, Lolly, if you don't mind. I really don't like taking those kinds of potions. You never know what's in them.'

'Nonsense, Tullia,' Lolly said, pulling out the cork and snatching up Tullia's cup from the table. 'It hasn't done me any harm, has it?' She tipped the bottle up and a thin dark liquid trickled into Tullia's wine. She added a spoonful of honey and stirred the mixture. 'Here, drink. What? Don't you trust me?'

'Of course I do,' Tullia said, taking the cup. She put it to her nose and sniffed. There was a faint odour of something not quite pleasant.

'Drink,' Lolly urged, 'drink.'

Tullia took a sip. Despite the odd smell, it tasted just like sweet wine. Glancing over the rim of her cup and seeing Lolly's eyes firmly upon her, she took a mouthful and swallowed, draining it.

'There,' she said, showing Lolly the empty cup. 'Happy now?'

Lolly sank back onto her cushions with a languid smile. 'Oh yes, sister, you've made me *very* happy.'

———

Everything was dark to her. Trying to open her eyes hurt and her lids fluttered like butterfly wings, batting feebly. Best to leave them shut, Tullia decided, turning her head on the pillow to the side where the coolness of the fabric momentarily gave ease to her feverish cheek.

Oh, how she hurt. Her very bones ached. She tried flexing her arms and legs to ease their muscles but the movement cost her dearly and she cried out in pain. She heard voices, female voices, and thought she recognised them. Was that her mother and Lolly? And then another voice, male, unfamiliar. Who was he?

Something touched her arm. It hurt and she tried to move her arm away but she had no strength, no power to defend herself. *Go away*, she mentally begged, *leave me alone.*

But whatever it was, it didn't leave her alone. It poked and prodded, forced her to open her mouth, felt around her head, and didn't seem to care that every touch was agony.

Lolly had been right after all, Tullia realised, she *had* been ill. And she deserved to be ill after all she had done. Perhaps this illness was a punishment from Vesta, for betraying both Lucius and Lolly with Arruns. If she recovered, she would end it, tell Arruns she couldn't continue to share his bed. She would be a better wife to Lucius and a kinder sister to Lolly. If only she would get better. She tried to move again and groaned. She had to get better so she could put things right.

She found the strength for a few words only. 'Vesta, forgive me.'

———

Lolly was quiet, staring at her sister who groaned and sweated beneath the bed sheets she had soiled. She wasn't sure what she had expected. That Tullia would go to bed that night and simply not wake up? But it had been days now and still Tullia was not dead. Lolly took hold of her sister's wrist and felt the pulse that beat irregularly beneath her fingertips. Surely, it could not be much longer?

The doctor had been sent for as soon as it was discovered Tullia was ill, but he could do nothing for her. Tullia would die, the doctor said, it was just a matter of time. But Lolly couldn't bear this waiting. She had even considered slipping the pillow out from beneath Tullia's head and forcing it over her sister's mouth. To stop the breath of her sister would be but the work of a moment; the slightest pressure on the pillow and it would all be over. But Tullia was never left alone. Tarquinia stayed constantly by her side.

Oh, just die, Tullia, Lolly thought. *It's tedious, keeping us waiting.*

'I blame you for this.'

Lolly looked across the bed to where her mother was sitting. 'Me? How is this my fault?'

Tarquinia's face was hard. 'You've brought her to this with your vile behaviour, you and that monster. She is being punished because of you.'

So, Tarquinia knew about her and Lucius, Lolly realised. And she thought they had been so careful. 'Lucius is not a monster.'

'You don't even have enough shame to deny it.'

'Why should I deny it?' Lolly said. 'It's no business of yours.'

'How can I have given birth to such a creature as you?' Tarquinia asked bitterly. 'You should have died in my womb or been left on a hilltop to be picked apart by wolves.'

The breath caught in Lolly's throat. She knew her mother didn't like her, but to hear that Tarquinia wished she had died was painful. She didn't know what to say, wasn't sure she could say anything. So she said nothing.

Tullia's ragged breathing suddenly quietened. Both Lolly and Tarquinia leant forward, ears straining. Tullia stopped breathing altogether a minute later.

With an animalistic howl, Tarquinia gathered up her daughter in her arms and held her sagging body to her chest.

Lolly watched her mother and dead sister. She had done it, she had killed and it had been so easy. The only thing that had gone wrong was Tullia taking too long to die. She hadn't used enough poison, that was all. She wouldn't make the same mistake with Arruns.

———

Arruns started up from the couch as soon as he saw Lolly enter.

'How is she?' he asked.

Lolly looked at him coldly, then shifted her gaze deliberately to Lucius, who was leaning against a column, arms folded, a frown creasing his forehead. She moved towards him and met his eyes. 'Tullia's dead, Lucius.'

Behind her, Arruns choked out a sob. Lolly kept her eyes on Lucius and he stared right back.

'I can't believe it, I can't,' Arruns said. 'I must see her.' He ran out of the room and they were alone.

'She's dead, Lucius,' Lolly said quietly. 'By Dis, Lucius, say something.'

His stare was intense, his expression unreadable. She was suddenly scared. Had he changed his mind? Was he sorry now he had agreed to Tullia's murder?

'You did it,' he said at last.

Was he accusing her? Her heart started to beat faster. 'Yes, I did,' she said, determined not to show her fear.

He unfolded his arms and made a grab at her. For the briefest of moments, she thought he was going to put his hands around her throat and throttle her. But he put his hands around her jaw, pulled her towards him and kissed her fiercely, his lips crushing hers. Lolly felt herself grow wet and she clutched at him as he broke the kiss, not wanting him to stop.

'You worried me there for a moment,' she gasped. 'I thought you'd changed your mind.'

'Bit late for that,' he grinned and helped himself to a cup of wine. 'Want one?'

She nodded and took the cup from him. 'Mother knows about us.'

'You told her?'

'No. I don't know how she knows.'

'But she does.'

'Yes.'

'Does it matter?' he shrugged. 'Does she suspect?' he asked suddenly.

'I don't think so.'

'Then the worst Tarquinia can do is tell Servius, if she hasn't already.'

'Father won't do anything,' Lolly said with certainty.

'Let him try,' Lucius said, giving her another kiss. 'So, Arruns next?'

'Soon,' she said, a little surprised at his impatience.

'How?'

'The same way. It will look like they both caught the same disease.'

He gave her an admiring smile. 'You've got it all thought out, haven't you?'

'I told you you could leave it to me.'

'Yes, you did.' He laughed and pinched her cheek. 'I'm glad you're on my side.

She took his hand and kissed the palm. 'I've always been on your side, Lucius, and I always will.'

———

Tarquinia gently placed Tullia's death mask alongside

Tanaquil's in the atrium. She stroked the cold, hard cheek and knew she was crying again. Gone. Tullia was gone. Her body was still in the domus, of course, washed and shrouded, but her essence, the thing that made Tullia herself, had left. And to have been taken so suddenly. Tarquinia hadn't even had time to say goodbye properly.

She wiped her wet cheeks with her fingers and sniffed. Crying wouldn't do any good, she had work to do. There were the mourners and musicians to hire, the funeral feast to order... She was glad of the work; it would keep her busy, not give her too much time to think.

Tarquinia turned at the sound of running footsteps. Arruns's personal slave, Silo, was hurtling towards her.

'What is it?' she asked.

Silo skidded to a stop. 'It's my master, domina,' he said. 'Please come,' and he ran off the way he had come.

Tarquinia ran after him, all thoughts of her work banished. The slave had run to the garden and its bright sunlight dazzled her. She shielded her eyes, squinting for Silo. She found him at the end of the path in the arbour. He was bending over, speaking to something on the ground. Tarquinia hurried towards him.

Arruns was lying on the dirt. His skin was flushed and sweaty, his mouth was open and spittle was leaking from one corner.

'Arruns,' Tarquinia whispered, falling to her knees. She gently lifted his head and lay it in her lap. 'Fetch the doctor,' she told Silo. He hurried away.

Tarquinia used a fold of her dress to wipe the sweat from Arruns's face. She bent her head and whispered that help was coming, that he would be fine, that this was nothing, he would be well soon.

Every word she uttered was a lie. Arruns was dead by the time the guards arrived to carry him to his bed.

———

'Are you coming to dinner?' Servius asked, putting his head around the cubiculum door.

Tarquinia was lying on the bed, her knees drawn up to her chest. She shook her head. 'I'm not hungry.'

'You should eat, my dear. Shall I have something brought to you?'

'No.'

Servius entered the room and shut the door behind him. 'I know you're upset—'

'Aren't you?'

'Of course I am, Tarquinia.'

'You didn't cry at their funerals.'

'It would have been undignified.'

Tarquinia sat up and sniffed. 'And we can't have that, can we?'

'What is it you want from me?'

'You know what I want,' Tarquinia eyed Servius squarely.

Servius rubbed his forehead vigorously. 'I can't believe it.'

'Because you don't want to. Lolly and Lucius killed Arruns and Tullia, believe me.'

'You have no proof,' Servius burst out. 'Nothing to support what you've said to me.'

'You have the proof of your own eyes, Servius. Did you see them at the funerals? Did you actually look at those two? Nothing, not one tear did either of them shed.'

'Because they, like me, knew it would be undignified. You cried enough for all of us.'

'At least I can cry,' Tarquinia said, proving her words true as tears fell down her cheeks. 'I have it in me to feel. Not like those monsters out there. I suppose they're eating? Stuffing their faces as if nothing's happened.'

'Tarquinia—'

'Your daughter killed her sister and then killed her husband,' Tarquinia shouted at him. 'All because she's rutting with that beast. I told you when you and Mother decided the girls would marry that Lolly wanted Lucius. I warned you against it and you didn't listen. You should confront them with the truth, see how they quail then.'

'And what then?' Servius said impatiently. 'What do I say to them: you killed your spouses, how very naughty you are?'

'You have them punished,' Tarquinia screeched. 'You have them dragged out into the forum and whipped for all to see them for the monsters they are.'

'Are you insane?' Servius cried. 'Our family will be entirely exposed. Every man in Rome who hates me will use such a scandal to speak against the monarchy. It will be said my family is corrupt, rotten to its core. It will be said I harbour murderers and whores within these walls. It won't matter that it isn't true—'

'It is true.'

'It will be said I am complicit in such deeds, and if there are those who are willing to think I played no part in them, it will still be said that I cannot control my own family, so how can I control Rome? The people will rise up, egged on by every man I've ever thwarted. We would be dragged from this fine house of ours onto the streets and stoned. And where would your mother's precious dynasty be then? Gone, just like that.' He snapped his fingers.

Tarquinia was crying now, mucus dripping unchecked

from her nostrils. 'I want them punished. I don't care what else happens.'

'Then you're a fool. And I won't listen to you when you're like this, Tarquinia, I absolutely refuse.' Servius yanked open the door and slammed it behind him.

———

Servius kept his hand on the door latch. He shouldn't have walked out on Tarquinia; it was cruel, knowing how upset she was. He wondered if he should go back in, say he was sorry and listen to what she had to say.

But he didn't want to. He didn't want to have to listen to Tarquinia say those hateful, awful things about Lolly. Where had she got the idea that Lolly had anything to do with the deaths of Tullia and Arruns? They had caught a disease, something new, something unknown, the doctor said, and it had killed them. They should be thankful the rest of them hadn't succumbed.

Servius could believe, did believe, Lolly and Lucius were fornicating. Lolly made her liking for Lucius so obvious. Whenever they were in the same room, it was him her eyes were always upon. Tarquinia was right there. He and Tanaquil should have listened to her and let Lolly marry Lucius. They would have been happy then and not have to love one another behind closed doors.

Servius let go of the door latch and made his way to the dining room. He wasn't hungry, either, but having dinner was something you did, even when you had just burned the bodies of two people you loved. As he drew nearer the dining room, he heard the voices of Lolly and Lucius and he hesitated before making himself visible to them. He didn't want to walk in on them if they were being intimate, it would be embarrassing for them all. He listened a moment for sounds that would send him away but heard nothing but murmurs. He went in.

'How is Mother?' Lolly asked when she saw him.

'She's gone to bed,' he said, sitting on the couch. 'She's not hungry.'

'She's very upset,' Lolly said.

'Yes, she is.' He took a deep breath. 'And how are you two?'

'Oh,' Lolly blinked, surprised by the question. She glanced at Lucius. 'Coping. Aren't we, Lucius?'

Lucius nodded, keeping his eyes on the dishes before him.

'Good. We shall all miss them very much.' Servius hung his head.

'Father,' Lolly said, angling her head to look up into his face, 'what is it?'

He gave her a brave smile. 'Nothing, really. It's just... I can't help thinking, you wouldn't know, but I can't help thinking of something that happened many years ago, something terrible.'

'You're talking about the curse,' Lucius said, studying Servius with interest.

Servius stared at him through misty eyes. 'You know about the curse?'

'Grandmother told us.'

'I didn't know.' Servius kept his eyes on Lucius. 'You know then what that woman cursed me with. Discord and strife. Pain delivered through my children. Is this it, do you think? Is this what she meant?'

'Father,' Lolly said with a little nervous laugh, 'you're upset.'

'Yes, I'm upset,' Servius said, 'I'm in pain, just like that woman wanted. I'm in pain and I'm upset because I've lost two of the beings dearest to me. Why aren't you?' He looked up suddenly into his youngest daughter's eyes.

'I am upset,' Lolly insisted, her breath catching in her throat. 'How can you say I'm not?'

'I've seen you shed no tears, daughter,' Servius said. 'Your mother—'

'What? What does Mother say?'

Servius glanced at Lucius, who had fixed him with a hard stare. 'Your mother…' He couldn't bring himself to say that Tarquinia thought Lolly had had a hand in murder. To say those words would give them life and meaning. 'Your mother is perturbed at your lack of sorrow,' he said instead.

'Is she?' Lolly said fiercely, her eyes blazing. 'What does she know of my sorrow? My heart is breaking, Father. I have lost my husband and my sister.'

'And I suppose you expect me to believe that you seek solace in the arms of your brother-in-law?' he retorted.

He saw Lolly grip Lucius's arm. Lucius did nothing but stare at Servius with what he suspected was amusement.

'Your mother wants me to stop you two. Wants me to have you whipped in the forum for your… for your fornication.'

'I won't listen to this,' Lolly said at last, 'and I won't be spoken to in this way.' She snatched her napkin from her lap and threw it on the table, pushing herself up from the couch and storming out.

'She didn't deny it,' Servius said, reaching for a date.

'Why should she?' Lucius said.

'For decency's sake,' Servius suggested. 'But I forget who I'm talking to.'

He expected Lucius to react, to move to hit him, to throw some insult back into his face. To his surprise, Lucius did nothing.

He shook his head. 'This is the curse working, I know it. I've been stupid. I had thought your grandmother's prayers and sacrifices had thwarted the curse completely. I have been lax in sacrificing since she died.'

'You put too much faith in a dying woman's words,' Lucius said.

Servius managed a cold smile. 'You speak brave, Lucius, yet I see you tremble.' He gestured at the hand that gripped Lucius's cup. 'You believe in the curse as much as I do. And you fear it.'

'The curse was directed at you.'

'You think Poena will distinguish between me and you? It's family that matters, Lucius, not blood. And you are my family.'

Lucius rose abruptly and strode around the couches, stopping in front of Servius. 'I'm not a Tullius, Servius. I'm a Tarquin, and the Tarquins are not cursed.' He walked slowly out of the dining room.

'That's right, Lucius,' Servius called after him, 'you keep telling yourself that.'

———

Lolly couldn't rest. Her father's words to her in the dining room had disturbed her. He hadn't said so, but she had seen and heard his hesitation when he talked of Tarquinia. She knew what that hesitation meant. Tarquinia suspected her and Lucius of murder, despite all her efforts, and her father wasn't willing to say so.

She began to wish she hadn't walked out. Lucius would tell her what had been said but Lucius was a man, he wasn't attuned to the little quirks and mannerisms that would tell Lolly what was really going on behind her father's eyes.

And she wanted to know what he believed. How safe were they, she and Lucius? She knew her mother had lost what little love she had for her, and of course, Tarquinia had nothing but hatred for Lucius. If Lolly were in her mother's place, if she had a daughter whom she suspected of murdering her child, she would not rest until she had vengeance. Tarquinia would be thinking the very same, Lolly knew. Even if Servius suspected and did nothing, Tarquinia would not rest. She and Lucius would not be safe until Tarquinia was dead.

But what did her mother matter? she told herself. Servius wasn't paying any attention to Tarquinia, so she didn't need to worry about her. At least, her father knowing about her and Lucius made things a little easier in the domus. They wouldn't have to worry now about being seen. Providing, of course, her father didn't try to separate them by marrying Lucius off to another woman and she to another man. That was a worry. She would, Lolly decided, have to secure Lucius before that could happen.

———

Lolly had stopped taking precautions and now she had what she needed. Lucius had seeded her womb and she was to have his child. It was time to speak to her father.

She found him, as usual, at his desk in his study. He was always working these days, even more so than before. It was strange, she reflected, how separate lives were being led in the domus. Servius spent most of his time either in his study or at the senate and she and Lucius shared his cubiculum openly. Tarquinia stayed out of the way, dining alone in her room because she refused to share a table with Lolly and Lucius and Servius had given up trying to change her mind.

Servius looked up at her and she noticed how tired he looked. His hair had turned a dark grey and there were bags beneath his eyes. He had lost weight, too. 'I need to speak with you, Father.'

'Is it important, Lolly? I've got a lot to get through today.'

'It's important to me. I'm pregnant.'

He dropped his stylus on the desk and sighed as he looked at her. 'Lucius?'

Her mouth tightened at the inference. 'As if you need to ask.'

'I suppose I should congratulate you.'

'I suppose you should.'

'Pregnant at last, after all those barren years with Arruns.'

'Lucius is more potent than Arruns ever was,' she said dismissively, thinking of the means she had taken not to get pregnant by Arruns.

'Not something I need to know,' Servius said, picking up his stylus.

'That's not all,' Lolly said, taking the stylus out of his hand. 'I can't be pregnant and a widow.'

'I see. So, marriage to Lucius. What you always wanted.'

'You should have let me marry him in the beginning.'

'At last, something you and your mother agree on.'

Mention of Tarquinia caused an uncomfortable silence. Lolly broke it.

'So, can I assume we have your blessing to marry?'

'If you feel you need my blessing. You always seem to do whatever you want with or without it.'

'You know, Mother's dismal moods are having a terrible effect on you. You should have the doctor see to her.'

'Your mother is fine,' he insisted.

'If you say so,' Lolly sighed. 'So, do I arrange my own wedding or shall I leave that to you?'

'A big wedding?'

'Quiet, I thought.'

'Then you don't need me,' Servius said, plucking the stylus back. 'Get it done. You can leave it to me to tell your mother. Oh, she will be pleased.'

PART III

538 BC–525 BC

17

Lucius kicked off his sandals and laid back, letting his legs hang over the end of the couch. What a tedious day it had been. All morning standing in for Servius to hear petitioners and then the afternoon inspecting the building works at the Temple of Diana, his father-in-law's big project that was finally nearing completion. Here he was, forty-two years of age, a husband, a father to four children, and still he was Servius's errand boy.

Lucius shouted for wine and a slave hurried to pour him a cup. He downed the wine in one gulp and held it out to be refilled. Resting his head on the bolster cushion, he closed his eyes, feeling the wine starting to loosen the muscles in his neck and shoulders. Ahh, that was better, that was what he needed, a little rest and some good wine.

'And a little peace and quiet,' he shouted as a baby's cry echoed through the domus. Was it too much to ask that a man be able to lay down his head and not be tormented by his children?

'What are you shouting for?' Lolly demanded as she came into the room.

'That noise,' he growled, pointing in the direction of the crying. 'Can't it be shut up?'

'That is your daughter,' Lolly said, picking up the empty wine cup and staring pointedly into it, 'and she can't help it, she's teething.'

'How can something so small be so loud?'

'All the children cried so when they were teething. You're just tetchy today.'

'I'm not tetchy, I'm worn out. Put some oil of cloves on her gums, that will help.'

'I do know what to do, Lucius. It will pass, we just have to be patient.' Lolly lifted up his feet to sit on the couch with him, placing them on her lap instead. 'You're brooding about it again.'

'No, I'm not,' he said sulkily.

'It will come, Lucius. Like with Cassia's teething, we have to be patient.'

'I am sick of being patient,' Lucius shouted, his body jerking with his vehemence. Lolly forced his legs to be still. 'How much longer do I have to wait?' He saw Lolly's eyes close briefly. She had heard this a hundred times before; he knew she was sick of his whining. There were times when he was sick of it himself. 'Sorry,' he said.

She patted his ankles. 'I know it's frustrating, my love. I feel the same about Mother.'

'Hoping your mother will die is not the same as waiting to inherit the throne.'

'I suppose all sons with a king for a father must feel the same as you.'

'Servius is not my father,' Lucius said through gritted teeth.

'You will be king one day, Lucius, but you could make it easier to become so, you know.'

Lucius groaned. 'Oh, not this again, Lolly, please.'

'If you can brood, then I can nag.' She gave him a meaningful look. 'Just being a prince will not guarantee the throne for you. Yes, the people are accustomed to kings now. Yes, you are the obvious choice, but you haven't done enough to prove yourself. You haven't been able to prove yourself in battle and you haven't pursued any policies of your own in the senate, only my father's.'

'Why don't you just say it?' Lucius said irritably. 'I'm a nobody as far as the senate is concerned.'

Lolly leant towards him and slapped his face. 'I won't have you talk like that. And I will not be the wife of a nobody, Lucius. I've worked too hard and sacrificed too much to end up as that.'

'You're a harpy,' he muttered, nursing his cheek.

Lolly fingered his right foot, then gently bent back the little toe, enjoying his cry of pain.

'What was that for?'

Lolly shrugged. 'I want to make sure you're paying attention. You need to work at becoming king, Lucius. You need to talk to people.'

'That's what I've been doing.' Lucius told her of all the people he'd seen that day during his time at the temple building site and in the senate.

Lolly nodded approvingly. 'That's good, but did you make any of those people your friends?'

'I don't need friends, Lolly.'

'You will, when the time comes. And it's never too early to start cultivating people who will be of use to us. That is one lesson I've learnt from Grandmother. She knew people could be valuable, Father told me. Learn from that. Oh, there's the children now.'

The sound of little pairs of feet could be heard in the

corridor. A moment later, three young children burst into the room and headed for their parents. The eldest, Titus, leant over the back of the couch, one hand idly playing with his mother's hair. The second eldest, Arruns, slumped on the couch opposite, slapping his stomach rhythmically as though it were a drum, and the youngest of the three, Sextus, climbed up on his father's lap.

'What do you want?' Lucius said in an indulgent tone.

'Can we dine with you tonight, Father?' Sextus asked, looking at him with eyes that were so like Lolly's.

'Absolutely not,' Lucius replied.

'But I'm upset,' Sextus pouted.

'Why are you upset, my darling?' Lolly asked, stroking her son's soft blonde hair.

'Because Grandmama hurt me,' he said and thrust out his arm. There was a thick red mark across the plumpest part.

Lolly grabbed his wrist and yanked it beneath her nose. 'Grandmama did that?'

'With the rod,' Sextus nodded, his chin wobbling. 'And I didn't do anything, I promise.'

'Of course you didn't,' Lolly said, pulling his face towards her and kissing his forehead. 'Lucius, do you see what she's done?'

'I'm not blind, Lolly.'

'What are you going to do about it?'

'I'm not going to do anything about it. It's only a mark. See, it's fading already.'

'I won't have her hitting my children,' Lolly said. 'How dare she. Lucius, you must tell her.'

'Tell her yourself, she's your mother.'

Lucius wished the children hadn't come in, wished Sextus hadn't told them about the beating. Lolly was going on about Tarquinia, Titus and Arruns were play wrestling over the couches, kicking the tables and knocking cups over in their fun, and Sextus was bouncing up and down on his bladder. He endured it for as long as he could, then decided he'd had enough. He told Sextus to get off him and Sextus clambered down, his little face threatening to crumple. He drew his legs away from Lolly's lap and rose from the couch. Lolly was only halfway through her diatribe against her mother when she demanded to know where he was going.

'To Cossus,' Lucius replied.

'To get drunk, I suppose?'

'That's right, my love. To get drunk.'

'If you end up with another woman, I'll know,' she warned, taking Sextus into her arms.

'Believe me, my love,' he said, tying his cloak around his neck, 'I want no other woman but you. I leave you to your children and your mother. Enjoy yourself, won't you.'

———

Tarquinia was reading in her cubiculum. It was getting harder to read, the writing growing ever more blurry with each passing year. She supposed there would come a time when she would either have to give up reading or hire someone to read to her. Maybe that would be better, she reflected, as she was sure reading aggravated her headaches. But reading was one of the few, perhaps the only pleasure she had left to her now and she was loathe to give it up.

She heard long, striding footsteps heading for her door and rolled up the scroll expectantly. They were Lolly's footsteps, she could tell, and she knew why her daughter was taking the unusual step of coming to see her. She raised her chin a little, determined to be defiant not conciliatory, strong not weak.

The door was thrown open – Lolly never bothered to knock anymore – and Lolly stormed in, dragging Sextus behind her.

'Look at that,' Lolly said, showing Tarquinia Sextus's arm. The red mark had all but faded.

'Why must I look at his arm?' Tarquinia said, keeping her eyes on Lolly's.

'You hit him. You hurt my son.'

'Yes, I did. I didn't hit him as hard as he deserved.'

'My son never deserves to be beaten.'

'That little monster,' Tarquinia jabbed a finger at Sextus who was attempting to hide behind his mother, 'threw a stone at one of the servants. It could have blinded her.'

'Oh, don't be ridiculous,' Lolly scoffed. 'A little stone won't hurt anyone.'

'It was not a *little* stone.'

'I don't care if it was a big bloody rock,' Lolly shouted. 'You will not lay a finger on my children or—'

'Or what, Lolly?' Tarquinia rose angrily, her determination not to lose her temper forgotten by her daughter's attitude.

'Or… or…,' Lolly blustered, her anger barely contained, 'or I'll have you dragged to the forum and whipped for everyone to see.'

Tarquinia laughed and sank back onto her chair. 'Oh Lolly, now who's being ridiculous?'

'I will, I mean it.'

'And you still sound like a petulant little girl.'

Lolly stamped her foot. 'I'm not a girl, Mother. I won't have you talking to me in this way.'

'You're not queen yet, Lolly, nor the gods willing, will you ever be. I hope Rome realises before it's too late that Lucius is not fit to be a king and that they elect someone who will do Rome good.' She was getting to her daughter, Tarquinia could see, and the knowledge sent a thrill through her tired body.

'Oh,' Lolly growled through her teeth, 'why don't you just die?'

'Like your sister did? Like your husband?'

Mother and daughter stared at each other for a long moment.

'You're old, Mother,' Lolly said at last. 'Your mind is going. Come, Sextus.'

Tarquinia was shaking as the door slammed. The way Lolly had looked at her was dreadful. There had been such contempt, such hatred in her eyes. Oh, why had she let herself say that about Arruns and Tullia? She hadn't meant to. She tried not to think about her dead daughter and son-in-law anymore, it hurt too much. Her nose was running and she tremblingly wiped it with her handkerchief. She was suddenly worried she had given her daughter a terrible idea.

———

Cossus threw a slice of meat from his plate to his dog at his feet, smiling as the animal swiftly devoured it and looked for more. 'You had a row with Lolly?'

'No,' Lucius said, helping himself to a plate of walnuts, 'I just had to get out of the domus. The children were making nuisances of themselves.'

'Why'd you have all those kids if you didn't want them?' Cossus wondered aloud. He had managed to become a widower before his wife saddled him with children and he had no desire to marry again, finding everything he needed in a woman in Rome's whorehouses.

'It's not that I don't want them,' Lucius said, 'they just happened.'

'Well, they will happen if you keep humping your wife.'

'You try and stop Lolly,' Lucius laughed, remembering how relentlessly Lolly had used him the previous night. He had spoken the truth when he said no other woman compared to her. He'd tried quite a few both before and after their marriage and he'd enjoyed none of them as much as he enjoyed Lolly. 'And besides, I need the children.'

Cossus rolled his eyes. 'Oh, that's right, I forgot, because you never mention the fact that you need your kids for your dynasty.'

Lucius heard the sarcasm in his friend's voice and chose to ignore it. 'I just hope I get a chance to sit on the throne before I'm too old to enjoy it.'

'I saw Servius the other day in the senate,' Cossus said, trying to extract a shred of meat from between his teeth with his fingernail. 'He looked in fairly robust health to me.'

'I know,' Lucius said sourly.

'So, you're just going to have to wait, aren't you?'

'Lolly thinks I should be making friends in the senate.'

Cossus laughed. 'She was talking about you when she said that, wasn't she?'

'Go boil your head,' Lucius said, throwing a walnut at him. 'People like me. You like me.'

'Ah, but I've known you for years,' Cossus reminded him, 'I know what you're like. And besides, I'm not the sort of friend Lolly means.'

Lucius wiped his mouth, thinking. Cossus was saying the same things as Lolly. Maybe they were both right and he needed to be more assiduous in making himself agreeable if he wanted to be king. Despite his protest to Cossus, he knew he wasn't the most likable of people. He was too abrupt, too sarcastic, too intolerant to be well liked. Not that he cared much. He had everyone he needed in Lolly and the few friends he had kept from his boyhood.

'Tell me then,' he said, 'how do I get the people who matter to like me?'

'You've got to approach it differently. If you ask me, there's no point wanting people to like you. Why do you want to be liked? Likable people are usually weak arseholes. I think you should work to show people you are the best option when it comes to succeeding Servius. You've got to show the senate how you will improve their lives as king. Do that and they'll like you well enough, I guarantee.'

———

'Prince Lucius, you honour my humble house.' Quintus Sanctus bowed to Lucius and Lolly and gestured for them to follow him through to the dining room.

'Remind me why we're here,' Lucius muttered to Lolly as they smiled at their host and followed.

'Quintus may be useful to us,' Lolly murmured, smiling at the other guests who all stood, waiting to greet them, 'and tonight is an excellent opportunity to start some rumours. Narcissa, how lovely you look. Is that silk from Phoenicia?'

Lucius let Lolly slip from his arm and watched with amusement as she feigned interest in their hostess's finery. Lolly could turn on the charm when she wanted, he knew. For his part, he felt a little exposed in this company. What exactly was he supposed to say to these people? He barely knew them and he certainly had nothing in common with them.

'Prince Lucius,' Quintus said, the slight lisp in his voice making Lucius's skin crawl. 'Please, do sit.' Quintus gestured towards the *medias* couch, which had been piled high with plump-looking bolster cushions.

It was the place of honour at any banquet and it satisfied Lucius that he had not been given a lesser position. At least these people knew how to treat a prince. He called softly to Lolly and held her hand as she climbed onto the couch. She shifted over to make room for him. Once he and Lolly were settled, the other guests took their places, Narcissa pointing to the couches each should occupy.

As the evening worn on, Lucius realised that had he come alone, as Cossus had suggested, making the dinner a male-only event, he would have managed the whole thing wrong. He would have grown bored with the talk of olive oil and grain prices, the gossip about neighbours and the deeds of foreigners that worked their way back to Rome. He would have tried to turn the conversation on to Servius's various faults and ineptitude too early and too obviously, rousing his hosts' and the other guests' indifference or worse, their ire.

Lolly knew better how to manage these things and Lucius was proud of the way she monopolised the conversations without seeming to, how she steered the talk onto political matters, but most of all, how she managed to imply that her father's policies had not been to Rome's benefit without ever actually saying so.

And Lolly had a wonderfully receptive audience. Quintus and Narcissa had good reasons of their own, Lucius supposed, for having no great love for Servius. What those reasons were, he couldn't fathom, nor did he care. They served a good dinner and Lolly was wrapping them around her finger.

'Of course, my father is feeling his age now,' he heard Lolly say. 'The duties have become a great burden to him.'

'But he does not do everything himself, surely?' Narcissa asked, pushing a plate of oysters towards Lolly.

Lolly took one of the shells. 'Lucius does all he can to help my father, of course. Father's eyesight is very bad and he asks Lucius to read him the foreign dispatches and draft replies, doesn't he, Lucius?'

'It's the least I can do for him,' Lucius said.

'And good training for you, I expect,' Quintus nodded sagely.

'That's not how Lucius sees it,' Lolly said, a little tartly. 'Lucius is very fond of my father and hates to see him struggling.'

'Does the Queen not help?' Narcissa asked.

'Oh,' Lolly waved her hand as if to suggest it was a foolish question, 'my mother has no interest in Rome.'

'But if she worries that the King is unduly burdened, then surely she would want to be of use to your father?' Narcissa persisted.

Lolly laughed, making her eyes go wide in innocence. 'Oh, no, I've never known Mother to worry about Father and his work.'

'Perhaps because she knows your father has your husband to lean on?'

'Yes, I expect so.'

Narcissa nodded enthusiastically and Lolly slid a sideways glance at Lucius as if to say, *It's as easy as that, my love.*

———

She had heard what they were up to and she was determined to stop it.

Tarquinia had spent the morning at her friend's house,

chatting pleasantly about this and that, until Restita had
pointed a finger and said there was Lucius coming out of
Cossus's house across the street. Tarquinia was not particularly interested in Lucius's whereabouts and had continued
examining Restita's latest purchase of hair combs, until
Restita said it was such a shame that work was taking its toll
on Servius and how fortunate he was to have Lucius.

Tarquinia had looked up then from the ivory combs and
asked Restita what she was talking about. Restita had given a
little embarrassed laugh and shrugged. It was common
knowledge, she said, that Servius's faculties were starting to
fail him and that Lucius had taken over a lot of his work. She
realised she had spoken out of turn, as she called it, because
she hastened to add that she knew Servius was still up to the
job, just that he needed someone to take some of the burden
from his shoulders. Tarquinia demanded to know who was
spreading these lies and Restita had swallowed nervously and
jerked her head at Cossus's house. *So*, Tarquinia thought,
*Cossus has become Lucius's mouthpiece in the city and no
doubt, in the senate, working hard to make out Servius is
struggling*.

Making her excuses to Restita, Tarquinia hurried back to
the domus, waving away the litter bearers who would not
move fast enough for her liking. She rushed through the
house, shouting for Lolly and found her in the garden.

'Just what are you two up to?' Tarquinia demanded, grabbing hold of Lolly's arm and dragging her around to face her.

'Let go of me.' Lolly tugged her arm out of her mother's
grasp. 'I have no idea what you're talking about, Mother.'

'Don't play the innocent with me. Do you think I haven't
heard what is being said about Servius in the city? You think I
can't work out who's spreading these rumours?'

'What rumours?'

'That your father is failing.'

'Well, that's true. Father isn't as sharp as he used to be.'

'Your father is as clear about his duties and his ability to carry them out as ever he was.'

'That's your opinion, Mother,' Lolly said defiantly, 'it's not the opinion of many people.'

'Oh, many people. By that I suppose you mean you and that wretched husband of yours.'

'Lucius has said nothing unreasonable. If he has intimated that Father is finding kingship difficult these days, then he is merely expressing an opinion out of concern for him.'

Tarquinia shook her head. 'Just who do you think you are fooling with all this... this nonsense? You forget, Lolly, I know you, I know what you are, what you're capable of and I won't have you or Lucius trying to undermine Servius. I won't have it.'

Lolly snorted a laugh. 'Oh, you won't have it? Oh, Mother, do stop before you make a complete fool of yourself. Lucius is his own man. He is at perfect liberty to say what he pleases about whoever he pleases.'

'He is a subject, Lolly, and he owes obedience and loyalty to Servius.'

'He owes Father nothing,' Lolly spat, 'least of all loyalty. What has Father ever done for him?'

'What has he done for him? He's looked after Lucius since he was a child, given him a home, given him both his daughters—'

'Father has made my husband little better than his servant.'

'Lucius owes your father everything.'

'And that's what we hate,' Lolly shouted, her breast heaving.

Tarquinia drew in a deep breath. 'So, now we get to the

truth, don't we? You're both frustrated and dissatisfied with your lot in life. You think Servius has held you back, you think you deserve more.'

'We do deserve more,' Lolly said, trying to calm herself.

'And you think this is how you're going to get it? I know what you're up to, I see your plan now. You think you can discredit your father and put your husband on the throne, don't you? I know it's your idea. Lucius doesn't have the brains to think of this.'

'How dare you speak so of Lucius.' Lolly's eyes burned with indignation.

'I'll speak how I like of that fiend,' Tarquinia retorted. She didn't see Lolly's hand come up and slash across her face. She just felt the keen sting it left behind.

Lolly was breathing fast, her face almost as red as her mother's inflamed cheek. 'You say that about Lucius again and I promise you, Mother, you'll get worse. I'll take a whip to you, I swear I will.'

Tarquinia held her hand to her face. 'You are no daughter of mine. I curse you, you and your husband.'

Lolly threw back her head and laughed. 'Oh, curse away, Mother. This family has nothing but curses against it. No god will listen to you and your whining. You have no power and you can't harm me or Lucius. You're old. You'll be dead soon and then Father will be all on his own. And so much easier to deal with.'

———

Tarquinia angled her face to the light, her bloodshot eyes on Servius.

'It's a little swollen,' Servius said and stepped away. 'Lolly did that?'

'You think I'm lying?'

Servius frowned. 'No, of course not, but why would she do that? What did you say to her?'

'It doesn't matter what I said to her,' Tarquinia said, staring at him in amazement. 'I'm her mother and she struck me.'

Servius returned to his desk, his eyes raking despondently over the scrolls that littered it. 'Well, yes, but what do you want me to do about it?'

'I want you to punish her. She's *your* daughter.'

'She's not a little girl, Tarquinia. I can't lock her in her room and refuse to feed her until she apologises.'

'You can have her whipped. That's what she threatened to do to me.'

Servius stared up at her. 'I don't believe you. She wouldn't.'

'Oh, you never believe she can do anything bad, can you? She's always your good little girl. Lolly is bad through and through, she always has been. How far does she have to go before you realise she is evil? I would have thought that after what she did to Arruns and Tullia—'

'Oh no, don't start that again,' Servius held up his hands to stop her. 'You never had any proof she had anything to do with their dying.'

'You and your proof,' Tarquinia scoffed. 'I know what she is. And I know *him*.'

'You've never liked Lucius.'

'With good reason, Servius. Why, why won't you see that pair for what they are?'

'Because I have too much else to do,' Servius shouted, suddenly angry. 'I have a country to run.'

'Listen to me, Servius, please,' Tarquinia pleaded, leaning over his desk and putting her face close to his. 'If you don't do something about those two, you won't have a country to run. They are acting against you. In the city, in the senate, Lucius is openly criticising you, your decisions, your acts. He is trying to turn people against you.'

Servius stared at his wife as she spoke, worried by the frenzy on her face. Tarquinia was becoming hysterical again and her tantrums, her paranoia, were always against Lucius and Lolly. He was sick of it. 'My dear,' he said quietly, not wanting to provoke her further, 'why don't you go and have a lie down? I think you're tired, overwrought.'

To his relief, Tarquinia didn't shout back. Her shoulders slumped and she straightened. 'Go to bed,' she repeated, raising an eyebrow. 'Is that all you can say? Go to bed, Tarquinia, and everything will be better in the morning.'

'It will be, my love,' he promised, leading her to the door. 'You will see.'

She went out without argument and he had closed the door on her before she had reached the end of the corridor.

———

Lucius had arrived home looking forward to a big dinner — he was hungry and he had been promised pork in honey — and a reading by his favourite Greek poet. What he got when he arrived was Lolly looking thunderous and the news she had cancelled both the dinner and the poet.

'We have to do something about Mother,' Lolly gave as an explanation and told him of her encounter in the garden that afternoon with Tarquinia.

'And for this I have to forgo my pork and poetry?' he said sulkily, throwing off his toga and flumping down on the couch.

'You should have heard her, Lucius.' Lolly leant over the

back of the couch and ran her fingers through his hair. 'She called you a fiend.'

'So? I've been called worse.'

Lolly smacked him. 'Will you take this seriously?'

'Why must I take her seriously, Lolly? She's a mad old woman. Let's ignore her, like we always do.'

'I've had enough of her viciousness towards me and you. She went to Father and told him I hit her.'

'And what did he do?'

'Told her to go to bed.'

Lucius laughed. 'See, even he's not paying her any attention. You're worrying about nothing.'

'She can hurt us, Lucius. She has friends who will talk to their husbands. And then their husbands will talk to their fellow senators. Any word she says against us will undo everything you've achieved in the senate so far.'

'Which isn't much,' Lucius mumbled.

Lolly tutted in annoyance at his words. She knew Lucius was dispirited by how slowly they were progressing. Cossus was doing his part well, speaking for Lucius against Servius in the senate, but there was only so much he could say before he became just a noise buzzing in the ears of the senators. When Cossus spoke, it was just gossip, opinions that couldn't be corroborated. When Lucius spoke, there was the idea that he had proof of Servius's failings behind his words. But she also knew how difficult and irksome Lucius found it to have to mingle with the senators, to pretend to like them and listen to their complaints.

'It's working,' she insisted, 'and we can't let Mother damage us.'

'What do you want to do then?' Lucius asked, resigned to act if it was what Lolly wanted. Lolly looked down at him and met his eyes. He understood her at once. 'Really?'

'Why not?'

Lucius nibbled on his lip for a moment. 'It would solve our problem. And make our home life easier.'

'Just what I was thinking, my love.'

'But not poison this time.'

'No,' Lolly agreed, 'poison would raise eyebrows. What then?'

'An accident,' Lucius said after a moment. 'A terrible misfortune.'

'Difficult to arrange, surely?'

'Not really,' Lucius grinned and lunged at Lolly. He grabbed her, pulling her over the back of the couch so she landed on top of him. She was laughing and trying, feebly, to fight him off. 'You leave it to me, my little tigress.'

———

The litter bearers kept stumbling on the road out of Rome. Tarquinia hated this part of a holiday, the travelling to get to wherever she was going. With every lurch, she had to remind herself why she was going. She was going because she wanted to get as far away as she could from Lucius and Lolly.

Servius hadn't believed her when she said they were making life unbearable, that Lucius and Lolly were doing all they could to upset her. It hadn't been in ways that Tarquinia could point to and say to Servius, 'Yes, they did this or that'. No, they were more subtle than that. They would make demeaning remarks to her friends that they knew would get back to her, such as how much food she was eating or how her dresses seemed to fit so much more snugly of late, how she had never contributed anything of interest or value to conversations, how the servants, even the slaves, had no respect for her. Seemingly little things that over time mounted up to upset her a very great deal. She hated Lucius and Lolly, hated them with an intensity she would never have thought herself capable of. And when Servius suggested that as she was looking a little worn, she should take a holiday by the seaside, she had said yes without hesitation.

Tarquinia felt her heart lightening as the walls of Rome grew smaller behind her. She was even glad to not have Servius with her. She felt free for the first time since... well, she couldn't remember when. She would enjoy her month by the sea. She would breathe the sea air, fill her lungs with its freshness, eat fish caught only moments earlier and drink all the wine she wanted without fear of censure from her husband. Oh, the bliss. Tarquinia closed her eyes and sunk into the cushions, not even minding anymore the relentless jolting of the litter.

She was woken by her head hitting the side of the litter. She cried out and pressed her fingers to her temple. As the pain receded, she realised the litter had stopped. Stretching out a plump arm, she parted the hangings. She looked out onto fields and trees, hedges and ditches. Rome was long gone. She must have been asleep for a while.

'What's going on? Why have we stopped?' she called.

No one answered. She leant out of the litter and looked around. There was no one there. Her heart began to beat faster. She scrambled backwards into the litter, letting the hangings fall together. What had happened? Why was she alone? She knew there were bandits outside Rome, desperate men ready to rob travellers and leave their bodies to be torn apart by wolves, and she wondered if she should make a dash for Rome if her litter bearers had been attacked. But she had no idea how far away Rome was.

Tarquinia heard a noise. It sounded like footsteps. She held her breath and waited. The footsteps came nearer. They stopped outside the litter. And then all she could hear was her blood pounding in her ears. She fixed her eyes on the gap in the hangings.

The hangings moved, slowly, an inch at a time. She saw legs, thick, hairy, and the end of a sword, dripping blood. Tarquinia opened her mouth to scream but then a head appeared. And she knew who it belonged to!

'Salve, my lady,' Cossus grinned.

'You're… you're Lucius's friend,' she stammered, her mind trying to make sense of what was happening.

'That's right, my lady.'

'What's happened? Have my litter bearers been attacked by bandits?'

'You could say that.' Cossus squatted, filling the aperture.

She pointed a shaken finger at his bloodied sword. 'Have you killed the bandits?'

'No, lady. There were no bandits to kill. I killed your litter bearers.'

'But– I–'

'And now I'm going to kill you.'

Tarquinia did scream then, but for only the briefest of moments.

————

Someone had put a large jug of wine on his desk, some thoughtful servant who knew he would need solace. The wine was strong, it hadn't been watered, and it felt good as it slid down his throat and warmed his chest.

Dead, in the blink of an eye, Tarquinia was dead. He hadn't even said goodbye to her properly when she left. His mind had been on a deputation due to arrive that afternoon from Cumae and he had kissed her cheek and wished her a safe journey before disappearing back to his office. He hadn't even bothered to wave.

Servius hoped Tarquinia hadn't suffered. The litter bearers' bodies had been found with their hands hacked off and their insides falling out, typical of the bandits that plagued the countryside, but Tarquinia had had only one wound to her heart. The doctor who examined her body assured him her death would have been quick.

It hurt him now that she had been so unhappy these last few months and that he had done nothing to make things better. He knew Lolly had been unkind to her mother, had seen it and done nothing, all because he didn't want to get involved in a row between his daughter and his wife. He had been tired of the discord, it had been going on for so long. The curse, he said to himself, it was the curse working. Discord and strife, that was what the woman had wanted and that was what he had been punished with.

He wondered if Lolly was feeling as guilty as he did now. Was she wishing she hadn't been so cruel to her mother, hadn't made all those unkind jibes, hadn't struck her? He didn't know, even though Lolly had made all the right noises when Tarquinia's body was brought back to the domus. She had cried in the street, seeming not to care she was being stared at. That was odd really, now he thought about it. Lolly was normally so conscious of her dignity. Lucius had been stiff-lipped as Tarquinia was taken into the domus, he remembered, but then Tarquinia and he had never got on. What did he expect?

Servius poured himself another cup of wine and carried it to the bed, his bones cracking as he bent his body to the mattress.

Lucomo, Tanaquil, Tullia, Arruns and now Tarquinia, all gone. Lucomo and Tanaquil he could understand. Though

Lucomo's end had been premature, he would have died sooner or later and it had been the same with Tanaquil. But the others, Tullia and Arruns especially, should still be alive, they should be breathing and walking around the domus, filling the rooms with their voices and their laughter.

He hardly ever heard laughter any more, tucked away in his corner of the domus. The grandchildren would laugh and play, of course, and it pleased him when he did hear their noise, but they could have been the children of the servants for all the affinity he felt with them. Though they had his blood in their veins, Lolly's children felt as alien to him as any stranger in Rome. He was alone, though constantly surrounded by people in the domus.

Servius drained the cup, grateful for the soporific effect the wine was having on him. He wished Tarquinia was with him, wished she were lying by his side so he could hold her hand and feel the warmth of her soft skin. But he'd never feel her touch again.

She was in Elysium and at peace now.

18

Aulus Flavonius watched Servius exit the senate house. The King seemed to limp a little. Servius had certainly aged since the death of Tarquinia. It was such a shame about his wife. By all accounts, she had been a good little woman.

'You look very deep in thought, Aulus,' Gallio Burrus said, pushing his way through the crowd to stand by his friend.

'Ah, salve, Gallio. I was just thinking about the King,' Aulus said, nodding at the door through which Servius had just gone.

'Ah yes,' Gallio said, 'not the man he was, is he?'

'Not since the death of his wife, no.'

'It has affected him badly.'

There was a note of disapproval in Gallio's voice that irked Aulus. 'How would you be if your wife was killed?' he rebuked.

Gallio bristled. 'There's no need to take that tone with me, Aulus. It was a terrible thing that happened to the Lady Tarquinia but it doesn't do to let grief unman one. But there's more to my meaning than that. I'm not just talking about how he feels but how the King is in himself. You heard him talk today. He was indecisive, rambling, feeble–'

'Everything, in fact,' Aulus said, fixing Gallio with a knowing look, 'that Prince Lucius has been saying about his father-in-law for the past six months.'

Gallio made a face. 'Well, he's been right, hasn't he? We've seen it today.'

'I won't deny that Servius has gone down a little of late, but he's been a good king. I'm not ready to throw him out just yet.'

'Neither am I, Aulus,' Gallio protested, trying to laugh. 'I'm just saying.'

'There are many of our fellow senators who are just saying, my friend. I'm not embarrassed to admit that the mood in the senate worries me just a little.'

'Why should it worry you?'

Aulus pupped his lips. 'Has it never struck you as odd the way so many of the Tarquins have died suddenly?'

Gallio shook his head. 'No. People die. It is the way of the world.'

'But think back. The first Tarquins lost both their sons, the king murdered, the grandchildren, Arruns and Tullia, both healthy and yet both died suddenly, one after the other. And then Tarquinia, killed by bandits on a road that hadn't seen any problems of that sort for a good few months.'

'What are you getting at?'

'It just seems,' Aulus shrugged, struggling to find the words to explain his unease, 'strange, that a family should suffer such misfortune.'

'You're forgetting, Aulus,' Gallio lowered his voice, 'the Tarquins are cursed.'

'They certainly seem to be,' Aulus said. He looked around the senate house and saw Lucius surrounded by at least seven senators, all hanging on his every word. 'Is he the future, Gallio?'

Gallio followed his gaze. 'That seems to be the way the senate is thinking. He has his followers and I expect he'll be the next king.'

'With or without an election?' Aulus asked wryly.

'I suppose it will depend whether one is necessary,' Gallio said unconcernedly. 'If Prince Lucius seems to be who the majority of senators want, why bother?'

'Why bother, Gallio?' Aulus asked, shaking his head. 'Are you serious? You would have Rome become a hereditary monarchy by default?'

Gallio sighed, unmoved by his friend's indignation. 'It works for other countries, Aulus. Why not ours?' He moved away, not waiting for an answer.

How easy Gallio found it, Aulus mused, to accept something that is by no means inevitable. And yet was Gallio right? Did everyone in the senate think the same?

'By all the gods, I hope not,' Aulus murmured to himself, 'for all our sakes.'

———

The three cups made a dull thud as they knocked together, and a few beads of wine escaped to bedew Lolly's skin. Cossus grabbed her hand and pulled it to his lips, his thick wet tongue flicking to lick the droplets away.

Lolly, keeping her eyes on his, slid her hand away. 'Lucius,' she said silkily, 'do tell your friend to behave.'

Lucius, who had seen what Cossus had done, laughed. 'Get your hands off my wife, you old lecher.'

'Not so much of the old,' Cossus protested, falling back

into his chair. He grinned at Lolly. 'I'm your friend too, my lady.'

'I suppose you are,' Lolly raised her cup to him, 'after what you've done for us.'

'Not entirely selflessly,' Cossus said. 'I shall expect great things from you when you're king, Lucius.'

'I know, and you'll get them,' Lucius said, shifting along on the couch to make room for Lolly.

He wished Cossus wasn't with them in the domus. He wanted to tell Lolly about his morning in the senate house, about the progress he was making with the senators. They had listened intently to him that morning after Servius had left. He'd heard them express their concerns that Servius was making himself ill by working too hard, and he had done what he could to fan those concerns. He'd had an eager audience and not a few had taken him aside and said they looked forward to the time when he would be king. He'd had to bite his tongue then, knowing those admissions were enough for now. Their words were something to build on. But how much longer would he have to wait?

'When will I get them?' Cossus asked and Lucius heard the steel in his voice that told the question wasn't an idle one.

'Soon enough, Cossus,' Lolly said, glancing at Lucius. 'We're not going to rush and risk ruining everything we've worked for.'

'Take too long and people will forget everything you've told them,' Cossus said. 'People have short memories. And Servius's health may improve. He may even marry again, have you considered that? And what if he does marry and has a son? Baby or not, it might be enough to convince the senate that son should be king.'

Lolly put out a hand to stop Lucius answering. 'Even if that were to happen, which it won't, a baby would need a regent to rule for it until it came of age. Lucius would be the obvious choice for regent.'

'Unless the senate ruled in place of a regent,' Cossus pointed out. 'It could happen.'

'Lolly!' Lucius said urgently.

She patted his hand to calm him. 'It could happen,' she said stiffly, subduing her anger at Cossus. 'It won't.'

'But if—' Lucius began.

'Have you forgotten your horoscope, Lucius?' Lolly said, twisting on the couch to face him. 'It said you would be king. King, not regent.'

'That's right,' Lucius gasped, grabbing her hand and kissing it in his relief. 'Thank the gods I have you, Lolly.'

Lolly turned her head towards Cossus, enjoying the sour look on his face. She understood Cossus much better than he realised. She knew his friendship towards Lucius was only partly sincere. He and Lucius were friends, yes, but Cossus was the type of man who always looked out for himself. His campaigning on Lucius's behalf was so he could reap the rewards when Lucius was made king. Cossus wanted to be Lucius's right hand when he sat on the throne. Well, he could forget that. Lolly would be the person Lucius turned to, not Cossus.

'That horoscope said you would begin your reign in blood,' Cossus said after a moment.

'How do you know that?' Lolly demanded.

'I swore that astrologer to secrecy,' Lucius cried.

Cossus threw back his head and laughed. 'You think that would stop me? I made that little runt tell me as soon as you'd left my house, Lucius.'

'How dare you!' Lolly declared.

Cossus's smile died. 'I dare do lots of things, lady. I dare to say treasonous things to senators, I give senators gold for favours, and I kill women who get in the way, all for your husband.'

Lolly swallowed down the lump in her throat. She felt herself trembling. She wanted to say something harsh, to admonish Cossus for his impertinence, but the words would not come.

'So, if I want to know the future,' Cossus continued, 'I ask.'

Lucius took hold of Lolly's hand and squeezed it. 'It doesn't matter, Lolly,' he said in a low voice. 'We can trust Cossus. Can't we, Cossus?'

Cossus took a mouthful of wine before answering. 'Course you can, old friend.'

'We can trust him to look after his own interests,' Lolly said, emboldened by Lucius's touch.

'We all serve our own interests, lady,' Cossus sneered. 'I do, Lucius does. So do you. So, let's not have any more of you two being on your high horse over what I know, shall we?'

Lolly and Cossus held each other's gaze for a long moment. Then Lolly said, 'Yes.' She glanced at Lucius, who nodded almost imperceptibly.

'So,' Cossus said loudly as if the quarrel had never happened, 'your reign begins in blood, Lucius. When shall we start the bloodletting?'

'I don't understand,' Lucius said hesitantly.

Cossus jerked a laugh and licked his thick lips. 'Yes, you do, you just don't want to admit it. Whose blood do you think the horoscope referred to?'

'My father's,' Lolly said quietly.

'No one else's,' Cossus agreed. 'Servius isn't meant to die of old age, is he?'

'What are you saying?' Lucius asked, his breath catching in his throat.

Cossus put his cup down and leant forward, his elbows on his knees. 'You're not scared of taking bold moves, either of you, and you're not sentimental about family. You've proved that, getting me to kill your mother. I say, why not do the same to your father? And in getting him out of the way, make sure there's no chance for an election to be held.'

'I thought all this palm-pressing I've been doing in the senate has been to make sure I get chosen at an election,' Lucius said. 'Why else have I been putting myself through all that?'

'That's insurance,' Cossus waved Lucius's words away. 'You're still going to need senators on your side once you're king. What I'm talking about is a show of strength. None of this namby-pamby asking people to like you. You should take the throne from Servius.'

'Are you so very tired of waiting, Cossus?' Lolly asked sardonically, raising an eyebrow.

'You bet I am, lady,' he said. 'And so is Lucius. And if you're honest with yourself, so are you.'

'Well, Lolly?' Lucius said. 'What do you think?'

Lolly stared at Cossus for a long moment, then slowly turned her face towards Lucius. She nodded. 'I think Cossus is right, Lucius. Father has to die.'

———

Sweat was prickling all over Lucius's body. It wasn't just the heat in the forum, though he wished he could put it down to that. He was nervous. No, he was more than nervous, he was terrified. It had been exciting to talk about taking the throne with Lolly and Cossus, and not only exciting but easy. Cossus had a way of making everything seem achievable; he never saw problems, at least none that couldn't be overcome by violence.

Lucius would have felt stronger had Lolly been with him. But women weren't allowed in the senate and she was forced to wait for him back at the domus. *Waiting to hear the good news*, he thought, bile rising in his throat. It suddenly occurred to him that he could go home, turn around, walk out of the forum and return to the domus, and no one would be any the wiser. He could do that, he thought, except that Lolly would never forgive him.

The previous night he had gathered Lolly up in his arms, kissed the top of her head and asked her if she was sure. She had angled her face towards him and thanked him for thinking to ask. For a moment, he thought she had changed her mind, but then she smiled and said she was certain, that it was the only way they could be sure he would become king. He loved her for those words. When Lucius thought of what Lolly had done, the sacrifices she had made just to give him his heart's desire, he could only shake his head in wonderment. Lolly was more than a wife; she was his other self.

Cossus came up to him, checking the buckle of his sword belt. 'Ready?'

Lucius took a deep breath. 'I'm ready,' he nodded, his eyes fixed on the senate house door.

'Don't be nervous,' Cossus ordered.

'I'm not,' Lucius snapped. 'Don't worry about me.'

'Easy for you to say, but I do worry. If you lose your bottle, Lucius, then we're all dead.'

'I told you, I'm fine.' Lucius looked over his shoulder at the men Cossus had assembled to act as bodyguards and a greater collection of thugs Lucius had never seen. Lucius wished he could have used the lictors, but Lolly had pointed out that they would undoubtedly prove more loyal to Servius than to him. Lucius nodded towards the men. 'Do they know what to do?'

'You needn't worry about them,' Cossus said. 'They've been told they're here to protect you, not to start a fight. '

'And if a fight breaks out?'

Cossus laughed. 'Then they've got my permission to enjoy themselves. But it won't come to that, Lucius. This is going to be a walkover. Believe me, there's no one in Rome who'll stand up to us.'

Lucius set his jaw and nodded. 'All right, let's go then.'

Cossus grinned and made a mock bow. 'After you, my king.'

Lucius started towards the senate house. He felt Cossus behind him and heard the men following, knowing they were being watched by the people. Some called out, asking Lucius what was going on. He ignored them, not wanting to be distracted.

The senate seemed huge without any senators to fill it. Cossus's hired men remained outside the doors while Cossus and Lucius entered, their footsteps echoing in the empty hall.

Cossus looked around. 'No one here but the heralds,' he confirmed. 'Now.'

Lucius took a deep breath and turned back to the doors, to the throne that stood in their shadow. It was a large wooden chair, straight-backed with the seat forming a semi-circle, curving up to become its arms. The wood shone for it was polished daily with beeswax. An immaculate fleece, kept white through washing and swiftly replaced when it started to deteriorate, lay across the seat. Lucius put his hand reverently on the back of the chair and stroked the wood.

'What are you waiting for?' Cossus asked, frowning.

Lucius's jaw tightened, annoyed at Cossus for trying to rush him.

But Cossus had never been good at being patient. 'Get on with it,' he growled, spying one of the heralds who stood guard in the senate heading for them. 'You've got an audience.' He jerked his head at the doorway. People in the forum were craning their necks to see what was happening in the senate house.

Lucius moved around the throne and lowered himself onto it, his body trembling. As soon as he sat, he felt enveloped by the chair, embraced by it, and it felt as if it belonged to him.

He looked across to Cossus and laughed almost disbelievingly. He would never have admitted it, but Lucius had half-feared Jupiter would strike him dead with a thunderbolt for daring to sit on the throne. But there was no thunderbolt. Jupiter was not displeased.

Lucius was not allowed to enjoy himself for long. Some curious folk had poked their heads around the corner of the doorway and rushed off to tell others in the forum that Lucius was sitting on the throne. Even now, Lucius could see people pointing and talking to their neighbours, the news spreading like ripples on a pond.

'My lord prince?'

Lucius turned. One of the heralds was standing by the throne, utter perplexity in his expression.

'Summon the senators,' Lucius told him, feeling Cossus move closer. 'Inform them their king wants to see them.'

The herald stared open-mouthed at Lucius, not comprehending.

'Go,' Cossus barked, drawing his sword a little out of its scabbard. The herald hurried out of the senate and down the steps, disappearing into the crowd.

'How long do you think we'll have to wait?' Lucius asked Cossus.

'Not long,' Cossus said. 'Word will have got around that we're here. Mark my words, all those senators who have been lounging on their couches, stuffing their faces this morning will be rushing here to find out what's going on.'

'I told the herald their king wanted to see them.' Lucius banged his hand on the arm of the chair. 'I should have said King Lucius. They will think it's Servius who's summoned them. I should have said King Lucius.'

'You're starting to panic, Lucius,' Cossus said unsympathetically. 'Don't. Keep your nerve.'

It was easy for Cossus to say but it was an anxious wait for Lucius, sitting there on the throne with a thousand eyes upon him. But he couldn't turn back now. He could do nothing but wait.

'Look there,' Cossus said when ten minutes had passed. Lucius looked up at him and saw him jerk his chin towards the Sacra Via's entrance into the forum. People were trying to get through but were being hindered by the press of bodies. 'They're coming. I told you they would.'

Lucius watched and waited until the toga-clad senators bustled into the senate, clustering around the throne. He felt like laughing. They all looked so confused.

'Senators of Rome,' Lucius said when the crowd had quieted, expectant, 'I have summoned you here to make a historic announcement. Servius Tullius is no longer King of Rome. I am now your king. I, who am descended from a true king, Lucius Tarquinius. You have all been defrauded by Servius Tullius, a man born of a whore and slave, a man not fit to govern noble men such as you. Servius Tullius took advantage of my grandfather's murder to install himself on the throne of Rome without recourse to your good advice and permission. He did not stand for election. Servius Tullius usurped the throne of Rome and has kept a firm hold of it ever since. But no longer. I am ready, with your consent, and the consent of the people, to take his place and become your king. Unlike Servius Tullius, I will respect your rights as patricians. I will not steal land from you and give it away to those who have no right or claim to it. I will not tax you so unjustly that you are unable to maintain your estates. In short, I will treat you with the respect you deserve, as I hope you will treat me.'

He felt he had spoken the speech well. He and Lolly had spent half the previous day writing it and Lucius most of the night learning it by heart. It was a good speech, succinct, direct. The senators should have liked it. So, why were they silent? He felt his muscles tense and he longed to jump up from the throne. But he knew he must not. He must sit still and not fidget. He must not give any sign that he was panicking. *But, please, someone say something*, he thought, *someone speak.*

Someone started to clap, slowly at first, then faster and faster. That clap was joined by another, and another, and another. Lucius's heart began to beat again, his muscles relaxed. Oh, the noise of their adulation was joyous. It was what he had been born to hear. If only Lolly could have witnessed this. How proud she would be. Lucius smiled beneficently on the senators.

And then Servius appeared in the doorway.

———

Servius stared at Lucius. 'What do you think you're doing?'

Lucius stared at his father-in-law, shocked into silence by Servius's sudden and unexpected appearance.

Servius was panting, trying to catch his breath and ignore the sharp pains in his chest. He had rushed out of the domus when his secretary had burst into his office and told him something was afoot in the senate house, that he had better see for himself. Servius hadn't even waited for his lictors to escort him but run all the way. He waved his arm weakly. 'Get out of that chair. It's not yours.'

Lucius found his voice. 'It is mine,' he shouted. 'My grandfather sat on this throne. My bloodline, Servius, not yours.'

'I was Lucomo's son,' Servius protested.

'You are the son of a slave,' Lucius cried. 'You usurped this throne and no one had the courage to pull you down from it.'

'Is that what you are doing? Do you think you can become king through this stratagem?'

'I am king now, you old fool. See, here I sit and say I am the King and none save you says otherwise.'

Servius looked about him, at the senators who stood nearby. 'They're waiting to see what will happen, Lucius, nothing more. You think they support you? Take away whatever it is you've bribed your so-called supporters with and they will return to me, I promise you.'

'They will not, Servius. They are mine, they will obey you no longer. And they will not stop me now!'

Lucius bolted from the throne and threw his arms around Servius's waist, lifting him off his feet. Servius cried out in astonishment and thrashed in his arms, but he was no match for Lucius. He struggled but could not free himself from Lucius's grip. He cried out for help, but no one came to his aid. Cossus stood with his sword drawn and his men behind him and they were enough to convince any man thinking of helping to think again and reach a different conclusion.

Lucius dragged Servius to the top of the senate steps. Bending his legs and making a great cry, he lifted Servius off his feet and thrust him from his arms. Servius fell, a groan escaping him with each stone step he hit. His body snapped and cracked as bones broke and splintered and blood daubed the stone. Over and over he went, stopping only when he came to the bottom of the steps. He lay motionless, one arm bent beneath his body, blood flowing from his mouth and nose.

No one moved. No one spoke. The crowd looked on the body of their king while Lucius stood alone at the top of the steps, chest heaving, eyes blazing, his face flushed and shining.

Servius wasn't moving. Was he dead? Lucius looked down on his father-in-law, not quite believing what he'd done.

He took his eyes off the mangled body and stared out over the forum. He saw the carts piled high with sacks, saw the oxen and donkeys that pulled them, their ears twitching. He saw the birds perched on the pediments of the Temple of Vesta and of Diana. He saw the people, his people, staring up at him, their mouths open.

What fools they looked with their vacant faces and wide, staring eyes. See how not one of them was brave enough to have stopped him. Was not Bellona truly his mistress and did he not fright his subjects so? Well enough. He wanted his subjects to fear him. He didn't want their respect. What good was their respect? It gave them leave to question, to rebuke. He wanted nothing from them but their obedience.

Lucius shrugged his clothing straight, smoothed back his hair. He turned and re-entered the senate, those senators near the door backing away from him. He met Cossus's eye. There was a glint in it, a silent appreciation for what Lucius had done and Lucius had to stop himself from grinning. He sat back down on the throne.

'Senators,' he said, gesturing for the men to take their seats, 'the reign of Servius is over. I am your king now.'

———

Hands were clutching his arms. He struggled feebly against their grip, thinking they belonged to Lucius. But then he heard voices and recognised none of them. It was not Lucius who bent over him or tugged parts of his body, not that fiend who had realised he was not yet dead and had returned to finish the job.

Servius was pushed up into a sitting position and the movement was agony. He felt pain everywhere: in the arm that hung uselessly by his side, in his bruised and broken ribs, in the skin that had been scraped and torn. Vomit rose in his throat and he belched forth the bread and wine he had consumed when he had been safe at the domus, soiling his disarrayed clothing and bringing with it a foul acrid stench.

'He's alive,' someone said and Servius was grateful for the confirmation. It made sense. To feel pain this acutely could only mean that he breathed still.

Oh, why had he left the domus without his bodyguards? This would not have happened had he only waited for them. He knew he had to get back to the domus, rouse his lictors from whatever torpor kept them and return to arrest Lucius. Lucius must have thought he was dead, otherwise he would not have left him here to be helped to his feet in this way.

'What do we do?' someone asked. 'Do we help him or leave him?'

'He's the King,' another replied.

'The Prince said he was king,' a fearful voice said.

'You want him as king?' the voice came back.

'The senators are with Lucius,' a young voice cried out. 'They're not here with him, are they? If they're not for Servius, it doesn't matter what we think.'

'You spineless cur,' the strong voice said. 'Go, go and wait to see what you should do. Wait for the senators to tell you how to think.' The voice came close to Servius's ear. 'Can you get up?'

I must get back to the domus, Servius thought. He nodded, leaning heavily on his supporter and managing to stand, though a jolt shot through his right leg and made him cry out in pain.

'Shall we carry him?' someone asked and Servius could not tell who spoke. He was fearful. Who could he trust in all this crowd? Someone might offer help only to complete Lucius's terrible crime and kill him dead.

'Leave me alone,' he croaked and tested putting one foot in front of the other. It hurt, but it was bearable. He would get back to the domus, he would.

'Let us help you,' the voice protested.

'Leave me,' Servius growled.

He was left standing alone, mutterings of his ingratitude fading in his bloody ears. He moved his legs again, slowly, painfully, waiting for the pain to ease before moving again. His eyes had become puffy — one was almost swollen shut — and he was unsure where he was going. He hoped he was heading for an exit; there were many of them out of the forum. He begged Fortuna that he would find one. He went blindly, his right arm out in front to test for obstacles. He did not see them but people moved out of his way and their bodies formed a natural corridor to an exit. He determined to keep a straight course and so find his way home.

Lolly was pacing the atrium.

It had been more than two hours since Lucius and Cossus had left for the senate house, almost an hour since she witnessed her father's departure, his toga held up above his knees as he ran out of the domus. She was proud of herself for having the foresight to tell the lictors to take their ease and not worry about guarding her father, her lie that he was content to remain in the domus for the rest of the day all too convincing.

Lolly had wanted to go with Lucius and Cossus, wanting to see her husband take his rightful place on the throne. She was not allowed, of course, no woman was allowed in the senate house. She knew why. Let a woman in to have a say in ruling the country and those old fools would soon see what quick action, decisiveness and power truly meant. All those feeble senators did was talk and debate; they never actually did anything. Well, that was going to change. Lucius and she would rule together and pay no heed to the senators with their stale wind. They would make Rome into what they wanted.

Oh, it was so frustrating, this waiting at home, not knowing what was happening in the senate. Was Lucius safe? Had he taken the throne? Did he have the support of the senators? And what of her father? That was the question most on her mind. They couldn't have predicted how Servius would act, that he would even hear of Lucius's actions before they had a chance to despatch him.

After her fifth dash to the front doors to see if Lucius was returning, she knew she could bear it no longer. She called a servant and ordered her chariot to be got ready. She snatched up a bronze platter from the table and examined her face, turning it from side to side to get a good idea of her appearance in the rippling metal. She patted the underside of her chin, cringing at the little extra flesh that made a slapping sound when she patted it. She would have to watch that, especially now. She didn't want to be known as a fat queen.

Lolly heard the rumble of wheels that signalled her chariot had come round. She hurried out to meet it. Synistor, her chariot driver, held out his hand to help her up onto the tightly woven leather straps. Synistor was the strongest man in the royal household, she choosing him for his muscles, honed during a youth spent felling trees and hacking stone out of the ground. He also had a great deal of knowledge about horses and had bought the two that were harnessed to the chariot. Lolly knew these horses were the best in Rome, probably among the best in the whole of Italy.

She wrapped her right wrist around the leather strap tied to the front of the chariot, a means to keep her steady and prevent her from falling off. 'To the forum,' she told Synistor, 'to the steps of the senate house.'

Synistor flicked the reins and the horses moved off. They were fleet of foot but the narrow streets of the city meant it was not possible to drive too fast. She told Synistor not to take the Sacra Via, knowing it was the route Lucius and Cossus had taken and not wanting to hinder them should they plan to return the same way. Synistor knew his mistress well and gave no quarter to the people who lived and worked on the streets they passed along. They had to move out of the way quickly or risk being trodden beneath the horses' hooves and the wheels of the chariot.

The chariot entered the forum and Synistor was forced to slow the horses to a walking pace. There was no cheering, no shouting, just an eerie stillness. Lolly looked into the faces of the people she passed and she saw wariness in them, not joy, not surprise, not any of the emotions she should be seeing. What had they to be frightened of, the fools?

Synistor drew the chariot up alongside the steps of the senate. Lolly unwound the leather strap from her wrist and stepped down. There was blood on the steps. Whose blood? she wondered and her heart missed a beat. Could something have gone terribly wrong? Could something have happened to Lucius?

She climbed the steps, sidestepping the blood so it wouldn't stain the hem of her dress. The doors to the senate were open; she could see inside but it was dark, the sun now behind the building. But she could see the outline of the throne and it was occupied, she couldn't see who by. But she could see Cossus and her heart leapt. If Cossus was standing by the throne, then Lucius must be on it. Lolly saw Cossus bend and whisper. The figure on the throne turned and looked over his shoulder at her.

Lucius had done it, he had seized the throne. He'd had his moment; it was time for hers. She raised both arms above her head.

Great king,' she called out in a strong, clear voice. 'So I will call you for so you are. You have done a great thing this day and the people of Rome thank you for it.'

Lucius was coming towards her now. *Slow down*, she thought, *you're walking too fast. It's undignified for a king to be in a hurry.*

But Lucius didn't slow down. He came right up to her and grabbed her elbow. 'What are you doing here? I told you to stay at home.'

'I couldn't bear it, being there and not knowing what was happening. But you've done it, Lucius. You have, haven't you?'

Lucius was frowning, looking over her shoulder. 'Where is he?'

'Where's who? Lucius, what is it?'

'Servius, he was there.' Lucius pointed to the base of the steps. 'He was dead. That is, I thought he was dead. Lolly, I threw him down the steps and he wasn't moving.'

'The people will have taken him,' Lolly said quickly. 'That's all. Lucius, look at me. You sit on the throne, do you not? Then it doesn't matter where my father is. Dead or alive, he's gone. He's gone, Lucius.'

'Find him, Lolly,' Lucius said desperately. 'Find him and make sure he's dead. I won't sit easy on the throne until I know he's dead.'

'I'll find him,' Lolly promised with a kiss. 'Now, go back in there. The senators are waiting for you. Be a king, Lucius. For me.'

He smiled thinly and re-entered the senate house. Lolly returned to her chariot, her eyes drawn inexorably to the blood. She wasn't sure what to do, whether she should question the bystanders as to her father's whereabouts or go home and get Cossus to send out his men later. And if she did find her father, what would she do with him?

Synistor held out his hand to help her back into the chariot. 'Lady,' he said as she stepped up next to him, 'I've been talking to some of these people. They've told me your father went off that way,' and he pointed to the Sacra Via exit. 'He was injured but alive.'

'We must follow him,' she said. She moved to tie her wrist to the leather strap again, then changed her mind. 'Give me the reins.'

'My lady?'

'I want to drive.'

'Let me—'

'No. I will drive. Stand aside, Synistor.'

Synistor handed her the reins, then moved behind her and tied his wrist with the leather thong. Lolly snapped the reins against the backs of her horses.

The crowd parted instantly. The horses lifted their hooves and the chariot soon reached the exit, making its way swiftly along the long, straight road. Synistor had taught Lolly well and she handled the chariot expertly. She enjoyed the thrill of controlling the two horses and the lightweight frame beneath her feet, and she almost forgot what she was supposed to be doing. But then, up ahead, she saw a figure in the middle of the street. As the chariot drew nearer, she saw it was a man; nearer still, she saw it was her father.

Lolly didn't stop to think. She snapped the reins again and the horses increased their speed. They were getting closer and closer to her father and had Lolly changed her mind, she knew she wouldn't be able to pull them up in time. But she wouldn't change her mind; she knew exactly what she had to do.

Servius heard the thunder of the horses' hooves and the rattle of the chariot. He stopped, turning to see the equipage bearing down on him. He lifted his arm to protect himself and his startled face was the last Lolly saw of her father before he disappeared beneath the horses' stamping legs. The chariot bucked and tilted as it passed over Servius's body and Lolly pulled on the reins. The horses responded and the chariot stopped.

Lolly turned the chariot around. Servius was on the ground, unmoving.

'You got him, my lady,' Synistor said. 'He's dead.'

'Let's make sure,' Lolly said and drove the horses on, on towards her father. Once again, she drove the chariot over him, stopping and turning it around.

'He can't be alive after that,' Synistor assured her.

'Give me your sword,' she said, holding out her hand.

Synistor drew his sword and gave it to her. 'You should let me,' he said.

'I have to do this,' she replied and stepped down from the chariot. As she walked towards the battered thing that had been her father, she became aware of faces at windows and around door frames. She held her chin a little higher. She would show them the kind of woman she was. Let any who dared try to interfere and just see how she would deal with them.

But no one did dare for they instinctively knew that Lolly did not walk down the street alone. Though invisible, the goddess Bellona was by her side.

Lolly reached her father and knelt beside his body. Synistor had been correct; Servius was dead. She pulled out his arm from beneath his body. Broken bones had ruptured the skin and it made a grinding noise as she pulled. She tugged it to lie flat on the ground, then lifted the sword and brought it down with all her strength. The sword cut easily through the flesh and bone and the hand came away from the arm, blood spattering her dress and pooling where she knelt. She felt the sticky, warm mess seep through the fabric, soaking her knees. She took hold of the severed hand and returned to the chariot.

'Dead, my lady?' Synistor asked wryly.

'Dead,' she returned. 'Take me home, Synistor.'

———

Lucius had said all he wanted to say to the senators. Now, he wanted to get back to the domus, get back to Lolly, find out what had happened to Servius. The only safe former king was a dead former king. If Servius wasn't dead yet, then he would have to be made so as soon as possible.

He and Cossus, and the hired men Cossus said they couldn't afford to dismiss just yet, took a circuitous route back to the Esquiline. The people stared as they passed but none called out 'Vivat Rex'.

'It will come,' Cossus assured him, reading his thoughts.

'Why are they not happy?' Lucius snarled. 'I've deposed a weak king.'

'It's too fresh. Let them reflect. They'll come to see this as good fortune soon enough.'

They reached the domus and saw there were four lictors guarding the doors. 'That's Lolly's doing, I wager,' Cossus said, pleased she had given a thought to their security.

'She has good sense,' Lucius said.

'She has more than that,' Cossus said admiringly. He turned away and spoke to the men, telling them to go around the back and wait in the yard. 'I wouldn't want to face her on a battlefield.'

'Where is she?' Lucius murmured, pushing open the doors. They had barely entered before Lolly was in his arms. Cossus stood by while they kissed, impatient for them to break apart.

'King Lucius,' Lolly said, holding Lucius at arm's length and looking him up and down.

'Are you hurt?' Lucius cried, pointing to her dress and the bloodstains upon the hem. 'Lolly!'

'It's not mine, Lucius,' she assured him as his hands felt her body. 'It's my father's.'

'You found him?'

'Found him. Killed him.'

Cossus stepped forward. 'You killed him?'

Lolly nodded, a smile playing upon her lips. 'I found him

on the Sacra Via. I ran over him twice and then I took a sword and I...'

'What, Lolly?' Lucius pressed, wondering what she was grinning about.

Lolly held out her hand to Lucius. He took it and she pulled him towards the shrine set in the wall of the atrium that held the household gods. She pushed him towards it. 'Look,' she whispered in his ear.

Lucius gasped. There was a hand lying in front of the small statues. There was a ring upon the little finger, the intaglio familiar to him.

'Servius!' he cried and spun around to Lolly.

'Yes,' she nodded. 'I cut it from his body.'

Cossus stepped up and looked at the hand. He laughed. 'Like I said, Lucius, I wouldn't like to meet your wife on the battlefield.'

'He is dead, then?' Lucius asked.

'Do not doubt me,' Lolly said. 'You asked me to find him and I did, and I killed him, for you.'

Lucius cupped her face and kissed her. 'Thank you, my love. What is that noise?'

Cossus hurried to the doors. He opened them just a crack and looked out. 'People are coming.'

Lucius joined him. 'Armed?'

Cossus shook his head. 'No. It's a cart.'

'Who is it?' Lolly asked.

'Nobody important. Wait here.' Cossus opened the door further and stepped outside, pulling the door to behind him.

Lucius put his eye to the crack. He watched as Cossus went to the man pulling the cart and spoke to him. A man at the rear leaned into the back of the cart and lifted a leather tarpaulin to reveal whatever it covered. Cossus looked into the cart and grimaced. He cast a look back at the doors, spoke a few more words to the men and then returned, closing the doors behind him.

'What is it? What is in the cart?' Lolly demanded.

Cossus looked at her. 'Servius. They thought you'd want his body to bury. It's clear they don't know you, eh?' He laughed but neither Lolly nor Lucius joined in with him.

'Tell them to go. And to take the carcase with them,' Lucius said, perturbed. 'They can bury him if they want, but we'll have nothing to do with him. I've had my fill of Servius.'

'Why not bury him?' Cossus asked. 'It'll cost you nothing and it will look good to the people.'

'After his own daughter killed him?' Lolly said. 'Talk sense, Cossus.'

'Every man should have a proper funeral,' Cossus protested.

'Romulus didn't,' Lucius said. 'Show me the tomb of the founder of Rome and I'll give a funeral for Servius.'

'Tell them to throw his body in the Tiber,' Lolly said. Cossus didn't move. 'Lucius, tell your friend to do as I say.'

'Cossus,' Lucius said, not meeting his friend's eye. 'Do as my wife says.'

'As you say,' Cossus said. He went outside again and Lolly and Lucius heard the cart leaving.

'Was I right, Lolly?' Lucius asked.

'Perfectly right,' Lolly said. 'You are the King, Lucius. We have no need to honour a dead man.'

———

Lolly had wanted Lucius to make love to her. The day's events had excited her, but they had wearied him. He had tried to oblige her, but his anxiety and exhaustion shrunk his member and she could not coax it to swell. She had given a loud, irritated sigh as he climbed off her.

'You're thinking again,' she said scornfully. 'Must you?'

'I can't help it,' he protested, knowing she was angry at him for his impotence.

'What can't you help, Lucius? Thinking? Or acting like a eunuch?'

'It's only this once. Must you taunt me, today of all days?'

'I think I shall find a man who can perform,' she mused. 'Synistor will do. I doubt he ever has any complaints.'

'I shall have him killed if he lays a finger on you,' Lucius said heatedly.

'So? I will have had him, wouldn't I? You can do what you like with him after.'

Lucius grabbed her throat. 'I will have your horses pull you apart if you so much as look at another man.'

Her smile was victorious. 'You do still love me then?'

'How can I not, you witch?'

'Then why would I even want another man?'

He released her. 'You taunt me.'

'I tease,' she corrected, 'to make a man of you.'

'Does my manhood lie only in my prick?'

'It's the only part of your manhood I can grab hold of,' she said and reached beneath the sheets.

He laughed as her fingers stroked his thighs and he fell back onto the bed. 'Oh, Lolly, what would I do without you?'

'Nothing. You would lie in bed all day and drink. But not anymore. No life of indolence for you, my King. There is much to do.'

'Is there?'

'Oh, Lucius, you've won today but we cannot pretend all

of the senators are on our side. There will be those who will speak out against us in the senate.'

He hadn't considered that there would be opposition now Servius was dead. The knowledge troubled him. 'We can't prevent them from speaking against me.'

'Oh my sweet, of course we can. We stop their mouths before they can open them. Now, lay down and go to sleep if you're not going to make love to me.'

'You expect me to sleep now you've told me of this?'

'The senators who oppose us will keep until tomorrow.'

But Lucius could not lay down his head and rest. He threw off the sheet and climbed out of bed. Ignoring Lolly's protests, he made his way to the cubiculum at the end of the corridor which Lucius had given to Cossus for the night. He burst in without knocking, causing the woman lying beside Cossus to yelp in surprise.

'What is it? What's wrong?' Cossus asked, sitting up.

'Get rid of her,' Lucius said and waited while the woman climbed naked from the bed, gathering up her clothes from the floor and exiting. 'The senators who will oppose me. Do you know who they are?'

'I know them,' Cossus said, thinking of the list he had drawn up of those men who had never spoken well of Lucius in debates or accepted the bribes that Cossus had offered.

'They must be silenced.'

'What, now?' Cossus cried.

Lucius nodded. 'Now.'

———

Aulus Flavonius watched the smoke rise into the night sky. The funeral pyre had been hastily constructed and had threatened to spill over and tip the half-burnt body to the ground.

But it had been propped up and now burned fiercely, heating the faces of those who watched and leaving their backs to freeze.

What a day it had been! Violent, bloody, and no doubt a sign of things to come. Whether he liked it or not, Lucius was king now but Lucius's reign had begun in blood and Aulus firmly believed it would continue the same way. Lucius was not a man of peace.

'Is Servius in Elysium now or in the Underworld, do you think?' Acacius Arco said, tightening his cloak around himself.

'If ever a man deserved to be in Elysium, it was Servius,' Aulus said.

'I never thought to live to see such a day, Aulus.'

'It bodes ill, Acacius.'

'Ay, it does.'

'Tomorrow, we must speak against Lucius.' Aulus waited. 'You say nothing.'

'Lucius has taken the throne, Aulus,' Acacius said resignedly.

'Exactly, he has taken it. We did not elect him. I know why you say nothing, my friend. You're frightened, and no wonder, when Lucius has that she-wolf by his side.'

'They are a fearsome prospect, Aulus.'

'Are we women, Acacius?' Aulus demanded fiercely. 'We have fought in wars, we know what it is to run a man through with our swords. Lucius will die as easily as any other man, I promise you.'

'I'm too old to go to war, Aulus,' Acacius said. 'I want to die in my bed, not on some battlefield, or even in the senate.'

'We would all like to have quiet lives, Acacius,' Aulus said, putting a hand on his friend's arm. 'But Bellona seems to rule in Rome, not Pax.'

'If the goddess Bellona favours Lucius Tarquinius…'

'Then the answer is simple. We must offer her more than he,' Aulus said. 'We will make a sacrifice tomorrow to Bellona and to Pax, Acacius, you and I, and all our fellow senators who honour Servius here with us.' He gestured at the men who stood by the pyre as it burned. 'We will pray to them to be reconciled. And they will hear us.'

'I hear you,' a voice behind them, 'and I'm not liking what I hear.'

Aulus and Acacius spun around. Cossus was grinning at them. Acacius gave a strangled cry of fright and tried to run, but he ran straight into one of Cossus's hired men, who held him, laughing.

'Lucius has sent you,' Aulus said, watching and understanding as the other mourners were taken by Cossus's men as Acacius had been.

'Oh, you are clever, aren't you?' Cossus said. 'I see now why you're a senator and I'm not.'

'I'm a senator because I'm not available for hire, unlike you,' Aulus sneered. 'If you are the kind of men King Lucius will have about him, I pity Rome.'

'That's all right. You won't have to pity Rome for long,' Cossus promised and thrust forward with his sword.

Aulus felt the blade pierce his skin, felt the keenest pain in his heart, and saw only Cossus's ugly, grinning face before he fell.

19

For no ordinary woman, the Sibyl arrived ordinarily enough.

She entered the city on foot, a shabby woollen cloak covering her head and body, a leather bag slung over her shoulder. She had no need for finery, nor for escort, for she was protected by the gods. Should anyone be fool enough to trespass within a foot of her person, they would see the wrath of Jupiter and Mars and Bellona in her eyes and quickly retreat, making the sign against evil behind their backs so she would not see and curse them all the same.

Her eyes were bright though they were black. They shone out of their pure white surround and stood stark against the dirt ingrained into her face. Her body was thin, scrawny, and it made her seem older than her twenty-four years.

She made her way along the Sacra Via to reach the Esquiline Hill and the home of King Lucius. Arriving at the doors, she told the guards she wanted to see the King, and they looked at one another, something telling them this person was no mere petitioner nor woman looking for work in the household. Though she was shabby, there was something in her bearing that made them open the doors and escort her into the atrium. Summoning a lictor, the guard told him what the visitor wanted. The lictor, having greater responsibility and daily access to a king and queen, was not so easily overwhelmed and demanded to know who she thought she was that she could command an audience with the King.

'Tell King Lucius the Sibyl of Cumae has come to make him an offer,' she said quietly.

Abashed, the lictor nodded, almost bowed, and hurried off to find Lucius. The guard left alone with the Sibyl stood uneasily to one side as if at any moment she might turn and deliver a prophecy about him that he would not wish to hear. Just when the guard was wondering whether he should offer her a seat or a drink, the lictor returned and asked the Sibyl to follow him.

———

Lolly laid the gold necklace she had been examining carefully on its protective linen wrap. 'Is she really the Sibyl?'

'I suppose we'll find out,' Lucius said, flicking his fingers at her to help him put on his toga.

She rose and slapped his hands away, setting right the heavy cloth. 'But why has she come here?'

'Will you stop asking questions you know I don't have the answer to?' Lucius snapped. 'Just be quiet.'

Lolly sighed and resumed her seat, irritated by Lucius's anxiety over the woman who had come to see him. He was ridiculously superstitious. So, she had a fearsome reputation, Lolly thought, what of it? Any woman could claim to hear the voice of a god or goddess and speak for them. Who was to say she was telling the truth and not just spouting any old nonsense that came into her head? And these women would have such reverence paid to them!

'Well, this better not be a waste of your time,' she said, breaking off as the lictor entered with a woman following slowly behind.

She was not much to look at, Lolly mused, taking in the woman's drab appearance, but she had to admit there was an aura about her. She understood why the lictor had spoken in hushed tones of her arrival.

'You claim to be the Sibyl of Cumae,' Lucius said, doing the woman the honour of standing in her presence.

'I do not claim to be,' the Sibyl said with a hint of amusement. 'I am.'

'And you travel alone?' Lolly asked, surprised, for the lictor had said the woman had arrived without any companion, a brave choice for any woman.

'I am never alone,' the Sibyl replied smoothly. 'The gods are always with me. They protect me from harm.'

Lucius gestured to the couch and the Sibyl sat. Lucius sat next to Lolly and she sensed his nervousness.

'You said something about an offer,' Lucius said.

The Sibyl allowed the strap of her leather bag to slide off her shoulder, catching the bag before it fell to the ground. She opened the flap and held the bag towards them. Lolly and Lucius craned their necks to see the contents. The bag was stuffed with scrolls, some of the wooden finials poking out the top of the opening.

'Books?' Lucius asked.

'Prophecies pronounced by my predecessor,' the Sibyl said. 'Nine books about the future of Rome. And of your future, King Lucius Tarquinius. I offer them to you.'

'Oh, well, I thank you—,' Lucius began.

'For the right price, of course,' the Sibyl smiled sweetly, her black eyes glinting in the light of the oil lamps that burned around her.

'And what is the right price?' Lolly asked after a moment, her voice arch, cold. The Sibyl was just another person with their hand out, then. How these people did come out of the woodwork.

'Five hundred aes,' the Sibyl said.

'Five hundred,' spluttered Lucius. 'Are you insane?'

The smile vanished from the Sibyl's face and Lolly placed a restraining hand upon Lucius's arm. He looked to her and her eyes told him to be quiet.

'That is a very great price,' Lolly said carefully. It was never wise to insult and offend a person of such reputation as the Sibyl, nor a woman who claimed she could call on the gods for protection, even if that reputation was dubious. 'How do we know your prophecies are worth such a sum?'

'You don't,' the Sibyl said. 'You will find out what they are worth when you buy them from me.'

'What will you do with five hundred aes?' Lucius asked, content to be silent no longer. 'What does a prophetess need with such riches?'

'Your contempt does you no favours, King Lucius,' the Sibyl said, fixing her gaze upon him. 'A prophetess must needs eat, clothe herself, keep temples to the gods in good repair. If a king needs riches, why not a prophetess?'

'I may need riches,' Lucius said, his temper rising, 'but I don't need books telling me about my future. I already know it.'

'Are you sure you know all?' the Sibyl asked, raising an eyebrow.

'I'm sure,' Lucius said, waving Lolly to be quiet. He rose. 'You can leave now.' He clicked his fingers at the lictor who stepped forward, his face still bearing an expression of awe.

The Sibyl closed her bag and returned the strap to her

shoulder. She smiled, unperturbed, and followed the lictor from the room.

————

The Sibyl walked out of the domus without another word, the guards holding their breath as she passed. She made her way to the forum, the hood of her cloak up, obscuring her face. She might have been any other Roman woman, and yet her presence was such that people made way for her, whispering behind their hands as she passed.

In the forum, she looked for a fire and spotting a brazier by the Temple of Vesta, walked towards it, opening the bag as she went. She took out three of the scrolls and placed them one by one in the brazier, standing back and watching while the parchment caught and burned.

————

The lictor hurried into the garden where the family were enjoying a puppet show. A Greek soldier was being hacked down by a Roman when he blurted, 'The Sibyl has returned and demands to see you, my lord.'

'Who's the Sibyl?' Sextus asked, knocking his feet against the legs of his brother's stool.

'She has the effrontery to return?' Lucius said to Lolly.

Lolly didn't answer. Her brow furrowed, she told the lictor to bring the Sibyl to the garden and the children to go to the nursery. Titus protested, but Lolly was adamant and the nurse shooed her charges away. A slave was told to remove the puppeteer and Lolly and Lucius were alone. Lucius's face bore an angry expression that Lolly tried to avoid, but the Sibyl's persistence worried her. What was in those bloody books that made the Sibyl so sure of herself? The sum the woman wanted was great, but Lolly was now thinking it was a sum worth paying to find out.

'I am not paying that woman five hundred aes for nine books I have no intention of reading,' Lucius told her.

'You won't be paying me five hundred aes for nine books,' a voice said, making Lolly and Lucius jump. 'You'll be paying me five hundred aes for six books.'

'What do you mean?' Lucius asked the Sibyl.

'I mean, King Lucius, that I burnt three of the books yesterday. There are six left. Now, will you pay me the sum I named?'

'You really must be mad,' Lucius said. 'If I wasn't going to pay you for nine, why would I pay you for only six?'

'Because you want to know what is in the books,' the Sibyl said as if the answer was obvious.

'Could we perhaps just look at the books?' Lolly asked, pointing at the leather bag over the Sibyl's shoulder. 'Just to ascertain that they are worth what you ask?'

The Sibyl gave her an unflinching stare. 'No, lady, you may not.'

'Well,' Lolly said, glancing back at Lucius, 'perhaps we could manage three hundred?'

'Don't pander to her, Lolly,' Lucius said angrily. 'We'll pay her nothing. You've had another wasted journey, Sibyl. You'll get nothing from me.'

'Very well,' the Sibyl said, seemingly not at all discouraged by Lucius's response. She once more followed the lictor as he led her from the domus, not even waiting for Lucius's dismissal.

'Lucius,' Lolly whined as they went.

'Enough, Lolly,' Lucius snapped. 'The woman's a fraud.'

'We don't know that. There must be something in those

books to make her so sure of herself. You're the one who worries about curses and prophecies. Wouldn't you rather know what the future held? Even if it does cost so much?'

'I already know my future. I had my horoscope read, remember?'

'But can you be sure that the astrologer told you the truth?' Lolly asked earnestly. 'After all, he told Cossus what he had said to you after swearing he wouldn't.'

Lucius didn't answer. Maybe he had made a mistake in dismissing the Sibyl, but it was done now and he wouldn't humiliate himself by having someone go after her and bring her back.

While Lolly and Lucius were arguing, the Sibyl made her way to the forum again, walked up to the brazier by the Temple of Vesta, and burnt three more of the books in her bag.

———

'She's back,' Lolly said quietly. 'She's waiting in the atrium. Here.' She waved a slave into the room and he deposited a small chest on the table before Lucius. 'There's five hundred aes in there. Give it to her.'

'No,' Lucius said shortly.

'Lucius.' Rushing to him, Lolly grabbed his chin and jerked his face towards hers. 'Give her the money. What she has may be nothing but I'm not risking our future and the future of our children for a few ingots.'

'It's not a few—'

'Give her what she wants,' Lolly pleaded.

'Wise advice, lady,' the Sibyl said behind her, having not waited for the lictor to announce her.

Lolly turned to her, her heart beating fast. 'There's five hundred aes in there,' she pointed to the chest.

'And there are three books left in here,' the Sibyl said, gesturing at her bag.

'Only three?' Lucius said.

'I burnt three more because of your intransigence. I would have burnt these last three if you had still refused to pay.'

Lucius gave a mirthless laugh. 'You cannot ask for five hundred aes for only a third of what you originally offered.'

'Can I not?' the Sibyl's eyebrow raised again. 'Then I shall return to Cumae, after I have burnt these three.'

'Wait,' Lolly called desperately as the Sibyl turned to leave. 'We will pay. Take the chest and leave the books.' She put out her hand to stop Lucius, who was about to grab the chest himself. She turned her face to him and her pained expression convinced him. He nodded and gestured to the Sibyl that the chest was hers. He fell back onto the couch, angry at Lolly.

The Sibyl smiled. 'You should have persuaded your husband to see sense before we came to this pass, lady,' she said, taking out the last three scrolls and placing them on a table by one of the couches. 'Much has been lost.'

Lolly picked up the scrolls reverently. 'There are no copies of those that were burnt?'

'None. That's what made them valuable.' The Sibyl bent and picked up the chest. It was heavy and she had to hold it in both arms. 'I hope you make good use of those, King Lucius, if you find anything of value in them.'

'Thank you, Lucius,' Lolly said, kissing his chastely on the cheek when the Sibyl had gone.

He softened. 'That better be the last we see of her,' Lucius muttered, 'and you can forget about buying any more silks or jewellery for a while.'

Lolly knew that was her punishment for defying him and giving in to the Sibyl rather than the fact they couldn't afford them. She didn't mind. 'Let's see what's in these,' she said, picking up one of the scrolls.

———

Sextus had seen the Sibyl leave and rushed up to his mother. 'Tell me what she said,' he said, bouncing around Lolly excitedly.

'Go to your room, Sextus,' Lucius said, holding out his hand to stop his son getting too near the valuable scrolls.

'You always tell me to go away when something interesting has happened,' Sextus whined. 'I can stay, can't I, Mother?'

But Lolly was too absorbed to pay her youngest son much attention. 'What? Oh, no, Sextus, go and play. Your father and I are busy.' She picked up one of the scrolls, untied the twine and carefully unfurled the parchment. It cracked ominously and she winced.

'Be careful, Lolly,' Lucius said. 'These cost a fortune.'

'I know,' she said through gritted teeth, pulling the paper a little further. 'Sextus, be careful!'

Sextus had knocked his mother's shoulder as he craned his neck to look. 'What's that?' he asked, screwing up his face as he tried to read the words.

Lolly looked over the top of the scroll at Lucius. 'It's in Greek,' she told him. 'I can't read these. Does your secretary know Greek?'

'I doubt it,' Lucius said, holding out his hand for the scroll. 'We'll have to get a Greek slave to read it. Do we have one?'

'You're mad if you think I'm going to entrust these to a

slave,' Lolly said, taking the scroll back as if she thought he was going to find a Greek slave there and then. 'We don't know what's in them.'

'Then what do you suggest?' Lucius asked, sitting back as Sextus forced himself onto his father's lap. He wrapped his arms around his son's waist and rested his chin on the small shoulder.

'Is there anyone we know who can read Greek and who we can trust?' Lolly wondered.

'You're not asking much, are you?' Lucius asked sarcastically.

'There must be someone,' Lolly sighed and they both lapsed into silence as they tried to think.

'Doesn't Uncle Manius speak Greek?' Sextus asked, picking up his father's wine and taking a sip. 'He tried to teach me when we went to his farm last summer.'

Lolly and Lucius looked at one another and burst out laughing. Sextus stared at both his parents and asked indignantly what was so funny.

'Nothing, my boy,' Lucius said, ruffling his son's curls. 'You've just managed to find the very person we need and you didn't even realise it. What a clever boy you are.'

―――――

Manius dropped his leather bag on the floor of the atrium and fixed a smile onto his face as Lucius came towards him.

He had received the summons to Rome four days earlier. The note, handwritten by Lucius, had been brief: *I need you. Come to Rome. You'll stay with us.* No mention of why he was needed and no consideration that it might be inconvenient to leave his farm.

It was inconvenient. Manius's father had recently died

and it had become rapidly clear that his old age and decrepi-tude had caused some mismanagement of the farm to occur. Manius was having to work twice as hard as normal to try to sort the farm out properly. Some suppliers had been paid twice for goods received and never owned up; other suppliers hadn't been paid at all and were talking about redress. Two of the head farm workers who hadn't been paid for months had left to take up work elsewhere and four of the slaves had fallen sick and died, leaving him with a labour shortfall.

Manius had considered writing back that he couldn't possibly come to Rome at such a time, but his wife had reminded him that one could not simply refuse the King, especially not a king with such as wife as Lolly, a woman who could drive over her father's body and cut off his hand without flinching. So, Manius had watched as his wife packed his bag with bread and cheese wrapped in muslin for the journey and ensured he carried a stout stick to protect himself.

'Manius, it is good of you to come,' Lucius said, embracing him.

'You said you needed me,' Manius said, 'and it's nice to be needed.'

'Come through.' Lucius put his arm around Manius's shoulder and led him to the garden. 'Lolly! Manius is here.'

She was still a pretty thing, Manius thought as Lolly came towards him with her arms wide. She'd only put on a little weight after having the children and her hair still looked thick and lustrous. He took her hand and kissed it.

'Manius,' she said with a smile that made her cheeks dimple, 'it's been too long. I've told Lucius he should have invited you to visit us sooner.'

So, we're pretending this is a friendly visit, Manius thought. 'Well, I'm not sure I could have come had you invited me. I've been so busy with the farm.' And still am, he felt like adding.

'Yes, of course,' Lolly simpered, taking his arm and leading him to one of the stone benches. As he sat his nostrils were filled with the scent of lavender. 'We were so sorry to hear about your father.'

'It was a relief, actually, when he died. He was in a great deal of pain towards the end. It's hard to watch your father suffering.' Manius saw Lolly catch Lucius's eye and he could have kicked himself. Lolly had had no qualms about making her father suffer. He hurried to cover up his gaffe. 'Anyway, what do you need me for?'

Lucius opened his mouth to reply, but Lolly spoke first. 'No rush, Manius. It's only a little thing, but we thought you were the best man to help us with it. Let's get you settled in and then we'll show you later. Come, I'll take you to your room.'

Lolly rose and Manius did the same, hooking his bag back over his shoulder. Lucius smiled at him as he passed, but there was a thoughtful look on his face that Manius recognised. It was no little thing they needed from him, he realised, despite Lolly's assurance, but they wanted to pretend it was. Despite his annoyance at being summoned so peremptorily, Manius found his interest was piqued.

———

'Well?' Lucius looked up at Manius. 'You can read them, can't you?'

Manius nodded. 'Yes, I can read them, but I'm not sure I'm understand them.'

'Why not?' Lolly said, moving her stool nearer. 'Are they in code?'

'More like riddles,' Manius said, drawing his finger along a line of text. 'You know, you really should get a priest to take a look. They'll understand more than I will.'

'No,' Lolly said sharply, then tempering her tone with a smile. 'These may be nothing. Foolish writings by an insane woman for all we know. A priest would probably want to make something out of it and then there would be gossip.'

'It's best we keep these, whatever is in these, to ourselves,' Lucius agreed.

'Not that we expect much,' Lolly said with a nonchalant shrug. 'We didn't think much of the Sibyl who delivered them, did we, Lucius?'

'What? Oh, no. Didn't look anything like you would expect.'

'What did you expect?' Manius asked sardonically. 'Sibyls come in all shapes and sizes.'

'Do they? And how would you know?' Lucius bit back, not liking Manius's tone.

'That's why, Lucius,' Lolly's tone was warning, 'we need Manius. He obviously knows about these things. So, what can you tell us?'

'Here,' Manius pointed to a line halfway down the exposed page, 'it seems to be referring to an enemy of Rome, one that must be defeated with cunning rather than arms. But I can't see that it says who the enemy is or when it will happen.'

'For Jupiter's sake, what use is that?' Lucius shook his head.

'And it goes on that the cunning person will not be revered but reviled.'

'But it doesn't say who that is?' Lolly asked earnestly.

Manius searched the text. 'Not that I can see.'

She tutted. 'Anything else?' Lolly tapped the parchment.

'Plenty of things I don't understand. But this one,' Manius pointed to the scroll he had in front of him, 'doesn't seem to deal with Rome much at all. This one has a bit more in it,' he said, pulling over another. 'You see, here, it says a child of Rome will bring shame on his father and bring down his house through the virtue of a woman. But again, it doesn't say when or give any names.'

'And the last one?' Lucius asked, growing bored.

Manius shook his head. 'As far as I can tell, there's nothing in it that relates to Rome. Plenty of talk about Egypt, but that's all.' He let the scroll roll up. 'You look disappointed,' he said to Lolly.

'No,' she lied with a drawn-out sigh.

'Well, I am,' Lucius said. 'Five hundred aes we paid for that load of rubbish.'

'Five hundred?' Manius was astonished. He had never seen such wealth, let alone have it to buy books with.

'We don't know what was in the other books,' Lolly reminded Lucius. 'If you hadn't made such a fuss about paying her—'

'Oh, so it's my fault,' Lucius said.

'Well, it isn't mine. I said we should pay her. Who knows what we might have learnt from those other six books.'

'If those three are anything to go by, nothing at all,' Lucius said, snatching up a fig from the plate on the table and biting down hard.

'Their meanings aren't clear to us now,' Manius said, thinking he deserved some thanks for his efforts and realising he probably wasn't going to get any. 'That doesn't mean they won't be understood in time.'

'Probably long after they might have been of any use to us,' Lucius said. 'Oh, put them away, Manius. I've had enough.'

'What will you do with them?' Manius asked, depositing the scrolls gently into a circular box and closing the lid.

'Throw them on the fire?' Lucius suggested.

'Don't be ridiculous, Lucius,' Lolly scolded. 'We'll have them stored in the temple. Manius is right. They may be of use one day.'

———

'Thank you for coming,' Lucius said, resting his head on the back of the couch.

Finally, Manius thought, pouring himself another cup of wine. The three books of prophecy had been taken away, Lucius's most trusted secretary given the task of transporting them to the temple, with strict instructions he was not to show them to anyone. Manius thought Lolly was being overcautious. The scrolls were of interest certainly as a literary, perhaps even historical, record, but only a priest or scholar would be able to glean any meaning from them, and then what good would it do?

Manius had always been scornful of prophecies, soothsayers and the like. His mother had consulted astrologers and soothsayers about the fortune of the farm and Manius had always held that its success lay in clever management, not the spurious predictions of mystics. More to the point, he doubted that had the scrolls explicitly said an action of Lucius's would lead to such-and-such event, that Lucius would be able to change his mind and act differently to avoid it. Manius knew his friend. Once Lucius's mind was made up, it was fiendishly difficult to change it.

'Still enjoying your life in the country?' Lucius asked.

'I'm busy, I told you,' Manius said. 'I never realised how much there was to do.'

'You have a farm manager, don't you?'

'He's new to the job. Still learning. I dare not leave him. Not yet.'

'How soon before you can?'

Manius frowned at Lucius. 'Why are you asking?'

Lucius nibbled on his bottom lip before answering. 'The truth is, I'd rather like to have you here in Rome.'

'Don't you have anyone to go drinking with?' Manius asked, tipping up his empty glass and looking around for another jug. 'Cossus is still around, isn't he?'

'I'm not talking about drinking, Manius.' Lucius passed Manius his own jug of wine. 'Cossus is good as a bodyguard, as someone I can use to threaten. That's what he's good at, but I can't really take him into the senate and pass him off as an adviser. He scares the shit out of the senators.'

The wine was doing its work and Manius felt warmed through from the top of his head to his toes. It felt good to sit here with exceptionally good wine — where did Lucius get it from? It was so much better than the stuff Manius produced on his farm — and be able to forget about lazy workers and mice in the grain stores and whether the harvest was going to be good or bad this year. Manius did like Rome. He liked the bustle, the shops, the temples. He even liked the people, the sheer quantity of them. In the country, on his estate, he could talk to his family or he could talk with the staff, and sometimes, neither appealed. And there were times when he felt he was rusticating in the country. All that education he had had, sitting alongside Lucius and Cossus in the schoolroom, somehow seemed wasted in the country. What had his father educated him for if not a life in politics?

'He scares the shit out of me,' Manius said, only half-joking.

'So, you don't want me to ask him to join us later?' Lucius asked with a cheeky smile.

Manius made a face. 'I'd rather you didn't. A little of Cossus goes a long way.'

'So, what do you think?'

'About what?' Manius's mind was becoming a little clouded.

'About coming back to Rome,' Lucius said irritably, 'about staying in Rome, being a senator, working with me.'

'You need my help?'

Manius saw Lucius's face darken a little and remembered how Lucius hated to be thought of as needing anyone or anything. How little his old friend had changed.

'Yes,' Lucius admitted eventually, keeping his eyes on his cup.

Manius relished the admission for a long moment. It was delicious — the King of Rome, Lucius Tarquinius — asking for his help. But then he remembered how Lucius had come to the throne, the brutality of Servius's deposition. The news had shocked Manius's small community, and his neighbours had stared at him and asked him how he could call a man like Lucius friend. 'I'm not sure.'

Lucius snorted. 'I said you wouldn't agree. But Lolly wanted me to ask you.'

'Lolly did?' Manius was surprised. He hadn't thought Lolly particularly liked him.

'She said you would be best. For what we have planned.'

Oh, so that was it. Lolly had looked at Lucius's friends and worked out who would play best with the senators, who was approachable and not intimidating, who best could make Lucius appear amenable, kind even. Manius didn't really want to be Lolly's tool, but curiosity made him ask, 'What do you have planned?'

'Well, I say planned. They're just ideas at the moment, really.'

'Tell me,' Manius prompted.

Lucius sighed. 'Make changes to the law courts so I have more direct authority. Reduce the number of senators so they actually have a chance of agreeing on policies rather than debating all the time. And make new alliances, strengthen our position.'

'Those are quite definite ideas,' Manius said, his eyes widening at the scope of Lucius's ambition.

'They're long overdue,' Lucius insisted.

'The first two will be unpopular,' Manius said, the fug of the wine beginning to clear. 'You'll be accused of tyranny, I expect, making yourself the chief authority.'

'I am the King,' Lucius pointed out indignantly.

Manius held up a hand to say he understood. 'The third, new alliances? Do you mean through treaties?'

Lucius licked his lips. 'Not necessarily. Conquest.'

'You want to go to war?'

'Why not? Rome can only grow great if we expand. And to do that, we need to take greater control of Italy. Our nearest neighbours are a thorn in our side, Manius. We need to bring them under control.'

Manius thought for a long moment. It sounded interesting, exciting even. He would quite like to be a part of that. But...

'I can't,' he said regretfully. 'There's just too much for me to do at home. The farm will go under if I leave.'

Lucius was looking upset. *Why does he always do this to me*, Manius thought, annoyed, *make me feel guilty about not doing what he wants? I'm not going to change my mind, I'm not.*

'I'll tell Lolly you said no,' Lucius said, getting up from the couch with a sigh. 'She'll be disappointed.'

'I'm sorry, Lucius,' Manius said, grabbing hold of Lucius's arm as he made to pass. 'If I would, I could. It's just you've asked at the wrong time.'

Lucius halted. 'So, once your farm is running well, you'll come to Rome?'

'Well…' he sputtered, wishing he'd kept his mouth shut.

'You just said—'

'Yes, all right,' Manius said, holding up his hands. 'When the farm is up and running, I'll come to Rome. But you find me a decent house to live in when I come. I'm not living in a pigsty.'

20

It had been a strange five years, Manius mused. Strange, engrossing, and in some respects, downright unpleasant.

He had returned to his farm after his trip to Rome to read the Sibyl's scrolls and thrown himself into his work. It occupied him completely for about three months, and then the farm had settled, had found its rhythm. The labourers were happy, or as happy as labourers ever could be, and the farm was surviving rather than failing. His farm manager, having come to grips with the job, began to resent Manius's interference and Manius found he was needed less and less. He began to grow restless, discontented, until his wife, fed up with his moods, begged him to take up Lucius's offer. She assured him that she had no desire to live in Rome nor be beholden to the Tarquins. So, if he went, he went alone.

Lucius had found him a house a few doors along from the domus on the Esquiline Hill. Lucius even bought it for him, which, so Lucius said with glee, had pissed Cossus off no end. Manius was grateful and knew he was expected to be so. But he didn't care that he was now under obligation to Lucius. He enjoyed being back in Rome, enjoyed using his intellect, enjoyed being Lucius's chief adviser and shaper of policy as Lucius came to rely less and less on the senate.

But Manius knew this was different. This was more Cossus's territory than his. This was conflict, face to face with a sword at his side, not a debate in the senate house with a wax tablet and stylus to hand. If they weren't at battle now, he had an uneasy feeling Lucius was heading towards it. He paused and almost laughed at himself. *Manius, you fool, you're getting old before your time.*

Lucius had meant what he said, Manius had discovered, about extending Rome's authority in Italy. Manius had been surprised that Lucius had extended the hand of friendship to the Latin tribes rather than the sword and they had been pleased to accept. Lucius had even married his daughter to the most important leader of the tribes, Octavius Mamilius, though she, by all accounts, had protested. Manius believed Lolly had locked Cassia in her room and refused her food until she agreed to go through with the marriage. When Manius had visited the domus to talk through some proposed legislation with Lucius, he had found Cassia crying in the garden. Uncle Manius was a favourite with the girl and she had welcomed his avuncular embrace, swearing she hated her mother and that she was actually glad she was to marry Mamilius as it would mean getting away from Lolly. Manius could sympathise; he had never found it easy to be in Lolly's company.

But despite everything Lucius had achieved in reconciling the Latins, there was one tribe who was reluctant to come into Rome's embrace: Aricia.

———

In Ferentina, Lucius was pissing against a tree. As the arc of amber liquid dwindled, he decided that it was almost time. Finishing, he let his toga drop and turned to stare out over the hill behind him. The sun would soon be setting and he had made them wait long enough.

They couldn't see him from the grove, even if they had bothered to look up. The trees gave him cover but allowed him to see through the branches. There were so many of them, he hadn't realised. All the better. When he arrived, he would be the focus of many eyes, not just a few.

He stared harder. Where was Turnus Herdonius? Skulking in his tent probably. Lucius looked over his shoulder and saw Cossus and Manius talking together. Although he knew they had never been friends, they had always at least tolerated one another. But over the last five years, even the facade of civility had gone and they openly loathed one another. The only thing that kept them from sticking swords in each other was Lucius; he had use for them both and they knew it.

'I want to get closer,' he called and they both turned in his direction, breaking off their conversation.

'How close?' Cossus asked as Lucius came towards them.

'So I can hear them,' he said.

'What are you hoping to hear?'

'Nothing in particular,' Lucius shrugged. 'I just want to get an idea of what they're thinking. Turnus is against me.'

'Turnus is against everyone,' Cossus said dismissively.

'I don't care about everyone,' Lucius said. 'Just me.'

'If we all go, they'll hear us,' Manius said.

'We'll leave the men behind for the moment,' Lucius said. 'Just us three. The trees will give us cover. We'll need dark cloaks.'

The necessary cloaks were found and donned and the three men made their way down the hill, going carefully, avoiding any terrain that would betray their presence. At the bottom of the hill, not more than twelve feet from the grove, they each found a tree to hide behind and waited until Turnus Herdonius stepped out of his tent.

Turnus made an impressive figure, Lucius thought with reluctant admiration. He stood a good head taller than most of his countrymen, was thickset without being fat, and had huge knuckly hands. He smacked those hands together as he emerged and immediately got his associates' attention.

'Where is he?' Turns bellowed. 'He invites us all here and then makes us wait. Does the arrogance of this king know no bounds? Is it any wonder his own people call him Tarquin the Proud?'

A rumble of laughter erupted from his audience. 'Not to his face,' someone shouted out and Turnus identified the speaker with an approving wag of his finger.

'They wouldn't dare,' he cried happily, revelling in the laughter he provoked. Then he turned serious. 'Who does this king think he is? Is he hoping that by keeping us waiting, we'll be all the more grateful when he does deign to appear? Is he expecting us to fall to our knees and submit our necks to the Roman yoke?'

His audience murmured.

'And if we do,' Turnus continued, 'what future do we have as independent Latins? Just see how King Lucius treats his own people. He came to the throne in blood; he murders any who oppose him. He continues to silence and put away anyone who speaks or acts against him. If King Lucius can treat his own people in such a way, what care will he have for us?'

The murmurs grew louder, more aggressive. Lucius signalled to Cossus to fetch the men.

'We should leave,' Turnus said and waited. He looked around the group. 'We. Should. Leave. We should pack up our tents, gather our men and go home. Let this king arrive, if he arrives at all, and find none of us here to listen to his false words.'

Lucius stepped out from behind the tree. 'Turnus Herdonius,' he greeted, holding his arms wide. 'How good it is to see you.' He kissed the astonished Turnus on the cheeks. 'You are in good voice, I hear.'

'You've been here all this time?' Turnus asked.

'Well, not all. I was up there,' Lucius pointed to the top of the hill, 'and then I was there,' he pointed to the tree. 'I heard everything you had to say, if that's what you're wondering.'

'Then I don't need to repeat myself,' Turnus said, folding his arms over his massive chest.

'No, you don't.' Lucius turned to the Latins who were watching their interaction with interest. 'Please forgive me for my lateness. I was called upon to act as arbiter in a dispute between father and son and so anxious was I to see them reconciled, I am afraid I lost track of time. And now, the greater part of this day is gone,' he gestured towards the sun that had half disappeared and which had turned the grove a deep orange, 'that I do not want to keep you from your dinner and your beds.' He smiled his most charming smile. "What say you all? Shall we resume in the morning?'

'Do we have anything to resume?' Turnus said, the remark a response to Lucius but directed towards the Latins.

'Oh, I think we do. Don't we?' Lucius appealed to the Latins.

'We've come all this way, Turnus,' one of the Latins said. 'We may as well hear what King Lucius has to say.'

His companions seemed to agree. Some of them had even started to walk away. Turnus watched them go with disappointment in his eyes.

'We'll stay then,' he said. 'But don't take me for a fool. I see you for what you are and I'll make sure they all do too. Till the morning, Lucius.'

Manius joined Lucius as Turnus went back to his tent. 'I didn't hear. What did he say?'

'That I can't fool him. That's he going to convince everyone to do what he wants.'

They both turned as Cossus strode into the grove, at least twenty armed men following.

'Can he?' Manius asked, ignoring him. 'Does he have that kind of influence?'

Lucius stared at his men. 'For the moment, perhaps. We need to change that.'

'How, before the morning?'

'What's going on?' Cossus said, looking around at the emptying grove. 'I've brought the men as you asked.'

'Not needed as it turned out,' Manius said with some satisfaction. 'Lucius talked them into boredom.'

Cossus scowled. 'Are you going to let him talk about you like that?' he said to Lucius.

Lucius ignored him. 'We need a plan,' he said. 'Let's go back to our camp and see what we can come up with.'

He led the way out of the grove, Cossus glowering at Manius, Manius suspecting Lucius already had an idea of how to deal with Turnus.

———

Lucius instructed Manius to arrange for food to be sent in and told Cossus to make sure the flap to the tent was closed. While they waited for the cold pork and beans to arrive, the three men made themselves comfortable on their camp chairs, listening to the talk of the men outside the tent and the occasional female laugh or shout from one of the camp followers.

'Turnus is never going to be a friend to Rome,' Cossus said, putting his feet up on the table and showing Lucius the dirty soles of his shoes.

'You don't know that,' Manius said, frowning at the liberty Cossus insisted on taking with Lucius. 'He agreed to listen.'

'Just to make himself look good,' Cossus said. 'You wait. Tomorrow, he'll spout more of the same shit and he'll take the rest of the Latins with him.'

'Lucius?' Manius asked.

Lucius was playing with a knife, twisting it in his fingers, catching the flame from the oil lamp on the desk in its reflective silver surface. 'Cossus is right,' he said to Manius. 'Turnus won't change.'

'So… what do we do?'

Lucius shrugged. 'We kill him.'

'We kill him?' Manius repeated, eyebrows raised.

'You got a problem with that?' Cossus asked.

'A bit of a problem, yes,' Manius shot back. 'We kill him and the rest of the Latins kill us. We're outnumbered, in case you hadn't noticed.'

Cossus and Lucius glanced at each other and smiled.

'What?' Manius said, infuriated.

'By Dis, you're stupid at times.'

'Cossus, Cossus, be nice,' Lucius said as Manius lunged towards Cossus. 'Manius, sit down. We thought it likely Turnus would oppose me. I just wanted to make sure before we acted.'

Manius glared at Lucius. 'Why didn't you tell me that?'

'Cossus is better at this sort of thing,' Lucius said.

'Better at thuggery.'

Cossus threw a cup at Manius and it caught a glancing

blow on his shoulder. 'Can we get on with it?' he appealed to Lucius.

Lucius nodded and Cossus rose, leaving the tent in two strides. 'Where's he going?' Manius asked.

'He's gone to fetch our means of getting rid of Turnus.'

Cossus returned a few minutes later, pushing a young boy in front of him. 'This is him. He's Turnus's boy.'

Lucius looked the boy over. He was about fourteen, he calculated, scrawny and blotchy skinned. There was a dark purple bruise across his left cheekbone.

'How did you get that?' Lucius asked.

The boy kept his eyes on the floor. 'My master did it, my lord.'

'He's a hard master, then?'

The boy nodded. 'He beats me often.'

'Do you know why you're here?'

'Not really. He,' he glanced up at Cossus, 'said you would give me gold if I did what you wanted.'

'He was right. Two pieces of gold for one night's work. Cossus, get the swords.'

Cossus moved behind Lucius and knelt, opening up a long wooden chest and taking out an armful of sheathed swords. He got back to his feet with a groan that showed his age and returned to stand by the boy.

'You see these swords,' Lucius pointed the boy to the weapons. 'You're going to hide those in your master's tent. And you mustn't let anyone see you do it.'

'I...I don't think I can do that, my lord,' the boy stammered, staring in horror at the swords.

Lucius sighed in irritation. 'Why not?' he said, his voice harder than before.

'I'll be seen.'

'We're paying you to be invisible, boy,' Lucius said. He

saw the boy tremble and took a few deep breaths to calm himself. 'You can do it if you try.'

'I suppose I could go in the back of the tent?' the boy suggested. 'But my master has retired. He's already in the tent.'

Lucius glanced at Cossus. 'Can we do something about Turnus?'

Cossus nodded. 'I'll go and invite him for a drink. Make him come out to the fire. The boy can do it then.'

Lucius returned his gaze to the boy. 'There. You can do it, yes?'

The boy looked from Lucius to Cossus and back again. 'Yes, my lord.'

'Good,' Lucius said. 'Cossus, give the boy something to cover those with so he's not seen on the way back to the Arician camp.'

Cossus nodded. 'Leave it to me, Lucius. Come on, boy.'

'When do I get the gold?' the boy blurted out, his eyes wide at his daring.

Cossus smacked the back of his head. The boy cried out and kept his face down, used to such blows.

'Cossus!' Manius protested. 'Leave the boy alone.'

'You don't tell me what to do, Manius,' Cossus growled.

'Enough!' Lucius slammed his hand down on the table. 'Cossus, go. Do what you have to. Manius, for Jupiter's sake, sit down and take some wine.'

Cossus left with the boy and Manius did as he was bid. He poured a cup of wine for himself and topped up Lucius's.

'Cossus is a brute,' he muttered.

'He's useful,' Lucius said.

'What do you hope to achieve with this?' Manius gestured at the tent flap which Cossus had left open. 'Putting swords in Turnus's tent?'

'Can't you work it out? That's worrying. You're supposed to be my clever adviser.'

'Just tell me,' Manius said, refusing to let himself be riled.

'I'm going to expose Turnus as having planned to kill me and all the other Latin leaders, hence the swords. When the other leaders see the swords, they'll believe me and agree that it is better to be led by Rome than stay independent. They're already halfway there. It's only Turnus who holds them back.'

'You sound so sure,' Manius said.

'I am sure,' Lucius said. 'I consulted a soothsayer before leaving Rome. He said I will be victorious and that Turnus will be crushed.'

'Is it necessary to crush everyone?' Manius asked exasperatedly.

Lucius stared at him. 'You know, I wonder about you sometimes, Manius. What's the matter? Are you turning into a woman in your old age?'

'Don't mock me, Lucius,' Manius said warningly.

'My lord!' Lucius bellowed suddenly. 'You call me 'my lord' when you address me. I am your king, Manius, don't ever forget that.'

Manius dragged his eyes away from Lucius. 'No, my lord,' he said through gritted teeth. 'I won't forget.'

———

'How do I look?' Lucius stood before Manius and held out his arms.

The toga hung well off Lucius's frame and Manius consoled himself with the knowledge that he had advised correctly. Cossus had said Lucius should go to the grove in Ferentina in his armour, but Manius said it would put a martial slant on the event from the very beginning and they should try to avoid that. Lucius had wavered. Manius knew he would prefer to stand in front of the leaders of the Latins in armour, showing off his physique and strength, but Lucius had relented and the toga won.

'Excellent,' Manius said.

'Good. And stop sulking,' Lucius said, 'it's irritating.'

Manius didn't answer. Lucius was right, he was sulking. The rebuke Lucius had given him the night before still stung. But that would pass, he knew, the sting would lessen. What wouldn't lessen was the feeling that what Lucius was about to do was wrong. Manius had meant what he said the previous night. Why did Lucius always have to conquer? Why could he not seek to make alliances like Servius had done? *Ha, diplomacy! Perhaps I am getting old*, Manius thought.

Cossus burst into the tent, looked Lucius up and down, wrinkled his nose at the choice of attire and asked Lucius if he was ready. Lucius affirmed and all three exited, their destination the grove of Ferentina.

It was early, the sun only just rising over the horizon, and all the Latins were still asleep in their tents or on their makeshift beds on the ground. They awoke quickly at the noise made by Lucius and his men, and they threw off their blankets, asking one another what was going on.

'Forgive me, friends,' Lucius begged, holding his hands palms up. 'I would not disturb your rest for the world but this is a matter that cannot wait. I have discovered you have all been betrayed by the very man you look to lead you.'

'What is this?' Turnus pushed his way through to the front of the crowd gathered around Lucius. 'Tarquin, what new trick is this?'

'No trick, Turnus, you know of what I speak,' Lucius said.

'I know you're talking shit. Again.'

Lucius heard Cossus curse, but he wasn't about to let himself be put off by Turnus's bluntness. 'I speak the truth, Turnus, as your countrymen will discover.' He fixed his gaze on the Latins. 'Turnus Herdonius was planning to betray you, my friends. He and a band of conspirators had schemed to kill you at this meeting I invited you to and take over all the Latin states.'

'Where do you get this from?' Turnus demanded, laughing, but Lucius heard the concern in his voice.

'From someone whom you thought you had cowed into obedience and silence. A boy who had nothing but blows from you. A boy brave enough to seek me out and tell me what you intended.'

'What boy? Who are you talking about?'

'Come forward, boy.' Lucius held out his arm and Cossus propelled the young boy forward. He looked more frightened than ever and tried to resist Cossus's firm hand on his shoulder. 'This boy, your servant, Turnus, came to me and told me what he had discovered. Swords, my friends. Turnus was storing weapons in his tent to attack you this very morning.'

'This is nonsense,' Turnus asserted, turning to his men. 'He's making it up.'

'Am I making these up?' Lucius said and nodded to Cossus. Cossus snapped his fingers and one of his men deposited the swords on the ground in front of Turnus.

Turnus stared down at them. 'I've never seen these swords before. They're not mine.'

'They were found in your tent. Hidden.' Lucius heard the murmurings from the Latins. 'Why were they there, Turnus? Why were they hidden?'

'They're not mine,' Turnus snarled, his face turning purple. He turned to the Latins. 'I have not been plotting against you. It's him.' He jabbed his finger at Lucius. 'He's a master of cunning and of deceit. He is lying to you. Every word he utters is false.'

He wasn't convincing them, Lucius saw that. The Latins were talking with one another but they weren't including Turnus. One of the men, Bellus, turned to Lucius.

'We need to talk about this amongst ourselves,' he said, deliberately ignoring Turnus who was trying to interrupt. 'Come back in an hour.'

Bellus didn't wait for Lucius's answer. He told Turnus to go back to his tent. Turnus retreated without a word, looking sourly at the men Bellus sent to accompany him.

'What do you think?' Lucius said under his breath.

'Worked like a charm,' Cossus grinned, his hand still on the boy's shoulder. He wasn't going to have the boy return to his camp and have the truth shaken out of him.

'Astonishingly easy,' Manius said. 'That they would believe you so readily.'

'They know they can trust me,' Lucius said.

Cossus and Manius looked at one another. From Lucius's tone, they could tell he actually believed that.

———

Lucius was impatient for the hour to pass. He wanted to get Turnus out of the way sooner rather than later, so he could move on to the next stage of his plan, his elevation to ruling all the Latin tribes. His tent was too small to contain his energy, so he made a show of inspecting the men and irritating Cossus by suggesting improvements to the men's armour, most of which were decorative and would serve no useful purpose, save to make fighting more difficult. It was Manius, ironically, who saved Cossus from having to tell

Lucius to piss off by announcing that the Latins were assembling.

They made their way back to the grove, Cossus and Manius having to hurry to catch up with Lucius. The Latin leaders were already assembled when they arrived. Bellus stepped out of their group, arm extended towards Lucius. As Lucius grasped it, Bellus pulled him to one side.

'We've talked over what you said about Turnus. Most are willing to believe it. Some need a little more persuading.'

'What else can I do to prove his treachery?' Lucius queried innocently.

Bellus gave a quick glance over his shoulder. 'I can persuade them. They'll listen to me.'

'Thank you, Bellus,' Lucius said earnestly and turned to go.

'Hold a moment, there, my lord king,' Bellus said, catching hold of him. 'I said I can, not that I will.'

'I see.' Lucius said, wondering how much longer he would have to wait.

'I don't think you do,' Bellus said with an ugly grin. 'If you did, you'd be making me an offer now.'

Understanding crossed Lucius's face. 'What is it you want?'

'All of Turnus's goods and properties. And to act as your deputy when I've made you King of the Latins. You won't want to be leaving Rome all the time to administrate your new kingdoms. You could leave all that to me.'

Lucius thought quickly. He had planned to make his eldest nephew, Titus, his deputy in the Latin states. Admittedly, he hadn't made any definite promises but it had been understood. His sister wouldn't be pleased when she found out it was not to be. But still, he could put up with that, if it meant Turnus would be got rid of this easily.

'Agreed,' he said, and held out his hand.

Bellus grasped it. 'Right then. Let's deal with Turnus, shall we?'

Bellus strode back to his countrymen and spoke in low tones to the leaders. Lucius watched them closely. There was a lot of nodding, some arm waving, but from what Lucius could see, there was a consensus. And then Bellus shouted, 'Fetch Turnus,' and a ruffled Turnus, his arms bound behind his back, was dragged from his tent and brought to stand before Lucius. He had been struck; Lucius noted Turnus's split lip and the blood crusted around one nostril. Turnus glared at Lucius but said nothing.

'So, Turnus, from the look of you, I see your fellow Latins trusted in my words. They know of your treachery and will deal with you justly.' He looked over at Bellus. 'How will you deal with this traitor, my friend? Will you put him to trial?'

'No need for that,' Bellus said. 'We know he's a traitor. Don't we?' A roar went up from the Latins. 'We know how to deal with traitors.'

Bellus winked at Lucius, then jerked his thumb at the nearest group of men. They grabbed Turnus and lifted him off his feet, two holding him under the arms, another holding his legs together while a rope was placed around his ankles. Bucking futilely against his bonds, Turnus was carried to the side of the small lake that rippled in the grove. There, he was laid on the ground and held fast while a willow hurdle was tied to him. Heavy stones were laid on the hurdle, making Turnus cry out in pain at their weight. Then Turnus was lifted, hurdle and all, into the air and lowered into the lake. He was pushed out into the water until the ground fell away and he disappeared beneath the water. Bubbles broke the surface of the water. Soon, the surface of the lake was still.

Bellus turned and strode back to Lucius. 'That's how we deal with traitors.'

The rest of the Latins had followed Bellus and were now looking at him and Lucius.

Bellus addressed them. 'We, the Latin tribes, had a treaty with King Ancus Marcius and King Lucius Tarquinius Priscus, in which we were treated no better than Greeks or Egyptians, subject to their whims and vulnerable to any nation who thought they could subdue us. That treaty lapsed in King Servius's time and we were happy to let it do so, believing we needed no such treaty. We were wrong to think we could do without Rome. We have suffered from the enemies of Rome, who dare not attack her but will content themselves attacking us. If we come under Rome's dominion, if we acknowledge King Lucius our king, then we will enjoy her protection and we will prosper. What do you say, my friends? Shall we accept King Lucius's generous offer and become friends to Rome?'

There was no hesitation. The Latins cried out their approval and sunk to their knees, bowing their heads to Lucius.

———

Lucilla gripped the pommels of her chair, wishing it was her brother's throat. How dare he! How dare he! She thought back to Lucius's return to Rome, how he had strode through the doors of the domus, all smiles and self-congratulation, and told them how, with just a few well-chosen words, he had fooled the Latins and had them kill their own leader before they all bowed down to him.

Lucilla and her family had been in the domus to welcome him home, all impatient to hear his news. She and her sons had been expecting to hear how they would benefit, how Lucius would fulfil the promises he had made them. And Lucius had smiled, quite brazenly, and told them things had changed.

So, her eldest, Titus, would not be given the power Lucius had promised. Worse, Lucius offered nothing else in place of that power. Titus, she knew, had been going around the city boasting of how he would soon be king in all but name over the Latin tribes. She'd even encouraged him to do it. Lucilla didn't dare think how much she and he had bought on credit on the promise of that power. Now, all the shopkeepers and merchants who had sold them goods would be calling to have their bills settled and there was no money to pay them. The money would have come when Titus was made deputy. Lucilla winced at the thought of their home being invaded, their possessions taken. They would be ruined, all because Lucius didn't care a fig about her and her family.

Titus had been so disappointed. They had left the domus, refusing Lucius's appeals for them to stay and enjoy the dinner they had been invited to. Lucilla knew Lucius didn't care one way or the other whether they stayed. She had told him the food would stick in their throats and told Titus and Iunius to follow her home. She had seen Lucius's sly smile as she walked away. How she hated him.

An idea began to form in her mind. Her family was not entirely without power. They had a voice and one that, as Tarquins, would be listened to in the city. Yes, that was it. They would speak out, speak against Lucius. She would do it the only way open to her by gossiping amongst her friends, but Titus could and would do it in the senate house. Together, they would relentlessly batter against Lucius's pride and authority, and he would realise what a mistake he had made in keeping her and her son so low.

———

Lucius gnawed on his thumb. 'What is he saying?'

Cossus checked his papers. 'That you should be deposed, that you were in league with our enemies. That you are hoarding gold here in the domus that should have been distributed amongst the senate. That you've kept gifts from our subjects that should have been placed in the temples.'

'Anything that comes into his stupid mind, in fact,' Lucius said. 'Are people listening to him?'

'He always gets an audience when he talks,' Cossus said.

'Titus is pissed at you,' Manius said. 'You promised him an office of state and you took that away and gave him nothing in its place. Find something for him to do and he will stop all this.'

'It's his mother, too, Lucius,' Cossus said. 'She's been talking with her friends, those bitches Martia and Lavinia, and they've been spreading her gossip around.'

'I don't care about the talk of women,' Lucius spat. 'But Titus is my damned nephew. He owes me his loyalty. Is Iunius speaking against me too?'

'Iunius is a fool, Lucius,' Manius said quickly before Cossus could speak. 'A half-wit, you know that. He doesn't even go into the senate. No one listens to anything he says. And Titus will shut up soon. He'll run out of things to accuse you of.'

'I won't have it,' Lucius rose and glared at Cossus. 'You hear me?'

Cossus stared at Lucius and nodded. 'I hear you.'

Manius looked at Cossus's grim expression and understand what was meant. 'He's your nephew, Lucius,' he protested. 'You can't.'

'Can't? What can't I do, Manius?' Lucius fumed. 'Am I not the King?'

'But… your nephew!'

'Then he should know better, shouldn't he?' Cossus said, rising. 'Tell me when, Lucius.'

'The sooner the better,' Lucius said.

'I'll do it tonight, then. We'll go to a whorehouse. One quick stab and it'll be over. Blame it on one of the other patrons.'

'Good. It'll serve him and his mother right. His reputation will be ruined, dying in a whorehouse.'

'It's as good as done,' Cossus promised and with a triumphant glance at Manius, departed.

Lucius eyed Manius. 'You're quiet all of a sudden, Manius.'

'Will you comfort your sister when she hears her son is murdered, Lucius?' Manius said, his voice breaking. 'Will you pretend you're sorry or will you admit you had him killed?'

'You know, Manius,' Lucius bent down to pick up a handful of walnuts, 'I'm beginning to worry about you. First, it was Turnus you became protective of, now Titus. Both my enemies. It makes me wonder just who you're loyal to.'

Manius's blood was running cold. 'I'm loyal to you, Lucius, I've always been loyal to you.'

Lucius cracked open one of the walnuts. 'I'm glad to hear it. Otherwise, I might be asking Cossus to take you to a whorehouse one night.'

———

Lucilla gently pushed back a black curl from Titus's forehead. He looked as if he were asleep, lying there on the bier in the atrium. Except for the skin, that didn't look right. There was no pink tinge to it, only a grey clamminess. Her gaze travelled down her son's body, her throat tightening at the bloody gash in his torso that had stained the edges of the torn tunic. One stab. That had been all it took to take the life of her son.

She felt the presence of another person behind her. 'Is that you?' she asked.

'Yes, it's me,' Iunius said, putting his hand upon her shoulder.

'I bought a new statue for his birthday next week,' Lucilla said. 'You know, the one he said he liked in that workshop near the Tiber.'

'I know,' Iunius said.

'Should I take it back, do you think?'

'We'll keep it.'

'Would you like it in your room?'

'Mother,' he said, turning her around to face him, 'you know who did this, don't you?'

She raised her puffy red eyes to him. 'A man in the brothel.'

'No,' Iunius said firmly. 'It was the King.'

'Lucius?'

'He arranged it, I'm sure of it.'

Lucilla gripped his hands. 'Don't say so, Iunius.'

'Why? Cannot you bear to hear it?'

'It can't be true. He wouldn't. His own nephew.'

'Lucius doesn't care anything for blood, Mother, you know that.'

'How angry you sound.'

'I am angry,' Iunius growled. 'And I'm not going to let him get away with it.'

He moved away but Lucilla lunged and caught hold of him. 'You think I want to lose another son?'

His mother's ferocity made Iunius pause. 'You can't mean to let him get away with this? Titus,' he pointed at his dead brother lying on the bier, 'was killed because he was speaking out against Lucius. This is what Lucius does to any who oppose him. We are not safe from him, Mother.'

'We are, Iunius, we are. Lucius thinks you are simple.' Iunius made a noise of annoyance but Lucilla continued. 'We know you are not. But your shyness has meant he doesn't notice you, and that is good.'

'I'll show him just how simple I am,' Iunius promised.

'You wouldn't say so if you had laboured to bring you into this world, and fretted over every cold and cough, and torn your hair out when you have got into fights. Iunius, I beg you, do nothing. We will be safe, I promise.'

Lucilla reached up and kissed her son several times, hoping she could convince him to heed her words. She knew he spoke the truth about Lucius, had subconsciously known it as soon as she heard her eldest son had been killed.

'Then he gets away with it,' Iunius declared hopelessly.

'He will be punished by Poena,' Lucilla promised. 'The curse will work and Lucius will pay. He will suffer in the Underworld while we are in Elysium. Promise me, Iunius, that you will do nothing, that you will continue to be quiet and let them think you are simple. Only in that belief will we be truly safe.'

Lucilla saw her son's lips purse and his brow furrow, his eyes fixed on the dead body behind her. She knew she was asking much of him, that he was struggling between wanting to avenge his brother and be a dutiful, loving son to her.

'I promise, Mother,' he said at last and Lucilla released him from her grasp, content he was safe from Lucius's wickedness.

21

'I want to go to war,' Lucius declared, putting his feet up on the footstool and cupping his hands behind his head. He watched Manius and noted the slight change of expression. 'Why not?'

'Wars are costly,' Manius said after a moment, not looking up.

'Wars are necessary, Manius,' Lolly said, examining her stitching on a cushion she was embroidering. 'They make Rome great. Greater,' she amended with a smile at Lucius.

'There are other ways to do that, lady,' Manius said. 'Treaties and alliances.'

'How like my father you sound,' she said, shaking her head. 'He always went on about alliances and how they secured peace for Rome. We don't want peace, do we, Lucius?'

'Peace doesn't make you rich,' Lucius said, arching his back and moaning as his spine cracked.

'Who do you want to go to war with this time?' Manius asked.

'The Volsci, to begin with.'

'The Volsci. They will be a formidable enemy, Lucius.'

'Then we'll be well matched. Our Roman ranks have been swelled by the Latins, haven't they? If we go to war, the Latins will go with us. Why do you think I staged that charade in Ferentina? I wasn't interested in making friends just for the sake of it.'

'No, I realised that,' Manius said, only just managing to keep the sarcasm out of his voice. 'You have a strategy against the Volsci?'

'We'll move against Suessa Pometia,' Lucius nodded. 'That's the richest Volscian city.'

'And carry off all their wealth,' Manius said, 'and do what with it?'

Lucius glanced at Lolly, but she was busy with her needlework and didn't look up. He had promised to buy her a new litter — she complained the old one smelt musty and the fabric was threadbare — and to give each of the children a slave of their very own. She would have those, of course, but Suessa Pometia, he felt sure, would provide enough wealth for his main project. 'I'm going to put what we get from the Volsci towards building the temple to Jupiter Optimus Maximus that Grandfather always talked about and never managed.'

'Does Rome need another temple?' Manius wondered.

Lucius knew Manius would prefer the wealth to be spent on making the streets better, covering the mud with stones so the people could walk on them without walking in sludge during the winter months, and in reinforcing the city walls, some of which were crumbling and leaving the city exposed. 'We cannot honour the gods enough,' Lucius said. 'And besides, my grandfather made a promise to Jupiter. If I don't do it, Jupiter will not favour us.'

'And the Tarquins need all the help they can get,' Manius

said with a laugh. The smile fell from his face as he caught Lucius's eye. 'I mean, the curse laid upon your family… all those years ago…' he trailed off.

'My grandmother successfully countered that curse,' Lucius said stonily. 'It has never adversely affected us.'

'And the people will be pleased,' Lolly piped up. 'The site for the temple has lain empty for years and has become a veritable midden. Every pleb throws their rubbish there and the senate has become riddled with complaints about the rats. Building the temple will mean the site will be cleared, solving that problem, and will provide work for very many people. So you see, Manius, Lucius only has the people's welfare in mind.'

'Yes, lady,' Manius said, 'I see that now. Thank you for explaining it to me so clearly.'

Lolly smiled sweetly. 'Not at all, Manius. We can't have you leave here getting the wrong idea about your king, can we?'

———

Lucius shielded his eyes against the sun and surveyed the area ahead of him. The site on the Capitoline Hill had been cleared of all rubbish, the last of the debris swept away and burnt three weeks previously. The site was not flat enough, and so Lucius had ordered the ground to be flattened, and the old, rotting Sabine shrines to be removed. This done, the diggers had now moved in and there were hundreds of them, made up of Roman workmen and Volscian slaves captured during the war and brought to Rome as part of Lucius's triumph. The foundations were almost complete and soon timber would be brought in and stone. How long, he wondered, before the temple would be finished? Five years, ten? It didn't really matter how long it took. He'd already achieved what he wanted for the plebs were already praising him for the project. How like children they were.

He had been right to war with the Volsci. His victory over them how brought him much wealth. Not only was the temple underway, but Lolly had her new litter and the children their slaves. There had been enough riches to redecorate the whole of the domus with new frescoes and new furniture, and stout money chests had even had to be bought to hold what was left over. And it had been so easy to beat the Volsci. They had all but given up when they saw how big an army Rome had.

Lucius walked around the building site, acknowledging the bows of the diggers as he passed. Someone called out 'My lord,' and he turned to see Manius hurrying towards him. He sighed. Lucius was growing mightily tired of Manius, always complaining, always criticising.

'What is it?'

'My lord king,' Manius said, careful to use the title in the presence of plebeians, 'the senate has received word from the Gabii. They've rejected the treaty you made with Bellus and the other Latin leaders. They refuse to come under Roman rule.'

Lucius snatched the paper Manius held out to him and scanned it. There was too much to bother reading. 'What reason do they give?' he demanded, thrusting it back at Manius.

'No reason,' Manius said, rolling the paper up. 'Perhaps they don't think they need to give one.'

'Bellus said they would all agree,' Lucius snarled. 'He promised me he would see to it.'

'We could send some senators to Gabii. Negotiate a treaty they will find acceptable.'

'Negotiate?' Lucius spat in his face. 'I don't negotiate, Manius. I rule.'

'But if they won't—'

'We'll fight them. Subdue them. Make them bow their heads to Roman rule.'

'Another war?' Manius said.

'Yes, damn you, another war. I'll have the Gabii wealth just like I've had the Volscian. And if you don't like it, Manius, then you can piss off back to your estate in the country.'

———

Lucius was beginning to wonder whether he hadn't been a little precipitant in declaring war on Gabii. It had seemed such an easy thing to declare when Manius had told him of their opposition that day at the temple building site.

But Gabii was different from the Volsci. The Volscian territory had been open, exposed. Gabii was a fortress, easy for the inhabitants to defend. Their walls were thick, perhaps as much as fifteen feet thick, and high too. The Roman ladders had been repulsed almost as soon as they were put to the walls, missiles ranging down on those attempting to climb and those at the bottom holding the ladders in place. Lucius had to order his men back and try a different strategy. He had tried to break down the gates and found them almost as strong. Their efforts had resulted in holes and splinters, but the gates still stood, defiant against the Roman army.

Manius had implored Lucius to give up, to forget about the Gabii and return to Rome. Let Gabii stand alone, he said. They would soon realise that such isolation was bad for trade. They would be the poorer for not joining with Rome. They'd probably be begging for a treaty in a year or two.

Lucius had heard enough from Manius about diplomacy. Talk, talk, talk, that was all Manius ever wanted to do. Lucius, enraged, struck Manius, telling him not to be a coward. Manius, clutching his face more in shock than pain, refuted the accusation, but it hadn't stopped Lucius turning his back on him. Cossus was standing at Lucius's side and had smiled with pleasure at the snub Manius received.

Manius had had enough. He was sick of Lucius and he was sick of Cossus. He asked to be relieved of his position as adviser and Lucius agreed without hesitation. Manius went to his tent to pack, stuffing his belongings anyhow into his bag. He would return to his country estate and stay there. Let Lucius have his wars and his temples. Let him drag Rome down. Manius no longer cared.

———

'We need a new strategy,' Cossus declared, surveying a crudely drawn map of the Gabii stronghold. 'We're not going to get in through the gates for a while. They can't hold forever but how long do we want to wait?'

Lucius didn't answer. Cossus twisted on his stool. 'Stop thinking about him. Manius was a pain in the arse. It's best he went back to his shit-hole of a farm.'

'It's not a shit-hole,' Lucius muttered. He shouldn't have lost his temper with his old friend. Now, he only had Cossus for company and advice, and as Manius had once sagely said, a little of Cossus went a long way. Lucius already wanted Manius back, but there was no way he was going to apologise.

'Whatever you say. But he's gone. Be glad of it. I bloody well am.'

'That's obvious.'

'We don't need him. Never did. Now, can I have your attention on what we're going to do about Gabii?'

Lucius walked over to Cossus and stared down at the map. 'Well, if we can't breach the walls nor the gates in good time, what else is there?'

'You're the military genius, you tell me.' Cossus shoved the map towards Lucius.

'Maybe…' Lucius mused, raising his eyes to the tent's ceiling. He didn't speak for a long while.

Cossus, bored with waiting, demanded, 'Maybe what?'

'The prophecy,' Lucius said cryptically.

'What prophecy?'

'The one the Sibyl sold me,' Lucius said excitedly. 'It said an enemy of Rome would need to be defeated by cunning. We didn't know what it referred to at the time but what if it meant this? Now?'

'You place too much faith in soothsayers,' Cossus shook his head and pulled the map back to lay before him.

'This wasn't any old soothsayer, you fool, this was the Sibyl of Cumae. Yes, this was what the book meant. The Gabii need to be defeated by cunning.'

'All right, so, you have to be cunning. That should be easy enough for you.'

The insult went unnoticed. 'Let me think,' Lucius said, pacing up and down the small tent. 'By means of cunning…'

———

Sextus yawned as he pissed into the pot. He wasn't at all sure he liked being a soldier. He missed his comfortable bed and his food being cooked the way he liked. He missed being able to rise when he felt like it and having clean clothes to put on. He wondered whether he should ask his father if he could return to Rome, but he suspected his mother would turn him around and make him come straight back.

His tent flap opened and Cossus entered. Sextus didn't like Cossus. He always felt Cossus was laughing at him for he made fun of Sextus's fair complexion and mocked him for his liking for soft living. 'You're up at last,' Cossus said. 'Come. Your father wants you.'

Sextus, wondering what he had done wrong now, followed Cossus out of the tent and to his father's. His father was waiting for him. *He doesn't look particularly grim*, Sextus thought, *so maybe I'm not going to be told off.*

'Cossus said you wanted to see me, Father,' Sextus said.

'My boy,' Lucius said, kissing Sextus on both cheeks. 'I need you to do something for me. Come and sit down.' Lucius led Sextus to a stool and they both sat. 'It's not going to be pleasant.'

'What's not?' Sextus asked warily.

'We can't break through the Gabii defences, so we're going to have to try something different.' Lucius rose and moved to a table at the rear of the tent. He stretched out an arm and picked something up. Sextus strained to see what it was. 'It will be painful for you. I'm sorry about that but it can't be helped. Oh, you look scared, Sextus. Don't be. It will be painful but the pain won't last long, I promise.'

'What, Father?' Sextus cried, his voice coming out high and girlish. He shot a glance at Cossus who grinned at him.

'You're going to be whipped, Sextus,' Lucius said quite matter-of-factly. 'The skin on your back will be broken. You will bleed. It will be a punishment.' He put a black leather whip on the table.

'What have I done wrong?' Sextus asked, eyeing the whip warily.

'You haven't done anything wrong, my boy,' Lucius assured him. 'But it must look as if you've been punished.'

'And if you shut up, you'll find out why,' Cossus growled.

'Don't talk to me like that, you dog,' Sextus shouted at him, but Cossus only laughed the harder.

'Sextus,' Lucius said calmingly, shooting a disapproving glance at Cossus, 'listen. You will appear to have left this camp angry with me. You will go to the Gabii and show them what I have done to you. They will be sympathetic.'

'Will they?' Sextus said doubtfully.

'They will,' Lucius assured him. 'You will tell them what a cruel father I am. Then, you will make them an offer. You will act as go-between. You will help them negotiate a peace between us. They must be growing desperate inside their city by now. They will worry their food will run out. They may even have sickness. They will want to negotiate, I promise you.'

'But why should they listen to me?' Sextus whined. He really didn't want to go to the enemy camp. Now more than ever, he wished he had been allowed to stay at home.

'They'll listen. You have charm, Sextus, when you choose. Use it.'

'Yes, Father,' Sextus said reluctantly.

'Good. Now, take off your tunic and we'll go outside. Cossus, bring the whip.'

Sextus followed his father outside.

'No blubbing, now,' Lucius said. 'I won't have you showing me up in front of the men.'

'I won't,' Sextus protested fiercely, wondering why his whipping had to be public.

Lucius held out his hand and Cossus put the whip into it. He eyed Sextus hungrily as if he wanted to lay the blows himself rather than let Lucius do it. Cossus tied Sextus's wrists with a length of rope and then led him to a thick stake set into the ground. Sextus's arms were raised above his head and tied to a metal ring. Cossus slipped a leather strip between his teeth.

'Remember what I said,' Lucius said as he moved behind Sextus.

Sextus's face creased with the anticipation of pain. The first blow hurt more than he could ever have imagined.

———

Lucius tapped his fingers upon the table and stared into the darkness of his tent. He couldn't get the image of blood running down his son's back out of his mind. But he had been right, hadn't he? It was the only way to break this impasse and gain victory over the Gabii. Sextus would be all right once the wounds started to heal. He had been proud of Sextus. He hadn't blubbed, hadn't cried out. He had taken the strokes like a man. But what would Lolly say when she found out? Lucius wondered. Would she agree with him? Or would she say he was a monster to have wounded his own son so?

'He'll be fine,' Cossus said, making Lucius start. He had forgotten Cossus was waiting with him.

'Will he?'

'He'll have some scars to show off. Women love 'em.'

'What if they kill him?' Lucius asked. 'The Gabii. What if they don't believe him and kill him?'

Cossus shrugged, unable to answer and not caring either. He turned his attention back to his sword, pushing the whetstone along its edge to make it sharp.

'Can't you stop that?' Lucius cried after a minute. 'That noise is driving me mad.'

Cossus curled his lip and threw down both the whetstone and the sword. 'Let's get out of this tent. You're cooped up, that's why you're so uptight.'

Reluctantly, Lucius followed Cossus out of the tent and to the field behind the camp. It was uncultivated and the grass grew high, almost to their waists. In between the grass, wild poppies grew, their bright red heads seeming to bow to Lucius as he approached. He wandered amongst the grass and flowers for a while, breathing in their scent, feeling his muscles relax a little.

'Lucius!' Cossus suddenly called and Lucius turned. With a start, he saw Sextus at Cossus's side, and he hurried forward, his arms outstretched.

'Sextus,' he cried joyfully, surprising himself at how pleased he was to see his youngest son. 'They didn't hurt you?' *Oh, the irony*, he thought, as he saw Sextus wince, his tunic probably rubbing against his wounds.

'No, Father, *they* didn't,' Sextus confirmed and gestured with his eyes to the man who stood a little behind him.

Lucius looked the stranger over, noting the twitchy hand on the sword hilt, the wary eyes. 'Who is this?'

'He's from the Gabii,' Sextus said. 'We're here to negotiate.'

Sextus was playing his part well. *No more concern*, Lucius told himself. *Get to business.*

'Forgive me, my son, for what I did.'

'I don't,' Sextus blurted, 'I can't.'

For a moment, Lucius wondered if Sextus meant what he said. But then he saw the smallest smile turn up the corner of his son's mouth.

'Then I shall not press you.' He looked at the Gabii envoy. 'What are your terms?'

'We don't have terms. I'm here to tell you to cease your

attack,' the Gabii envoy said. 'You can't get in to the city. You are wasting your time.'

'I don't think I am,' Lucius said. 'I think your people are suffering.'

'We're not suffering. We're more than able to defend ourselves.'

'If that's so, then we have nothing to say to one another. Tell your masters I will not give up. I will have Gabii.'

The Gabii envoy grimaced. 'You think on what I've said, Tarquin. There's no victory for you here. See sense and leave.' He grabbed Sextus's shoulder.

'Take your hand off my son,' Lucius growled.

'He's coming back with me.'

'No, he isn't.'

'Yes, I am,' Sextus shouted at Lucius. 'I'm not staying here for you to whip me again.'

Lucius met Sextus's eye. Deliberately, he half-turned and began swiping his arm against the poppies. The red heads broke from their stalks, hovered a moment in the air, then fell to the ground.

'I will show no mercy to those fools you're hiding behind, Sextus,' Lucius said, looking back at his son. 'They'll be like those poppies. You understand me?'

Sextus licked his dry, cracked lips. He met his father's eye. 'Yes, Father, I understand.'

Lucius and Cossus watched Sextus and the envoy go.

'You should have just told him what to do. All that,' Cossus gestured contemptuously at the poppies, 'playacting.'

'It's called subtlety, Cossus. I don't expect you to understand.'

'Oh, really? Do you think he understood what you meant?'

'We'll find out, won't we?' Lucius said, keeping his eyes on his son until he disappeared from sight.

———

The doctor peeled off the bandages and Sextus hissed as the linen pulled at the dried blood. By Jupiter, his back seemed to hurt even more now than when the whip had first struck. He bit the pillow and tensed for the next removal.

'That looks painful,' a voice said and Sextus angled his head around, forced to look out of the corner of his eyes at the speaker.

It was Rufus, the Gabii leader. He was peering at Sextus's back, his expression more of interest than pity.

'It is. Very,' Sextus said, closing his eyes.

Rufus sat down by the cot, resting his hand on his knees. 'My messenger said you did well with your father today. You didn't give in to him.'

'I'll never give in to him. He's a brute. Do you think I'll ever be able to forget this?' Sextus jerked his head at his brutalised back.

'I couldn't whip my son,' Rufus mused,' no matter what he'd done. What had you argued about? You never told us.'

Sextus had known this question would come; in fact, he'd been surprised it hadn't been asked earlier. 'We were talking about the siege and I said we'd never break through. That we should negotiate a truce or retreat. He didn't like that. He said I was a coward. That's when he had me dragged out and whipped in front of all the men.'

'He's got quite the temper, hasn't he, your father? Of course, we've all heard about him. The tyrant of Rome.'

Sextus buried his face in his pillow. How dare this fool talk about his father like that? If he didn't have a job to do, he would have grabbed Rufus's own sword and stabbed him in the heart.

'How would you like to pay him back?' Rufus asked after a moment.

'What do you mean?'

'You know how Tarquin's arranged his men, you know what strategies he intends. If I give you command of one hundred men, you can be part of our attack.'

Don't agree too quickly, Sextus told himself, feeling his heart quicken. 'You, give me command? When you still have guards watching my every move?'

Rufus laughed. 'What do you expect? That I let you wander around the city unguarded?'

'Either you trust me or you don't. Do you really need guards to watch me sleep?'

Rufus stared at Sextus for a long moment. 'Very well. No more guards.'

'Thank you.'

Rufus nodded and rose. 'Get some rest. We'll talk more about how you can help us in the morning.'

The doctor left with Rufus. Sextus quickly rose from the cot and hurried to the door, opening it just a crack. Rufus had stopped a few feet away, halted by one of his men, an oaf named Vulso. Sextus strained his ears.

'You're leaving him unguarded,' he heard Vulso say. 'You've gone mad.'

'Keep your voice down,' Rufus said, flapping his hands to shush him. 'Sextus is harmless. His father knows it, that's why he doesn't care about him.'

'Harmless or not, he's still a Roman. He's still our enemy.'

'The Tarquins are all the same, Vulso. Give them something they want, something they value, and all previous loyalties are dust on the wind. I've offered Sextus a troop of men, a command of his own. He doesn't care who he fights for. He'd fight for a donkey if it promised to make him important. He'll fight for us.'

Sextus returned to his cot, fuming at what he had heard. Face down, he lay on the rickety bed. He wasn't tired. He had no intention of getting some rest as Rufus advised. He would let the camp settle down for the night and then, with no guards to watch him, he would make his move.

And then, Rufus would pay for his insults.

———

The barracks had fallen silent. Sextus climbed off the cot and opened the door, a little at first, checking there were no guards posted outside. Satisfied he was unguarded, he tiptoed out and made his way to the room at the end of the corridor, the room where Rufus slept.

Rufus looked almost like a child, his eyelids fluttering as he dreamt. What was he dreaming about? Sextus wondered, as he slid Rufus's sword out from beneath the pillow, careful not to make any movement that would awake its owner. Was he dreaming about killing Lucius? Well, if he was, it would be the last dream he would ever have.

Sextus pointed the sword at the vein throbbing in Rufus's throat. He held his breath as the point gently touched the ruddy skin. Rufus didn't stir. Using both hands on the sword's hilt, Sextus drove the blade through the skin and muscle. Rufus's eyes opened wide, his hands flailed helplessly at Sextus. No sound other than a low gurgle came from him as blood flooded his mouth. Blood sprayed Sextus's face. He licked the copper-tasting liquid from his lips and twisted the sword. Rufus's eyes locked on Sextus, his hands twitched once and then the arms dropped back to the bed. Sextus waited a few more seconds, then tugged the sword free from Rufus's neck.

Wiping the sword on the blanket covering Rufus, Sextus took a deep breath and headed out of the door, moving from one room to the next, killing the Gabii leaders just as his father had shown him when he had taken the heads off those pretty poppies.

Wouldn't his father be pleased in the morning when Sextus told the Gabii citizens their leaders were all dead and the siege was over? Wouldn't his father be proud when Sextus opened the gates of the city and told Lucius the city was his?

Yet another victory for King Lucius Tarquinius.

PART IV
511 BC–509 BC

22

The temple of Jupiter Optimus Maximus was complete.

The edifice rose above Lucius high into the sky, blocking out the sun that shone behind it. Lucius had hired the finest Etruscan stonemasons to carve the decorations that lined the pediment, and the four rearing horses that crowned the roof were a wonder to behold. It had been worth the wait, he decided, and worth the money, even though it had gone well over the original estimates. He had been warned by the senate that the treasury was close to empty and that something would have to be done to fill it again. He would raise taxes again and he could make the men working on the circus seating and the sewers work for nothing. If they complained, he would remind them it was for the good of Rome.

Rome could go to war again, that was always profitable. In fact, now Lucius came to think abut it, it had been a while since Rome had had to fight anyone. The treaties put in place with the Aequi and the other tribes were still in place and they seemed to be perfectly happy to keep them working. All except the Rutuli. They'd been making a lot of noise lately about the treaty terms being unfair. The senate had been

debating how to respond. Maybe treating with the Rutuli
wasn't the answer. Maybe he should show them who was in
charge, once and for all.

Lucius gave the nod to the priest to get the dedication
ceremony under way. It was a tediously long process but it
had to be endured. He looked around at his family. Lolly
looked magnificent in her purple dress and gold coronet. It
was remarkable, he suddenly thought, seeing her in the full
glare of the sun, how little she had aged since they married.
Her skin, though a little rougher than it had been, was still
taut, only the smallest suggestion of her age around her throat
where the skin was a little looser. How did she do it? He
knew that he had not aged as well. His blonde hair had grey
in it and his face was lined all over. He'd even found a liver
spot on his hand the other day. Maybe, he thought with
amusement, she had special potions that kept her young. That
would be like her.

His eyes moved on to his sons. Sextus was so like Lolly,
not just in looks but in temperament and he certainly had
inherited her sense of loyalty. Lucius had never been able to
forgive himself for the whipping he had given Sextus, but to
Sextus's credit, he didn't seem to harbour any grudge. He
never mentioned it, never brought it up to wound Lucius
when they had a row. Titus was more like him, which is why
he supposed they argued so much. Even now, Titus wasn't
paying attention; instead, his gaze was over the crowd who
had gathered to watch. And then there was Arruns who
Lucius never really paid much attention. He never spoke up
when the family was together, just went along with whatever
Sextus and Titus said or did. *Reminds me of my brother*,
Lucius thought and swallowed down the lump that rose in his
throat. Arruns was something of a disappointment but at least

he knew where his duty lay. Arruns, at least, was paying attention.

His sister and her youngest son had been invited to the ceremony, too. Lucius hadn't wanted to invite them — he couldn't stand the mood of resentment Lucilla always brought with her — but Lolly said it wouldn't look good if they weren't there. At least Iunius wasn't embarrassing him by dribbling or something equally repulsive. Lucius knew his nephew was an idiot but what exactly was supposed to be wrong with him? Lucilla had never said. He seemed to be preoccupied with something now. Just what was he staring at?

Lucius followed his nephew's gaze. Iunius seemed to be looking past the priests and the other officials, beyond into the shaded interior of the temple at one of the columns. His curiosity piqued, Lucius squinted, cursing his poor eyesight. Something was there, on the floor, moving. No, not moving, writhing. Lucius felt his skin prickle. Unable to stop himself, he moved out of the family semicircle and behind the priests, who didn't seem to notice or care.

He drew nearer, the strange object coming into focus the closer he got. He gasped. It was a snake, wriggling its way up out of a crack in the pillar.

Lolly caught up with him and laid her hand upon his arm. 'Lucius, what is it?'

Lucius pointed.

'It's a snake,' she said, wondering what had got into him.

'It's a bad omen.'

'You're sweating,' she said, wiping her hand across his forehead. 'Stop this, everyone can see.'

'What does it mean, Lolly?' Lucius asked as she tried to turn him away from the snake.

'I don't know,' she said. 'Oh, come on, Lucius.'

But he wouldn't move. She let go of him and hurried towards the snake, stamping her foot. It slithered away, towards the edge of the floor and disappeared over the side. Lucius felt he could breathe again.

'Now, come,' Lolly insisted and she led him back to the others. 'We'll consult the soothsayer when we get back to the domus.'

'This is too important a portent to trust to a soothsayer,' Lucius said, shaking his head.

'Oh, curse you and your superstitions. Well, what do you suggest then?'

'I must consult the Oracle at Delphi.'

———

Titus and Arruns were laughing about something. They found the most stupid of things funny and Iunius wasn't in the mood, either to laugh along with them or be the butt of their jokes.

As they travelled along the dusty road, his legs aching, Iunius tried to work out how long it would be before they would be back in Rome. He missed his home and his wife, missed his children and his mother. He even missed the noise and the stink of the streets. His homesickness wasn't helped by the company he was with. They may have been his cousins, but Iunius really couldn't stand Titus and Arruns. It was just his luck to be chosen to go on this journey to Delphi with them. He was sure Lucius said he had to go with them just to annoy him.

Although, Iunius had to admit to a mild interest in seeing the Oracle of Delphi. He had heard stories of her, of course, of the Pythia, the High Priestess of the Temple of Apollo. It was, he supposed, an honour to be chosen to represent Rome in this way, even if he had to go with his two obnoxious cousins. *I'll look on this as an adventure,* he told himself.

And it was an adventure. They had been given a very rough map to guide them to Delphi, but it left a lot out and they often had to ask the people they passed if they were on the right road. It took almost three weeks to reach Delphi and a few more weary hours to find suitable lodgings. By this time, any old hut would have done for Iunius, so dirty and tired did he feel, but true to form, Titus and Arruns would only accept the best accommodation in town.

While their baths were made ready and a warm meal cooked for them at the cleanest tavern they could find, Titus wrote a note and despatched it to the temple officials, advising them they would be at the temple on the morrow to consult the Oracle.

———

They set off early next morning for the Temple of Apollo. It was an old temple, and there were weeds and grasses growing between cracks in the stones and much of the paint was peeling from the walls and columns. Compared to the new temples in Rome, it didn't look all that impressive.

They walked past the queue of people, who like themselves, desired an audience with the Oracle. Unlike themselves, these people had to draw lots to see when they would be admitted, if they were to be admitted at all. Iunius, Titus and Arruns, as members of the royal Tarquin family and representatives of Rome, would be allowed to move to the head of the queue, providing of course, their offerings to Apollo were of suitable quality and worth. Lucius had given his sons two goblets made of solid gold to give to the temple.

Iunius remembered with bitterness Lucius's instruction

that his gift should not be anywhere near as grand as that presented by Titus and Arruns. How he had had to bite his tongue and swallow down the anger and hatred he felt for his uncle, ever mindful of his mother's fear for his life. But he would be damned if he was going to be humiliated at so important a place by his stupid cousins.

So, he had secretly sold some of his property, not even telling his mother, and ordered a solid gold staff to be made, hiding it inside a larger, hollowed-out wooden staff, which he knew neither Titus nor Arruns would show any interest in. If they had picked up the wooden staff, they would have wondered at its weight, but they never paid him or what he carried any attention.

The two priests who stood guard at the entrance to the temple waved them over. Titus took the two goblets in their protective leather wrapping from his satchel and passed them to the priests. The priests examined them closely, declared them a fine gift, then looked to Iunius. Iunius handed over the wooden staff, trying to hide his smile from his companions. The priests looked doubtfully at the gift, but their expressions changed when they passed it between them.

'Remove the top,' Iunius said to the priest who held it.

The priest stared at him for a moment, then did as Iunius said. He peered down the barrel, his mouth curving in a surprised, satisfied smile. He upended it and the golden staff slid out.

'You sly bastard,' Titus whispered in Iunius's ear. 'You wait till Father hears what you've done. You'll pay for that.'

Iunius gave him a smug smile and said nothing.

'You may all enter,' the priest said and gestured them towards the temple's entrance.

They passed the columns, heading deeper into the temple, until they came to a large stone throne. Upon it sat a woman.

To Iunius, she looked disappointingly ordinary. Her dress was of white linen and she wore a purple veil over her head. They knew the protocol and all three prostrated themselves on the floor before her.

'Welcome, sons of Rome,' the Oracle said, lifting her veil to reveal her face.

She was around thirty-five, her face unlined and her hair was jet black, although Iunius saw it was shot through with white. But if the rest of her was unremarkable, her eyes were extraordinary. They were a startling, piercing blue, but no blue Iunius had ever seen in eyes before. It felt like shards of ice were piercing him.

'Ask your question,' she commanded.

It had been agreed that Titus would speak to the Oracle. With a nervous look at his brother, he stepped forward and told of the snake appearing from a pillar of the new temple of Jupiter Optimus Maximus. On his father's behalf, he asked what such an omen meant for the future of the Tarquin dynasty.

The Oracle seemed to consider his request for a long while, so long that Iunius thought maybe she wasn't going to oblige them. But then she raised her head and looked at each of them in turn before returning her gaze to Titus.

'The snake is a symbol of guardianship,' she said and fell silent.

Titus and Arruns frowned at one another. 'Could it mean then that our father is taking good care of Rome, being a wise king, building the new temple?'

The Oracle suddenly shifted her gaze to Iunius. He felt his breath catch in his throat. Those shards of ice again!

'He who first saw the snake is the true guardian of Rome,' she said.

Iunius knew he had been the first to spot the snake, not

Lucius, as Titus and Arruns believed. *Me, Rome's true guardian?* His legs suddenly felt like jelly and he wanted to leave the temple, get away from the Oracle and her penetrating stare. But Titus was speaking again.

'Oracle, tell us, which son of King Lucius Tarquinius will succeed him to the throne of Rome?'

The Oracle did not hesitate. 'The first to kiss his mother will be the supreme power in Rome.'

'But—,' Arruns began.

The Oracle thrust out her hand. 'You have had your answers. Go now.' And she pulled her veil down, hiding her face from view.

———

Back out in the sunshine, they thanked the priests with the briefest of nods and hurried past the queue of hopefuls. The queue had grown since they first entered the temple and Iunius couldn't help wondering if they knew what they were letting themselves in for if they were granted an audience with the Oracle. It had been an unnerving experience.

'What will Father think of the Oracle's answer?' Arruns asked his brother.

'No idea,' Titus said dismissively, occupying himself rearranging the items in his now half-empty satchel.

Arruns looked to Iunius as if he was going to ask him the same question, but then looked away. Iunius knew what that meant. Arruns figured that Iunius, being the family idiot, wouldn't know and wasn't worth asking.

'Let's go back to our room, pack up our things and be on our way,' Titus said. He strode off, heading up the path.

'Why the hurry?' Arruns asked as he and Iunius hurried to catch up.

'Because Titus wants to kiss your mother,' Iunius said mockingly, unable to help himself.

'Shut your face, Iunius,' Titus said.

'Sextus will probably kiss her first,' Arruns said in a low voice so Titus couldn't hear. 'Or I might.'

'Not if your brother can help it,' Iunius said. 'If I were you, Arruns, I'd watch my step on our journey home. You might have an accident.'

'Don't be stupid,' Arruns laughed, but Iunius heard the note of unease in his voice. 'Titus wouldn't hurt me.'

'You're sure of that, are you?'

'Of course I'm sure. You're an idiot, Iunius, what do you know?' Arruns smacked Iunius on the shoulder. 'Come on. He'll moan if we slacken.' Arruns hurried off after Titus.

Iunius kept back a little, thinking. The Oracle's answer to Titus's question had been surprisingly, uncharacteristically straightforward. It was easy to take it at face value and that nagged at Iunius. He couldn't believe the answer was that obvious. All the next king had to do was kiss his mother? Really? And then it came to him. The mother in the Oracle's answer wasn't Lolly, the Queen of Rome. It was the universal mother, Gaia.

'Come on, Iunius,' Titus called, breaking into his thoughts, 'or we'll leave without you.'

Iunius quickened his pace, but then managed to trip on a stone and fall flat on his face.

'You great fool,' Titus said, giving him a not too gentle kick in the thigh. 'You're a bloody embarrassment. Get up.'

Iunius pressed his lips to a seam of dirt between the stones. There, he had given his mother a kiss. *It can't hurt*, he said to himself, *even if I am wrong about what the Oracle meant.*

———

'Oh, my boys.' Lolly hurried towards Titus and Arruns, her arms outstretched, as they arrived back at the domus. She leant in to kiss Titus, then recoiled. 'Ye gods, you stink.'

Titus grabbed hold of Lolly and kissed her cheek with a loud smack. Releasing her, he cast a triumphant look at Arruns, who was threw down his bag with a groan.

'Don't be so rough,' Lolly said, wiping her face where he had kissed her and examining her hands.

Arruns stepped forward and pecked his mother's cheek. 'Pleased to see us, Mother?'

'Of course I am,' she said, smiling at him, 'but you know how I hate dirt.' She clapped her hands and a slave stepped forward, his head bowed. 'Prepare baths for the princes immediately. Have you eaten?'

'Not a thing since this morning,' Arruns said. 'Titus was in a hurry to get home.'

'Ah, he wanted to see me,' Lolly cooed, missing the look that passed between her two sons. Her face fell. 'Oh, Iunius, I didn't see you there.'

Iunius stepped out of the atrium into the light. 'Lady,' he said, bowing his head.

'Is he staying?' Lolly asked Titus.

Titus shrugged. 'He may as well.'

'A bath for him too,' she told the slave who scurried off to get the baths ready.

'Where's Father?' Arruns asked, flopping down onto the couch and snapping his fingers at another slave for a drink.

'Oh, he's at the senate. Sextus is with him. They'll be back soon and we can all dine together. Lucius will be pleased to see you.' Lolly sat, watching every mouthful

Arruns took of the wine. He drank too much, in her opinion. 'He's telling the senate Rome needs to go to war.'

'Again?' Titus cried, snatching the wine jug from Arruns and pouring himself a cup. He waggled the nearly empty jug at Iunius. Iunius took it and poured what little was left into a cup for himself.

'Well, the new temple cost a fortune and now there's no money left in the treasury. He's raised taxes but it's not enough. You know your father doesn't like to be poor—'

'Poor!' Arruns laughed at the very idea.

Lolly cast a reproachful look at Arruns. 'And the Rutuli have been making trouble of late.'

'So, Uncle wants to go to war to get his hands on their gold,' Iunius said, forgetting for a moment he was supposed to be stupid and should never make any noise, especially in front of Lucius or Lolly, that drew attention to himself. 'Forgive me. I should not have spoken.'

'But it's true,' Titus laughed. 'Why work when you can steal is my father's motto.'

'Titus, don't be vulgar,' Lolly scolded.

'You notice Mother isn't saying it's not true,' Titus said, leaning over the couch to Iunius, 'just that it's vulgar to say it out loud.'

Lolly gave an exaggerated sigh. 'And to think I missed you when you were gone.'

'Well, I'm all for war,' Arruns said. 'It will be good to give those Rutulis a good thrashing.'

'It won't be an easy war,' Iunius said. 'They'll defend their riches hard. They won't just let us take it from them.'

'Oh, listen to the master strategist here,' Titus rolled his eyes at his mother and Arruns. They laughed. 'All the better, Iunius. Who wants an easy victory?'

'That's assuming Rome will be victorious,' Iunius muttered.

'Ye gods, Iunius, you're such a pessimistic prick,' Titus said, throwing a cushion at his cousin. 'You know, I really don't know why we let you tag along with us.'

'For comic value,' Arruns said. 'We can always rely on Iunius to give us a good laugh.'

Iunius smiled thinly, taking their insults as he always did, as he was expected to do. But his mind was on the Oracle and the kiss he had given Gaia.

Someday, maybe, he would be the one who was laughing.

23

Lucius banged his hand down on the table, making it creak ominously. 'Stop your excessive drinking, Sextus. You're turning this camp into a tavern.'

Lucius had persuaded the senate and Rome was at war again, this time with the Rutuli. But the Rutuli had learnt a lesson from the Gabii victory of years before and refused to come out of their citadel, forcing the Roman army into another siege. Lucius was forced to adopt a waiting strategy, hoping the Rutuli supplies would soon run out and they would have to surrender to ensure their survival.

'But there's nothing to do,' Sextus protested, fiddling with the hem of his tunic. 'If we're not going to fight, we have to do something to keep ourselves amused.'

'Find something else,' Lucius snarled. 'I won't be in command of an army of drunks.'

'I don't let the men drink,' Sextus said. 'Only the commanders.'

'I don't care. You stop, you hear me.'

'Or what? You'll have me whipped? Oh, Father, I'm sorry,' Sextus said quickly. 'I didn't mean that, I didn't.'

'You can go,' Lucius said, turning away, but as he heard Sextus lift the tent flap, he called, 'Sextus, do you hate me?'

'Of course not, Father,' Sextus said, and Lucius could tell he had embarrassed his son by the question.

'That's good,' Lucius said. He waved his hand. 'All right, you can go. Remember what I said.'

Lucius yawned. By Jupiter, he was tired. He wasn't young anymore, however much he tried to fool himself, and he hadn't anticipated how draining this campaign would be. He should have stayed at home with Lolly this time, sent someone else, sent his sons to wage the war alone. This would be the last time, he promised himself. He'd beat the Rutuli and then he would go back to Rome and stay there.

He just had to beat these damn Rutuli. *It never used to be this difficult*, he thought. *Time was when I faced an enemy, I cut them down easily. Now, I have enemies who openly defy me, and not just here. In Rome, senators debate me, criticise me for my policies, my actions. I can't silence them all.*

Lucius stared into the dark corners of his tent and another thought came to him, one that made him shiver. Was the Rutuli resistance evidence of the curse working or of the Sibyl's prophecies coming true? He hadn't made any propitiatory sacrifices of late, he'd just been so busy. He should write to Lolly and tell her to sacrifice a bull to Jupiter. That would surely appease the great god and Jupiter could persuade Poena to be kind to him. Lucius took out a pen and sheet of parchment from the small chest on his desk. He began writing to Lolly, telling her to make the sacrifice and to pray for a speedy conclusion to the war.

———

Sextus leant back and belched loudly, sighing with pleasure

as the gas left his body. This was more like it. This was better than sitting alone in his tent and being a good soldier as his father wanted. He reached for the wine jug on the floor beside his chair and lifted it to his lips. The liquid spilled out, soaking his cheeks and tunic. Laughter erupted around him.

'There's none to compare with her,' Sextus heard Collatinus say when it died down. 'Not one in Italy, let alone Rome.'

'Who you talking about?' Sextus asked, cradling the jug.

'Lucretia,' Collatinus replied, 'my wife.'

'Never seen her,' Sextus said dismissively. 'Can't say.'

'Sextus, you have seen her,' Collatinus said impatiently, turning to lean over the back of his chair. 'She was at Opiter's party last month.'

'I don't remember,' Sextus frowned.

'I don't suppose you do,' Collatinus smirked. 'You had your face pressed between Virginia's tits the whole evening.'

Everyone laughed, including Sextus. He remembered Virginia, a young woman whose very ample breasts he'd decided he wanted to explore, and he'd dragged her off to the garden and pulled her dress from her shoulders. She had protested a little and kept looking over her shoulder to make sure no one was watching, and he knew she had let him do what he wanted only because he was the son of the King. Being a prince certainly came in handy. He had left her in the garden half an hour later to make herself respectable and staggered back to the party. Now he thought about it, he remembered seeing Collatinus standing by a column with a woman at his side as he went back into the house, but she had been so quiet he hadn't bothered to see if she was pretty.

'Is she a goer then?' he asked, thrusting out and waggling his tongue. It pleased him to see the smile leave Collatinus's face.

'She's my wife, Sextus,' Collatinus said severely.

'She can still be a goer,' Sextus said, innocently wide-eyed. 'There's a whore inside every woman, let me tell you.'

'Not in my Lucretia. Don't judge her by your own paltry standards.'

'You were the one who brought her up,' Sextus said, 'saying she's incom… incom…'

'Incomparable,' Sextus's friend, Elerius, provided, hiding his smile behind his cup.

'That's the word,' Sextus waved his finger triumphantly. 'But I bet we can find a camp whore to compare with her. What do you say, Collatinus? Shall we go and find us some women?'

'Not for me. I don't want a whore.'

'Why not?'

'Because I happen to love my wife, Sextus.'

'Bully for you. Doesn't mean you can't dip your prick anywhere else, you know.'

'It does for me.'

Sextus blew a raspberry at Collatinus, spraying him with spit. 'Do you know, I think I ought to see this wife of yours again. See what all the fuss is about.'

Collatinus wiped down his tunic and turned his back to Sextus. 'I don't want you seeing her.'

'Why?' Sextus grabbed his shoulder and squeezed hard. 'You worried she's not as virtuous as you make out and I have her on her back before you can blink?'

'No, I'm not,' Collatinus said, pulling himself away. 'I don't want her being bothered by a boorish drunk like you.'

'D'you know, I bet she's being serviced right now,' Sextus went on. 'I bet she's riding one of your big African slaves this very minute.'

Collatinus sprung to his feet and grabbed Sextus, yanking

him out of his chair. 'You're going to apologise for that, Sextus. You want to see my wife? Then, let's go now.'

'Now?' Sextus said, having to stand on tiptoe to stay on his feet.

'Right now, and you'll see the kind of woman you'll never have,' Collatinus promised.

———

Sextus sobered up on the ride to Collatia. He and Collatinus had left the camp secretly, Sextus knowing his father would forbid it. The jolting of his horse was making Sextus feel sick, and twice he had had to call to Collatinus to stop so he could dismount and throw up. He wished now he hadn't suggested seeing Lucretia. What did he care if she was beautiful and virtuous? He had considered telling Collatinus he was prepared to accept Lucretia was beautiful and chaste, but Collatinus would insist on a public apology and princes had no need to make apologies. The journey was inevitable, so Sextus kept his mouth shut and just prayed that it would soon be over.

Collatia was not far and it was early morning when they arrived at Collatinus's home. They rode into the courtyard and dismounted, Sextus walking stiffly as Collatinus gestured him into the house. He had expected Collatinus to lead him to his bedroom so he could see Lucretia lying abed and alone, but instead, Collatinus led him through the house to the atrium. Sextus blinked at the sunlight coming through the open front doors.

'There,' Collatinus whispered victoriously, pointing.

A beautiful young woman was sitting in the atrium, wholly absorbed in spinning her basketful of wool. She had thick, light-brown hair made golden by the sunlight. Her skin looked perfect, not a blemish nor a freckle upon it and her arms were pleasingly plump. Around her were three of her maids, also spinning. A more perfect picture of wifely industry could not have been found and Collatinus knew it.

'Husband,' Lucretia called excitedly, seeing Collatinus in the doorway. 'Where did you spring from?'

Collatinus went to her and kissed her full on the mouth. Sextus saw a blush creep up her neck and flood her cheeks, making her appear even more lovely.

'Is that the Prince with you?' she whispered to Collatinus, her big brown eyes on Sextus.

'Yes, I wanted Prince Sextus to see how lovely you are,' Collatinus said. 'He didn't believe me.'

Lucretia's blush deepened. 'You must stop teasing me, husband,' she remonstrated, smiling sweetly at Sextus. 'Good morning, Prince Sextus.'

Sextus couldn't speak. She really was very lovely.

Lucretia looked up at Collatinus. 'Are you staying, husband?'

'No,' he said regretfully, kissing her hand, 'we have to get back. Just time for a quick bite and then we must be away again.'

'Oh, that is a pity,' she said. 'I will tell the kitchen.' Excusing herself, she moved past Sextus, just long enough for the scent she wore to waft up Sextus's nostrils and enchant him.

'I told you,' Collatinus said smugly, seeing how Sextus was moved. 'Is she not the most perfect creature you have ever seen?'

Sextus nodded. 'She certainly is.'

———

Sextus and Collatinus had ridden back to the camp. Their absence had been noted and Sextus was called before his father to explain himself. Sextus offered no explanation which enraged his father, but Sextus endured Lucius's anger without a twitch of anger or resentment. In fact, Lucius's words had barely registered for Sextus's mind was too full of the most perfect woman he had ever see: Lucretia.

He had to see her again. No, he didn't just have to see her, he had to have her.

The military situation hadn't changed. Rutuli was still holding out and Lucius was still in a foul mood about it. Collatinus, having proved his point, made it clear he no longer wanted to be in Sextus's company and stayed away from him. It seemed to Sextus that Fortuna was on his side. He could leave the camp and Collatinus would never know where he was headed.

What he was going to do once he arrived at Collatinus's house again, Sextus wasn't really sure. Would Lucretia, like Virginia, not dare to say no to a prince and so respond to his advances? Or would she tell him to leave and threaten to tell her husband? She had seemed to be impressed by his being a prince when they had met. Perhaps that would be enough to win her over.

Sextus pretended he wanted an early night, much to the derision of Elerius and his other drinking companions, and made a pretence of retiring to his tent. Once out of sight, he mounted his horse and set off on the road to Collatia. He didn't spare his horse, so eager was he to arrive. He kicked the mare's sides whenever she seemed to slow and she was foaming at the mouth when he drew up in Lucretia's courtyard.

Sextus threw his reins to a slave who hurried forward to meet him, demanding to another that he be taken to their mistress. The slave, recognising Sextus, hastened to obey and led him through the house to the tablinum where Lucretia was busy tidying her husband's desk.

She looked up, startled, at his entrance. 'Prince Sextus! Why... I was not expecting you. Is my husband with you?'

'No, my lady,' Sextus said courteously, his heart hammering as he gazed on her beauty, 'I am alone. I was passing through and thought I would do myself the honour of calling on you. I hope it is not inconvenient.'

Sextus could see from her expression that it was inconvenient but Lucretia was too polite to say so. Instead, she assured him she was honoured he felt able to call as a friend. She dutifully played the hostess and gave him dinner, a really quite miserable meal for it seemed she ate simply when her husband was from home. As the slaves cleared the table, Sextus asked if Lucretia could give him a room for the night.

Lucretia hesitated, which angered Sextus a little. He had expected her to agree immediately, pleased a prince of Rome would be content to rest his head under her roof. Lucretia's hesitation lasted only a moment. She said he was welcome to sleep in her home and ordered a servant to make a room ready for him.

When the oil lamps were lit, Sextus decided it was time to retire. He wanted to have some time to himself, to work out how he was going to proceed. His ardour had not diminished in the hours he had spent in Lucretia's company. Quite the opposite, in fact, he wanted her even more. But she was so damn virtuous. He had flirted and complimented, and she had accepted the flattery with a shy smile but had resolutely not played the game. She had shown him to his room, and he had watched her walk away, slipping into her own bedroom at the end of the corridor.

Sextus lay down on the unfamiliar bed still wearing his

tunic. His eyes focused on a crack in the ceiling, his mind on his hostess. There was only one way he would have Lucretia tonight, he decided, and that was by force. He closed his eyes and imagined her naked body next to his. It was delicious, just the imagining of it. How much more satisfying it would be to experience it for real.

Sextus waited until the noises in the house ceased. Then he crept out of his room and tiptoed down the corridor to Lucretia's bedroom door. He lifted the latch and, hardly daring to breathe, stepped inside. An oil lamp burned on a table by the bed and in its flickering light, Sextus saw Lucretia lying asleep.

She would be startled when she awoke and saw him. She would cover herself with her sheet and tell him, perhaps beg him, to leave her room. She would call on his honour, remind him of hers and her husband's. Those were words he didn't want to hear.

Sextus took out the small dagger he had put in his belt and saw its blade shimmer in the lamplight. He sat down on the edge of the bed and the small movement of the mattress woke Lucretia. She blinked, the dark lashes gently brushing the delicate skin beneath her eyes. Her eyes fixed on Sextus. The cry she made excited him and without thinking, he pointed the dagger at her throat.

'Don't speak, Lucretia,' he whispered. 'You know what I want. If you fight me, I'll kill you and put a dead slave in your bed. Everyone will believe you rutted with a slave who killed you before I killed him for the dishonour you both did to your husband.'

Despite the blade at her throat and his instruction to be silent, Lucretia spoke. 'Prince Sextus,' she gasped and there were tears in her eyes, 'please, don't do this. I beg you.'

Sextus pulled away the bed sheet she was trying to hide

behind, the blade digging into her throat, making a shadowy indentation but not breaking the skin. He switched the dagger to his left hand, leaving his right free to explore the naked legs showing beneath her nightdress. He felt her trembling beneath his touch but she did not kick out at him. *Perhaps she wants this too,* he thought, *and only needs to make a show of resisting.* The thought urged him on. His hand moved up under the thin linen and squeezed her thigh. He felt her legs press together and he smiled to himself. He edged his hand over the top of her thigh and pushed his fingers down between her legs. She cried out but didn't move, and he saw her eyes were shut tight, her face constricted as his fingers forced her legs apart.

Sextus lifted his body over hers and settled himself between her legs. He pressed the dagger a little harder against her throat as he pushed into her.

———

Lucretia cried as she wiped her thighs with a damp sponge. Sextus had used her roughly and her private parts ached, the delicate skin rubbed sore.

But the physical pain was nothing to the anguish she felt. She could not forgive herself for allowing her violation to take place. She had understood Sextus perfectly when he had flattered her during dinner, had comprehended his meaning and decided to ignore his remarks, secretly flattered a prince should find her beautiful. And so, it was her vanity that had led to her terror of the night before. She had been to blame.

Sextus had left her bed before dawn, thanking her for her hospitality as he dressed and sheathed his dagger. She could smell him on herself and no amount of washing with rose water seemed to be able to cleanse her skin of him. What was worse was the knowledge that he might have left a part of himself inside her, something that couldn't be wiped clean. The thought of bearing Sextus's child made her vomit.

Lucretia knew what she had to do next. She dressed herself and tied her hair back simply, not waiting for her maid to attend her, and made her way to the tablinum. She sat down gingerly at her husband's desk and wrote to Collatinus, beseeching him and a friend to come home to her, but not telling him why. He would come, without question, he would come, Lucretia knew.

And when he came, Lucretia would restore his honour to him the only way she could.

———

Collatinus had received his wife's message later that day. His mind frantic with worry, he didn't ask for leave from Lucius. He jumped on his horse and made for his home, remembering only too late that Lucretia had asked him to bring a friend. Why, he couldn't fathom. Fortunately, he met Iunius Brutus on the road, himself having left the Roman camp a few hours earlier after delivering a message from the senate. Collatinus begged Iunius to accompany him to Collatia and Iunius agreed without hesitation.

When they arrived at Collatinus's home, they found the servants and slaves unusually quiet. They eyed their master curiously as he demanded the whereabouts of his wife. 'In her cubiculum,' the slaves replied, and Collatinus hurried there, telling Iunius to follow.

'Lucretia?' Collatinus asked, opening the cubiculum door. 'What is it, what's the matter?' Lucretia burst into tears. Collatinus started towards her but she cried out with such fervour that he halted in the middle of the room. 'My love, what is it?'

'Iunius Brutus,' she said through her tears, seeing him hesitating at the door, 'you must hear this too so you can confirm what I say and do.'

'Anything for you, lady,' Iunius said, stepping inside.

'Husband,' Lucretia said, turning her eyes to Collatinus, 'you have been dishonoured. If you were to examine this bed, you would see the evidence of your disgrace. But please believe me, only my body has been the cause of your dishonour, not my mind, nor my heart.'

Collatinus looked with horror from her to the bed on which she sat. 'What do you mean, Lucretia? Have you lain with another man?'

'I have, husband,' she confessed, 'but not through lust or desire. He came here, claiming the rights of a guest, and as my prince and your friend, I obliged. I gave him dinner, I provided him with a bed. No, listen, hear me, Collatinus. I did all this for him so as not to dishonour you in his eyes. And he took advantage of me. He stole in here by night, held a knife to my throat and vi…,' she stumbled over the word. She took a deep breath. 'He violated me, threatening to kill me and put a dead slave in our bed to shame me further. Forgive me, but I allowed him to have me.'

'Lady,' Iunius said, 'rest easy, there is nothing to forgive.' He appealed to his friend who had not spoken. 'Is there, Collatinus?'

'You see, Iunius,' Lucretia said miserably as Collatinus covered his mouth with his hand. 'My husband is dishonoured and cannot forgive me.'

'Collatinus,' Iunius pleaded, 'say something.'

'I'll kill him,' Collatinus growled.

'No, you must not,' Lucretia cried, falling to her knees

and clutching her husband's hand. 'The King will kill you and I couldn't bear to be the cause of your death. Please, Collatinus, just say you forgive me.'

Collatinus knelt and took Lucretia in his arms. He buried his face in her hair and Iunius heard him murmuring his forgiveness. They stayed that way for a few minutes and Iunius shuffled his feet, wanting to leave and afford them some privacy.

But Lucretia saw and she pulled away from Collatinus, clambering back onto the bed. 'No, do not leave, Iunius. Not yet. You must witness this. Collatinus, I have your forgiveness but it cannot undo the shame I will bring on you when this affair is known. There is only one way I can do that and it is this.'

Iunius and Collatinus watched in mute horror as Lucretia withdrew a dagger from beneath her pillow and plunged it into her heart. The cry she gave was small, pitiful. She fell back onto the bed and only then did Collatinus find himself able to move. He pulled his dying wife upright and pulled the dagger from her body. The blood flowed freely, staining her perfectly white dress, and she died in his arms.

Collatinus stared up at Iunius. 'She used my dagger.'

———

Iunius could hardly believe what he had been called upon to witness. That a woman so pure, so very lovely as Lucretia had died before him and in such a manner, convinced she had done wrong, all because his wretched cousin had violated her!

Collatinus was in shock, Iunius realised. He hadn't moved since Lucretia died. The dagger had fallen from his hand onto the floor and Iunius snatched it up. Lucretia's blood was fresh upon it. The whole affair was monstrous and Sextus's violation couldn't be allowed to go unpunished.

'By the blood of Lucretia,' Iunius swore, 'I call on the gods to witness my oath.'

'Iunius, what are you doing?' Collatinus croaked, still clutching his wife.

Iunius didn't answer him. 'My oath is this. I shall avenge the death of this sweet lady. I shall pursue relentlessly the foul creature that violated her. I shall bring down the proud tyrant, King Lucius Tarquinius, who engendered him. I shall punish the Queen who brought him into the world. They will not escape my vengeance. I make this promise. Oh gods, hear me.'

Iunius thrust the dagger into Collatinus's hand. 'Swear the same oath, my friend. Avenge your wife and let us free Rome once and for all from this accursed family.'

Iunius saw a new intensity in Collatinus's eyes. He felt his friend's fingers brush over his own as Collatinus gripped the bloody dagger. 'Swear it,' Iunius ordered and Collatinus repeated the oath. When he finished speaking, he drew the blade across his palm. Iunius took the dagger and did the same.

Their hands clasped one another, their blood mingled, the oath was sealed.

———

Iunius and Collatinus took Lucretia's body to Rome. They laid her out, still dressed in her ripped and bloodied dress, in the forum for everyone to see. The people gathered around her corpse and shook their heads in dismay. The senators came out of the senate house and stared at the body of such a beautiful woman and asked each other what had happened.

Collatinus watched in silence as Iunius mounted the rostrum and called the citizens to attend him. He recounted what Lucretia had told them, of how Sextus had come offering friendship to the chaste wife of one of Rome's most loving and dutiful sons, Collatinus, how Sextus had dishonoured Collatinus and ravished Lucretia, and how that pure-hearted lady had killed herself to wipe out her husband's shame.

'But who is shamed here?' he cried. 'It is not this poor lady,' he gestured at Lucretia's body before him, 'nor is it my friend, Collatinus. Prince Sextus is shamed. At last, he is shown to be what Rome has always suspected but not dared to speak. That he is a debaucher, the son of a tyrant, the son of a murderess.'

He turned around to see if the senators were paying attention and they were. They were staring at him in unconcealed astonishment.

'I know what you are thinking,' he said to them. 'You're thinking what is this idiot doing, addressing us like this? I assure you, Iunius Brutus is no idiot, nor has he ever been. What I have been, I'll admit, is a coward. For the sake of my mother, I played the fool. She did not want to see me killed as my brother Titus was killed, for nothing more than speaking out against the tyrant, King Lucius Tarquinius. But I cannot play the fool any longer. The time for keeping silent is done. When tyrants can act without impunity, and the sons of tyrants can violate pure woman like Lucretia, then the time to look the other way is gone. We must stare this tyrant in the face and tell him no more. We must say we will suffer no one man to rule over this state of ours. We must not bow our knees to a king any longer. What say you? Are you with me in ridding ourselves of the tyrant?'

The response was overwhelming. The people, whom

Lucius had treated with contempt, enforcing their labour when they had no money to put bread in their children's stomachs, who had increased taxes when they hadn't the money to pay the taxes already levied, roared their assent. The senators applauded. Collatinus hid his face so he could cry.

Someone in the crowd cried out, 'Let's kill the tyrant,' and the cry was taken up.

Iunius held up his arms. 'Let us not shed more blood. We cannot cleanse Rome of the Tarquins' foul deeds by more killing. Let us act instead as civilised people. This city has gates. Let us shut them upon Lucius Tarquinius and forbid him entry. Let his right to rule be revoked by law, so he can never legally claw his way back to the throne.' He paused to catch his breath before delivering his final plea. 'Good people, let us have no more kings in Rome.'

———

Lucius could not believe what he was being told. One of his men, whom he had sent to Rome with a letter to deliver to the senate, had returned with a proclamation. Lucius had told him to read it out, knowing his eyesight was too poor to see the scribblings of the senate's scribes. The messenger had stumbled over the words, his eyes darting warily to Lucius, fearing what the King would do, remembering how roughly he had been treated when in Rome, pelted with mud and filth, simply for being Lucius's man. He considered himself lucky making it out of the city alive.

'Prince Sextus raped this woman?' Lucius asked.

'That's what I was told, my lord,' the messenger replied.

'Bring him here. Now,' Lucius barked and the man hurried away, pleased to be out of the King's reach.

The Sibylline books, Lucius remembered. They had said he would be brought low by a child of Rome through a woman's virtue. This was that moment. There had been truth in those scrolls after all.

Sextus entered the tent. 'You wanted to see me, Father.'

'Did you rape the wife of Collatinus?' Lucius asked quietly and heard Sextus's gasp of surprise.

'I had her,' Sextus said after a moment. 'I don't know about rape.'

'Don't lie to me. Did you violate her?'

Sextus licked his lips, then looked his father straight in the eye. 'Yes. I did.'

Lucius fell into his chair, his hand on his heart. 'You've brought me down,' he whispered. 'You, my child, just like the prophecy said you would.'

Sextus frowned, aghast as his father's reaction. 'What prophecy? What do you mean I've brought you down?'

'Rome is locking her gates against me. The senate has revoked my right to rule. They claim I am no longer king.'

'But they can't do that.'

'They've done it,' Lucius hurled the senate's proclamation at Sextus. It struck Sextus in the face. 'They mean to exile me. And that means they've exiled you. Oh, by the gods, your mother.' Lucius struggled to his feet. 'What have they done with your mother? Have they killed her?' He pushed Sextus out of the way and hurried outside. Sextus followed. 'You there,' Lucius called to one of his guards, 'go to Rome. Find out where the Queen is. See to it she is safe. If necessary, bring her here.' He turned on Sextus. 'I swear, if your mother has been harmed because of your actions, Sextus, I will whip you, and this time, I won't stop until you're dead.'

———

Lolly's maid had been in the forum when Iunius addressed the people and she had rejoiced in his words. She hated her mistress who was always ready with a sharp word and hard hand to punish her for the slightest mistake.

The maid rushed back to the domus and confronted her mistress, telling her with great delight that she would follow her orders no longer. Lolly raised her hand to slap her for her impertinence but had frozen in shock when the maid grinned at her and told her to go ahead. Soon, she said, it would be Lolly suffering such punishment. Iunius Brutus had spoken against the Tarquins and the people were with him.

Lolly watched in astonishment as the maid sauntered out of the room, marvelling at what the wretch had been talking about. Iunius had addressed the people and the senate? That idiot nephew of Lucius's? Oh, it was ridiculous; the maid had been wrong.

Then one of Lucius's secretaries had entered, his face ashen. With a trembling voice, he related what had taken place in the forum and Lolly listened without interrupting, hardly able to believe her ears. But there was no disbelieving the man's sincerity. There was a move afoot to unseat the monarchy and he was sure, he said uneasily, that it would succeed. Lolly, realising she was no longer safe in Rome, set out for Lucius's encampment under cover of darkness with only her oldest and most faithful maid for company.

———

Lucius's heart lightened when he saw his wife alive and unharmed. He kissed Lolly fervently, scarcely allowing her to draw breath, and gave thanks to all the gods he could name for protecting her on her journey. He asked Lolly for news but she could tell him nothing he didn't already know. Sextus greeted his mother enthusiastically, knowing she would be on his side and pleased he now had an ally against his father.

Lolly, Lucius quickly realised, was angry with him. He wanted her to stay with him, eat, drink, talk through a strategy to get the throne back, but Lolly declared she was exhausted from the journey, a journey that would not have been necessary had Lucius kept a closer eye on Sextus. As far as Lolly saw it, Sextus had been misled by Lucius's crude, low-born soldiers and Lucius should have been more careful about who their son associated with. Sextus protested to his mother that Lucretia had led him on and she believed him. That stupid girl Lucretia had obviously given herself to Sextus and then changed her mind. What woman would kill herself if she was the victim of rape? Lolly took Lucius's cot bed for herself and refused to speak another word to him.

A messenger from the senate arrived an hour or two after Lolly. The messenger, who didn't bow when he was brought before Lucius, who didn't call Lucius lord, told him that the senate had decreed Lucius was King of Rome no longer. What was more, if Lucius tried to get back into the city, he would be opposed by armed men; if captured, he would be executed. News spread swiftly through the camp of the senate's message, and even as Lucius watched, men deserted, shouting that they were returning to Rome to take up the cry of 'Down with the tyrant!'

EPILOGUE

The Sibyl's prophecy had come true. Lucius had been wrong to think the gods had favoured him and his family all this time, he realised that now. They had just been biding their time, waiting until he was at his highest to make the fall harder to bear. The curse had been upon the Tarquins the whole time. He had been deposed, exiled from his own kingdom, left in possession of only whatever riches were in the camp and which hadn't been taken by the deserters. He and his family could sink no lower.

But this sparked a thought, an idea of hope in Lucius. Maybe the curse was now broken. He had been driven out of Rome, he had suffered. Maybe that would be the end of it. *Yes*, Lucius thought, his heart swelling with this new idea, *we shall go where we will be welcome, perhaps Veii or Tarquinii, muster an army of loyal men, an army to break down the gates of Rome and we will subdue the ungrateful, rebellious populace.*

Bursting out of his tent, Lucius shouted into the darkness, 'What do I care of gods and prophecies? What more can you do to hurt me?'

He thrust his arms wide, and as the storm-clouds above him burst, lifted his face to the pelting rain and cried, 'I have ruled Rome for twenty-five years and I make this promise, you gods. I, Lucius Tarquinius Superbus, will return to be King of Rome again.'

AUTHOR'S NOTE

Rome's regal period, or Archaic Period, as it's sometimes known, is shrouded in mystery, so much so that there isn't a consensus among historians that Rome even had kings in the centuries before the Republic was created. One theory put forward is that Romans during the Republic created their kings (who were mostly tyrannical) to show how better a governing system a republic was. The kings believed to have ruled Rome may therefore be as fictional as King Arthur or Robin Hood.

Researching this book, I relied heavily on the writings of Livy (Titus Livius) to provide 'facts' about both the Tarquin kings and King Servius Tullius. However, because this is a work of fiction and its primary objective is to entertain, I had to make some choices about how I presented this story. In some histories, Lucius Tarquinius Superbus is the son of Lucius (Lucomo) Tarquinius Priscus, but this makes little sense of the accepted chronology, i.e. the second Lucius would have been extremely old (perhaps impossibly old) by the time of his deposition and expulsion from Rome. For this reason, I chose to accept another theory and depict the second Lucius as the grandson of Lucius Tarquinius Priscus.

Romans were very unoriginal when it came to the bestowing of names to children, especially to daughters. For example, the two daughters of Servius Tullius and Tarquinia were named Tullia Prima and Tullia Secunda (literally, Tullia One and Tullia Two) and not only was Tarquinia the wife of Servius, but a Tarquinia was also the sister of Lucius and Arruns, as well as a daughter of Lucius and Tullia Secunda. To avoid confusing the reader, I have changed the names of some of the players in this drama. Therefore, Tullia Secunda I have called Lolly, sister Tarquinia became Lucilla and daughter Tarquinia is Cassia. The Dramatis Personae at the beginning of this book reflects these choices, but should you want to see a (reasonably) correct family tree of the Tarquins and a full list of sources used, please visit my website: www.lauradowers.com.

PLEASE LEAVE A REVIEW

If you have enjoyed this book, it would be wonderful if you could spare the time to post an honest review on Amazon.

Reviews are incredibly important. Your review will help me bring my books to the attention of other readers who may enjoy them.

Thank you so much.

JOIN MY MAILING LIST

Join my mailing list to stay up-to-date with my writing news, new releases and more, and receive a FREE and EXCLUSIVE eBook, *The Poet Knight and His Muse*, a short story about Sir Philip Sidney and Penelope Devereux and one of the greatest love poems of Queen Elizabeth I's reign.

It is completely free to join and I promise I will never spam you – I'll only be in touch when I have something I think will be of interest to you. You can easily unsubscribe at any time.

You can join here: www.lauradowers.com

ALSO BY LAURA DOWERS

ACKNOWLEDGEMENTS

I'd like to thank my Advance Reader Team for taking the time to read this book and provide feedback. Your comments were very useful and greatly appreciated.

I'd love to hear from you. If would like to comment or ask a question about one of my books, then get in touch. You can find me at:

www.lauradowers.com
laura@lauradowers.com
Facebook.com/lauradowersauthor

Printed in Great Britain
by Amazon